YIELD

Book #5, Pierced Hearts

by

CARI SILVERWOOD

Editing:
Nerine Dorman find her on Twitter @nerinedorman
Lina Sacher http://www.linaedits.com
Cover design: Thomas Dorman – Dr. Benway on Deviantart and Facebook
https://www.facebook.com/Dr.Benways.Page

To join my mailing list and receive notice of future releases:

http://www.carisilverwood.net/about-me.html

If you'd like to discuss the Pierced Hearts series with a group of other readers, you're welcome to join this group on facebook:
https://www.facebook.com/groups/864034900283067/□

This series is now available in boxset collections
Pierced Hearts, Volume 1 includes Books 1, 2 and 3
Pierced Hearts, Volume 2 includes Books 2 and 3
(for those who already own Take me Break me)
Pierced Hearts, Volume 3 includes Books 4 and 5

CONTENTS

ACKNOWLEDGMENTS

To all my wonderful beta readers, friends and fans a big hug and Mwah! But especially to my number one fangirling 'piglet', Emma Rose, who read everything as I wrote. Also a huge thank you to Angel Brat, Jennifer Zeffer, who helped me immensely despite her evil day job, and to Jody Rhoton, who helped me figure out what was right and what needed fixing.

Thank you to my editor, Nerine Dorman for her facts on hook suspension – she's assisted with some suspensions. Lastly, thank you Zmish (fetlife name), for her wonderful information about the ins and outs of hook suspension and how thrilling the insertion of those hooks can be. What an awesome way to have an orgasm!

About Yield

This book is part of a dark erotic fiction series and may disturb readers who are uncomfortable with dubious consent or graphic violence.

If you've processed that and are headed onward, strap yourself in and hang on tight. The twisted fantasies in this story will take you to the edge of the abyss.

Disclaimer

THE BEGINNING

Wren

I played with the napkin next to my plate. The late afternoon sun came in low, glinting off the tableware and making the place so glary it was difficult to see the man weaving between the other empty chairs and tables. For a little roadside pitstop eatery up in the Papua New Guinea mountains, the décor was...cute. My napkin had Bart Simpson on it and none of the chairs matched. And the waitress had vanished.

I glanced at my hulking bodyguard and he nodded reassuringly. Not a single black hair was out of place. James Bond and Hugh probably exchanged texts and anti-villain plans, but my father always had employed the best. Hugh had insouciance down to an art. Nothing fazed him, except maybe the tropical heat. He had a thing for being properly dressed in at least long pants and buttoned shirt. Today was a day for sweating.

Even in my tank top and denim knee-length pants, I was feeling the heat. More sweat dribbled down my spine. If we stayed any longer, I'd melt and stick to the timber. I took up the napkin and used it for a fan as the new arrival reached the table. Surfer shorts and T-shirt. Good. I hated being the underdressed one. Student life at university had been like diving into my ideal environment. No one had ever dressed up except at parties or functions.

A flight of parrots shot past a few yards away, squawking.

"Hello." He put his hand on the back of the chair beside me. "Wren Gavoche?"

1

"Yes."

The British accent sounded wonderful and never failed to give me an instant rapport with the speaker. It was just...cute, even when attached to an alarmingly large man. Despite my instinct that looking more pointedly might give him the wrong impression, because really he was not within light years of being inscribed in my little book of possible BF's, I looked...and looked.

I let my gaze cruise over the swell of his biceps with the mysterious tatt peeking from under the sleeve, took in the breadth of his chest, his scent, the solid *don't fuck with me* way he stood, those huge hands, and those palest ever blue eyes.

Ooops. Caught staring. His minimal yet knowing smile seemed to rivet me to my seat.

"Hi." I pasted on an innocent grin. "You're Richard? No last name?"

That was so odd but I had Hugh. Safety in numbers, and concealed firearms.

"No." He removed his baseball cap, revealing a perky, light blond mohawk, pulled out the chair, and sat.

Then he waited.

"You contacted me, Richard. You said you had information." About what I had no clue but this search for what was behind my father's death, at a place designed to turn women into sex slaves, had so far gotten me one step past the starting post. "Do you know anything about my father's death? About this woman Jazmine Foulkes? I think she was abducted and kept there and that she escaped."

Jazmine, hotshot journalist, had written a damning article on my brother revealing how he was stealing millions from the government. But it wasn't that which had made him suicide, no, it was the other information she'd revealed. A blind person could see it was a personal attack. She'd found out about his cross dressing fetish.

That he'd killed his family as well as himself...

I didn't know for certain why Jazmine was at that slave house, but with my father being found dead there too I'd gradually come around to suspecting something perverted had happened to her on my father's orders. It was such a twisted idea and I hadn't quite wrapped my head around it.

The chair squeaked as Richard reclined. His focus was entirely on me, as if the menacing Hugh wasn't sitting beside me. "Perhaps. I don't know her whereabouts but I can help you find the man who set your father up to die."

"Oh." I tensed. This was what I'd been looking for. A breakthrough. "Who?"

He gestured at Hugh. "Get your watchdog to move away and I'll say more."

Damn. Was this safe? Hugh shook his head, grimly. But I dived in. Nowhere was where I'd gotten so far.

"Hugh, please?" I raised my eyebrows.

"Ma'am..." But he took in my expression then nodded.

Once he'd risen and seated himself at a distant table, one with the wall behind him, I nodded at Richard. Clever Hugh. Always seeking out the safest places. Could he read lips?

Richard, or whoever he was – I didn't believe it was his name for an instant – leaned his forearms on the table. His nearest hand ended up resting inches from my left hand. My breaths turned ragged. Just that proximity had made warmth suffuse between my legs. This man attracted me, no matter that he was clearly out of bounds. Fantasy territory – like lusting for the tatted-up, muscle-bound biker stalking through the pub on a Saturday night.

With my friends, I'd ogle after this type of man then turn aside and giggle about what he'd be like in bed.

"Well?" I pulled my hand away a fraction, but the electricity of his presence drew me still.

"The man you want is called Vetrov." Ugh, and even his voice seemed to stroke between my legs. Testosterone concentrate.

I swallowed and made myself listen.

"He organizes human trafficking. I know where to find him."

To business. I'd get the person who had done this and to hell with my life until I did. No brother, no mother, no father – only I remained. Most days I wanted to weep despite the millions Dad had left me. My vet science degree could wait. This money, what better thing to do with it than destroy the man who'd killed my father?

"Give me his name, where he lives, and I'll pay you very well. Once I know for sure he's the right man, one hundred thousand is yours."

For the first time he truly studied me. When his eyes lowered, my breasts tingled, my nipples tightening until they were aching and hard.

They'd be showing through my skimpy shirt. *Focus. Business.*

His mouth twitched and he lifted his hand and trapped mine. What the hell?

"Remove your hand." I tugged but he held on tight. The creak of the chair warned me that Hugh had noticed. I shook my head at him and he subsided into his chair.

"First hear my terms. Two hundred thousand. You're going to need me with you to help fine tune the location of Vetrov."

I frowned and was still considering when he spoke again.

"Also, I want you."

Time shivered. "What ?" I'd heard wrong.

"You." His smile was hard, uncompromising, and so lethal every hair on my body stood on end. "I want you in my bed. Once. After that, you won't want to leave. No you. No deal."

He didn't wink or move in any way, just waited while examining my face, and that floored me. Arrogant bastard.

Was this blackmail? Yet he intrigued me. I shook my head, jarring myself out of the state of shock. "Ummm."

One eyebrow rose. "Dare to take a chance for once, Wren. Life is better with surprises."

One night. Why was I even thinking it was possible?

I blinked, running through crazy thought after crazy thought. What would it be like to have sex with such an overtly dangerous man? All my past lovers had been students. Young *safe* men who'd never done more than go to university, parties, maybe the beach.

Insane to say yes.

I opened my mouth and was caught by how he stared at my lips. His large hand squeezed down harder until where his thumb pressed hurt. The pain brought another level of scariness to this. Now I was aroused and afraid in equal proportions.

The words seemed to blurt out without my mind having much say. "Once, only. And it's one hundred thousand if you want me as part of the deal." *Let's see what the smart ass thinks of that.*

"Done." He drew my hand to his mouth, kissed my knuckles like a gentleman, then he singled out my forefinger and sucked on it.

I could feel the movement of his tongue.

In one second, my finger became hot and wet and his.

Tremors ran through my pussy. Breathing halted. My eyes must be so very wide. The man had turned me on so much with that simple action, as if it were a button to my sexuality.

Holy fuck.

His murmur rumbled past my last defenses. "Keep looking at me like that and I'll bend you over this table now, pull down your underwear..."

...and fuck you. I could hear those unsaid words in my mind.

He released my hand. I snatched it away.

What had I just agreed to?

*****

Moghul

"Moghul! Problem."

At the sound of my name, I shut off the phone and swung back to the naked model my rigger had suspended from the ceiling by hooks. Her frantic pleas to be let down were worrying my men but the film crew kept to their task. Randy was working methodically to get her down.

The ropes lowered the last foot. Her bound breasts, then the rest of her front, gently kissed the floor.

"Way to go," I muttered. Maybe I could salvage something from the footage.

Not all the scripts worked, especially when we tried something new, like hook suspension.

The crew relaxed and Randy went to one knee beside Mel to extract the shiny hooks.

"Thank you, Randy!"

The Texan gave me a thumbs-up then resumed soothing and freeing the girl. The man was a find and a half with all his skills – big attitude, bad jokes, and big dick. If anyone else had been handling the submissive, she'd have been screaming the room down.

My second phone buzzed and I walked carefully backward until I found the wall.

I did a last check on the scene.

There was nothing sexy about the next part. Not with her panicking. Maybe if we were a torture snuff porn site but Kinkaverse was a straight up BDSM porn site. Domination, humiliation, and bondage of every sort while the models got fucked every which way. All above board and legal.

5

I pursed my lips and, just for a second, allowed myself the leisure of imagining Mel being made to stay up there. Enticing situation. Suspended on hooks, with her arms bound and anchored to the wall by other ropes, blood trickling from the points of entry, gagged maybe. Then she could be fucked by the Texan, and one or two others.

I smiled and let the little vision slip away.

It wasn't often I let myself dwell on the possibilities. Not while at work. My employees would be aghast, but not at my fantasies, at my realities.

"Got ya, sweetheart." Randy removed the last hook then cuddled her to him.

I snorted and glanced down at the message on my screen. Military-grade encryption but it never hurt to be careful. Someone reading over my shoulder could be as disastrous as the message being sent in plain text.

The woman in Moresby is not a friend of Jazmine Foulkes. She's Gavoche's daughter, Wren. She's trying to figure out her father's death. Dangerous if she links you and the House.

"Fuck," I said softly.

The spotlights in here were overcoming the aircon. I wiped my forehead with the back of my arm then stared up at the ceiling for a while.

The slave House, in Papua New Guinea, I'd written off. The place was being closed down anyway and the only liabilities, my men there, had been killed by the men who'd rescued Jazmine Foulkes. Those rescuers had also killed Wren's father.

Which was good, really, even if the man had been a friend.

I smiled thinly. No one left alive could connect me directly to anything as illegal, immoral, and depraved as sex slavery. Vetrov was a name I kept in quarantine from the legal, if dirty, businesses I ran as Moghul.

What were the odds Wren would connect me to the House? Low, as in very.

I should have her killed. It was final. It was sensible. People were loose ends because of their nosiness and Wren had met me, even if she knew nothing of her father's fetishes. Once all the immediate family was gone, no one was likely to see anything except an old man's kinkiness exposed in a tawdry fashion by his death in Papua

New Guinea.

I grimaced. What a waste. The last time I'd seen her, the girl had blossomed into a beauty.

The hooks called to me. Someone needed to try them out properly.

I never took things that far on my home turf. Absentmindedly, I tapped my finger on the mobile phone.

Yet a woman caught on those hooks, for me, just for me... Definite possibilities there. It would be karma in a way, considering Andrew's proclivities.

CHAPTER 1

Glass

The last flicker of the white painted metal of Wren's four-wheel-drive showed between the heavy green leaves of the trees.

What a woman. What a surprise that'd been – her agreeing to get in bed with me. I grinned. The buzz from that might take a while to die away.

That road wound down the mountain for miles and miles then back to the coast and Port Moresby. I whistled once. With the driver's side door of my Land Rover propped open with my boot, the sound carried well.

From the jungle to my right, Pieter emerged. His leonine dark locks had been tied back, revealing the heavy bones of his face. He was a man who looked like a brick to the face would barely dent him, and that he'd then apply that same brick to his attacker and make him wish he was home in bed. His looks told no lies.

He jogged over, yanked open the door, and slid into the front passenger seat, making the car creak.

"Lose some fat, man. You're killing the suspension."

"Har har. It's muscle not fat." Pieter pulled out his shiny Glock and laid it across his lap.

Seconds later, Jurgens appeared from behind the vehicle and hauled his ass into the back seat. Enough ink on the man to make a tattooist salivate. Enough metal to set off detectors at fifty feet. South Africa had lost a couple of predators when these guys left the country.

8

Their doors slammed and I pulled mine shut.

"Go," murmured Pieter.

"What did you find?" I turned the wheel and gently accelerated.

"Two men in the bush watched while you spoke to her. They must have their own car back there. We took them both down. Ziptied them. We've got everything from their pockets –

phones, and a camera, wallets. We chucked away their weapons. Next time we won't get to sneak up on them so easily."

That was the drawback of not acting while we had an advantage. I'd known this and yet I still hadn't given the go ahead to terminate them.

As I steered around the long swooping bends of the track, the bumps of a poorly maintained bitumen surface shuddered up through the seat. Birds whooped and whistled above the subdued growl of the engine. I settled my hands on the leather steering wheel cover. Land Rovers had an elegance to them even when they were working hard.

If I didn't tell Wren what had happened...

I fished my phone from my pocket and tossed it to Pieter. "Text her that they're back there. Where you left them. Tell her no security when we meet in town or the deal is off."

A few minutes later, Wren's vehicle passed us going back up to the café.

"You should've let us take them." Pieter cocked his head.

Yeah, maybe I should've.

"Why didn't you?"

I took too long figuring out my answer and Jurgen popped in with his view.

"Glass isn't into killing ladies. None of us are, come to think of it. *Fokken* bad business that is."

From the corner of my eye, I spotted a nod from Pieter.

"True." The man shifted his shoulders to lean into the doors and angle himself toward Glass. "But we had other plans for her, didn't we?"

"*Ja.* I think she confused Glass. That one could make you think with your cock instead of your head. Pretty little thing."

Pieter grinned. "Was that it? Though, hell, taking her would've solved that problem right smart."

"Taking her?" *Bloody hell.* It *had* been the plan. I grunted and kept steering. They let me have the silence.

Good men. Despite the joking, none of us thought lightly of kidnapping Wren or killing her guards. We were all ex-military with jungle actions in Africa under our belts. We'd killed, close up, many times. War had toughened us but it had also made us aware that death was final and life wasn't something you extinguished on a whim.

I glanced across at Pieter. "Did they get pictures?"

"Probably."

Shit.

"There's no internet access here though. Once these are gone we're okay." He pulled out a phone then dismantled and mutilated the sim card. "Jurgen, we may as well toss these out here."

"Sure."

To let them throw the bits as deep as possible into the jungle, I pulled over for a few seconds.

I didn't mind killing, when I absolutely had to, to keep my friends and employees out of jail and healthy. Wasn't that. Admit it, I had reservations about doing anything to a woman. Made my bloody toes curl.

But...I'd let Pieter do whatever he'd wanted to Jazmine. They'd deserved each other, though. From the first moment I saw Jazmine, her devotion to Pieter had shone through. She might not have seen it in herself, but it'd been there. Now she was his happy little slave. They were in love, for whatever strange reasons rocked their world.

Pieter and Jurgen deserved an apology. "I fucked up. I'm sorry. We've lost the initiative."

Concealing ourselves from any police inquiries was the prime, A-grade reason for this meeting. We needed to stop Wren chasing down clues. Even if it hadn't been a bullet from my own sniper rifle, I'd been in charge of the assault that had freed Pieter and Jazmine and killed Wren's father.

We should've stayed away from her and prayed she found no witnesses, no clues.

As if. I smiled to myself. As if praying was ever going to be our first line of attack for any problem.

Besides, if we'd stayed away, I'd never have met her.

A rich little spoilt bitch in the middle of the New Guinea Highlands searching for the answers to her father's death. If ever there was a man who deserved death it was him. Perverted sick bastard.

Would she still follow through with the meeting? Fuck, I hoped so. Still driving, I drew on memories. *Petite*, that was the word for Wren. She'd acted bold as brass but with that neat black hair flipping across her shoulders, and those big eyes peering at me when I'd suggested anything shocking...and that body, she seemed ripe for the next unscrupulous bastard to take advantage.

What was it about boobs, body, and cleavage, that enticed a man when he'd seen it a thousand times on porn sites on the internet and on every woman who'd ever graced his bed?

Nothing but her had existed as I'd threaded between the tables and chairs on the approach to her table.

That bright lipstick was such a contrast when the rest of her was faded denim shorts, white T-shirt, and pale skin. Red on cream. When she'd spoken, I'd imagined kissing those glossy lips, shoving her against a wall and kissing her.

Instant hard-on material.

Wasn't there some theory that women's lips were supposed to remind you of their pussy? I could go with that idea.

But kissing? Only kissing? How undirty and unnasty was that? I was slipping.

She looked like some innocent hidden away from the world for most of her life. Unsullied. The report said she was twenty-six. She probably knew every sex position in the book.

Who gave rat's ass? Just *looking* that innocent grabbed my attention.

Man, I was in trouble.

The vehicle hit a bigger bump and veered off course. I tugged it back into line and cleared away all the visions clouding my mind, or tried to.

My cock ached with the possibilities. I didn't feel right about kidnapping her, or killing her, just to tidy up my world...and how messed up were my morals that I'd even considered that? Pieter would be surprised to hear me question my moral code but it was true. There was a line I never wanted to cross and I'd found it the day we'd thought about killing Jazmine. Today had only reinforced that line.

Yeah, deep down I was a little angel with a halo made of stolen gold...and I had so many dirty things I wanted to do to pretty little Wren...over and over and fucking over.

CHAPTER 2
Wren

In my hotel room, I packed my handbag under Hugh's vigilant eyes. The Beretta, with an extra magazine, made the bag weigh a ton already. My wallet was in there too, as well as everything else a woman needed on a dirty evening assignation, like red lipstick and pepper spray.

Hugh put a small packet in my hand. His facial expression was as disgusted as that of an opera singer asked to do rap. We'd argued for hours. Apparently, what I was about to do was the equivalent of throwing myself off a cliff. There was no one whose opinion I valued more. Hugh had been a cross between my bodyguard and babysitter for years. When he'd finally agreed to help me, I'd been torn between wanting to give him a big hug and smacking him.

I turned the packet over. A condom?

"When did you become my mother, Hugh? My creepy mother, come to think of it?"

He raised a brow. "I'm being practical."

Agreeing, taking it, seemed to say, first of all, that I was indeed having sex with this Richard in exchange for information. Ugh. What had I been thinking? Second, that I should not expect him to provide the condom...or condoms. Wasn't that traditional male territory?

"No." I placed the packet on the glass-topped sideboard. With my forefinger, I pushed it away a few inches.

His brow stayed up.

"No thank you, Mother, I have other plans." I did too. Let's see what mister tough and arrogant Richard did when faced with insubordination. Wrong word...not insubordination, no. A redefinition of his clause. I didn't really expect to need a gun. My guards had been left intact, just gagged and bound.

The man could have hurt us both. Hugh wasn't a superhero – just a super-good friend slash bodyguard slash security organizer.

I reached for the last item on the sideboard – a knife – and slid it from the leather sheath, then turned it over. The blade danced with light.

Knives with their long, sharp steel, and their potential for penetrating the human body, were endowed with an unearthly promise that never failed to send cold shivering through me, down my spine, between my legs, to my sex.

The things a knife might do.

"I don't think you need this either."

What? I frowned. Sometimes, Hugh had a thing about letting me near knives, as if he sensed when they affected me badly. As I mostly did, I gave in. Gently, Hugh took the knife and sheathed it.

Snatching up my bag, I marched to the door, and threw a few last words over my shoulder, "You are odd. Guns get a big tick of approval but knives make you jittery?"

"I don't get jittery. Today is a day when you make me think you'll be careless. Your pistol has a safety catch."

"Hah." I pulled open the door. After Hugh followed me out, the luxury hinges huffed closed slowly.

With the Beretta, I could hit a bull's eye at twenty yards with ninety-three percent accuracy. A knife required close-up encounters. It required me being near enough that an assailant could wrench it from my hand if I made a mistake. No matter how much training I had in self-defense, a man was more dangerous up close. Hugh's logic argued the opposite, that I might hurt this Richard by accident. Maybe it was best I not be tempted.

"I'll be in the bar for a while, talking to a possible informant. If you need me, do not hesitate to press the emergency button in your handbag. We can track you to a degree with the location service, but here, in Papua New Guinea, it's not going to be as reliable. We may lose you. Be careful."

"Sure. I will be. You remember, no surveillance of us meeting at his car."

"I agreed to that, and if this goes wrong and all he wants to do is to ransom you, you'll lose millions."

I nodded. Nothing more to say, really. We'd gone over this ground many times. This was not in Hugh's handbook on keeping me safe.

I needed to know what had happened to Dad. Even if he was...had been, an utter bastard of a parent on most days of my life. Love didn't obey logic.

I heaved in a breath.

There was one other couple in the corridor, also heading for the lift.

My black high heels made no noise in the carpet. Such a quiet place. Behind all those doors, people were probably fucking their little hearts out while tied to the beds, being spanked, cropped, snorting cocaine. Even if I didn't partake, I knew of fetishes, kinks, and addictions. It had hardly been a secret after dear brother showed me a video of father whipping one of his mistresses. I'd been ten. Such a sweet brother, and I'd loved him too, despite his flaws.

If I died tomorrow, I'd be the end of the family line.

The family line being extinguished bothered me little. Our...my Gavoche family was about as close to Heaven as the murderous medieval Borgias. It was sadness that flattened me. My mouth turned down as I contemplated the past.

Children, a baby or two, might be nice, one day. At twenty-six, I could finally declare myself responsible enough to be a mother. No one else was left. Father could no longer deny me.

Babies... Huh. I clamped down on bad memories but a tear or two threatened to spill. Funny, how a still birth bit so deep, even though it was a person who had never quite been born. I sniffed then swallowed past the tightness in my throat. The pluses to being the last one left standing. Fuck, there had to be some, right? As well as the excess of money?

The handbag slapped against my side, no doubt making the crushed red silk of the dress even more crushed.

A few yards down the street from the hotel's circular drive, barely within the pool of light from a streetlight, Richard waited. Arms folded, he leaned on the hood of a black corvette – an old, remodeled one from the looks of it.

I glanced about, betting this spot was outside the hotel's video surveillance range. Far enough to be safe for me to walk, but also discreet.

"Enter." He waved at the Corvette.

Once I was sitting in the car, he leaned over and drew down the safety belt at the same time as I put my hand to it. His larger hand engulfed mine, pulling down the belt to click it in place while I stared at the stubble on the side of his face, stricken with both fear and arousal. This close, smelling him was a given. Whatever pheromones had kicked in, they were doing unwelcome things to me.

If he leaned his elbow on my lap, I'd possibly self-combust.

"I can do this myself."

"Just making sure." He resumed his seat. "Wouldn't want you getting hurt."

No smile, just that assessing appreciation that strayed downward to my breasts, for a second, before he met my gaze again.

Smug bastard. I blinked and pretended to straighten my skirt. Scary bastard.

Smart rejoinders could wait. Right now, this second, I was still humming with the effect of his proximity. Breathing steadily needed my concentration to the nth degree.

I simply hated men who could do this. It reeked of me losing control, them gaining it. Father had been good at that – control, and most men who attempted to make me do what they wanted only triggered a rise of temper. Sometimes when it was the stupid thing to do.

I had to say something or seem an idiot. But what?

He started the engine, clicked on his own belt, and pulled away into traffic.

Saved.

"We're going to a friend's house. Not mine. Not far from here."

After driving in what seemed circles, no doubt to check for my men tailing us, he stopped at the side of the road with a small bridge just ahead.

"Is there anything in your handbag that's important to you?"

Suspicious, I gripped it tighter, on my lap. "Why?"

"It's going into that river."

Fuck him. "Why?"

"You know why."

He put out a hand, imperious, expectant – and having it there in front of me, waiting, annoyed me no end. My gun – I'd lose that.

"The deal's off if you don't give me it."

Could I claim my phone as precious? No, he wasn't that stupid. "My wallet has all my credit cards, my driver's license."

"I'll keep those for you." His hand stayed out.

"And pills. There's a packet of them in there I need. I don't have another prescription."

"They're prescription? Not crack, uppers, downers? I'm not saving your fancy little rich girl designer drugs."

Shit. This man... I had thought him hot, now I knew better. Just another asshole.

"I don't do drugs. I have a sleep disorder. I sleepwalk."

"Sounds like fun. I'll find the pills."

My temper simmered down from molten to bubbling.

"You'd better be trustworthy." Because if he wasn't, I'd drive his bloody Corvette keys through his eyes before I'd give in to any demands.

"I am."

"You really expect me to –"

"I do. Trust me or it's off."

And so, after another twenty or thirty seconds of stonewalling him, and fuming, I relinquished the bag. Then I watched him find my wallet and pills, take out the cards, and declare me a bad girl for having a gun. Asshole. He drove closer to the bridge and exited the car to hurl the bag into the water.

The splash died away, leaving only the throb of the engine then the slam of the door as he reentered.

Gone. On my own. It had been nice knowing I had a gun if I needed it.

Glass might be a recruiter for one of those slave houses. I could end up locked away forever as some man's sex slave. I risked a sideways look and his set expression gave me no reassurance. I could be dead tomorrow too. Shut up doubts.

"Damn you," I whispered, staring out the window at the stonework of the bridge. "Damn you to hell."

"I'm already going there. Save your breath."

Hugh needed to invest in a GPS tracker I could insert up a body cavity. And wouldn't that be fun on a date night. Making light of this wasn't going to fix anything but it made me feel better.

"Now we can have our night in privacy. I'm allergic to people barging in with guns."

"Really? I'm not so gauche as to let Hugh do that." I slumped back into the upholstery. My orneriness surged to the fore. Fuck him ten times over. "Besides, I have an emergency beacon elsewhere on me."

"Oh?" I couldn't see much of his face as he drove, but amusement showed in his tone. "Then I will have fun searching for it, with you naked."

I glared. If looks could kill, he'd just been stapled to the seat with a hundred knives. Sharp fuckers. I could see the blood soaking that fancy dark shirt. The handles wedged deep, right up to his chest. Well...almost see them. Let's see him call that fun too.

I kept my eyes open as he maneuvered through the streets, fairly certain I could find where he was taking us on a map. Until he pulled over and made me sit still for a blindfold to be tied on. Deal or no deal. I had to say yes. This was getting more and more like a bloody game show.

At one point, I sneaked up a hand to raise the edge. He stopped me with one uh-uh and threatened to tie my hands. Now that rang alarm bells.

So I was good, outwardly, while inwardly adding some knives to the collection in his chest.

The echoes and creak of a metal door winding up said he'd driven into an underground car park. Somewhere secure then. A compound for foreigners probably. They were a common way to be safe here, what with the high crime rate against foreigners.

When he led me up and around some flights of stairs and through a door, then lifted off my blindfold, I found myself in an immaculately decorated apartment.

"What a pity," I sighed out.

That drew a sharp look.

I studied him as he ambled from the short entranceway into a living room to toss the blindfold onto a giant glass and metal chessboard. Ferns and small palms added greenery, their fronds hanging from small pots. An ocean theme encompassed a sand and blue color scheme, paintings, and furniture like a driftwood-inspired coffee table. There was even a small rowboat upended and fastened upright to one wall.

"A pity? Why?"

I shrugged.

To the left was a small but modern kitchen that ran along the wall. Beyond him was an opened wall looking out onto the night sky. Folded back shuttered doors were concertinaed at either end.

"Call me Glass. It's friendlier than Richard."

"If you want." Was this another fake name? Glass, it sounded like a nickname.

He propped his hand on the wall beside the boat.

For a moment I admired the way his arm muscles bulged and flexed under the sleeve of his dark gray shirt. Glass had that physical solidness of a man who could effortlessly fill a room with his presence. Had it in spades. Curiosity kept me looking far too long.

I tore myself away and answered his first question just to see his reaction.

"I was hoping to see a few knives in you when you removed the blindfold. My imagination amused me on the way here."

"Bloodthirsty."

"Yes. That's me."

He studied me. "Snap. Me too. We'll make a great couple."

"I'm paying you a lot of money. Don't trivialize this."

He snorted. "I'm not toning down my jokes for you. Be happy I'm not trivializing your quest to find your father's killer."

Stalemate.

Slowly, he approached, his tread measured, his gaze as nonchalantly menacing as a leopard that's found a fear-paralyzed bunny in its territory.

I steeled myself not to back away and dug my nails into my palms to make myself focus.

Look at him. Do not take your eyes away, do not blink, it shows weakness.

"You made me a promise yesterday." He stopped a foot away, glowering down at me while I strived to keep my tongue from straying onto my lips.

When nervous, I licked them or even ran my tongue under my top lip. I wasn't nervous, just...just...fuck. My toes curled as he reached out, slow and deliberate, toward my face.

My response was automatic. "Do not touch me."

At that, one brow inched up, but he still took my chin in the cup of his hand. I rocked back, gasping at the contact. His subtle smile transfixed me as much as the feel of his calloused thumb running lightly along my jawbone. Such warm skin, as if his body were several degrees hotter than mine.

Heat spread from between my legs and my nipples ached and tightened.

"See."

God, the way he watched me...

I swallowed surreptitiously, "See what?"

"You can take my hand on you. I don't bite."

Something about those words broke the spell. The assurance that I'd stand there for him, perhaps? When he moved his hand to caress my hair at the side of my face, I stepped away.

"Oh but I do. I bite."

To my consternation, that only made his mouth quirk at one corner.

Fine. Did he want me to think him made of rock? Emotionless?

This seemed a good time to set boundaries. Was it reckless, considering where I was? Perhaps. But I'd been rock climbing, kayaking, done my share of hiking through wilderness and even tried parachuting, once. I had a father who'd scared me so much I nearly puked, once, when I did something he detested. Damn though, my pulse went crazy as I found the bedroom doorway to the right and entered.

"Is this the main bedroom?"

"Yes." He came up behind me, close.

"Good." I went and sat on the edge of the king-size bed, sinking into the heavy quilt, then bouncing up and down. "Care to take a seat?"

Though he looked suspicious, he sat beside me, merely inches away.

Goose bumps. All my hairs stood on end. I hadn't considered he'd sit this near me.

I lined up the right words in my head, enunciated them carefully. "You said you wanted me to join you in bed before you'd help me. Well, now I have. My part of the deal is done, apart from the money. I never said it meant sex. Now, you have to fulfill your side of things."

I waited, my lips set in a line. My impulsive decision at the café had been thrown down and ground underfoot. If he was angry, I'd offer to pay more.

If...

What if he wanted to rape me?

Those – rape, death, kidnapping – were what Hugh had railed at me about, for hours. I didn't care. My psychologists would be aghast, but I plain didn't care. Maybe I would care if it happened. Of course I would. Logically, I knew it. But rape and assault seemed distant, far-away concepts. My father's death had ushered in a weariness, which came and went like a gray tide.

If bad things happened, at least I'd be done with this man; I'd know what he was capable of. Perhaps it would bring me peace, as if a penance had been paid. God knew, I owed a lot. It often seemed as if I'd been waiting to pay my whole life.

Bravery was easy when you were numb.

I waited still. What was he doing?

With his thigh almost touching mine, and the dip in the mattress, I had to be careful not to topple into him. I listened to his breathing, smelled him. My awareness seemed to sharpen. From the corner of my eye, I saw the muscles of his arm, and I wondered. What if...he did try something?

I must be mad. I think I wanted him to.

The urge to look at him intensified.

CHAPTER 3

Moghul

Op1
to Vetrov (decrypted)

7.43 pm Wren G observed entering black Corvette. Surveillance ceased after driver (blond male 30 to 40yrs approx) began evasion. Male unidentified at present. Do you wish his identity?

A video was downloading.

Did I? I held the phone to my chin, staring unfocused down the flight of stairs. I was annoyed at myself. I didn't have any rights over this girl or her body. Then why my reaction to the knowledge that a man was taking her on dates?

My meandering thoughts took me down the stairs. I hadn't been to my island house for years. No reason. My private playing area held no interest for me. Any subs I took up with at play parties were happy being little exhibitionists and flogged, fucked, or whatever, in public.

Was it fortuitous, some subtle nudge of fate's hand that the text about Wren had come through while I was visiting?

I could sell this place in a month. I was considering it. Sunlight streamed in through the thick plate glass wall. I glanced across, through the tinted glass, at the blue on blue horizon. The views over the ocean were spectacular. It would need some cleaning, some removal of kink equipment, unless I wanted to shock the real estate agent. I leaned on the rounded steel railing encompassing the rectangular hole in the tiled floor and peered over the edge. The pit of despair, as my last submissive had labelled it, was full of dead bugs, dust, and cobwebs. How spiders got into an air-conditioned, sealed home was inconceivable, as Vizzini might have said.

The brushed steel was cool under my palms. My architect had done well. Outside was searingly hot.

I was fantasizing about a pretty woman when there were a million of them out there. A pretty woman hung on hooks, with an audience of one. I could see myself making her come despite her predicament...her writhing and screaming, then I'd tease her endlessly and make her come again and again. Sadism plus orgasms – my favorite recipe.

Whoa. Lips pursed, I let out a long breath. I was getting a hard-on just thinking about it.

A Vetrov affair should not invade my legal, if very kinky, Moghul world. It was as if Alice in Wonderland had popped out of a rabbit hole in my living room, though Wren did have a tenuous link to me through her father.

The high-res video downloaded onto the screen and I clicked play. As she walked toward his car, her red dress frothed about her legs like waves washing onto a forbidden shore.

What the hell. Just this once. I could follow what she got up to with impunity. In Papua New Guinea, my affairs were all cleaned up.

Of course, if she wandered into my territory here, now, that would be a whole new ball game. It would be irritating. I sorted through my emotions. And interesting and tempting, definitely tempting. But I could see no route she could take that would lead her to me. No one knew my alter egos.

I shook my head. All hypothetical. After twenty years building my little empire I wasn't about to jeopardize it on a whim.

Vetrov
to Op1
Yes.

*****

Glass

Was this Wren girl suicidal? I hovered between laughing at her antics and just grabbing her.

Her light blue eyes were dilated, though maybe that was the low light. A little muscle on her jaw twitched. She held my gaze despite toying nervously with the cloth of that dead sexy red dress.

Balls, steel lady balls, even if she was crazy.

She had no idea who I was, except that I'd said I could help her track who had killed her father, and she knew I had men capable of neutralizing her security. I wasn't your average guy on the street with a deep respect for the law.

I could kidnap her and beat the crap out of her for bugging me.

The neighbors wouldn't hear much, if I gagged her first and tied her up. I had to admit she tempted me. I could do anything. Pieter had showed me the other side. The dark possibilities: ever since I saw Jazmine kneel to him, they'd been like a siren song.

Wren blinked and ducked her head again.

Especially when she acted submissive like that. *Jesus.* I stared down at the top of her head, as if struck by lightning along with an earthquake and a small nuclear device.

"You expect me to roll over and agree to that?"

Her back stiffened and she unleashed a glare on me. "Two hundred thousand is not a pittance."

"Gone back to two hundred, hey?" Compensation. She knew she'd done wrong, and that glare, it was like a kick to my brain and my balls.

So I grabbed her. I clenched my fist in the back of her hair. Her eyes snapped open.

Revelation rolled in. This was *nice.*

Soft hair. A woman in my hand. While she was still gasping, I relentlessly pulled her backward until she hit the bed, then I anchored my elbow near her and waited to see what she'd do.

Her hands came up to pry mine off. One after the other, I trapped them and clasped them to her, below her breasts.

Another glare.

"Let's cut all the fucking around." I didn't expect her to give in.

When she arched as if to kick me, I laid my thigh over hers. After a few more seconds of curses, and trying to wriggle loose, she lay there panting.

"You fucking bastard!"

"A fucking bastard? Bastard, maybe. The other? I promise you'll know when that happens."

The wrestling had done nice things. If breasts ever heaved, it was now.

"That dress would make a blind man want to rape you."

She fell silent.

Was there fear in her eyes? Or just anger?

"Why? Why'd you change your mind?"

"I don't. Want. To fuck you." Those words came out through an angry sneer.

Nasty. I snaked my fingers deeper into her hair and got another gasp for my efforts. I twisted my wrist and turned her to face me more. I could see the appeal this had for Pieter. Controlling her was a damn aphrodisiac.

"You don't want to fuck me," I deadpanned.

I wasn't impervious to this woman squirming under me. I had a hard-on tenting my pants.

Maybe her mind had problems with fucking me, a lowlife mercenary living in New Guinea, but I'd bet my two hundred K that her pussy was wet and wanting me.

"You're damn lucky," I said, grating out the words with my mouth two inches from hers. "That I'm not into rape."

"Oh." She blinked while her mouth closed from making that *Oh*.

Disappointment, I swear, written in big red letters. What the hell?

Oh baby, I'm going to convert your confusion into a yes tonight.

"This was a business deal. Not a date. You want to renegotiate? It takes two."

"It wasn't signed and sealed."

"In my universe, our agreement was as good as signed in blood. Want to argue?"

Under my hand, her wrists moved as she flexed her fingers and her tendons shifted. I let her go and jumped to my feet. My maneuver seemed to have stunned her and she lay there looking up.

I leaned over her, steadying myself with a hand to the quilt by her hip. Then I smiled.

"You want to get out of this deal, Miss Wren?"

She nodded.

"Then I get part of you to play with tonight."

"What?"

"Let's see. Which bits?" I did an insolent appraisal of her body, sliding my hand upward from her hip, over her belly, to the undercurve of her breast. She quivered enough that I registered it. "Your mouth?" I bent and brushed my lips over hers, then pulled away, slow, conscious of how her breathing had ceased.

So soft. Her mouth was lush, fertile, like maybe I could give her babies just by kissing.

"Wait," she said huskily, her palms pressing on my chest. "Wait now. You're talking kissing? I guess...I can do that."

My knee had ended up against the edge of the bed, squashing the dress material between her legs.

I slid my hand to her dress and started gathering fabric in my fist, making it slither up her legs. "Best of all, after I play with you, you show me your panties. If they're wet, I get to fuck you."

Her hands whipped down and she tried to hold down the dress. "Hey! No! No agreement. No way can you do that!"

"Why? Afraid you're already in violation? Show me or I'll assume you've got the hots for me anyway. I'm being lenient."

I shoved up the dress, baring a smooth expanse of upper thigh and the lowest point of a triangle of red lace. Damn. The swell of her mons showed above that. I could bury my face there and not come up for a month. Move aside that elastic and I could...

I coughed. Back on subject. *Shut up, dick. Later you'll get your turn.*

"This is perverted," she said, quietly alarmed.

"You're lucky they're not black. With black, I couldn't tell from looking. Red is good." I nudged with my leg, applying pressure to the inside of her knees, encouraging her to spread them. "Red goes dark when it's wet. If they weren't red, I'd have to take these off and feel your pussy with my fingers."

"This is..." Her throat moved and her tone had lowered to a whisper. "It's totally crazy."

There was a fevered look to her face that hadn't been there before, a blush on her cheeks. She wasn't resisting enough for a woman who really, truly meant no. Maybe she thrived on reluctance? Maybe she wanted a man who would simply do what he wanted to her. I could run with that. Run a long fucking way.

"Are you wet, Miss?" Miss? Where'd that come from? I'd never called a woman miss before. "Show me. Now."

She made a weird noise in her throat – half whimper, half question. I fixed her with a determined glower. "Now."

"Glass..." But her ass did a subtle squirm, and this time she gave in. Her leg muscles stopped pushing against my palms. Slowly, they fell open.

I straightened and took in the scenery, wishing I had a camera.

Her blue eyes were half closed. Her red dress was scrunched onto her stomach. Her thighs had opened, revealing those red panties. One yank and I'd have them gone. The crotch area showed a quarter inch wide line of darkness. If I bared her pussy by rolling aside the cloth, my finger would find more than enough moisture to sink effortlessly into her.

Now I knew.

Did she know how aroused she was?

She lay under me looking distressed, flushed, a little perplexed even. Expectant.

This was too easy. I wanted her on fire, *dying* to have me inside her. I didn't want some miserable victory that she'd forget tomorrow. I wanted total surrender. If I didn't get her to scream out a climax loud enough to give someone a heart attack, I'd missed my mark.

How wet could I get her? My cock could wait while I stirred this little miss until she was begging me.

"Outside. Now. I'm starving."

"What? Dinner?" she blurted, staggering as I towed her out of the bedroom to the broad balcony and a set of table and chairs.

"Yes, dinner. Sit. Stay. Miss Wren." I hauled out her chair.

When she was sitting and had arranged her dress, I bent over. "Hold still."

Then I gave her the first kiss, making her part her lips and holding her under the jaw lightly. Just enough pressure to keep her there. Just enough to say, *right now, you're mine.* When she raised her hand and touched my shoulder, I pinned it to the table. Her breathing hitched.

The more I held her still, the more she reacted. Or so it seemed.

Her eyes followed me as I lifted away and she was panting. That red-lipsticked mouth. One day, I needed to fuck it.

I stroked her hair, ran my finger down her ear, and smiled when she shivered. "Now, forget what I mean to do to you. Enjoy the night."

Tell someone not to think about something and they will. I wanted her worried and thinking.

Her mouth opened and closed, then her tongue poked around at her top lip in an adorable way. "I cannot believe I let you do that. You are incorrigible, Mister Glass."

"Mister Glass? Sounds like a promotion."

She made a dismissive noise. How wet had that kiss got her? How often could I check her panties? Figuring that out might kill me.

The smell of the takeaway food drifted past and her stomach growled.

"I need to rescue the food from the microwave."

When I returned with the plates and the Champagne bottle under my arm, I found she'd angled her chair to look out over the roofs to the bay. Most cities had an allure at night, when the grime and crime was disguised by sparkling strings of streetlights. Below us the swimming pool water slapped at the sides as someone did laps.

She turned and simply sat for a few minutes staring at me. I let the silence be, figuring she was adjusting to what had happened, justifying her reactions somehow. Besides, I was happy watching her back.

At last she inhaled deeply and leaned in to peer at the plate before her.

"Thai. Best I could do. This is Moet Chandon however..." I brandished the bottle and uncorked it, poured us both a glass before sitting.

"Champagne?" She cruised her fingertip through the moisture already dimpling the outside of the glass. "If I drink this, I can't take my pills. I have a sleeping disorder."

"Go without for one night."

Wren lifted the glass and swirled the liquid, tilting the goblet as if fascinated by the play of color. "Once, I walked down to our garage and started the car while asleep. I'm told some people can drive even when sleep walking."

"Really?" It seemed incredible. "It's worth it to drink some Moet." I indicated her champagne. "If you drift off I promise I won't give you my keys."

If I tied her to the bed she wasn't likely to sleepwalk far.

I sat back and picked up my fork while she tasted the wine.

"This *is* nice. I haven't had Champagne for so long." She took another sip.

We ate and shared a few stories, dancing around what was not okay to tell each other. As the scene in the bedroom ebbed from her mind, she grew more confident.

I took possession of her hand and held it as often as I could. Tracing between her fingers while she tried to talk about some sensible thing let me watch the subtle changes on her face. Her eyelids fluttered. When I lifted her hand to my mouth and kissed each finger, one by one, she glanced down at the table and shifted position. The chair creaked.

I wondered if I was arousing her. I hoped so.

"I can't eat, easily, when you do that." A little crease formed on her forehead.

"I'm done." I gave her hand back to her, trying not to smile when she fumbled and dropped her knife.

"What do you do for a living?" I forked up noodles. I knew the answer but figured I should ask.

"I'm studying veterinary science at Sydney University. You? Killing people?" Her smirk said she was trying to tease.

"And here I was polite enough not to ask if you spent your days counting money."

Wren shrugged. "When you have more than you need, it means little."

"When you have almost none, it means everything."

"Are you saying you're that poor? Somehow I doubt it. Besides, isn't money the root of all evil?"

"That philosophy is a little overrated, otherwise we'd all be giving our money away not struggling to get more."

Wren swirled her goblet, staring at me as if surprised I knew the word philosophy. I doubted she'd ever struggled for money.

"So if you're not simply killing people?"

"I'm ex-army. I went to officer training at Sandhurst then the SAS for a short time before I was injured and retired."

The arch of her brows was perfect. "So, you're British? You don't quite sound it."

"I am. Or I was. Now I'm..." I waved a hand. "A bit African, a bit Papua New Guinean, a bit Aussie. I haven't been back for thirteen years. You're Australian?" I knew she was. I knew a lot about her.

"No. No. I'm a bit of everything, like you."

Seemed like she was saying she had no idea who she was. I let it pass...and I wondered why it bothered me. Her accent seemed private school when she concentrated, but when I caught her off guard in a joke, she lapsed into something less posh. A few times, I caught her staring at nothing, her mouth downturned, as if she relived a painful memory.

I was seized by moments of *her*. Her lips nudging the edge of the glass. The sway of her breasts. The curves revealed and sculpted under the silk. Black hair, red lips, cream skin. Like a china doll with cracks you couldn't see.

Something was riding her. She had demons, same as me, which only intrigued me more. A sleeping disorder? I could guess why with a father so immoral I'd felt dirty seeing his corpse. A brother with his own perversions, too, from what I'd heard. Where did she fit in all this?

Her knife and fork were scraped across the plate and neatly arranged. Done eating.

What the hell was I doing experimenting on her by trying to emulate Pieter?

What the hell was she doing here? For all her money and her paid security, she was here with me. I had an inclination to wrap her in my arms and fix whatever was making her sad. And I wanted to throw her down on that bed in there and fuck her. Why hadn't she run from me when I started controlling her?

I shoved away my chair roughly enough to make it screech and rose to my feet, ignoring her startled expression. "We're going swimming."

In a closet, neatly packed away, I found a few bikinis, the tags still on them.

It was a muggy, humid night and the coolness of the pool would be welcome.

"One of these should fit you." I put the whole bunch of them in her hands. "The bathroom's that door." I pointed.

Then I went and leaned my head on the wall in the bedroom.

Was this me? Maybe if I banged my head a few times, I'd see sense? This woman didn't need me to abuse her, she needed someone to stop her falling over the next cliff. Throwing herself over even.

She's an adult.

I wrenched on the boardshorts I'd found – the pair with the condom packet still in the pocket.

She met me in the hallway, wearing the blue bikinis with the tassels.

They fit her like a dirty depraved glove that covered her like body paint, and showed everything that needed seeing when her nipples peaked. I could even see the shape of her pussy. Not looking would've taken a court order.

Fucking hell.

I checked inside my head for those doubts. Conflicted, man, conflicted.

If I had a conscience it was a damn fornicating voyeur of a conscience. My libido was taking me somewhere my brain had rejected.

In her hand was her dress and a red bra, the straps dangling, and those panties – I could just see the edge of them. As I approached, I think my stare was close to nailing her to the wall behind her, because she gaped at me then stepped back and hit that same wall.

"Wait." She held up a hand, waving it palm out. "Glass, I thought you'd changed your mind. You were so civilized at the table."

Civilized? What man was civilized?

I'm pretty sure I growled.

My little victim.

In one stride I was in front of her. I could see myself fastening her to that wall with my hands on her neck and my leg between hers. I could *feel it.* I flexed my fists. *Don't.*

I pressed my forehead to hers. What better route into her mind than through her eyes – through the trembling of her eyelashes and the shifting shades of blue in those irises.

"I was thinking of letting you go home untouched. Then...this."

I trailed my gaze down to her cleavage and beyond. Every curve led to another and downward, her breasts, her hips, that cute belly button I wanted to stick my tongue in, the slight mound of her stomach. She was a sexual puzzle with the best ever prize when you solved her.

Eyes wide, mouth open, she didn't even bother to try to stop me. Her hands were splayed against the wall either side of her as if she needed that to stop her falling.

Her clothes had landed in a pile at her feet.

She hadn't run.

Maybe I could do this without breaking her.

Maybe? What was I letting myself become? She wasn't some disposable sex creature.

I put my mouth to the side of her face and my lips moved on her ear as I spoke. "You're fucking with my head. I do all kinds of shit to you, and you don't run? You don't scream or panic or look for the door? From now on, if you stay, I'm going to do what I like to you. Fuck etiquette. Hear me?"

CHAPTER 4
Wren

The pound of my heart and the rumble of his up-close words took me from a world where it was right to be alone and lonely, to his world, where I could be anything he wanted me to be. It was fearsome and wrong and ever so right...for me.

I couldn't answer. Not yet. Not in words. I had this ferocious man before me and my head was in a thousand pieces.

He was right.

I could've, should've run. I hated controlling men. Jesus. He fingered my throat.

"I gather, you're staying."

"Uhhh." I squeezed shut my eyes, opened them. He was still there.

I was fucking with his head?

"You can't..." I croaked. "Wait."

"Wait?" His brows rose and I saw something amazing, something I don't think I'd seen all night – a real smile. I didn't care that it had a freaky aura of triumph about it. It was a smile that also had humanity.

The man could be nice. He'd looked almost as shaken as I felt, before he cornered me.

The wall at my back had no give, alas, because I wanted to sink into it as much as I wanted to push myself at him. God, god, god. Like a weird, black-hole, gravitational mass he was sucking me toward him. I couldn't resist, could I?

Yes.

Considering my hate of controlling men, why him? He was right.

After what he'd done to me on the bed, I should've left.

I liked it. Not just liked. It absorbed me, what he was doing.

Shut eyes again and pray, but I couldn't keep doing that.

I stared back at him.

My color. He had pale blue, almost gray eyes, like mine.

Don't. Do. This.

"You can't —" My voice collapsed and I had to start again. "You can't expect me to agree to that."

"Then go." I could see his nostrils widen as he said that, his gaze hard. Like this was a death sentence.

The two of us were caught in some unearthly spiral.

My eyelids moistened, heralding tears. Say it before you chicken out. "I don't want to go."

"Oh?"

Surprise. Fucking surprise showed in his tone. Hallelujah. I needed to see some weakness. No matter how much I was dying to succumb to this, I couldn't, not if he was purely asshole. I didn't understand why any of this was doing what it did to me, except that I'd never encountered a man like this.

Forceful. Sexual dynamite.

Obsessed with me. Fuck, that was hot. Even if just for one night.

But he was also...confused.

I wasn't stupid. I wasn't.

He's dangerous.

Tentatively, I put my hand out and felt his jaw, the bristles rough on my skin.

I'd never go down a set of rapids without some idea of what I was doing, of the hazards at play.

"Can I trust you?"

For a microsecond, his face changed in some infinitesimal way. "Can you trust me?" As he said the next soft words, he found one of my wrists and then the other and held them to the wall beside my head. "Absolutely, to the ends of the earth. And not at all. If you stay, I'm doing what I want to. Not what you want."

I tried to wrench from his grip and couldn't budge at all. The strength in this man's hands flattened me. I drifted far, far away. To the ends of the earth.

Spellbound.

Heartbeats counted the languid rhythm of my wayward thoughts.

He unraveled me.

This...was the same as when he'd made me spread my legs and show my underwear to him, while I'd lain exposed like some slave girl thrown before her master. It seemed I had a thing for this, when it was Glass. I'd never, ever let another man to do this.

The meaning of his actions and words came to me: He could take physical control of me without asking. He wasn't some deranged killer, but he might go somewhere that turned him on more than me.

I wasn't sure I'd mind that at all.

If my translation was wrong, this could be a disaster, but what was the point of being an adrenalin junkie without an occasional fix?

"I'm staying." My tears spilled as I spoke and I felt the cooling tracks run over my cheeks. I was insane, clearly, completely, insane.

"Good."

"Do what you want to...with me."

The words plummeted to earth, like the fall of a missile.

Then he kissed my tears. Dear god, he kissed them.

Then he kissed my mouth. "I'm going to make you scream."

Oh my. If he wanted to make me scream in pleasure, I was okay with that. If in pain, I was strangely okay with that too.

He covered my mouth with his, denying me oxygen in a kiss that was an assault, not romantic foreplay.

His larger body crushed me slowly to the wall. With every breath, my breasts pushed into his chest. The harder he crushed me, and the harder he kissed, the more I tried to resist. Every breath became a fight, yet it was background noise, as his tongue shoved into me.

Seeing loses importance when you're kissing, really kissing.

I tasted this man, and felt his tongue probe my mouth, felt him breathe hotly into me, and his bites on my neck. I'd never had a man dare to hold me with such perfection. No matter what I did, or how much force I used to try to pull loose, he kept me in place, beneath him.

I vanished into some other place where I was...his.

I could hear myself groaning and breathing hard. Feel the twist of my body as I struggled to escape even though I couldn't and didn't want to. I felt the press of his thigh between mine. The rush and heat of blood. The screwing, twining, pumping of pressure inside me until I was gasping for relief. Do me. Fuck me. Be inside me.

"Please." I cried the word, in a shameless way. "Please.

Then he stopped kissing me.

"What do you want?"

"You." I opened my eyes again. How did you say this? I kept going, hoping my brain would find the words, no matter how embarrassing. "You. I want you...in me."

He laughed softly. "Not yet. Not until I say. Are your panties wet now? Are you?"

Why couldn't he want this like I did?

"Yes?" I said hesitantly.

"Let me see. Let me feel you." He stepped away a foot. "Pull aside your bikini."

The bump in his boardshorts advertised his eagerness. Just doing what he said was as impossible as throwing myself out the window behind him, naked. I simply...couldn't. I reached for him, already knowing it was wrong.

Like I expected, like I wanted, I realized, he grabbed my hand, and stopped me, tightening his fingers in on mine until it hurt.

"No. Do what I said."

"Or what?" I asked, breathless and hoping. "Would you hurt me?"

The seconds burned past, leaving a trail of lust.

The walls in here were going to be steeped in our pheromones when we were gone.

Around his eyes crinkled. "I'll spank you red. With some bites for extra. And since it will be my first time doing that, you should be fucking scared."

"You've never..." I flushed, knowing my hushed tone had betrayed my excitement. What was wrong with me, wanting this? I hadn't even been able to say spanked.

"Never wanted to."

My wrists were hurting from twisting in his grip. The sting reminded me, exquisitely, of what he could do.

Reality – he'd not done this before. That I was his first was scary, a good sort of scary. What would it feel like? Why did I even fucking want to know what it would feel like? And when he'd said he'd bite me, a sexual thrill had twisted in. Not just because of me imagining him doing it. I'd heard such wicked anticipation in his voice. Both of us had our souls out raw, on the block, for each other to see.

He folded his arms and his biceps strained the sleeves of his shirt.

His hands had impressed me from when I first saw him at the café

– big, calloused. Testosterone would be more common than blood inside Glass. He'd have no trouble figuring out how to hurt me. I think I had a mini orgasm right then and there. Damn. Why didn't I know this about myself?

"You have five seconds." He didn't count out loud, or look at his wristwatch, which made it worse. I had to guess.

I blinked. Then I took a deep, deep breath. The beginning. I'd asked for this. I slid my shaking hand downward until my fingers met the top edge of the bikini. When I moved to pull it down, he shook his head.

"Uh-uh. Don't take them off. Just pull the crotch aside."

Fuck. This was more than a little humiliating. But, as I shifted the thin scrap of cloth, I realized how wet I was. I'd soaked the crotch of the bikini bottoms despite only having only put them on a few minutes before.

I fumbled and my fingers slid across my lower lips. The attention of this man on where my fingers were made me even wetter and my swollen labia tingled at my own touch. I waited, red-faced, knowing my pussy had spasmed in while he watched. Hopefully, the angle meant he hadn't seen.

"Push out your pelvis. I want you to finger fuck yourself." His gaze flicked to my face.

We hadn't even had sex and he wanted something so intimate?

I shut my eyes, shocked, and yet, I was going to do this. Did he wonder if I would? Or was he so arrogant that he knew?

I searched his face.

Oh yes, he was sure. Arrogant bastard – Glass in two words.

But I loved it. I desperately wanted that arrogance.

My breath hitched as I bumped my finger over the swollen contours of my pussy. I found the tight circle of my entrance and inserted my middle finger, gasping a little as I explored myself.

"That's it. Good girl." He grunted. "Keep going – keep fucking yourself – until I say stop. Use your thumb on your clit. I want to see you panting, Wren." All said with that fierce concentration.

God. This was so arousing. I delved inside myself, my finger slipping in easily on my moisture. When the skin between my fingers hit my limit, I pulled out that finger, and stuck it back in. So slick was I, the sucking and sliding sounds travelled. The smallest friction of that finger inside me was a hundred times better than when I'd masturbated before.

He watched my face and my hand equally, going from one to the other, one to the other. The small smile that showed in his eyes, amped my pleasure and made me even crazier. I went past the point where I cared what he saw and groaned, shoving my crotch at him as I fucked myself. I squeezed in a second finger and thumbed my clit harder, doing vigorous circles over just the right spot.

The obvious erection in his boardshorts made me grunt and slow. I gasped a few times then braved his criticism, my fingers still deep inside. "Please? I'd rather... You?"

I'd never ached for cock like this.

God, my clit and pussy were pulsing, and I was dying for release. Just a few more seconds, or a ride on that dick straining at his shorts. I could feel it in me, sliding in, fucking me.

"No. I want you to pull out your fingers. Put your hands above your head and wait."

Wait for what? The zombie apocalypse? I needed this man inside me or I was going to explode. And I was already messy enough.

"Glass, this is –"

"Grounds for spanking?" That smile went away and he nodded slightly, as if he was imagining doing it.

The connection between us went from hot to on fire in two seconds flat.

There was sex and there was whatever the hell this was. Analyzing it was not happening, though I tried, my logical thoughts were snarled up with my desires. Raising my hands would make me feel like a pet fucktoy being exhibited and somehow that was good. No. Wait. His pet fucktoy. That was the important bit.

I left my bikini where it was, rolled to one side. Without losing his attention one iota, I put my hands above my head, aware my hand was sticky and glistening with my juices.

"You are so beautiful."

"Thank you?" I think I squeaked that out. Fuck. Do me, man.

He took a step nearer, and went to one knee before me. Then, with excruciating slowness, he found the edge of the bikini and placed it back over my pussy, covering me. Oh you bastard. When he slid a finger dead center down my slit, squashing the cloth into me, I quivered and let out a small moan. My fingers curled and my toes scrunched in and, as subtly as I could, I moved on his finger.

YIELD

If only...

Frozen with hope, I watched him rest his hands on the front of my thighs, then lean forward, with that gleam in his eyes, and breathe on me. The warmth permeated through the cloth, heating my clit.

"God damn," I croaked. My legs shook but I said nothing more. There was some intangible...reward in not asking. In waiting for his decision.

"You're going to come down to the pool with me now. Like this." He nodded. "All wet and ready to be fucked." He stood, sliding his hands up my mostly naked torso and stopping with them curved into my waist. "And I'm going to know what you're feeling. How fucking wet your cunt is because of me."

Dirty, dirty man. I shuddered.

That was it. Nothing more.

Mouth agape, I watched as he turned and walked to the door, picking up his towel from the floor on the way. Then he held the door open and cocked his head at me.

Incomprehensible combustion, that's what they'd call how I died. I sighed and followed him. Every second was rendering me ever more addicted to this arrogant man.

CHAPTER 5
Glass

We took the concrete stairs and went down to ground level. After watching Wren's small feet negotiate the bends and take a few of them wide, I guided her with my palm on her hip or ass. Two glasses of Champagne and she was tipsy. Two and maybe I wasn't thinking straight either. I'd just complicated everything a hundredfold.

Employer and employee relationships didn't normally involve spankings like this one might. I'd begun this affair at the café to get her out of our hair. To eliminate a threat. I hadn't been thinking straight. Though the news earlier today meant maybe I'd have been better off staying away? Wait. She might've ended up dead. No way would that have been acceptable, even if I hadn't gotten to know her.

When I again guided her, Wren frowned at me. "You don't need to do that. I'm okay."

"You're not." I tightened my fingers on her ass to remind her I could do what I liked tonight. Her gasp and fleeting look of shock pleased me. "I don't want to risk you falling."

Manipulating her was my newest obsession. I tipped her chin up then kissed her lightly while running my finger along her slit. My finger sank almost an inch into the groove of her pussy, when I used enough pressure. Through the material, I could feel her slickness.

When I probed especially deep with that finger, she squealed and wriggled. "Glass! This isn't fair. It's public."

Wriggly woman. Mmm. My balls were going to be so blue.

"No one here, Wren. Except us. Keep still." I pulled her head back by her hair and kept her backed against the railing, while I played with her pussy some more – long enough to get her groaning quietly. If I wasn't fuzzing her brain with lust, I was happy doing it to mine.

I let her go and she hung there, hands clinging to the metal, seeming spun out in some pre-orgasmic space. Now that was pretty.

"Come on." I took her hand, tugged until she focused on me, and started down the stairs.

"If you keep doing that," she muttered. "I'm going to need therapy. More therapy, I mean."

I snorted. "And the more you complain the longer I'm going to keep you like that."

Her next look was perplexed.

Whatever her question, I had no answer, yet. Wren had some appeal I couldn't measure. I'd had pretty women before. Wasn't that. Daring? Rich? I think it was the kinkiness shining through whenever I challenged her.

Yeah, that was a big part of it.

What I was doing to her seemed to have fried her synapses too. Just a smidgeon. A hot woman who'd given me carte blanche with her body. Every man's dream.

She was still mostly an enigma to me. I knew little of who she was, apart from the public details about the millionaire heiress. Whether I fucked her or not, and who was I kidding, it was a foregone conclusion, surely? Either way, I had to get her away from Papua New Guinea. Away from the mess here that might hide clues for her to find. Or people wanting to kill her over them. I'd lure her to Australia, on the pretense of finding Vetrov. After that, I'd have to see what I could make happen.

Anything. Why think small?

I peeked through the square of frosted glass on the pool area door. Still no lights on inside. Then I unlocked the door and ushered her through, watching the sway of that pert bottom.

The pool area was unlit except by the moon smiling above and the streetlights washing over the wall and leaking through gaps between buildings. Water shone on the limestone paving, where someone had crossed while dripping. We slung our towels on a sun lounge and dropped into the shallow end, raising twin geysers of water as we plunged in.

Wren submerged and slipped away underwater, rising from the

depths after a few yards to swim freestyle to the far end and back. Though her strokes seemed precise, I reached down and caught her shoulder when she returned.

"That's deep up there. With that Champagne in you, you're not swimming laps."

She rose from the water and shook her head, using her hand to sweep away some hair that had fanned across her face. Even wet she was gorgeous. Hell, with the water making the bikini become her skin, I was going to need help getting my dick to go down or it might stick that way, permanently. Maybe her mouth could suck it dry. Now that was a thought.

"Come with me?" She backed away, as if ready to swim off again.

In the darkness it was hard to be sure but her smile wasn't provocative, more unsure. She was delaying what I'd set in motion – her seduction.

Fuck that.

"No."

"You're worried about my safety? It's been a while since anyone but Hugh truly cared if I lived or died."

"I said I want you here." I grabbed her hand.

"Wait. We need to finalize our agreement. Before...anything."

"Anything?" Business first, hey? Procrastinating, for sure.

Slowly I reeled her in, keeping her coming my way, as I walked backward to the steps that led from the shallowest section. The water made musical sounds as it flowed around us. Cool in here, and it had made her nipples peak even higher.

"The agreement. I help you look for Vetrov in Australia. You pay me one hundred thousand. Another hundred when we have concrete evidence. Done."

Headlights flickered through part of the fence and across the pool.

"Are you afraid of me, Wren?"

"I'm not some street-working bimbo."

I studied her. Having second thoughts or just reminding me of how much of a sacrifice this was to her? I didn't suppose she often went to her knees before men, and that was what she'd done, in a manner of speaking. She'd descended to my level from her lofty throne in her tower in the clouds.

Bullshit. I was a man. She was a woman. She'd gotten off on me telling her to fingerfuck herself upstairs.

"I know you're not. You're a beautiful woman with more dollars than some small countries. But this isn't a stock market transaction. I'm the only way you're getting closer to Vetrov and after all this time searching, you know that."

She didn't try to argue. Good.

"That's one half of what this night is about. Now you can forget it. Answer my question. Are you afraid of me?"

Her throat worked. "Some. If I had a gun in my hand, less so."

The return of the feistiness. "Guns are cheap courage. You haven't got one. It's just me and you. I think a little fear is good for you."

"So I get to scare you too?"

I laughed. "Try me. Besides, when I said you, I meant you specifically. You've got some sort of thing for me making you do things while I threaten you. Coincidentally, I like doing it."

"That's not..."

"Are you going to lie?" Oh denial was a bitch.

She drew in a long breath. "You make it sound crazy."

"We are what we are. Everyone is a little crazy inside." I reached the steps and sat. "Sit in my lap."

She tugged at my hand and I resisted easily.

"Sit."

She sucked in her lip. "No."

I dragged her lower and said my next words into her ear, rumbling, and probably a little threatening, which was the whole point. "Sit the fuck down or I'll do something you'll regret."

"Huh." Her answer seemed to barely escape her throat and I felt her shiver under my hand. "You wouldn't."

"No?" I smiled. "Short memory, Wren. Five seconds."

Her wet hair had swung across her face again. All I could see was the movement of her lips as she mouthed curses under her breath. Water plinked into the pool.

Then, after one last huff, she gave in. Though she tried to sit with both legs to one side of me, I stopped her, tapping her nose. "No, sweetheart, straddle me. I want to be able to touch you properly.

"Oh." She shifted and ended up how I wanted her – legs either side of my lap and her facing me. The water lapped at her belly button. Droplets cruised down her front from her wet-through bikini

43

top. We were under the building here, since it overhung the shallow end. A fluorescent in the stairway cast light through the glass door and onto her body.

What was going through her head? I could see she had her bottom lip caught between her teeth. From how she'd reacted upstairs, taking charge with a fucking vengeance was my best move.

I thumbed away some hair from her cheek. Even that seemed to make her lips relax and part.

Being an officer had drummed into me the advantages of knowing your situation. I came to a conclusion I'd been halfway to deciding was true anyway. I could hypnotize Wren with dominance and threats.

"Don't say anything. Don't move. I want to look at my property."

The sharp intake of air as if she meant to interject made me stare down at her. She remained silent, only shifting slightly on my legs.

"The games we can have," I murmured. "Make that, the games I can play with you."

Then I put my hands up and ran my thumbs slowly down the inner edge of the cups of her top where they framed her cleavage. Though her breathing became heavier, she sat still for me, very still, apart from her thighs squeezing in on mine. The girl did like this.

I peeled the cloth aside, tucking it beneath each breast to bare them both. Her tits moved as I adjusted them. My poor aching cock tried to grow another inch. This game beat monopoly and poker, hands down. When I had sex, I normally admired the woman, but never with the same leisure as now. I'd never had someone be happy to be my little plaything, as Wren did, or be so enraptured by it. It was exhilarating.

Smoothing my thumbs around the dark coins of her areolae made her clench her thighs again.

"Pretty girl." I did two more full, slow circles while I studied her face. "Keep being so good and I'll reward you."

Not a protest escaped her, just a single, almost inaudible shaky moan.

I decided my manifesto of the day was to touch every place on her, every perfection and imperfection. All of her drew my hands, from her shoulders to her slender fingers, to her thighs beneath the water. I felt like a sculptor feeling his way over stone, looking for the heart of it, deciding what was hidden in a piece of exquisite marble.

I ran my skin over hers. I ran her hair through my fingers. I caressed the sides of her face, her lips, and even her ears, marveling at the intricacies of the curves of such delicate parts of her. She kept me entertained with her measured sighs and how she leaned into each touch. Lastly, I held her breasts, those full mounds that said woman as much as the contours of her waist, the succulence of her ass, or her cunt.

"Remember, don't move."

"Mmm. What if I —"

"Nope. Or talking." I dragged her to me by her nipples, ignoring her yelps. Then I bit her breasts, hard, one then the other, leaving dark, circular marks. Her burst of fuck, fuck, fuck and the clawing of her nails into my biceps were incredibly amusing and hot.

"You're lucky I'm not sure fuck is a real word."

"Mmm!" An indignant sound if ever there was one.

"Or that." So cute when she was horny and angry.

When her panting lessened, I parted the lips of her pussy and nudged my fingertip in, an inch or so, wiggling it in and out of her cunt, until I figured her eyes might pop if I delayed fucking her any longer. But the temptation to tease her, just a few moments more, sucked me in. I thrust two fingers inside her at once, slowly at first then faster and with more gusto. With my thumb, I toggled the tiny engorged bump of her clit from side to side.

"Oh!" Wren stiffened.

"Like that?"

"Fuck. Gla —"

Whoa. Small mistake. One I didn't regret as she wriggled on me making small noises, before she arched and cried out like a goddess in the throes of a supreme revelation. Climaxing.

I missed not a second of it.

Her grip would leave bruises on me. This goddess I could worship forever.

Should I make her come again? I got her close, playing with her pussy and fucking her thoroughly with my thick fingers.

If only I could video her writhing. Another time.

"Please! I need to. I need to." Her whispers grew louder until I wondered if our neighbors had noticed. Her fingers dug into my biceps again, but she was hanging on, not trying to pull my hand away.

"Put your arms behind your back and hold your wrists."

She hesitated.

"Now."

Though looking unhappy, she did as I asked.

I wrapped my hand about one breast and squeezed until it must be hurting. She whined. Yet even underwater, I could feel the warmth as her moisture leaked past my cunt-submerged fingers. Her inner muscles clamped down hard.

Curious. Wren was definitely a masochist.

"When I take out my fingers, you're going to lie down, ass up, over the top of these steps."

The throb of my cock reminded me there was more to this than biting and fingerfucking.

I pulled out my fingers and shifted from under her.

I half expected a tsunami as she threw herself down. Instead I got this panting wreck of a woman standing on the step with her bikini askew, staring at me with hair stuck all over her shoulders and face.

When she moved, it was a luscious version of a crawl as she got down on all fours and flowed like a bitch on heat up those steps. My eyes were accustomed to the low light and I could see her pussy since the bottoms were still rolled away. Fuck this.

If she was teasing me with her sex, it had worked.

When she stopped and waggled her ass at me, while sprawled down those top steps with water under her knees and belly, I unclipped her top then used it to tie her left wrist to the lane ring.

"What are you doing?"

Rhetorical question? "Tying you the fuck up so you can't get away."

"I wasn't..."

"Talking again?" I gave one ass cheek a stinging smack.

Her mouth formed an O and I kissed her hard. Then I yanked down her bottoms. Those I used to fasten her other wrist to the base of a metal safety railing.

"Now try waggling that butt." I whipped down my shorts, taking the condom from the pocket. I ripped the packet open and rolled the condom onto my cock in record time. She peeked back at me, watching my every move. "If you were planning to run," I teased her. "You can't."

"Can I talk?"

I nodded.

"I might. I would. Just to see you get mad." That ass of hers swayed seductively again. I swear the moisture on her pussy glistened in the next sweep of headlights.

I covered her with my body and probed for her entrance. The tip of my cock sank in like it had found the promised land of milk and honey – inches deep, with ease. When I did a forceful fuck that slapped into her and hit bottom, she collapsed onto the step.

"Oh hell." Wren groaned and pressed her ass back into me. "Oh...ohhh."

"You like that?" I said to her ear.

Her first reply was more a whimper. Then: "Can't...talk."

I chuckled. "You poor thing. I'm going to take you now like a whore." And I fucked her as I said it. In and out of that precious hole. Her pussy spasmed on me when I again shoved my cock in especially deep.

"Oh god. Yes. Yes." She tucked her head down as if to hide.

None of that. I sank my fingers into her hair and dragged her head back, using it as a convenient anchor. My thrusts grew ever more violent. Her moans grew louder. The water slopped at me as I used her, plunging deep and hard, fucking her like I'd bought her for the night and wanted my money's worth. I'd figured she'd like me making her a whore and I was so right. At her scream and the extreme arch of her spine when I pounded one spot, I fixed my cock on that target and bruised the hell out of her pussy. As I came, her even louder scream and the convulsions of her body made me smile like a fucking lunatic.

Done. Done and fucked.

I bit the angle of her neck and shoulder as I recovered. Then the other side. She squealed but barely moved. She was too busy sucking in air. Sweet exhausted girl. Another mark of mine on her.

Before I untied her, before she emerged from that orgasmic space she'd ventured into, with her every muscle limp and wrung out, I asked her one last question.

"Are you my whore, Wren? Are you my greedy little whore?"

Her eyelids flickered and she licked her lips, still with her eyes shut. Her voice was steady if husky. "Yes. Oh yes. I am." Then she opened her eyes. "I am."

Talk about gladdening the heart. Mine was having a party,

balloons and streamers and stuff. No strippers though. I had a weird feeling of exclusivity about Wren – like she might be the one and only. Pity I had no real notion of what she felt. I'd snuck up on her with this question. Whore... In hindsight I should've phrased it differently, made it more romantic. Dumbass.

For a while, I lay with her on a sun lounge, with her cuddled to my chest, thinking about what this all meant for the future.

The few buzzing mosquitoes trying to suck our blood seemed paltry harbingers of doom.

How did you ask an heiress if she meant it when she said she was your whore?

I needed to tie her up again soon and get more answers.

"Glass," she whispered, snuggling herself closer, if that was possible when we were skin to skin. "That was..."

I raised my head. "What?"

"Hmm?"

"It was what?"

Her breathing steadied, slowed.

A few minutes later, she began snoring.

I considered pinching her but relented and instead, lay there star watching with her curvy body in my arms. I put my nose to her wet hair and inhaled. She smelled like heaven and sex.

"Twinkle, twinkle, little star," I began softly.

CHAPTER 6
Wren

The morning after a bout of scorching hot sex takes on a whole other meaning when you've let your partner tie you up.

I awoke in the massive bed to find him lying on his side, elbow propping him up, looking down at me from only inches away. The sumptuous mattress had conspired to sink me into a hollow.

My sky seemed to be composed of his naked chest and that eighth wonder of the world, the thick, intertwining muscles of a man's arm. I smiled. No fan of the male physique could see such sights without swooning a little, even with the hairy armpit. The tattoo that had intrigued me since I met him was revealed in the soft light. It was a lion's head with some small letters flowing over a banner. Not SAS, as I'd thought. Some leftover of his mercenary days? Across the room, a timber blind rattled quietly in the breeze.

"Hello." Glass traced his finger across the seam of my lips, tickling and making me shiver. His eyes narrowed and he pushed past my lips to run his finger along my teeth and onto my tongue. I sucked on his finger and the suction seemed to pull excitement into my lower belly.

What other one-night-stand lover would dare to be so forward?

Only, was Glass that or more?

He removed his finger then painted my nose tip with wetness.

"Ugh! No." I wriggled.

"Why the frown?"

"Before you poked my nose?" I resisted rolling my eyes. Men, they were worse than dogs sometimes... I grimaced. "I was just thinking."

"Regrets?"

I drew a breath. That he even bothered to ask raised him in my estimation. I'd loved his alpha male act, but if he'd simply wanted to do it and move on, with no concern about my reaction, I'd be gone so fast. Out of this bed. Gone.

"No. Not yet."

He leaned down to kiss me, holding my throat in a light grip as he did so.

Magic. It reminded me of how he could be, and had been last night. The room focused in. Just a kiss, yet more. A little bit of dominance went a long way.

"You going to tell me if that was a first for you? I was pretty rough." His eyebrow tilted but he kept his hand there at my throat.

I was crazy fucking hypnotized by this. Already I was aware of my involuntary sexual reaction – I was taking deeper breaths and between my legs warmed. No act, not him. Glass was pure alpha, but I hated admitting that I liked it in words. It seemed a betrayal of myself.

Honesty is the best policy. Most of the time. I counted out the seconds and managed to convince myself.

"First." I swallowed, my throat moving against his fingers. He was still stroking me. Way to confuse me. I suppose that might've been his plan. "I liked it."

"I figured that, Wren." His smile birthed a happy glow in my heart.

"I've never thought it would appeal to me. My father gave me an allergy to controlling men." I searched his face but saw nothing bad. No arrogant triumph this morning, though that had its place. Just...a man thinking?

"That answer and that you're still here, in my bed, I figure gives me rights." His smile twitched, then he threw back the sheet that had half-covered me.

"What?" I frowned and tried to lunge for the sheet only to have him gather both my hands, straddle me, and pin my hands to the pillow above my head. My natural orneriness reared its head. "Presumptuous of you. We need to talk."

I twisted my wrists to get free. Unsuccessfully, of course.

Voila, I saw my true motivation in a flash. I wanted to see what he would do if I provoked him. Teasing this man would surely have consequences.

He sat on me harder, worming his leg between mine, forcing them apart. "We will. Like I said though, since you're still here, I'm taking my owed-to-me morning sacrifice. You."

His pause was devilish and electric. We both knew he was checking to see what I'd do. Instant telepathy, for once. Fuck. This was hot. If I played it too nasty, he'd stop. I could feel that, though I wanted him to just go for it, no matter what. Even if I tried to claw his eyes out.

What was wrong with me?

Maybe next time. After that talk.

I lay there panting, staring up at him, and holding back the fight. At last I whispered the words I had to. "Don't let go."

"Not happening." Such intensity was there, in his eyes. "Lift your legs until your knees are up near your ears." When I hesitated, deliberately, only slightly moving them, he slapped my butt. I swear I could feel every scorching finger imprint. "Now!"

Oh fuck.

I raised my legs and he rearranged his grip on me, one arm at a time going to the outside of my legs then regaining that wrist hold.

I ended up pinned like a butterfly to a display case but doubled up, my feet tapping the headboard with his shoulders keeping me there. My pussy was out where he could penetrate me as he wished.

So vulnerable to whatever he wanted.

Condom! He was about to...

Damn.

I didn't want to speak again. That would ruin this. He let go of my wrist with one hand.

But I had to. Already, I felt the wetness from his cock bluntly poking into the crease where my leg met my ass. "Wait!" You need to... Those last words only echoed in my mind. His free hand had come out from under his pillow.

Without taking his gaze off me and my wide-open pose for more than a fraction of a second, he put a condom packet to his mouth and tore it open, then rolled the condom down his cock, one-handed.

The man planned ahead. Oh my.

That he'd been so sure I'd acquiesce was both disturbing and thrilling. He plunged into me, and my eyes rolled up as I felt the brutish slide of his cock, shoving in, invading me without mercy. It felt bigger than before. All the way...in. I grunted as he sheathed himself fully and banged into the flesh of my ass.

"Don't expect to come." That was almost a growl. But I'd shut my eyes and wasn't opening them just to see if he'd morphed into a beast. "I'm going to fuck the hell out of you."

He ground himself into my pussy, his thighs shoving into the undersides of mine. He was as deep as any man could get into me. My groan was heartfelt. I didn't get to come? I didn't care. Fuck me until there is no tomorrow.

So I lay there with my head being shunted into the pillows, half buried, my feet thumping on the wall or waving in midair, while he took his pleasure. The room itself shook for all I knew.

I couldn't escape and that was exactly how I wanted it.

With Glass heavy breathing and grunting into the pillow that'd fallen on my head while he fucked me hard, I blissed out.

When he came, he shouted a little. Made me grin, despite the throb and ache inside. I could feel his cum in there, condom or not. That made me feel like I was His.

So odd. I'd never wanted to be anyone's before. Never.

He released my wrists and legs but stayed on top of me and moved away the pillow.

"Now we can talk?" I whispered in his ear. I bit it then nuzzled his neck. I couldn't get enough of how he tasted and smelled.

He snorted but turned his head to look. "Soon. Soon as I'm done with you."

"Soon?"

"Yes."

There was more, I found: Being soaped up in the shower while he kissed me and manhandled me. Being made to come with his mouth on me while I clung to his shoulders, my legs trembling, as I tried not to fall over in the water. Being told to kneel and kiss his cock then to open my mouth while he fucked it. What a morning. No talking at all had been done and it seemed as if a world of time passed when next I checked a clock. I figured we were doing some important dialogue already.

Breakfast was late and involved toast and eggs. He cooked.

"My university student cooking skills aren't up to your standards?" He waggled the spatula at me, where I sat wrapped in a bathrobe on the kitchen counter. "You said you burned eggs."

"I did. I do." I smiled, struck by the silliness of his pose. Big, nasty man with spatula. At least he had on a shirt and shorts. I could imagine the damage if the oil from the pan spat at him while he was stark naked like he had been half an hour ago, in front of me, with his cock out...shoving it in my mouth. Damn. I squirmed subtly, squeezing my thighs together. Forced BJs turned me on? "I can't believe I'm doing this."

"Letting me cook for you?"

I guess this was our talk. I blinked then forged onward. "Letting you dominate me in bed."

Again, there was that thoughtful look I'd caught on him sometimes. Enough times to reassure me he wasn't some Neanderthal. I'd known the man had to have brains to run whatever business he had here. SAS officers were selected from thousands of candidates. It was nice to see continued evidence, though.

"I have friends into this. Domination. Submission. Slaves even, some of the women call themselves."

Slaves? I closed my mouth. "Uh-huh."

He levered the eggs from the pan and placed them on the plates with the fried tomatoes and toast. There wasn't a lot of variety in the fridge but neither of us had wanted to go out looking for cafés. Discussing murders and perhaps human trafficking, maybe other illegal acts, none of these were things to be chatted about over coffee. Neither was our relationship.

I slipped off the counter and followed Glass to the table.

The eggs were overcooked but I'd done enough teasing, and I'd cooked worse eggs.

"An A for effort. And the knives and forks are pretty." I turned them over, admiring the silver fruit motif on the handles. Then I began eating.

I'd face what he said head on. "You said slaves? That's so odd."

"Not for you?"

"Uhh." Seriously? "On principle, no."

"Weirdly, I can see love in the relationship I know of." He shook his head. "And I'm told it all depends on the couple."

Which implied the slave got a say in how things were organized. Inside, I shuddered. I didn't want to give him ideas or explore something so repulsive. Again, me, gone, if he so much as mentioned he liked this.

"But, whatever they do, it's not my thing." He sat back, considering me. "I like you Wren because you strike me as a woman who loves her independence." Now he leaned in and I started, caught with my fork halfway to my mouth. "And yet you like me taking over."

"I..." Without much thought on my part, my fork ended up placed on my plate, with the precision of an aircraft landing. "Okay. You must have noticed this is difficult for me to say out loud. And fuck you for laughing." I covered my eyes. "I do, yes."

He engulfed my other hand in his, where it lay on the table, pressing down reassuringly. "If I'm looking like I'm amused, it's because I'm happy. That's all. I'd never laugh at you."

"No?" I peeked at him.

"Not unless you trip on a banana peel or something." Glass smiled. "Look, it's not shameful. It's us. Me. You. That's it."

"I'm supposed to be a strong independent feminist who kicks guys in the balls if they try this shit. Jeez. I took a wrong turn somewhere."

"No." He squeezed my fingers. "Besides, I surprised me too. I had other ideas. They didn't work out."

What was that supposed to mean?

For a while he said nothing and I could see he'd gone away in his head.

"I was wrong. Very. Never try to be someone else."

His vague revelation sobered me up. I didn't know what he referred to, and he didn't seem about to tell me. I moved my fingers out from under his.

What did I know about him? The real him? My natural cautiousness, that'd been reinforced by years of being taught what was safe, sidled back in and tapped me on the arm. I'd fucked up my life once. Twice might qualify me for a Darwin Award. I needed to go slower.

I assessed him again. Chances were he wasn't who my hormones were trying to make him out to be.

"Glass. Our biggest problem is that I need you to find my father's killer. I don't know how this...us will affect that."

"You're saying you'd drop the 'us' in this deal if it meant a tidier world?"

I'd put this out front and center. Did I really want that?

"I'd rather both, Wren. I think you would too."

Huh. He was right. I would like to have both but I'd be a fool to let that be the basis of a business decision. I might've failed my father's standards of negotiation, but I was still good.

"Hugh would be horrified." This was a security nightmare. I stared at my hand and his, now inches apart. But me? Glass had presented me with a whole new adventure. "Maybe we need distance?"

"Should Hugh make your personal decisions?" His hand sliding away, he sank back in his chair. Though his expression was less open, he wasn't needling me, much.

If anything, being a couple would tie Glass closer to me, the same as it did me to him. That was cold logic.

Could it backfire? I guessed so. But surely no worse than it might if we stayed distant? If anything, the more I came to know Glass, the more honorable he seemed to become. Perception only? Or was I affecting him?

Now that would be odd.

A true security nightmare would be him getting angry at my change of mind. No one knew where I was. I looked him over. I could do little if he decided to hurt me. This was, in a way, a test of character.

Or a test of how much he wanted my money.

Then again, he could get far more by ransoming me.

Nightmare.

"One day, that's all. We've been in bed one day. I don't even know your name. Is Glass even anything like it? Or Richard?"

"Wren, here's a truth." He nodded. "If any other woman had baulked like you are, I would have walked away. I don't need complications. Not normally."

"So my money is making you stay?"

"Stop trying to anger me."

I found myself blushing.

"You are making me stay. But I have men who rely on me to keep their names out of the news and off the radar of anyone who might want to harm them. Much of what we do relies on being low in visibility."

"That still means you won't tell me your name. I don't think..." I shut my eyes for a second, horrified at what I had to say. The loss was eating a hole in my stomach and I hadn't even said it yet. "We can't have a relationship, if I don't know who you are."

The moment became some horrible, twisted, silent thing. I could feel something good and wonderful slipping from me. I wasn't sure what I was doing. If I didn't trust him, telling him I didn't was stupid. Wasn't it? I twined my hands together and my fingers went a funny mixture of white and pink from the pressure. Not looking at Glass seemed wise.

Guess I didn't deserve this. Happiness. Or a chance at it. Jesus, it was one night, but I was stupid thinking I could make myself think he meant nothing to me.

I sighed. Messed up.

One night in bed with him? He does mean nothing. It's just my fantasies getting in the way.

"I am Richard Oakham." I jumped. The man had sneaked up behind me. "Thirty-nine years old. Born in Birmingham." His hands landed heavily on my shoulders. "My nickname is Glass and it began as Glass Dick. I got that because a girlfriend sent me a glass dildo and half the bloody regiment saw it when it fell out of the packaging.

"If..." He bent low, leaning his chin on my shoulder. "If you try to back out of this us, so help me god, I will spank you. Whether we are in a relationship or not. I'm trusting you Wren. Just not your Hugh. I can see you want to give this a go. Be brave. Do it. We can always tell each other to fuck off if it doesn't work out."

Tears dribbled down my cheeks. I resisted wiping them away for a few seconds then I did, with my knuckle.

"What have you done to me? I never cry."

"Well. I think you should do it more. Since I like seeing it. It shows you care, Wren. I was wondering if you were a robot, for a minute. After all that happened, this morning and last night, and then you switch and pretend it was nothing?" He dragged a chair closer, and sat beside me, then pulled me onto his lap.

I considered protesting, for all of half a second.

"I'm sorry." My muffled words were said half into his shirt. "I don't want to be a robot. It's just..." I struggled to express something that went against the raison d'être of most of my life. "You just seem too perfect to be true."

"What?" His chin rasped in my hair as he shook his head.

56

"Interesting that you regard what I did as perfect."

Oops. My eccentricity was showing.

"I'm not perfect. Nothing like it."

He was, though. Or he seemed to be. Fuck it. Women were supposed to articulate better than men, but this confounded me. I liked being here, in his lap, but trusting him was so difficult. I merely grunted, as if agreeing.

"I've got a serious urge to do bad things to you every time I see you, Wren. Which goes so well with this urge I have to keep you safe from all the bad ogres of this world, even if I am one. You don't want to see inside my head."

"It's got to be nicer than in mine."

He chuckled.

As before, doubts arose. "You really feel that way?"

"Yes. Yes, I do." The puzzlement that came through in his voice, as if he'd surprised himself, made me smile.

"I'm glad you do." I knew I wasn't giving as much as he was, and I felt the tug of regret. I wanted to. I just couldn't. Not yet.

"Me too." His hand patted my thigh. "Tomorrow, we're going to Australia, in my plane. You can phone Hugh and tell him that today. When we arrive at our destination, you can phone him again."

Tomorrow? I jolted upright. Though it was nice being on his lap, I had things to do.

"My passport. It's in a safe at the hotel."

He pulled me back down. "You don't need it. We're going illegally."

"Shit." I'd not done anything illegal for years. "I can't."

"Can. Shut up and kiss me."

Well, if he put it like that.

CHAPTER 7
Moghul

I left the munch early. The hotel was swarming with newcomers eager to learn about BDSM, but I was tired and had business to attend to. I'd missed the late night shoot for Kinkaverse too. Jeff could deal with that. On the drive home, I pulled over to the curb to answer his call. The model had protested doing the anal hook scene with the new hook we'd ordered just for the damn scene. I okayed a bonus payout, made a note to get it in the contract next time, told Jeff not to use her again, then set off home.

Things. There were always things needing doing.

Once upon a time, a munch had been a good way to sink back into the semi-normal world as well as check out potential new subs, maybe find new talent for Kinkaverse. Not today.

I uncapped an ice-cold lager and sat at my desk in the downstairs study. My Vetrov emails, the ones that dealt with the illegal side of work, had attachments, videos. At least one would be verifying punishment had been dealt with at the new House Two.

There was no pleasure for me in these; I wasn't like some of the men I employed. My manager at the first House in Papua New Guinea had taken sadomasochism to extremes I'd never suspected him of appreciating. Skinning a cop had been exceptionally brutal. Luckily that manager had died when the place was overrun. I would've had him executed if he'd survived.

These videos were a duty not a pleasure. I lined them up and clicked play.

Early days at House Two and I'd instructed my manager to be particularly vicious in this punishment to demonstrate the foolishness of breaking rules. A guard had been caught fucking one of the girls. Didn't matter if she was newly acquired or abducted weeks before and well trained. They were all off limits.

A room with no visible windows. Well lit. White walls. Whips, ropes, and chains hung from the wall behind the gagged and naked man tied to a timber St. Andrews cross.

I'd never been there but it was almost familiar due to the resemblance to a room at one of my play parties. Such small differences could color a room fun or evil – such as a sharp knife and an unwilling tied up victim. I had no doubt this room was evil, because I'd made it so.

"Guilty," proclaimed a man off to the left. At his nod, another man applied a circular clamp to the base of the former guard's balls and cock, as a tourniquet. His screams were muffled. With the efficiency of a stock hand castrating a bull, my manager used a knife on the guard. Only a few drops of blood spattered to the floor. After a few minutes of agony, the maimed man was executed by strangling him with a garrote cord. Shooting was too normal and never had the same deterrent.

This whole scene was to stop others copying what the guilty man had done. He had no use for his balls in Hell and the brutality was an effective deterrent. Better than simply killing. That it worked was all I needed to know.

The next vid was of a new technique for breaking in a girl. I okayed it, moved on.

This third one was a routine vid automatically gathered from the house Chris and his comfy ménage a quatre occupied. Chris, my naughty, kinky, immoral accountant. One day I would hand over some of my business to another. The only way I knew to make a man trustworthy was to have him by the balls first. Chris was looking interesting. Protégée potential. Only he was a bit of a pussy when it came to his little submissive family. I had enough evidence of the man fucking a woman who had been reported kidnapped to put him away for his whole life, if I chose to use it. I didn't. It was merely leverage. Chris had a history of being able to see sideways and around corners, where crime was concerned. No one could do my taxation books for years without knowing something of what they were getting into.

"Come to me, said the spider to the fly," I murmured then clicked on stop. I'd seen him screwing his women a hundred times. Only Chris wasn't a fly. He was more another big hairy spider with a liking for a particular kidnapped woman. Ideal really. Smart and flawed.

Was he was aware I was still taping him? I doubted it. The wiring of the house he'd bought from his former boss had been done in secret while he was away acquiring his victims. Planning ahead was one of my fortes.

Yes. It was.

I cleared my throat and closed that video window. Nothing new, just blond-haired, pretty Chris and his partner in crime fucking their slaves.

Next.

My desire, itch, whatever it was, to watch this fourth video annoyed me. Fucking Wren. Maybe I should go visit House Two incognito and get this new fetish out of my system. If I wanted reality, I could find some there.

Unwise. Very unwise. I couldn't do that.

I sifted through the email info. Glass was a retired former SAS officer. Richard Oakham. Starting a war with a man who commanded his own semi private army was not wise either. I focused on a line of data. The name of one of his men was familiar – a Pieter. Pieter was one of his mercs...

Well, well, well. I'd lay bets this Glass had something to do with the assault on and elimination of my first House. He'd cost me a lot of money if that were true. That explained his interest in Wren and her one-woman crusade to solve her father's murder. A smart man would've led her astray without contacting her. Or he'd dispose of her. Did his desire for her money exceed his common sense?

I had a private army of sorts also. Using them would be like drawing a big red arrow in the sky saying I was worried he'd find me.

I shook my head. No. Not going there. I never ever guided my business with revenge in mind. Not unless he looked to be capable of, or inclined to, interfere with my business again.

Then, only then, would I lift my hand.

The video was of her and Glass approaching a seaplane – one my spies had placed under surveillance, once they found out who Glass was. The still at the beginning was mostly of her back. Did she turn around to face the camera at some point in this video?

Fuck. What was I? A little boy contemplating a new Christmas present?

No, I was an adult and adults tended to get god-awful Christmas presents from relatives who should know better. Why did she intrigue me so much? Her looks were partly the cause. Her pale skin versus bright lips and clothing made me think of a vampire from some gorgeous artistic film aimed at a Cannes nomination. I could see her sucking someone's blood. I could see myself sucking hers. And what an instant hard on that gave me.

Also she was rich. The sort of woman who would cut most men down to size purely by displaying her casual regard to her wealth.

With my boots on an open drawer in the desk, I swung the chair under me back and forth in short arcs, thinking. No, not a boy with an oncoming present. I guess I was more of a collector.

What was my dirty subconscious dreaming of doing with this little work of art? No video for me. I tossed the computer mouse in the bin, in the full knowledge I'd have to fish it out again later.

Behind me was a window opening to a downhill view across Cleveland Bay toward Magnetic Island. I swung the chair to look out. I'd sell the damn house over there. No keeping women for me. I was past that sort of idiocy. Fools messed around in their backyard. Wise men did it in other people's backyards.

That the last line of the email said the plane was heading for Australia meant little. I knew from a report by my IT expert that, at one point in my history, my IP address would lead investigators with some *nous* to this town. It wouldn't lead to me. Picking me out from two hundred thousand people was not going to happen, no matter how smart Mr. Glass turned out to be.

I could rest easy, play it safe. Be cool. And I could sell my old house so I couldn't get tempted.

CHAPTER 8
Wren

The blindfold was expected, since Glass had warned me he needed to protect the identity of his pilot. It was a civilized blindfold, a pair of wraparound, completely blacked-out sunglasses. This time there were unexpected benefits to the blindfold – I had him beside me.

The roar of the engines as we bumped over the ocean might have panicked some. I'd been in a thousand aircraft, some big, some small. If I couldn't trust the pilot then *que sera sera*. Once the plane had taxied off the water, he reinforced the blindfold with some sort of elasticized tape that covered where I could have looked over the top or bottom of the glasses, if I tried hard enough. The rest of me was free, apart from the safety harness. My murmured protest was met with a kiss to my cheek.

"Shhh. Be calm. I'll take care of you."

A little patronizing? I didn't, quite, mind.

I was getting used to Glass and his manner. He kept me on my toes, off balance, and after all, being in a cocoon isn't living.

That *be calm* etcetera had been his summary of what needed doing when we'd sat on the jetty earlier. I'd stalled. Flying in his seaplane to Australia blindfolded because he needed a pilot to fly the plane back here and that pilot needed to stay anonymous? It had made me uneasy. I had no backup. I was alone. Hugh had been furious as it was, when I'd reported I was going to meet him in five days in Australia. Quietly furious, as he often was if I thwarted his security efforts. I didn't blame him.

This was unsafe.

After half an hour of Glass basically telling me he'd be with me all the way, and wouldn't let anything bad happen, I'd said yes. I'd climbed to my feet and followed him. No extra information. Nothing new swayed me. I just decided, what the hell, I'd already trusted Glass with my life and he hadn't failed me. If he was going to take advantage of me, such as ransoming me, he could've done it already.

So. Here I was.

His hand had engulfed mine since take off. I loved how he made me feel small. Big man, big hand, and big cock. I grinned and kept my face down to disguise my sudden amusement.

Him taking advantage of me sexually had already happened though, and *damn*, I could live for a year on the memories. I could masturbate for a year on the memories. Seriously, I must be sick.

I shifted on the seat and let my eyes shut under the sunglasses. I sighed, reliving when he'd made me stand against the wall and do dirty things to myself.

I guess I looked a little too happy because Glass nudged me with his shoulder. "What are you thinking?" He must have leaned in close, for I felt his breath on my neck.

Evil man.

Should I say? I was directly behind the left-hand pilot's seat. I'd seen where I sat, before the pilot had arrived and I'd been blindfolded. With the heavy drone of the engine, the pilot wouldn't hear a word unless I spoke too loudly. I might not shock Glass, but I could tease him and I had the perfect excuse. The man had asked.

I turned my head, finding he'd maneuvered himself so his ear was next to my mouth. "I was remembering when you made me stand against the wall and pull my bikini aside. How you made me..."

I hesitated, never before having said anything this sexual aloud where others *might* overhear me. The temptation overrode my prudishness. I could imagine how it might affect this man.

And so, I added more. "You made me put my fingers up inside. Made me fuck myself." I couldn't see him but I was sure he was listening, *really* intently. What fun. "Watching you watch me until I almost came...I remember how wet I was. And then you kneeled and touched my... My..." My tongue was stuck on the four-letter word. It always flipped my curse meter to high. "Cunt. That was so hot."

He cleared his throat.

"Did I say that right?" I was going from grinning to straight-faced spasmodically, as I tried not to show how hilarious I thought this was. "You did ask."

"You are a little cock-tease. I should pull you over here and make you sit on me."

The threat froze my heart. *Crap.* Sitting was not just *sitting.* He wouldn't dare.

He lowered our clasped hands into the lap of the short, pleated, black skirt he'd helped me buy at a market. "Part your legs," he murmured.

I went from zero to lust speed in one second. "Uhhh. What?" What was he thinking of doing? "The pilot," I hissed.

"He's busy. Can't see. He won't hear you if you're quiet."

He was expecting me to make noise? Expecting moaning, maybe?

"You're crazy! I am not. *Not.* Doing this."

"If you delay any more, I will tie your hands and fuck you on that seat. I guarantee you, he will see that."

Seconds slipped past in some other universe. My thoughts whirled. If I didn't do it, would he fuck me here, in this plane? I could imagine that happening, in exuberant color and sound. I'd watch that movie. I could feel that movie happening to *me.* And what was wrong with me? *Nothing.* A fantasy, that's all it was. Triggered by his threat. I didn't actually want the pilot to see anything. That would be so damn dirty. But Glass...from what he'd done before, he might carry through with this.

I felt heat unfurl and swell, low in my stomach, as surely as if he were already doing filthy, dirty things to me.

"I..." I began, then I halted, confused.

I couldn't fool myself. This excited me.

If I was sick, I wasn't sure I wanted to be cured.

I stopped resisting and let him drag my hand downward. With our combined fists, he put pressure on my clit for a few leisurely circular motions. He let go but surprised me with one last encouraging press that drew a gasp from me. The sneak of the skirt up my right thigh told me he was inching it upward. I considered my options again, but my thinking blurred the instant he tugged aside my panties and slid his thick finger along my slit.

"You're wet again," he said matter-of-factly.

"You bastard." An automatic objection. A second later, I parted my thighs another half inch. In that moment, I was a wanton slut.

Whether he heard my words or not, he casually slipped that finger into me. Then he fucked me for a few strokes. One place high inside became a hot button to fun. *Zing.* I swallowed a choking noise and tried not to move as a wave of *ohmigod* spread. *Hold it in. Hold. Oh, oh god.* I arched up an inch. *Back fucking down. Into the seat.*

I was clutching the seat to either side.

Maybe I had a G-spot after all.

"Did you call me a bastard?"

What? I blinked madly under the taped over sunglasses. Nothing but blackness there, and *him*, touching me, him inside my pussy, with another man a few feet away. *Please keep flying. Don't look.*

And why did he ask that? Yes, I had. So?

His finger sucked out, slowly, my pussy muscles clamping on it like they could keep it there as a hostage. I bit back a giggle. I was aching so much to have him back in me. Beg? *No. Absolutely no.*

But I wanted. I wanted that finger so much. This time I did giggle at the absurdity.

"Giggling? You need punishment. You don't get to call me a bastard, Miss Wren." A drawled threat.

Psssh. "Live with it," I muttered, feeling daring, as if I'd climbed a mountain for the first time. The adrenalin high was awesome. The pilot hadn't shifted in his seat. Or I hadn't heard him do so. As long as he didn't have some strategically positioned mirror, I was safe.

Glass pushed apart my legs again. There was something else down there, between my legs that wasn't his hand. Something hard but the size of his finger...no, bigger, probing for my entrance. I squirmed away, or tried to, but he increased the force, screwing it upward while the base of his hand rested heavily on my mons. My clit and the top of my thighs – where his hand had trapped and pinched some skin – hurt and throbbed, all at once.

"No!" I said in a strident whisper. "No."

"I fuck you, or this does."

"Wait." The thing moved inward a half inch, pressing back my walls with its ungiving hardness. A plastic or metal something. Not a dildo. It was too inflexible. I clenched my hand on his wrist and tried to pluck it away with pure strength. I failed. I dug in nails.

All done on the quiet, without abrupt movements. With my face still.

"Stop, Wren. Put your hands on the seat. Now." When he said

now his tone lowered, like he was on his last tether.

The plane droned on. Without sight, our little scene seemed as obvious as a play on a stage. Maybe not. Be *shush*.

"Wait. Wait, wait, wait." Yet I had my palms on the seat as I spoke, as he wriggled the thing further in. I was a little scared. Not knowing what it was, left too much to my imagination.

I'm Wren Gavoche, I could buy a thousand of these planes, and here I am letting him do this to me?

I did know why. I did. The deeper me knew. Because letting him do this bound us together like a vine around a tree. Like a captive princess and a black prince or a damsel in a dark dungeon with her torturer. If he needed to punish me, I needed to be his victim. Win...win...lose, in some weird ever-tightening circle.

He seated the thing in me all the way. Poked his finger up and shoved one last time to make sure then removed his finger. The thing had disappeared up there. My entrance had closed. Deeper in, the rest of my pussy clenched down on the bitch thing so tightly it hurt. Was this a glass dildo? But no. It had an end. Too short. All of it was up there.

I turned my head, praying he was there, listening. "Now, please? Take it out?"

He patted me lightly, then tidied up my panties, but he left his hand between my thighs, as if claiming my pussy. His thumb tip brushed across my clit in a barely there way. "It's staying inside you until we land."

Fuck. Really?

The feathery touches of his thumb distracted me, until arousal made me clamp down again then I felt *it*. Rigid. A painful and foreign thing.

I turned down my mouth. "Not fair. Or nice."

"Next time don't cock tease or swear at me. Keep your hands where they are. Be good."

That male rumbling monotone giving me little orders was something that sneaked in under my hard-won defenses. I had a revelation that if he hurt me in the name of orders, I'd yield on an instant, that I'd like that reinforcement. No one except my father had ever truly dared to oppose me. Except Hugh, and that was different. I'd never allowed any man to even vaguely contemplate doing this, commanding me.

Glass though... I shivered, and waited, growing ever more aroused.

He nosed my ear lobe then bit and stayed there biting and sucking while his thumb kept on circling and circling, under my skirt, skating over my poor clit, sending me higher with each and every second. My fingers clawed at the seat cover.

How could the pilot not know? How could I sit here and...oh crap, I didn't *care*.

"Ssss." My teeth clenched. My fingers curled in harder.

His teeth released my ear. "Are you going to come just from this?"

Just from?

From him fingerfucking me while I was blindfolded then making me sit still so he could insert that, insert that...*whatever* into me and now he was assaulting my clit? Sarcastic comment needed.

Not. Right. Now.

I had my head pressed back into the upholstery by then and my lips sealed. I wasn't going to squeal or do anything unladylike the pilot could hear. I swore it.

But I did come and, since my brain shut down for those few vital climactic seconds, I had to pray like mad I'd been silent. I think I tore a small hole in the seat cover when I came, or maybe it was already there.

Damn. I listened to the sounds I was making while trying to get enough oxygen through slightly parted lips.

Attempting to breathe quietly, in the wake of a full on but restrained orgasm, is an exercise in futility.

"There, that wasn't so bad."

Glaring from under a blindfold was not effective.

Whatever was inside me, I adapted to. I ignored it, as much as I could, even though it annoyed me that he wanted it to stay there.

For much of the remainder of the flight, Glass kept his hand on my thigh, or he took my hand in his, so that I curled my fingers within his fist. Sometimes, I moved mine to reawaken the sensation of being held in that warm cave of his hand. Fingers, just my fingers, but it was enough to make me feel safe. I discovered, I remembered, how much happiness there was in touch.

Two years, no, it was more, since I'd felt this way. A long time without connecting to someone like this. I resisted clawing my hands in and my nails into Glass. I should tell him about my past. I would.

They said I wasn't dangerous, that I hadn't done anything, but I had to tell him. Besides, I doubted I would ever believe them, not really.

I'd woken up with my lover dead and bloodied at my feet, with a knife buried in him. Hard to get past that, no matter what the police report had said about angles of knife entry and forced entry signs. If someone had stepped forward and said, I did it, take me away, perhaps I'd have reconciled my illogical guilt. They hadn't. Alas. My obsession with knives didn't help. Sharp things attracted me and I'd never even been a cutter. The doctors had said I was different. I agreed.

CHAPTER 9
Glass

Once the plane was taxiing away across the sea, I unwound the tape from her sunglasses. Nine AM and the sun reflecting off the water had me squinting, despite my own aviator glasses.

"Ready? It's blinding me even. I've got you another pair of sunglasses."

We'd done some limited shopping yesterday. Clothes, shoes, toothbrush – all were in my backpack. I couldn't let her return to the hotel, not without making it extremely likely Hugh would be on my tail.

"Yes."

Before I did so, I took in the sight of this beautiful creature I seemed to have acquired. The movement of her lips fascinated me; the rest of her might send me into a coma. Maybe I'd better not rip all her clothes off, yet.

Hell, she reveled in me doing whatever I wanted to. I pulled her in close and kissed her.

The subtle give in her lips as she succumbed was always a delight. Her spine curved backward and her sighs filled my mouth. The kiss, the small waves frothing past our legs, the sand squeezing between my toes and under my thongs, or flip-flops, as my Americanized girl sometimes called them, and the deserted beach behind me...I wanted to stamp this as a moment of paradise. This was a forever day. I knew I'd take it out, in the days to come, and turn it this way and that, sucking all the goodness from it.

I vowed I would make more days like this, with her.

A little soon for deep sentiment, but I'd been holding back for what seemed ages, since she'd first laid down on that bed for me.

"Can I take off the glasses? The plane's gone?"

"Yes. It has. Wait though. A little longer. I want to look at you."

"Oh."

Then she waited, with a hint of a smile tugging at the corners of her mouth. She smiled just because I'd asked her and because she loved obeying, loved knowing I was looking at her – I'd bet my life that was true. That obedience and attitude, I could pluck from the air and put in my box with this forever day also.

Her smile said so much. Fuck, I was done for.

From her face, I brushed some hair sent flying by the wind.

I understood the allure of a submissive woman now. Only I needed one with fire in her still, like Wren. Where was the fun in being with a person so placid and obedient they might as well be a blob in the shape of a woman? But I needed someone I could connect with in other ways too and I didn't even know what color toothbrush she preferred or if she liked sunsets or horror movies. We'd gone from the ground floor to the top of the building without stopping at the places in between.

Was that so bad?

Yes. If we never went back and looked at the other floors. I'd fix that, soon.

"Here. Shut your eyes." I removed one pair of glasses and slid the other pair into place. Her eyes looked bleary. "See me?"

"Uh. Yes. What else? I was tempted to scream monster and run away. Buuut I won't." Her bottom lip was drawn between her teeth as she observed me. "Now?"

"What?" I raised an eyebrow. I knew what she wanted.

"You know what. Damn you." She frowned then pouted, and the little ridge between her eyes made me want to kiss it.

"Damn me? You sure that's what you meant to say? Almost a monster was bad enough." I waggled my eyebrows. Couldn't help it. Somehow her pouting had made this descend from high dominance to silliness.

"Uhhh. I can't call you bastard or say damn you?"

"Nope."

"Oh." A somber look settled on her. "What about fucktard or dickwad?" A snort escaped and she sprinted past me for the beach.

Spray splashed up in her footsteps.

I took off after her only to find her stopped in the shallows, giggling and bent over with her hand under her skirt.

"Ohmigod. Oh god. I do believe I want to kill you, Glass."

"Having trouble?" I reached down and caught her hands in mine, and put them both at her back. "Is something trying to fall out? You'd better not lose that. It's my favorite torch."

"Torch?" Her face fell then froze. "Oh! I've been around Americans for too long. A flashlight? That's what it is?"

Her wrists turned under my hand but she stayed in one place, peering up at me. The red top was cut in a way that cupped every curve of her breasts. The sprint had left her a little breathless.

"I should make you run again."

"Why?"

"The view is better when these are moving."

"Pfft. They're nothing wonderful."

"Don't say that. They're perfect." Starting at her collarbone, I drew a line down her cleavage. "But...this first." I bent to reach under her skirt, slipped my fingers into her panties, and probed inside her. That got her dancing on her feet.

"Hey!"

I ran my finger in further, up beside the torch, stretching her. Easy to do when she was already so wet. "I have to get finger and thumb around it. Seems like your little cunt doesn't want to give it back. Dirty girl."

"Am. Not." Her denial was accompanied by a wide-eyed innocent look.

I chuckled, noting her last squirm as I pushed my thumb in too, in an effort to grab the thing. "If you've squeezed any of your cum past the waterproofing, if it doesn't switch on, I'm spanking you. Got it." I extracted the torch, noting with some amusement the last bit of pussy suction resisting my pulling.

"Cum? Women don't have cum. Idiot. Oh. Oopsie."

"Oopsie?"

I kept my hold on her wrists but eyed the on-off switch. All the messing about hadn't turned it on inside her. I clicked the switch and a weak light glowed from the bulb.

"Is it working?" She went up on tiptoes to look. "Wow. It is. I cannot believe I let you do that. I should've pulled it out myself. I should get compensation. Storage fees or something."

One handed, I rinsed it in sea water and tucked it in my shorts' pocket. If it went rusty, at least I'd had good use from it.

"Storage fees? And you called me idiot. Tsk." I peered down at her, looming as if I was thinking of calling down Armageddon on her ass. Her amusement stirred something in me. I was amused too, but her taunts made me want to wreak some nastiness on her. Nasty. Dirty. Both would be best. "That smart ass comment says you want something."

She stilled. "It does?"

"It does. I think I'm figuring out your language. You know why you didn't remove it?" I tightened my grip on her wrists and pulled her into me.

"No." The soft word could barely be heard above the wash of the sea. Her mouth stayed parted as she waited for my answer. The longer I held her in this iron grip, the more tension ebbed from her muscles.

"For the same reason you shouldn't have called me an idiot. The penalties. Want to know what they are, my princess whore?"

I felt her fingers flex and watched her let out a long breath. Hypnotized, and so cute when she fell into this spaced-out place of hers. Then she shivered and seemed to awaken. "I'll pass. By the way, princess and whore aren't compatible."

"For you, an exception is made. Come."

I pulled her, protesting, up to the beach. My thongs were not the best footwear in the sea and I almost left them behind, stuck in the shifting wet sands. I threw the backpack onto the firmer sand then towed her to where a fallen tree had left a convenient trunk looping into the beach at chair level. I sat and put her facedown over my lap, in spite of her nonstop attempts to argue her way out of this.

"No. Wait. No. What are you doing? Glass?"

I did a last check of our surroundings. This was a beach in the Far North of Queensland and nobody was likely to be here, except my friend who should've dropped off the car and left by now. Nothing moved or made a sound except the sea, the terns and seagulls, and a lone crow on a pandanus palm.

When I pushed up the skirt, her pristine ass appeared, as if by magic. In pretty white lace panties too. I sighed. "When did they make it legal to look this sexy? This ass, I need to make mine."

"Sorry. Prior owner. Me."

"Guess I need to re-educate you on that." I wiggled the panties down until the line of lace revealed a hint of her pussy. Having something inside her had definitely aroused Wren and her labia were puffy, as well as soaked with her moisture. I smacked her hard, on one cheek.

"Ow!" Wren arched and tried to peer at me.

With a palm on her upper back, I pushed her down again.

"Should I be letting you do this?" she grumbled.

Letting? Now that said a lot. Mainly that she had a choice. "You already chose to let me do what I wanted to do to you, so yes."

"That was for one night."

She'd stopped trying to get off my lap, so this seemed more her checking where we were at.

"And I haven't heard you revoke that. So until I do..." I grabbed a handful of her hair. "I'm doing what I like."

I took off one flip-flop and smacked it on my leg to knock off sand and test how if felt. *Ouch.*

Maybe she was right. This was a good time to rearrange what we were doing, just a bit. I wasn't Pieter. I wanted something different, but he'd taught me the ropes, so to speak. I could speak kinky language like a Dom with the best leather pants.

"You know what a safeword is? It's a word that says stop to your Dominant, your Dom. If anything freaks you out, you say it."

"Dom?" Tentatively, she put a hand up to where I'd tangled my fingers in her hair, as if to check I really held her. After a shiver, she added, "We're going there?"

"We've been there since we met, Wren. You like me doing things like this." I gave her head a shake and she was silent for several seconds, her hand slipping from her hair to support her on the sand.

"Oh. I guess..."

"Give me your safeword."

"Sand." She gave that funny snort I heard her often make when something struck her as funny.

I caressed her ass in big circles, loving the give and the shape of her flesh. "Sand. Fine."

A safeword was another step. A good one.

I smacked her with the flip-flop, heard her yelp, and an under-the-breath curse then I watched the thong-print go from white to pink.

Pretty, but even better was the whine as she wriggled on me.

She was letting me do this – punish her. If my cock didn't poke a hole in my shorts it would be a miracle.

Spanking, or was this flip-flopping or thonging? It had a definite appeal. *Fuck*. Honestly, it rocked my world having her where she was, and taking it, semi-happily. I did nine more until I had her panting in between her screeching at the whack as the rubber came down on her.

Some grains of sand had abraded her skin and a little blood seeped. Oops indeed. I shouldn't be going that far. I touched her skin below the tiny bleb, intrigued that I'd caused this.

No, I shouldn't.

She was panting still, her head low, and her outstretched arms propping her up off the sand.

I drew her into a sitting position on my lap and dusted the sand off her. After kissing her hair, I rested my chin on her head. My hands found places on her to move upon and pat. This sort of cuddling with her in my arms satisfied some deep need I never knew I had.

"How did that make you feel?"

"It hurt." She sniffed then shifted her butt. "Still does. I think you bloody well sanded my butt." She inhaled then let it out steadily, as if giving herself time to think. "It turned me on, sometimes."

I grinned into her hair. "Good to know. It turned me on too. Your little cunt tempted me, every time I smacked you, but fucking you here would lead to cock abrasion or pussy sanding, or worse."

"That statement," she muttered. "Is so dirty I don't know where to start complaining."

"Nowhere, if you're smart. Unless you want more flip-flop?"

"No! It was different but no." She buried her face in my shirt. "Even if it got me hot."

Such an adventurous woman, if this was her first time exploring kink. Some of my previous girlfriends, I'd been lucky to get more than *fuck me* out of them. I rethought that. I couldn't, wouldn't, call Wren a girlfriend. She was something more, if I could manage to keep this functioning as a relationship.

Was it just first lust? Did I truly want to keep this going? Did she? Why the hell would she? I was a hired hand who'd shown her some kink.

My own head was still wrestling with what we were doing. Hers? Perhaps more so.

Like I'd told her, we could always change our minds later. Try my fucking hardest. I never was one for aiming for failure.

"There's a car waiting for us beyond those dunes, but I want to talk to you. I want, Wren, to make this last. Me rolling over the top of you is only going to get me so far. I know that. Even if right now I have you so turned on I could get you to hand me the keys to the Bank of England. You're rich, studying to be a veterinarian, and have probably never gotten worse than a parking ticket. I've shot a lot of people for money or my country, and I've got more illegal activities under my belt than a monkey has eaten bananas. I'm a bad man for you to be around."

"Ah." She paused and her reply came out in a hard focused tone. "I'm not all good, far from it. I could tell you stories. I don't care about your past, Glass. Really. There are reasons, but I hate labelling people. Hate it." She shifted my hand, from where I had rested it on her hip to her lap, and toyed with my fingers. "And I don't have a key to the Bank of England."

"Damn. I was betting on that."

I waited to see if she'd address the core of my statement.

Another wriggle before she plunged in. "I would like to keep this, us, going. I think I would."

Think? That was a good beginning. I could work with that.

"Then tell me more about you. Let's begin somewhere cute. You must like puppies. You're going to be a vet."

"Puppies! Of all the things." Wren giggled. "I do, though I'm as interested in other animals. Like I know this time of day is bad for croc attacks and that over there is a mark in the sand that might be a crocodile drag mark."

"Fuck." I sat forward. "Where? I missed it."

"Got you. Made it up. Told you I was bad."

"If we weren't in chat mode... I'll save that one up for later punishment."

"It was a joke!"

"A bad one. Now. Puppies? Or would you rather I flip-flop you again?"

I was going to get to know her, even if I had to extract it by torture.

"Pfft. Won't work. 'Sides, You don't hit that hard."

"Yeah?" I gave a short rendition of an evil laugh. "Next time, I won't hold back."

"Then I shall rephrase that. You're a fantastic flip-flop wielder."

The next few days were going to be fun.

My one niggling problem was that I was the man responsible for killing her father, and here I was supposedly helping her investigate his death. I was lying to her, bigtime. If I put a foot wrong, I would lose her. If I told her that her father's last act before he died had been to force his cock into Jazmine's mouth and to order Pieter mutilated, would that have altered things for the better or for the worse? Her father had been methodically torturing Jazmine. Hard to see any of him in Wren. Thank god.

She might simply think I was lying. We were on the edge of making something good from this relationship. Shocking her might make her turn away from me. Now wasn't the time to tell her anyway.

Those thoughts made me sit there cuddling her for way too long. I couldn't see a simple solution, though I turned my dilemma this way and that. A darker air shrouded the day despite the brightness of the sun.We were both sunburnt by the time we drove off in the rust-bucket Subaru toward Cairns. My old army mate wanted the car in Cairns, within three days.

I clunked through the gears as we bumped over the road leading out to the Bruce highway.

"I'll take you to a restaurant once we get to our final destination. There's one on the water, looking out over the strand. The Red Gecko. Unless it's shut down."

As long as no rivers flooded on the way down the coast, we could make it easily. The weather at this time of year was often erratic.

CHAPTER 10
Moghul

I pulled over to the curb on my bike to check the text that'd come in, propping my foot on the pedal to steady the bike. I had an offer for the Magnetic Island house from a Chinese buyer. The man would be over in two days to see it in person. Some of them bought off pictures, this guy didn't. It was a good price, though.

I texted back the okay to the real estate agent and set off again. The road was quiet this early on the island – steep inclines in places as it rose into the hills, but I liked pushing my muscles to the max.

I could imagine the Chinese buyer turning my pit of despair into a big goldfish pond. After all, there was drainage and a water supply already installed.

Or I could imagine *her* in there. I wheeled to a halt again, took the water bottle from the carrier and drank.

I stared ahead, focused on nothing.

She'd be crying, looking up at me, tears running down her face. Only not from that happy mixture of pleasure and pain my subs normally had. I was a good Dom to them.

Wren was simply crying.

Fuck.

I jammed the bottle back into the holder.

She and this Glass had arrived in town yesterday. My best option might be to let the surveillance be run by my men so I could forget about them entirely.

No. That was a step too far. Since my operatives didn't know who I was, it was impossible for them to accurately assess the information they gained. I'd have to keep looking at it, audio transcripts and all. Put a transponder on their vehicle too, if it seemed safe. They wouldn't be expecting their target to be tracking them by satellite. The wonders of science.

I pushed away, wobbling at first until I built up some speed, my legs burning as I plowed my frustration into working the pedals.

Obsession. I knew all about obsessive men. It never ended well.

Don't mess in your own backyard.

I had to keep it clean though and there was a difference.

*****

Wren

I paused on the front doorstep and watched Glass hike across the deserted road to the path that led between houses to the beach. The fishing rods led the way. We'd bought them yesterday along with bait, other fishing gear, knives to cut up the fish we meant to catch, as well as various holiday stuff such as sunscreen and a bikini. This had segued into a beach holiday as much as a detective affair. Surreal, at first, but it had simply happened. We stepped off the ferry and tumbled into this languid tropical paradise.

Six AM and no one sane was up yet. The crazies included a few joggers and people into fishing, and possibly, from their accent, a couple of German tourists who'd forgotten to get blind drunk the night before and wanted a beach walk.

I didn't know how Glass managed to get Australian cash and the two cars we used to dogleg our way here and I didn't care. Hugh would've cared but it didn't seem worth getting curious about. The house he'd magicked up was in a street one back from the beach at Horseshoe Bay on Magnetic Island – a very average house, even by my student experiences.

No credit cards were allowed to be used. Nothing that required anything that might be tracked. Someone else was doing the renting. Always a friend. If we drove and were stopped for a minor traffic offense, did he have a fake license to show police? Glass hadn't said, but neither of us was supposed to be in Australia.

So here I was with a man who by his own admission was bad, having illegally entered my own country. Maybe because he wanted me here on his terms? I think mostly he wanted me for a few days without Hugh, my security nanny. If anything went wrong, I might end up with a police record.

It had made me stop and think, last night, while we sat out in deckchairs on the upstairs balcony, feeling the sigh of the wind and watching the palm trees sway and the white tops of the waves as they rolled in.

Bizarre, feeling so relaxed. I should've been excited about being closer to finding the man who'd orchestrated the slave house where my father was murdered. Instead, I was in a prolonged state of contentment.

My search for Dad's killer had been more about assuaging guilt and finding closure than revenge or a true need to know. It had taken this, a revelation about my sex life and a man who seemed to understand me and, at the very least, like me a lot, to let me see my reasons.

Father had died a dirty death. Photographs had been leaked onto the internet, if not the Sydney newspapers. In this day of the ever-present camera phone, someone had taken pictures. It'd been the back end of Papua New Guinea, the Highlands where people still had small tribal wars, and someone had a camera and access to the web. The ignominy of your last legacy to your child being found dead at a slave house where women were systematically abused, lying face down with your genitals out, was not what he'd have planned. Shit happens.

"Coming?" Glass yelled back. A neighborhood dog began barking.

Today we were conferencing at the beach, I'd been informed.

"Sure!" I smiled and trotted after him.

Being a pseudo-detective was having strange benefits. I'd never healed from the death of my fiancé in Europe. I'd not expected to. The scars went so deep. Here, now, I felt the hint of promise on the horizon. If Glass did end up being only a flash-in-the-pan boyfriend, I think he'd still done me more good than any of the psychiatrists or the whole ton of medicine they'd poured into me for months. I hadn't taken a pill for days. I hadn't sleepwalked. Though maybe having Glass wrapped around me most nights was helping with that.

I grinned. Yeah, it was.

He'd threatened to tie me to the bed if I did, but he hadn't. I was tempted to pretend to sleepwalk.

I caught up to him, hopping when a bit of gravel sneaked into my sandals, then had to try to extract the rock while standing like a flamingo on one leg.

Glass waited patiently. The beach beckoned at the end of this short track between the houses. From the other side of the fence to the right, a red cattle dog wagged its tail at us.

I tossed away the pebble then reached over the fence and offered the back of my hand to the dog to sniff. When he proved friendly, I gave him a few pats.

Glass came up beside me. "Take care. He might've bitten."

I scoffed. "I'm going to be a veterinarian. I think I've got more experience with dog language than you."

"True. If you're okay with walking across the rocks, we can go there."

He pointed to the right of the beach, where a jumble of boulders speared out into deeper water.

At my nod, we wandered down the track and over the road to the beach. We reached the softer sand and I took off my shoes. The cool crunch of sand underfoot said *be you*, more than anything. Salt air, late crabs scuttling to their holes as us humans tromped past, and the debris from higher waves wet under my soles, and Glass, a man who seemed to just take everything in his stride. I could feel the last of the anxiety ebbing from me. I was always anxious. How light could I get without all that worry? I might float away this morning.

Life was good. Tears pricked my eyes. I had no clue what was happening except that I was happy.

When we'd settled the gear on the rocks, and Glass began hooking on the bait, I sat, hands in my lap, or on the smooth rock to either side, listening to the waves while watching the deft movements of his hands. He knew I wasn't much of a fisherperson. Sharing this was more about just sharing than about fishing to me. I'd learn a little, and be with him.

Glass wasn't just growing on me. He was seeping into my being.

He glanced up at me. "Today, I'm going to contact a hacker who has contacts on the inside of the ISP involved with the email tracked here. If we can get access to the database, we should be able to narrow the origin of the message further."

"Okay." I nodded.

I wasn't sure why we had to come here personally to do all that, but I'd go with the flow and let Glass do this his way. I was paying him a hundred thousand for this so there wasn't much point in me trying to direct things. In a few days, if we weren't getting anywhere, perhaps I would call this off. After vowing to spend a year doing this, I'd lost my motivation. Glass had helped me see it in perspective against the landscape of actually living my own life.

When I looked at this rationally, I'd been prepared to let my father control me from beyond the grave. Not good.

"I even have..." He paused. "Some contacts in the police force here. That may or may not pan out. And one of my men will be here soon too. I don't like being your only guard until Hugh arrives." His gaze turned thoughtful as he tied the knot in the line. He opened the packet of what was apparently preserved worms.

I pulled a face. Definitely no fishing for me. I could dissect a formalin-preserved dog but worms were just too icky, unless someone was demanding I do it for an exam question.

"Do I get a name?"

"J? As good as I can do." He grimaced. "Sorry. I have an aversion to revealing who my men are. I'll get past it, once I know Hugh isn't going to try calling the law down on us."

It was a good point. He and his man were more vulnerable than I was. I had an excuse for being here. And I'd learned from Father. I knew ways to twist the law to my advantage. Hugh had contacts of his own I could call on. Not direct bribes, no. Favors. They were good for most things. From bending a politician to your will, to someone lesser.

"I understand. However, I will be instructing Hugh to be civil to you and not to interfere."

"Good." He threaded the worm onto the hook, bit by bit then stepped over to a rock nearer the water. "If I catch anything, will you eat it for breakfast?"

"Sure. I'll even try cooking it." Though getting the bones out might be beyond me. How to fillet fish was a mystery I'd not solved.

"You might regret that if I catch a shark or a stingray."

I rolled my eyes. "We'll be throwing those back."

The line whizzed as it curled through the air and out over the ocean. There was Glass, all manly and athletic, muscles showing nicely through that white T-shirt, and here was me trying not to drool.

"How did I get so lucky?"

"Huh." He half-turned, eyebrow up.

"To find you. You're a catch too, you know."

"Flattery won't save you if you're a bad girl," he murmured, eye on the line as it washed back and forth in the waves.

How was it he could make me shiver with such a casual phrase?

"Which reminds me. What if something happens to you? Not that it will. But what if you end up in jail or fall off a cliff and break a leg? Will Hugh be understanding then? I need you to explain this to him. He's not to go off halfcocked for any reason."

That stunned me, until I realized this was Glass at his professional best – assessing future threats and planning.

He put down the line and jumped to my rock to sit beside me. "Hey. I saw the sad face. I'm only being practical. If I bring...Jurgen here, I need to be able to guarantee he's as safe as possible. He might be a merc, but I take care of my men. I also take care of you. You won't be falling off any cliffs."

He'd said that name deliberately.

"I figured that already, though you did worry me for a second." I smiled half-heartedly as he gave me a one-armed hug. "Thank you for trusting me with his name. I won't tell Hugh, but I will tell him what you said about co-operating. Good enough?"

"Yes. Thanks." He kissed my head. "I'm taking you to the Red Gecko for lunch. It's across the bay in town. European cuisine, so expect anything from burgers to roulade of pork with a sauce of overripe figs done with caviar bon-bons."

"Oh. My. God. You made that up, totally. Though I will be disappointed if they don't have caviar bon-bons."

It turned out to be lucky we had bread, avocados, and eggs at the house since all the fish in the sea were partying elsewhere. By the time lunch came around, Glass had towed me across the town, from one end to the other, speaking to his sources and I was ready to eat a chef.

The Red Gecko was on stilts out over the bay. Nothing made me happier than eating while being able to look out over water. I was a bit of a water baby and had visited many upper-echelon restaurants sited like this, as well as surf lifesaving clubs up and down the east coast of Australia. Always, it was for the view, since the food at the clubs was rather hit or miss.

With my fork half way to my mouth, carrying flakes of grilled salmon, I had another of those moments of happiness. Seeing Glass shovel food into his mouth was strangely satisfying.

"Fuck," I muttered.

"What?" he asked past the mouthful.

"I think I'm having a maternal moment over you eating."

"Say again?" He slowed in his chewing, frowning.

"Never mind. I'm being silly."

Disconcerting, though. I'd never ever wanted to see a man eat, just because it made me feel good. Was that a sign of love? I guess I could suppress my urge to stick a fork in my eyes.

Love...foreign concept. My brother had been the only person I could attach that emotion to...since Nathan had died. And then my brother had died too. Sobering. Maybe love wasn't my best game.

"Hey." Glass had reached over and squeezed my hand. "Looking glum here might just be a spanking offense."

"It's nothing." I smiled back. "Memories."

A man across the room was staring at me. Suit and tie sort with a stern disapproving expression. A face of stone. My dress perhaps? The pink gown with the feathers motif was mid-calf and had the most plunging cleavage. If I leaned too far, something might fall out, considering I hadn't found a bra to suit it.

Some amazing dresses had called to me at a small stall in a shopping arcade over on the island. Next time wear the revealing dresses at nighttime? No. That was stupid. I'd never let others determine my clothes. I wasn't going to start now.

Look all you like, mister. I shot him a look of tired insouciance as if I'd just gotten back from Paris. *Fuck you, sir.*

Now that cheered up my day immensely. Next time I'd wear a bikini. Around here, it was surprising no one else had tried that.

As we ate and exchanged small talk, a revelation of sorts sneaked in, then came down *wham* like a hammer of doom. I wasn't stupid. Top of the class at times, though university was more challenging than high school. What Glass had been doing, what he'd said, it seemed smoke and mirrors. I knew something about tracking down people on the net. This conclusion had arrived in my head all on its own. It was a familiar way to learn, for me – complex knowledge learned at lectures, or through textbooks, sometimes hit me like this, when I least expected it.

Was this all smoke and mirrors? There was more magic here than how he conjured up money, friends, and houses. He was pretending to help me.

I stared at my plate and stirred the rice into a small pile, then nibbled a few grains.

Don't say anything. Not yet. I'm wrong. I must be.

If I was right though, what the hell was Glass to me? If he was lying to me about that, was the whole lover and Dom thing pretend too? Please let me be wrong.

"Dessert and coffee?"

I glanced at him. This man had flipped back into stranger slash predator territory. Was everything false? My stomach squeezed in. Queasy was the best word for how I felt.

Vomiting was a distinct possibility.

"No." I flashed a smile. "I'm full. Can we go?"

"Sure."

On the way out, I passed the table where that annoying man sat. He was busy on the phone and I'd been forgotten.

My awareness rolled for a moment then settled.

Glass walked at my elbow, talking to me, and yet all of me felt forgotten and separate from the world. The walls had come up, again.

CHAPTER 11
Moghul

It was her. Wren. As she walked past with him, I was certain. Even across the room, and with her tanned and happier than in previous videos and stills, I'd been ninety-nine percent certain.

The Chinese buyer was in town. I was supposed to meet him in an hour. I eyed the text on the phone screen and ignored her as she walked past. Excellent subterfuge there – stare at the woman and man trying to track you down.

I'd lived years without getting messy and thought myself smart, because I guess I was smart. And now, I was contemplating taking that step off that cliff into air.

What if I could do this with my usual meticulous preparation? Lessen the risk to almost zero.

I rechecked the phone screen where my reply text waited for me to press send.

Sorry. Changed my mind.

I won't be signing the contract. Please apologize to the buyer.

I shut my eyes and simply sat there *anticipating* for so long a waitress came over and tapped my shoulder. Her heels had clopped across the floor and I'd smelled her perfume long before she touched me. I may have startled her when I opened my eyes, as she blanched and leaned away.

"I'm sorry, sir, but are you okay?"

"I'm fine." I nodded slowly. "I'm far better than I've ever been and in a day or so, I think that will be surpassed."

"Oh." She looked nonplussed.

"I'm fucking good. That work for you?" I dabbed my mouth with the napkin, threw it down, and shoved back my chair.

"Of course, sir." She backed away some more.

I loved how waitresses called a man sir.

I walked to the desk, sorting through who I could call in for this one.

My businesses were all humming along and could do without me fine-tuning things for a week, maybe two, three. I could send a few instructions for them then be done.

First the acquisition, then the transfer of my new possession without risking anyone identifying me, then her installation. It would work.

There was property and there was *property*.

I paid some cloned receptionist whose face I forgot as soon as I turned away.

I pressed the send button. Done.

Now, onward, fucking onward. Release the hounds. Cry havoc. All kinds of bad things were in the offing.

My shoes echoed on the hardwood floor on the way out, then on the concrete of the pavement. I was navigating by sound and half-hearted memory, because what was inside my head was far more scintillating.

I was looking forward to this in the worst possible way.

*****

Wren

The walk along the beach that night helped me clear things up in my head. Glass and I should talk. I was probably wrong, just getting cold feet. He'd never shown himself to be anything except a caring man, once you minused out the sex machine. I grinned. Yes, talk. It was the brave and the right thing to do. I'd never lacked for bravery before.

If I had, I'd never have been out on the beach with only the moonlight to guide me.

If...

Footsteps sifting sand had made me turn halfway toward them. One person wasn't a danger.

Only they moved swiftly and wrapped themselves around me. Something hard and sharp jammed into my arm muscle. I felt the cold and expanding pain of an injection. Whatever it was, I had to get free before the effects hit me. I had ages, didn't I? Most things took longer than the movies showed. I panicked though, thrashed about. Kicked. Tried to scream past the wadding over my mouth and eyes. Too many arms. More than one man, surely?

Maybe it was a long time. Maybe a second. It seemed like forever, afterward.

Memories surfed in my head as I bounced about in some vehicle. I'd struggled, I think, but ended up halfway to the beach before everything, and me, floated off into nowhere and nothing.

My mouth was full of dry paper. My head ached with the rush of a hundred prickling needles. Someone far away whispered nonsense. Was it me? All irrelevant and wrong. My tongue poked at dryness. *Here* was somewhere that made me sleepy. Drifting off was far, far easier than...thinking.

CHAPTER 12
Glass

After half an hour, I became worried and trekked across to the beach in the dark. The torch illuminated dunes, waves creeping up the beach to the shush of water shifting sand, and a long, empty expanse. Horseshoe Bay was a huge arc of a beach, miles long, but she'd never have wandered far. Wren wasn't that foolish.

She didn't have a gun – nothing, just her in her shorts and top when she'd walked out that door.

For once being silent and sneaky might be the wrong thing to do. If she was hurt, she might hear me and yell back. If she was being dragged away, she might make an extra effort and scream. Whoever had her would be alerted but...I weighed it up, and I yelled.

"Wren! Can you hear me? Yell if you can."

I listened, again, quietly turning.

Shit. Fuck. Shit-fucking hell.

I jogged farther down the beach, praying, while listening. Only the rough scuffing sound of my feet came to my ears above the crumple and wash.

Though the upper beach was a mass of churned sand and footprints, down low the tide was going out and the sand was flat and gleaming in the light. Except there, a few feet away.

I squatted to look, touching the damp sand.

The bare footprints were the right size for a woman. I followed along the beach and found a place where several bigger prints merged into a small flurry of dug-up sand. After that, the bigger shoeprints went toward the road, where they'd come from, and hers ended.

Nothing more. I turned on the spot with the torch shining out into the dark. Nothing.

When I followed the new prints they crossed the dunes to the road. There were no cars parked here, perhaps a smell of car exhaust, or maybe I was imagining.

"Wren! Wren!" I listened again and heard crickets then I screamed my loudest, "Wren!" Further down this street intersected with a more major street that swept on to the shops. Headlights cruised there. But here. Nothing.

I put my hand to my sore throat. That last yell had almost ripped off the lining.

"Fuck, woman, what's happened to you? Where have you gone?"

I dug out my phone to take some pictures before the sand blew away and obliterated evidence. I'd need to call Hugh. The police, maybe.

She'd been a bit unhappy with me, for some reason, I'd sensed it, but this? It couldn't be a part of that? Why would she disappear? I put my hands on my head, giving the street one last survey.

What the fuck had happened?

Something bad. Maybe something like Vetrov.

If it had, I was going to find him and shove his dick down his throat, fill him full of holes, then stomp in his fucking face.

CHAPTER 13
Moghul

The surreal feeling began when I picked her up at five AM. The low-light camera that I'd strapped to a tree showed her abductors had abandoned the car by the side of the small road, as arranged, and driven off in another. I drove up, drew on gloves, and popped the trunk.

The lightbulb in the trunk had been removed, but the moonlight angling in past my shoulder and the penlight I flicked on showed me enough.

There she lay. It was indeed her.

Wren. Such a pretty name for such a beautiful woman.

Her hair had strayed in dark swirling tangles about her neck and face. Her shirt had bunched up and showed midriff. Her shorts revealed the lower curve of her ass and were as indecent as the peekaboo neckline of her dress at the restaurant. I already knew what the edge of her areolas looked like, courtesy of that dress.

At the time, being aware Glass was seeing her body the same as I, had thrown me into some weird jealous mood.

No longer. The man had lost her.

I hesitated for all of half a second before tugging off one glove and pulling down the T-shirt and the cup of her bra with two fingers, reacquainting myself with the appearance of her areola. My leisurely aim painted circles of light across her breasts, on her parted lips, her eyelashes, and on the leather cuffs about her wrists where they'd fastened them at her back.

Fuck.

Putting clamps on her tits would be one of the firsts.

I'd never been such a perverted fuck until now.

I'd done all sorts of shit by proxy over the net, and kink in real life to willing submissive women, but this, tonight... It caught me up and whirled me off into some predatory space where I was ultra-aware of her and me and this car trunk, and of nothing else.

Had the world been turned into irradiated mist? Maybe. All I cared about was now and here.

Focus on what needs doing. I took in an indispensable lungful of oxygen, having forgotten to breathe while I stared.

The dissociative sedative was still circulating in her bloodstream in high concentrations and would be for a few more hours. She was awake but barely aware of her surroundings.

Even so, any drug was a risk. I leaned in and listened, while resting my palm on her chest then I fumbled at her neck until I found the bump of her carotid artery pulse.

Breathing – good. Pulse – good. Relief poured in.

So odd, to be able to touch her.

I clicked off the light and straightened, still aware of her seductive scent and remembering the soft give of her skin underneath my fingers. My heart thumped heavily.

Not obsessed, hell no. I scoffed at my own naivety.

I worked my arms under her and carried her to my own trunk, crunching stray leaves under my boot and grinding them into the bitumen surface of the road. Then I gently lowered her and tucked her legs up to accommodate the temporary soundproofing. The partition between the trunk and the back seat had plenty of gaps and air would be plentiful. She could breathe. In daytime she might've cooked from the sun beating down on the metal. Nighttime was perfect.

There were no human sounds here, in this eucalypt forest north of town, just an owl, some bugs making bug noises, and distant cars grumbling along the highway.

I slammed the trunk shut, walked to the open driver's side door, and slid into my seat.

Then...I freaked, a little.

What the hell was I doing?

Rules, limitations, boundaries, being sensible according to what my brain said was best – these had formed my compass for surviving for the twenty-five years since I hit teenager times. I *lived* my rules.

"Holy fuck," I muttered, thinking of her back there and me here, holding the wheel, staring out at the darkness.

In one day, I'd turned everything upside down.

The drive back to the island and over on the ferry wasn't nerve wracking. Confusing would sum it up best. The chance that anyone would find out I had a woman in my trunk was infinitesimal. I had on my faded T-shirt, shorts, and the gym shoes I wore when boating, fishing or hiking. The sleeping bag and backpack piled on the back seat made it look like I'd been camping.

No one would stop me.

I had Wren.

Every time I recalled that, most of my blood likely rushed to my dick, or my head, or both. I felt like a king and that was something I hadn't felt for years. Guess I was world weary. Tired of what I did, no matter how crazy it would be to any onlooker. I'd done it all, but mostly kept my worst fucked-up-edness situations outside my ten-mile zone of exclusion. It was always over there. Never here.

The people around my car on the ferry were clueless. This was easy.

Deciding what to do with her was the difficult part.

My meticulous planning had been all about the acquisition. The future was where my problems began.

*****

Moghul

By nine in the morning she was stirring. I had the syringe of Valium ready, in case she developed muscle spasms. Sometimes recovery caused those. I wasn't keen on having to find a vein and do this. Scared I'd fuck up and kill her. It wasn't likely, since Valium was about the safest thing about this whole situation, still, it scared me.

That was the crux of my problem.

I'd lain here for hours, in the subdued lighting, in this enormous room devoted to fucking, flogging, and restraining submissives, and I'd worried. A foreign concept that, to me – worry of the sort where you were swearing at yourself.

Slowly, everything had sorted itself out in my head. Killing her, accidentally or on purpose was not happening. Yet, it was one of three future possibilities. The hard crunch of facts, the application of logic, told me so.

Clearly, I'd flunked serial killer school. Seriously badly, flunked it.

I rolled off the leather-upholstered platform. Built for restraining my girls and for easy cleaning, it made a good bed, though it was hard on the back.

I paced to the distant controls and turned up the recessed ceiling lights, and completed a last survey to make sure nothing was out of place. The leather collar on her neck had steel reinforcing inside and was locked together. Only my key would get that off. Same with the chain leash I'd attached to the wall. The burgundy wrist and ankle cuffs were also reinforced and locked on.

For now, she was free to move except for the leash. All the equipment was far out of reach.

Wren lifted her head from the red leather of her bed, coughed, and rubbed her eyes.

I checked the fit of the black mask I wore then picked up the plastic cup of water. I'd hacked away most of the leather from a gimp mask so it only went around my head at nose and eye level. Ragged, but it would do. Wearing a proper gimp mask fulltime was a pain in the ass. I'd dyed my scruffy brown hair black. Luckily a twenty-four hour chemist had been open. All done with a smidgen of anger because my actions said I *might* let her go. But I was never one for denying reality.

In a few weeks I'd have to decide.

Kill her. Train her until she obeyed me absolutely. Let her go.

Those were my options. I'd seen all the trouble Chris had been through with his women. Training a woman until you were certain they were bound to you irrevocably was like trying to catch a storm and bring it to heel.

Submission in BDSM was different and consensual. The submissive could walk away from the relationship at any time, and many did, the same as any vanilla relationship, no matter what labels you applied – slaves could still walk. No law could hold someone to any contract signed between kinksters. Slaves could become not-slaves.

This had to be permanent. Obedience needed to be ingrained and automatic, so that no matter what I did to her, she would remain so – a difficult task and one that would need a new approach. Beating her or humiliating her until she shrank away to a shell of a person was repulsive to me. The key to this would be personalized to Wren. I *needed* to find that key.

Everyone had flaws and weaknesses. With enough time, it should be possible?

Maybe. Guaranteed? No.

I should've fucking seen this. I guess I hadn't wanted to.

I'd never kill her. Would I? I really doubted that I could.

The man I'd killed recently had been my personal first. Bad enough. A woman...maybe. Wren? My head ached at the idea.

Fuck no.

Wearing the mask and dyeing my hair let me keep those options open.

"Who...are...?" She blinked, her arms propping her off her side, elbows flexed, her eyes still dull from the drug, and her gorgeous hair trailing over her shoulders. "Who are you?"

I slowly approached her, considering my first words. I'm sure I wore my sadistic smile. My subs had told me I often did, when contemplating how to I was going to use them, what I was going to do to them.

Like a man about to take his first step on the moon, I wanted to get this right.

"I'm the man...who now..." My boots tapped the timing of my words on the big, white tiles. "Owns you."

CHAPTER 14
Wren

Owns you?

Shit. Even in the fuzzy state my mind was in, terror splintered my heart. Where was I?

The room was minimal in furniture and huge, and so clean it somehow reminded me of a hospital, a luxurious one. My terror escalated. Alone. I kept looking, sweeping from left to right while watching this guy. His five feet distance still invaded my private space because he fucking wore a black leather mask. Only covering the eyes, mostly. But that was enough.

Who wore masks? What had I done last night?

Nightclub?

A small sunken pool to the left, white tiles, distant door, him, tiles...I blinked. Beyond him, a lovely mural of some sort. On the wall to the right... Jesus. Whips, chains, things made of leather that dangled from hooks. More things that looked ugly and as if made to hurt. Bits of furniture I didn't quite understand. A cross.

I'd been kidnapped.

Bizarrely, I catalogued his clothes. Plain gray shirt with buttons. Black cargo pants. Did serial killers wear that?

Maybe. What was he planning to do with me?

Terror took flight and became something worse. My chest hurt from the way my heart struggled to beat fast enough for me to run.

Only, one problem. I swallowed and put my hand to my neck, found the leather collar there I'd suspected, and peeked sideways. That cold metal dribbling off my arm a moment before? A leash.

"I'm not a dog," I whispered, harshly, scared at how my throat hurt. What had he done to me while I was unconscious? My clothes were still on. Nothing seemed sore or wrong, apart from some bruised spots on my arms.

I rallied. *Be brave. Tell this fucker how it is.* "Are you aware of who I am? Release me and –"

"I know who you are, Wren Gavoche, to the last million, to the number of times you've flown overseas, and to how many years you've been at university."

Oh shit.

"I know you."

My hopes sank. Not random then. But perhaps, despite my surroundings, it was all about money?

"If you're looking to ransom me, I can tell you who to contact?" My eyebrows rose jerkily, more willing to show my hope and desperation than my head was. Embarrassing body reaction. He shook his head. "No?" My voice cracked and petered out. "Millions, I have..."

"No. Drink this." He held out a white cup.

My mouth was so dry my tongue was having trouble moving against my lips. If that was water? I craned my head to see inside it, my elbow collapsing under me, a little, from weakness. Clear fluid.

"It's only water."

"Uh-huh." I didn't have a lot of choice here. I took the cup with a shaking hand and gulped down the contents, feeling strength ebb back into me. "More?"

My toes curled as I heard myself begging. Thirst was too basic a need to resist.

"Soon. I need to ask you a question."

His tone was so measured, so normal, it skittered through me, and my nipples tightened. I wasn't tiny, but he was the equal of Glass in height and that said he'd hit six feet. A little less muscled, though. Maybe I could do him some damage if I used all my training?

Maybe I'd get hurt, and where was I going to go when I was tied here? Some metal device locked my collar. My fingertips found the keyhole.

"You won't get that off. Complex lock and the keys are not on me."

Where, before, everything had tumbled in and piled up in my head so fast I could barely process it, now the certainty of the trouble I was in hit me hard.

My forehead ached from the effort of not crying.

I dabbed my nose with the back of my hand and sniffed back those tears.

The black leather mask and the stark confidence in his brown eyes said, *I can do anything to you.* This room, the collar on my neck – they spoke of organization and planning, of a man prepared to spend time and money to abduct me. Yet he didn't want money in return? The accumulated facts reduced me to a wreck.

Would I get out of here alive?

"Now, my question. How does Glass plan to find this man you seek?"

He knew about Glass?

Of course he did. *He knows about my past. This man's been following me for ages.*

I blinked at him, stunned, trying to run down the logic while not revealing my confusion to him.

Disaster though. Knowing he knew so much about me, while he was a blank, put me on even rockier ground.

Wait. This was *him*? Surely it was? This must be Vetrov. The man who sold women like cattle. I gasped and backed up, shuffling my legs and belly along the smooth leather, feeling it stick to my stomach where my T-shirt rode up.

"No," he spat, and he reached for my hair, halting my retreat with the pain of a wrenching grip that seemed likely to tear out some hair by the roots.

I grabbed at his hand, compelled to tear loose by any means – nails, strength, and god, that was so not working. His hold didn't budge.

"Stop clawing me, Wren." He lowered his head to stare level into my eyes. "Or I'll give you your first punishment."

Fear. Pure fear. So many unknowns here that my imagination made everything screech to a halt. What punishment? My throat seized. I stopped tearing at his hands and lowered mine. My breaths were shaky and my hands too.

Where my hair was near to twisting from its roots, the hurt throbbed outward.

"Good girl."

Glass had said that. Not this monster. I coughed to bury a sob. I wasn't some weak bitch. *Woman up.*

I glared. *Fuck you.*

"Look at me like that and I punish you. Calm yourself."

I shut my eyes to escape him. Think. Doing what he said didn't mean surrender. It was sensible. I needed to survive to escape. I needed to be healthy. I sucked in a breath and forced my anger deep. Even this he took from me.

Didn't *matter.*

I looked at him and measured my breaths to distract myself. In. Out.

"Well done." He nodded. "Now answer my question."

He released my head and rose to his full height.

After a second, I sat up on my knees and felt instantly vulnerable. When I went to put my legs over the edge to sit properly, he caught me with a headshake.

"No. Stay there. I like you kneeling."

"It hurts my legs —"

His smile was a knowing one. "Nice try. No. Behave as I tell you to. Answer."

He seriously wanted me to reveal the plans of Glass when they might be my salvation? What if what Glass was doing wasn't pretend? I shook my head.

"You'll never get me to tell you. And if I did say something, how will you know if it's the truth?"

"I will know. Last chance. Tell me."

Smart ass. He was bluffing.

But, last chance? What did that mean? I flicked my gaze to where all those kinky medieval-looking things waited, hanging from the wall, where the black benches stood on four legs with silvery chains and leather cuffs dangling...lurking like creatures ready to pounce.

He'd have plans with those. I swallowed, steeled myself.

"He said his next step was to interrogate Mickey Mouse and Barbie. How the fuck will you know? If you torture me with..." I gestured dismissively at the equipment. "With that, I'll only tell you more lies, you stupid prick."

His smile broadened, though I was pretty damn sure his eyes had narrowed. Evil gleamed there. He slapped me, rocking my head to the side. It was more a shock than anything. "Your mouth just got you in serious trouble."

I dwindled inside, wishing I could make my last words vanish. My cheek stung. I shouldn't have called him that. Why did I say that? I intertwined my fingers on my thighs for reassurance and tried not to shiver.

"Let me be clear. I won't harm you irrevocably and I don't plan to kill you or chop you up. I want you alive, here, as my little fucktoy and pleasure slave. Understand? And even if you tell me lies, Wren, I'll enjoy torturing you. Why else do you think I wanted you? I'm a sadist, a hardcore sadist, and making women scream and squirm brightens my day."

He reached down and with finger and thumb pinched my lower lip and stretched it outward. The small pain combined with his intense stare froze me in place.

I was appalled, but not just by fear. Warmth had flooded me, my sex, my face. His words had both scared and excited me. My pussy had squeezed in. I knew the signs from how I'd reacted to Glass. I'd become sensitized – my dumbass body linking dominant men to sex.

This was so very, very wrong, yet I had to consciously resist squirming on my knees.

He put his finger to the center of my forehead and ran it lazily down my face, bumping over my eyebrow, my nose, to my hurt lip before he bent down to murmur, "You'll be such a good girl once I'm done with you."

Me? Me?

The crazy arrogance of this bastard.

He had no clue. Scare me. Do bad things. I would spring up and put a knife in his heart when he least expected it. I'd base-jumped off a mountain, once.

This was child's play...

Then he stalked over to all that black leather and steel, and began to gather various implements that clinked.

Shit. Okay. Rewind, please.

That raggedly cut black mask rendered him into a thing from Hell, from the neck up. The cargo pants, not so much. The last horrible porno torture movie I'd glimpsed, *Hostel*...he'd fit right in. The woman in that had been hung upside down and gutted, blood pouring from the slashes on her body and flooding onto the floor.

I should close my mouth, slow down my betraying heartbeat.

I trusted him not to harm me as much as I'd trust a wolf pack not to hunt me down.

He returned, arms loaded down with a rolled cloth, like some shepherd from the desert, visiting the savior, bearing awful gifts.

This time, my retreat was impossible to halt. I ended up on my knees on the bed with my back and the soles of my feet pressed to the cold wall.

Scared had overwhelmed that initial tinge of blasphemous excitement.

His mask... I focused in. It was enough of a disguise that I might never recognize him with it gone. If I escaped, I might pass him on the street and not realize I had. That would be a crime.

My courage revived because I bitch slapped it.

I needed to get the mask off him. Dangerous. But I *was* going to get out of here and whatever this man did to me I would repay him in spades.

He laid everything in a neat row on a white towel he'd stretched across the floor. The first instrument he picked up, I recognized as a crop. He swished it to and fro, smiling.

"I wasn't going to use anything on you. It's your first day and you're possibly affected by the drug." One brow crept above the mask's edge. "But swearing at me needs correcting. This is a small punishment. Say 'thank you Sir for my punishment' before I begin."

What The. Fuck. "Seriously?" I squeaked out, eyeing his fist where it tensed on the handle. "You've got to be joki –"

Shut up. Shut up. He's already planning to hurt me.

That look in his eye had intensified.

"Get off and kneel on the floor. Put your head and your forearms on the bed." He shoved the rolled-up sleeves of his shirt, higher up his arms.

I couldn't. I'd been prepared to grit my teeth and bear whatever pain he doled out with his stick, but say those dumb words? It went too far for me to simply acquiesce.

Fight or flight, and flight was a bit difficult.

I knew trying out my Muay Thai would be a mistake. I just knew it. Even if I kicked a few teeth in, he had more weight on me, double maybe. More muscles. His biceps were twice as thick, but I was going to try. Saying those words would make me vomit.

I pushed off with all the power in my curled legs, prepared to get in one jump kick to that ugly face...and my legs failed me. I half crumpled, half launched onto the floor, tripping on my tangled legs, and hit my head on the tiles.

The thump reverberated.

The benefits of being drugged. Head butting floors. I was rolling about groaning, clutching my head, when he scooped me up and sat down on the bed, still holding me.

Through the splitting pain, I peered up at him.

"Well. That was interesting. If stupid. You might've hung yourself if the leash had been shorter." His scowl wrinkled his forehead. "I'll delay your punishment."

"Uh." Scintillating reply but perhaps it was best to act dumb and hurt. Act? That was a thought that seemed a good one, even as the pain stomped through my brain like a football player with studded boots.

Act...I needed to do more of that. I could pretend, mislead him, if only I could control my need to spit back when he angered me.

The crease in the middle of his forehead said he was worried.

Why was he worried?

"You're going to have a bump. I'll get you an ice pack."

"Uhhh." Surreal.

"Stupid girl. I told you I wasn't going to chop you up. I need you intact. When you feel pain, I'd rather it be my pain."

How...nice.

True to his word, he got up to find an ice pack. The temporary respite left me pondering.

I needed a plan to get out of here. Maybe two or three plans, to be on the safe side. A knife would be good too. They always were.

Fuck, my head hurt.

CHAPTER 15
Moghul

What was I trying to be? Her goddamned daddy Dom?

I fed her lunch and dinner, let her think herself safe, and took her by leash to the bathroom. Let her recover. The lump on her head was small and she had no signs of concussion. Had she been planning to run or to attack me earlier? She couldn't have run with the leash at her neck. Fight then? Her history sheet said she'd trained in martial arts, joined a Muay Thai group at university. Interesting, considering I'd had Chris teach me his MMA moves. One day, perhaps, I'd let that man in on who I was, apart from Mr. Nice-as-Pie Moghul.

Whatever, I could overpower the little bitch easily.

At ten that night, while she was half asleep, I walked in, dragged her from the bed by her hair, and forced her to her knees. Her screams gave my balls ideas, demonic ones involving fucking her until she was a limp mess. Wren screamed well.

I guess twisting her hair into a knot tight enough to make my fist go red and white was the cause. Or it could be the grip on her throat. Or maybe the fright at being woken so harshly. Poor girl. Not.

My smile quirked. Fun.

With my teeth beside her ear, I grated out, "Quiet. I have far, far worse I can do."

She fell silent, apart from a few whimpers, and I hoisted her upper body onto the bed. When she stayed there, I released her hair, hauled her wrists to the small of her back, and locked the cuffs together.

I stood. I stared.

Familiar territory. A tied-up woman. A whimpering, quivering, tied-up woman.

I'd figured out my shit. The lack of consent had thrown me. Strange but true. No longer. Once I got her into orgasming while I gave her pain, I'd be happier still. Nothing beat that. Fucking *nothing*.

And obeying me, though there was an addictive spice in dominating brats. I turned that over in my head. If I let Wren think she could defy me on occasion, wouldn't that make this impossible? Maybe not. I liked having a good excuse for my punishments.

Now though, I needed to set a baseline.

"You behaving for me now, Wren?"

"Mmm." She nodded rapidly, her face turned sideways against the bed. There were tears on her cheeks.

I planted my bare foot on her back, squashed her to the leather. "Good."

Feeling her chest move through the shirt as she panted – awesome. I was king again.

I could do one better than this – her naked.

The lights were dim. I fished out the remote and turned them up bright.

Then I leaned in to deliver my message. "I've been soft on you and I really don't want us to begin on the wrong foot. I'm not soft. I'm hard, so hard I'm going to ram my cock up your ass before this week is over. If you haven't had anal before, I have butt plugs to cure that virgin asshole."

Ruining her was not my aim.

"Wait. Wait."

Her gasped words were desperate. Good.

"No waiting tonight. Punishment. But first I need these clothes off you." Her renewed wriggling just meant I needed to cram her down with my foot more. I did so then pulled my knife from my pocket and opened it. The big six-inch blade would do.

I showed it to her, inches from her face. "This is being used on you. Move and I will cut you. I have no tolerance for stupidity. Understand me?"

Nothing.

"Understand me?" This time I put the point an inch from her eye.

She only blinked, but her answer was husky. "Yes. I do."

Ahh. Now this time I had it right. Nothing like being a big, scary man, with a big, scary knife to set the tone.

The point was newly sharpened. Ready for flesh, clothes, and scaring the fuck out of girls who wriggled and made my cock hard. Or didn't wriggle because I told them not to.

I almost came at the sight as thread by thread I undressed her. Slow and steady, as the saying went, with the edge turned away from her. The back of the knife *could* seem just as scary, with the right psychological impetus.

Her staccato breaths bumped my hand and she gasped as I reached the neck of the shirt.

"Did you move?" I murmured. "Like me to use it the other way round?"

Her quiet, mouse-like answer came a few seconds later. "No. No, of course I don't. I didn't move." She licked her lips. "No."

But I pulled the knife from under the cloth and flipped her over so I could talk with her eyes on me. "That was a lie."

"No, no, no. It wasn't. I didn't. I *swear* I didn't." Those pretty lips were licked again before she trotted out, "Maybe you need new glasses?"

"Fuck." I chuckled. "You do ask for it."

Her gaze fixed on my blade.

"Shiny?" With my palm jammed between her breasts, I showed her the slicing edge. "This is going next to your skin. Obey me. Don't move."

That brought me a whimper. My cock twitched.

The T-shirt was already cut down the middle of the back and the shoulders, so I pulled that out from under her, baring her cute white bra.

When I shifted my palm and settled it over her pussy, her face flinched into some new expression then back into such a quiet, almost stony, facade that I wondered. Her breathing had gone from panting, to stillness, then to a measured, deeper pace. Turned on?

By my hand?

I ground the heel of it onto her with increasing pressure, observing my obstinate captive.

Nothing.

Edge up, though she couldn't see that, the knife meandered its fearful course, curling past the whorl of her belly button, over her quivering stomach, to slide light as the roll of a blood drop to the drawstring waist of her shorts. Wriggling it let the tip insinuate between cloth and skin and severed the first threads.

I eyed her, dubious. All her body signals made me think of tension, of a coiled-up energy, waiting and ready to erupt.

Maybe it was the current lack of breathing.

Maybe it was that she'd stopped talking or blinking.

I had her utter attention.

Arousal, or fear?

I swiveled my palm. Where my fingers splayed between her thighs, I felt her muscles move. Perhaps undulate was the better word to use.

I still wasn't certain. The knife carved through the cloth of her shorts like a shark through water. She'd know the sharp edge couldn't be against her skin. Yet she'd levered her head off the bed and was staring. Her lips seemed fuller, her eyes dark.

What secrets lurked in her mind?

The material fell from my blade, revealing her white underwear. I continued, cutting, shifting my hand from her mound to fasten down her thigh. When I reached the apex of her thighs, I turned the knife so it stood on end, the tip poised above the soft swell of her mons. If it fell, the blade would split her, intimately. My attention divided between the flutter of her eyelashes and what my hand was doing, I lowered the tip, until the business end kissed her panties.

She sucked in a breath then shuddered the next ones. Lovely. I waited, only stroking her thigh with my fingers. Just to see. Just to watch. Around her jaw, muscles clenched.

With my big, nasty weapon, I pressed down on her to caress where her clit should be, certain I could see the engorged bump pushing upward as if to greet the knife. A few threads frayed but cloth remained between the honed metal and her mons.

Her thigh strained beneath my hand.

"Is this turning you on?" I said, in a monotone, as if the question were insignificant.

"No," she blurted. "Fuck no. Get it away from me. I like my bits where they are."

"No?"

Her swallow was obvious. "No."

"What if I press harder..." Instead, as I spoke, I scraped tiny, slow circles around that bump.

Wren only grunted. With her hands bound under her back, I could do anything and she was helpless. Most subs loved the helplessness.

Not all liked the terror of a knife. She seemed to like *something* about this.

Novel. I'd not thought I'd get to her this easily. Punishment, smunishment. This was meat and bones to me. Turning her on, damn straight I would explore this until I was sure.

Struck by a notion, I sat next to her and covered her eyes with my hand, shoving her head to the leather and blocking out sight. After one startled squeak, she was quiet. I went to my elbow and circled her clit some more, watching my hand on the knife and the curve of her legs. The shallow angle at which I viewed her thighs let me see how she tensed and relaxed – a subtle concealment. I imagined her kneading the floor with her toes, unable to stop that small reaction.

Delicious, if true.

"Such a bad, bad girl you are. Are you hiding from me?"

Only a strangled sound came from her mouth.

"Moving now, little Wren, would be real bad."

As I kept playing with her clit, her breathing intensified into what seemed close to what a woman did when building toward climax.

I could growl some dirty words in her ear, or just keep watching. Trial and error.

Damn, though. She was pressing upward with her mound, and from the way her legs moved and the sounds of her feet unsticking from and then tapping on tile, she'd braced them on the floor.

And now...a quiet, almost inaudible moan. Done through her closed mouth. I laughed to myself. Still suppressing her reactions.

How I wish I'd bared her tits. Why not? I sat up a little and shoved down both cups, before blindfolding her with my hand again. I pinned her more thoroughly by wrapping my leg over her thigh and inserting it between her legs, gripping her like stone, then I resumed my gentle but insistent knifeplay with her clit.

"Now I've got you. I could tie you down some more and fuck you with this knife."

After two or three frantic gasps, her body went into full-on arousal mode. Her muscles tensed. Her body exploded upward an inch or two, despite my crushing hold. I had to raise the knife in unison or cut her.

Not being able to see, or that extra restriction on her movement, it had done something.

Her mouth opened and a series of moans accompanied the jerky movements of her belly. So beautiful. I dared to mutter some quiet dirtiness. Whispering.

"That's the way. Come for me. You are such a pretty, pretty thing. My pretty whore. My knife is on your clit, almost cutting you and it's going to make you come. Round and round, and round." As I said those words, I was doing exactly that with the tip.

When another burst of gasps hit her, I quickly reversed the knife and used the butt on her clit instead. Then I leaned over and sucked her nipple into my mouth. I bit down, hard, my teeth staying fastened there as...

She came. She arched into the knife and my mouth, and came. Those noises she made... Incredible. Fuck me, she'd come from the knife.

What had I found? A little masochist?

My little masochist.

CHAPTER 16
Wren

Shame, frustration, anger, they whirled around in my mind while I lay on my side and breathed heavily into his chest. He held me, still, his leg wrapped over my body, his arm pressing me close and his fingers toying with mine where they were cuffed at my back. Such a contradiction of madly brutal and soft. Of cruel and kind. I'd come while he watched, and it had been so amazing I'd not forget anything about this, ever, and I wanted to kill him for doing it to me.

God, I so hated him.

He'd pushed my shorts down my legs so that I was held to him mostly naked. Vulnerable, so vulnerable, and at the back of my mind I couldn't get over the fact that I'd come in front of him....because of the knife.

The dirty talk and the way he'd fastened me down had contributed, but it was the knife that threw me past the point of no return.

I'd loved that rollercoaster of fear and arousal and just loved how he...

I clenched my jaw and calmed myself. No.

Fuck.

I hate him.

But at the back of my mind thoughts drifted, of how I liked dominance and control, and of how my other man...my real one, had awoken me to that. *Not going there. Not.*

Then he kissed the top of my head and began to speak.

"Don't try to keep secrets from me, pretty thing, I will find them out. Thank you for coming for me. You'll learn I can do that to you when I want to, especially now I've proven you can. You're fighting me..."

Such condescension, but I was tired.

I felt his breath on my hair and his voice was so warm and close that for a moment I wanted to sink into him. I snapped my eyes open. *Fuck him.*

"...and I don't care. Fight me."

What?

"It only gives me reasons to punish you."

Uh-huh. Whatever, mister arrogant.

"That reminds me. I haven't punished you."

He jumped to his feet, leaving a void where his body had been. My feet weren't tied so I moved to wriggle and slide off the bed on my stomach. Sitting still for this punishment? No way. The cuffs, unfortunately, weren't coming off without that elusive key. Was it on him now, or not?

If he turned away... Shit, no, I'd never be able to kick him and knock him out with surety. Not with the one kick I could get in while tied up.

My feet hit the floor, but I had no time to figure out how to rise.

"That's far enough." His foot squashed down on my back like it had before.

Air whooshed from my lungs. What was I? His private footwarmer?

"For the swearing."

The first strike whammed down on my butt hard enough to feel like a burning steel stick had hit me. I screeched, surprised and hurt. Painful heat lanced outward.

Swiftly, he hit me there several more times. The crop must have been brought in earlier and left on the floor. Despite my attempts to squirm away, I was stuck in place, his target. I managed not to scream again but my ass burned like hell by the end.

"Fuck." I hissed. "You —"

"Shhh." He slapped his hand on the burning places and this time I did screech. "You want this twice?"

Shit. Crap. I will kill him ASAP and STAT. With a pistol, an axe, and the candlestick in the library or anywhere else I can do it. Cluedo had popped up with a vengeance. Where was the damned butler when I needed him?

I panted into the leather and tried not to think of how wet my pussy was, of how much I was aching, inches from his foot. It was the orgasm. Nothing more. Move along there, nothing to see.

I needed a cock to slide onto *so* badly.

If this had been Glass...

I panted some more, wishing he would remove his foot. It was too much. Too much *there*, his presence. Solid. Weighing me down. The weight seemed to radiate into my abdomen and my sore butt, adding to the ache.

Then his foot lifted. I waited and figured I should raise my head, because that's what an aware, aggressive, non-victim woman would do.

"This next, is for your smart ass, you-need-glasses comment." My feet were seized and I heard the ankle cuffs locked. "And it's for me."

When I craned my neck to look back, he was running a cream rope between my wrists and the ankle cuffs. He made a swift tie then began to tighten it so my feet were inexorably drawn toward my hands. All I could do was watch, until I ended up with much of my weight on my knees.

What was he up to? I didn't like this, no, not at all. Fear trickled down my spine.

"A hogtied woman makes forced blow jobs so much easier." He sat on the bed, a foot away, smiling, and swept his gaze down my body. "Damn, that lingerie. Hot."

Anger flared. Though I knew it was dumb, I couldn't stop. "Don't you fucking da —"

The sudden claw hold in my hair and stinging slap to my face halted me. The up-close stare into my eyes paralyzed me completely. My protests faded from my thoughts and I was left in limbo, mouth open.

"Whoa. Now, that's nice." His thumb carefully swept some stray hair from before my eye. "Those soft eyes. A picture of submissiveness."

I drew a blank at first. Thoughts ticked past.

What? Never. Ever, ever.

Well, maybe, for Glass.

While I was still processing what he'd said and trying to remind myself to fight, he hoisted me back onto the bed, onto my side. Then he sat next to me, grabbed my shoulders, and pulled me onto his lap. There was no way to resist, except by backchat and that seemed a futile way to go about this. *Act. Remember?*

Act how?

While I chased my own thoughts around in the labyrinth of my mind, he was unzipping his pants and pulling out his cock. The thing stuck up before my nose, waving like some flagpole waiting for a flag. Cocks were so stupid looking.

Well now. Definitely biteable.

You really expect me to do that, a BJ, and not bite you? Man you are...

He'd hurt me if I did. Badly.

Where were the easy solutions?

Biting him was senseless. If I chewed it off totally, ugh, he'd still kill me before he bled out, or ran off to a doctor, or whatever. And I'd be stuck here, dead or whatever.

"Before I fuck your mouth, this." He leaned over, kissed me fiercely, stinging my lips, then leaned to the side. "And this."

His shirt got in the way of seeing what he did.

I felt him grab one breast before pinching both nipples, over and over. Something tinkled and I knew, I damn well knew, what was coming. Nipple clamps. Who hadn't seen those on the net? Wearing them was another matter. I preferred my nipples unflattened, unchewed, unhurt.

And dammit, *pain*, there it was. I couldn't help gasping. I still couldn't see past his body, with my head almost buried, but I could tell hard metal teeth had been clamped onto each nipple.

Determined not to react too much, I screwed up my face, and took sharp breaths, but said nothing out loud.

Inside though, *bastard* was getting worn out. The tears squeezing past my shut eyelids were involuntary. If I could've made them go away, I would've, since they showed he was affecting me. Climaxes, pain, I wanted all to go away, and the best way was to make him, the man whose lap I lay on, to vanish.

Abracadabra. Piss off.

If only.

Wasn't working, though the *ow* factor in my nipples was building.

"Beautiful," he murmured, almost to himself, then he tightened something on the clamps, so I had to bite my lower lip to keep in the squeal. I swiped my face across his shirt, praying he was occupied.

He must've noticed.

His hand fastened on my jaw and he twisted my face upward, toward his gaze.

Still bound tightly, my hands and feet touching, my spine forced into a bow shape, I could only glare...or not glare.

Not glare. My expression slipped to neutral. I wanted no more pain.

One side of his mouth curved upward.

"Good girl. I saw that. And you're crying. Tears please me." He shifted back on the bed and placed me so my mouth and his erect cock were barely an inch apart.

I clicked my teeth, a subtle movement. I was tempted, still.

"Let's have a talk, shall we?" His grip on my jaw crushed in enough to make me cry out and flinch. "You're smart, Wren. What would I do if you used your teeth and bit me? Hmm?"

Answering was an uncomfortable notion and yet another mark of surrender. I could feel myself sliding down some imaginary staircase, becoming smaller, each time he won.

He shook my head a little. "Answer me."

I shut my eyes. What else could I do? "You'd hurt me back."

"Exactly. I'm going to put my cock in your mouth and I'm going to leave it there as long as I wish to. Do anything bad and know you will regret it. I may not cut you into pieces but the shit I could do to you, for hours on end, would make you very sorry. Understand me? Say, yes Sir."

Fuck. Why'd he have to ask that last part? My tongue felt wrapped in plastic. I would gag on those words.

"Wren." He slapped my cheek.

It rocked me, smacked sense into me, I guess. No one had ever dared slap me like he did, and the shock of it was foreign, like coldness splashing into my mind.

I gulped. Tried to lower my head, and couldn't.

"Say it." His tone had lowered to a threatening level – he was a human storm about to roll over me.

After one, small, reinforcing breath, I said it. "Yes... Sir."

Done. I'd obeyed. If he smiled...

He didn't but the intense examination of my face was as bad, if not worse.

I blinked up at him, and secretly squeezed my thighs together, ever so aware of being tied up and bent to his will.

Frightening. More than anything he'd done. I was losing *me*.

"Good. I'm getting somewhere." God, my toes scrunched in at that. He directed his cock to my mouth. "Lick it then suck in the head, and hold it there."

Would I? Could I? More tears leaked from my eyes, rolling sideways and dropping onto his shorts. I shuddered.

Another slip down that staircase.

I had to. I opened my mouth, inched out my tongue, and licked his cock. I licked it again, circled it with my tongue tip, feeling the skin slide under my tongue. At least he tasted clean.

"More. Take me in your mouth."

At his nudge to the back of my head, and I realized he'd put his hand there to guide me, I pushed forward and drew him inside, engulfing only the head, as he'd asked.

This wasn't so bad. I could stand it. To survive I would have to obey, sometimes.

Most times. Yeah, but the future was another world. It wasn't now.

"There. Good girl." He stroked my neck, patted my hair.

And waited.

He didn't fuck my mouth. After a while I ventured a sideways look up at him, only to find he was waiting for me to look up.

Ugh. His cock in my mouth became even more an instrument of something wrong. Torture? No.

Dominance? Yes.

Mind games. The man was good at those. I still didn't know his name and I couldn't ask, not with my mouth full.

"I want you to suck on me some more, while I watch you. Don't shut your eyes. Don't look away."

Oh god. This was like having him stare into my head.

After a second or two, I did as he wanted me to. As I sucked on him, he rocked into my mouth. I had to blink, but otherwise I looked into his eyes, and to my disgust, I was getting wetter, hornier. I was sick in some weird way, to get aroused at him fucking my mouth.

Though one hand stayed in my hair, after a while he searched in a pocket then leaned over me again. Something pushed between my legs, perhaps a dildo, slipping from back to front, in the swollen groove of my pussy.

"I forgot to bring lube but you're very wet down there." He

peered at me. "Your cunt knows what to do, even if your mind is being bad. Lucky for you, I like bad."

I frowned and grunted at him with my lips still mostly sealed around his cock. It was inches inside so I could barely breathe, except through my nose. If he slid further in, maybe I could barf on him. My gagging reflex was excellent.

"This is going in your ass." He showed me a glistening butt plug and I frowned harder, wanting to speak but knowing he'd only do something worse than what he was. Like a bigger plug.

Then he probed with his finger, found my asshole, and pushed there with the point of the plug.

The feel of it screwing into me, squashing against muscles I barely knew I had, made me cough and struggle to remember whether I was breathing, squealing, or sucking his cock.

He stopped moving it inward.

A searing heat pulsed from where he tried to make it enter me. It was bigger than he showed me, surely? I whined.

"Shhh. It'll go in eventually. This is tiny. Push out. *Push. Out.* If you don't try to accept this I will just shove it in and that will hurt more. Trust me on this."

I didn't want this, at all.

"Wren." His hand in my hair tightened. "I'm doing this by feel and I need you to be good and sensible."

I blinked past more of those horrible hot tears. Crying was such a cop out.

"Nod to me, then push out. Now."

I shivered.

Survive. It's okay to do this.

I nodded and pushed out down there, and finally felt the thing slip into me. The abrupt pop of it past that constriction surprised me and I gasped.

"Yesss. Excellent. It's in. Now, let me look at you."

He wasn't asking permission. When he pulled from my mouth, his cock wobbled there, wet from my saliva, before he stood.

My body was turned around so I hung off the bed again. A familiar position, then I felt him pull apart my ass cheeks. He sighed, as if the sight pleased him immensely.

While I was puzzling over that, he loosened the hogtie rope and his body covered mine, his chest pressing my wrists into my back and me onto the bed. The nipple clamps twisted and sparked pain. His cock arrived at my pussy entrance, poking, moving my lips aside.

Pleasure tingled through me, hard, insistent, a crazy overwhelming wave of sensation.

I wanted him. Such a betrayal. I almost sobbed.

But I didn't have to let him know. I was capable of control. I stayed rock still as he glided his cock back and forth in my moisture. My inner thighs grew wet but the one obvious thing I was unable to control, happened: I breathed *lust*.

Fuck me. Fuck me hard was said by every shuddering inhalation and every shaky exhalation.

His words arrived, stirring the fine hairs of my neck. "I'd love to nail you to this bed. I can tell you are dying for it."

"No!" I shook my head.

It didn't stop him, but then I'd known that.

Fraction by fraction, as if getting this wrong would upset the order of the universe, he wriggled in the head of his cock until it was barely inserted in me. He'd parted my lips then he'd stopped.

He awoke excruciating need.

Oh. I bowed my head, utterly absorbed in where he was, in how close he was to slipping deeper. Meanwhile I, the clever, clever woman who had decided to be stone to his advances, was so near to arching into him, to give him better access.

Be still.

He seemed enormous. I think my pussy had grown new pleasure cells – all the better to feel his fucking huge pulsing cock.

My mind was in the gutter.

And I loved being there.

Make me your thing, your sex object. Degrade me with your perverted desires.

I wanted to cry that out, and I did, in my mind. I throbbed everywhere – pussy, nipples, ass cheeks, asshole, even my mouth was sore from his kisses. He'd taken every part of me except where a man was supposed to put his cock.

I bit back a groan. My knees trembled.

"You want me, Wren. Say it."

I croaked out some unintelligible word. Even I wasn't sure what it was. Then I roused myself. "No. I don't. I will *never* want you. I'll never say it."

"Then I'll use your other holes until you beg me not to."

Bad, very bad. I'd miscalculated.

He bit my shoulder, his teeth seeming intent on meeting in my flesh, to keep a piece of me forever. I shrieked. The accumulated pain unhinged me.

Even as I forgot what I was supposed to be doing, and thrust backward, he slipped away.

While the fire in my shoulder and my lost opportunity for cock still ruled me, I heard him pace around the end of the bed. The first I knew of his intent was when he dragged me by my hair and my bitten shoulder across the leather, like a fresh kill.

My status as victim was underlined with agony and casual force.

My head reached the other edge.

"Open." The growling command made me snap my gaze upward. His deadly eyes slew thoughts of doing anything except obeying.

I opened. He stuck his cock to my mouth and forced himself past my teeth while I gulped and spluttered.

I'd never been used so casually. He fucked my mouth, without saying a word, for ages. His thrusts sped up and he began going all the way to the back of my throat and past it until I gagged. Struggling to get air, I wriggled and tried to move away. He held me there, fucked my mouth three more times and somehow came down my throat.

I drooled and gasped, my head over the side, sightless.

By the time he came back from doing whatever he'd done in the nearby bathroom, my eyelids were drooping shut. I was exhausted. Untying me rocked my body. I simply took it, limp.

When he unlocked the leash from the wall and carried me into the shower, I refused to stand, instead I curled up on the floor and let the warm water pound into me. I didn't care. The butt plug was slipped from me. The nipple clamps unclipped. I didn't move or open my eyes during any of it and he didn't speak.

There was no surrender in this, I vaguely convinced myself.

Whatever else he did, I couldn't remember much of it the next morning. He'd toweled me dry, I guess. My underwear though, was gone.

I'd have to do better than this if I was to escape. I stared at the ceiling, unfocused, feeling obliterated.

No mercy.

Find a weakness.

I could do this. I'd ruled one of Father's boardrooms once. A bunch of ornery men in suits who knew far more than I did had been ten times harder to deal with than this...a man who liked to kidnap, whip, and facefuck women who denied him.

I thought that through, aware of my nipples crinkling in as if from cold. He terrified me. I figured I'd only seen half of what he was capable of doing to me.

Yeah, I was wrong. Father's suits were pussies compared to this man.

I could still do this.

CHAPTER 17
Glass

Through the window of the passenger lounge, I watched the wings of the white-and-red plane level off and the wheels touch down. First plane of the morning and the sun shimmied off the metal to the backdrop of a stark orange sky. Hugh had arrived by small, chartered plane and I had to tell him she was gone. I wasn't sure how to explain it to myself, let alone him, and so I hadn't texted him more than to say, come ASAP. Her phone. She'd left it on the bed and I had the password due to having bought it for her and insisted. That had been...satisfying, that she'd let me have that much of a look in at her life. Especially considering I'd chucked her last cellphone in the river.

Nothing ever happened on Magnetic Island. It was a fucking idyllic paradise. The most you had to be wary of were the stinging jellyfish in summertime, the winding roads, and sunburn. Even the waves were laughable due to the Great Barrier Reef protecting the east coast of Queensland. Crystal clear water, fun in the sun, and some evil bastards had taken her.

I ran my hand through my now very black hair. My mohawk was gone and I'd dyed my hair ASAP, along with my eyebrows, soon as I figured out the cops might be needed. I'd be the prime suspect, if they found me. Big guy, blonde Mohawk, shit, I stood out like flare on a battlefield. I'd be in jail for a whole mess of other things I'd done, even if they decided I was innocent of abducting Wren. I didn't want the cops to know I existed, if possible, if we had to involve them.

My worries slammed in. Where was she? What was happening to

her? Was she hurt? Or worse, was someone hurting her? Wherever she was, if she wasn't dead, she'd be afraid. For the hundredth time, I clamped down on the associated emotions. I couldn't function, couldn't help her, if I was a wreck.

Now all I had to do was convince Hugh I was innocent. This was going to be one bastard of a conversation.

Just being here was a big plus though. If I'd done it, and I was sane and intelligent, I'd be gone. I'd be texting ransom notes not *please come* messages.

Four men disembarked with him and all were his; they marched in tandem and I remembered a couple of them from PNG. I had Jurgen behind me, ten yards back, sitting in the passenger lounge seats. He knew the facts. I couldn't, in all fairness, expect him to risk himself on something like this without knowing why. Our friendship was strong though and he'd only shrugged and asked where I wanted him.

We weren't armed, of course, neither would Hugh be. This was the safest place to begin discussing her disappearance. From what Wren had said, I had a fair idea the man regarded her as his little sister as much as a client. He couldn't blow my head off until he found himself a gun.

They came in through the sliding doors, off the tarmac, and paused while all of them searched the milling crowd. That no one spotted me until I was close gave me some faith in my simple disguise.

"Morning." I held out my hand to Hugh and we shook, both of us wary.

His dark trousers and classy business shirt weren't matched by his men. All, bar one, were in jeans and T-shirt, like I was. Though I probably looked like something the cat dragged in, ate, then threw up. No sleep since she'd gone missing, so I was dead tired. All my training in sleep deprivation was long ago. Besides, this was different. Like chalk and cheese. Like cutting your hair versus cutting off your leg and watching yourself bleed.

"Where is she?"

"I need to talk with you somewhere private, alone. Please."

After a moment of appraisal, he nodded. Straight to the point, I liked that. Pity he was going to want to kill me in a few minutes.

I'd found a small, sheltered picnic-type area outside that was still vacant. Too early for breakfast, but I had picked up two coffees on the way past the airport café. His men stayed back, pretending to wander the small garden area while Jurgen leaned against a fig tree and watched us with that lazy yet alert air of his. The shadows were heavy and long, and the rising sun colored the sky like some classic postcard holiday snap. I slid into the steel bench seat and passed the other coffee to Hugh, raised mine, took a sip.

Good barista coffee. A noisy miner fluttered in and landed on a springy twig to peck upside down at a red bottlebrush flower.

Coffee, birds, sunrise...life. Signs that things were turning for the better? I needed more than that. I needed Wren in my arms and whoever did this dead with a bullet through their head.

"What's gone wrong, Mr. Glass?"

He knew my name? Or at least my nickname. Both probably. Expected. The man was in the security game. I wondered what had led him to me.

"Wren has vanished. I think she's been kidnapped."

He shut his eyes for a second then opened them to fix me with a hard stare. "Give me the details."

I leaned on my elbows and placed the cup on the table. "You don't want to kill me?"

"Not yet." The man edged forward. "If you'd done it, you'd have to have the intelligence of a snail to be sitting there. Plus I've never seen such a hangdog look on a man's face. Tell me details. After I hear them, I may kill you for putting her at risk. Was he the only other protection you gave her?" He inclined his head toward Jurgen.

"No. Just me. I fucked up." Admitting that was strangely good. Have my guilt trip then do what I had to do – find her. I sucked in a breath.

"You don't say."

"We were staying at a house at Horseshoe Beach on the island. She went for a walk on the beach and never came back. Dressed in shorts, T-shirt, sandals. After thirty minutes, I went looking for her. By torchlight, I found some scuffed-up sand, some footprints leading back through the dunes to the road, no vehicles, nothing dropped. I took photos that night and this morning. Did a thorough search. Nothing. There's been zero messages, or contact from anyone. Though she was a bit out of sorts that night, I don't see this as normal behavior for her. She has no money, no phone, no clothes."

He nodded. "Any ideas who it might be?"

"Not from the evidence, no. Because there is none. It's all sand there and nothing stays put. Windy that night too, so there were no good footprints even when I saw them. However...I think it's him." I locked gazes, took a sip of coffee, swallowed. "I think it's this Vetrov. Nothing else adds up."

"So you brought her here, to this town where you suspected he might live, gave her no real security..." He heaved in a breath. "Fuck. I don't swear, Mister Glass, but fuck."

I pulled a face of disgust, screwing up my mouth. "I didn't believe he lived here. There are two hundred K people and no reason to think he'd know we were here. If it helps, I'd hand you the gun to shoot me, if I thought it would get her back."

My eyes stung for a second. Damn I was serious about that.

"And I'd do it in a heartbeat. If it would help. I know what you've done in the past. You're a criminal eking out an existence, well, making good money perhaps, in Papua New Guinea the most god-forsaken place I've seen recently. Why did you bring her here? Did you want her kidnapped? I don't buy the *I need to track the IP address* excuse, she told me about. I don't know why she did. Wren is smart."

"I could just tell you she likes me, but it's worse than that." I tapped the cup with my fingers. "That part's none of your business except to know that she means a helluva lot to me. I don't volunteer to be shot for all my customers."

"Let me guess. You're in love with Wren, a millionaire who can buy you a life you've only dreamed of?"

I reined in my impulse to punch him. I understood the whys of his sarcasm. "Let me give you another fact. That last day she and you were loose in PNG, you were going to a rendezvous up in the mountains."

"Yes."

"You were going to be killed. Getting her out of there was my way of saving her life."

He angled his head. The coffee hadn't been touched. "I don't buy that either. You'd only just met."

"It was love at first sight, you skeptical bastard."

"Hmmm."

I regarded him steadily. If he didn't believe me, he could go kick his own bollocks. It was close to the truth. Even if I hadn't known it at the time.

After a while, his mouth twitched. "You've sold me, for now. I know you don't really need her money, and you don't strike me as a typical money grabber. What have you got in the way of a plan? Give me something. Because in one minute, I'm contacting the local police, unless you have a very viable alternative. They can do a lot of things, I...we, cannot do. I also am not sure this isn't an abduction just for rape by some random strangers. In which case, the cops are our best chance. They can do a massive search. She could be lying somewhere in the bush on the island, or in a house, injured." He sighed. "If it turns out to be that and you've made mistakes..."

He left the sentence uncompleted.

Fuck, fuck, fuck. He had to say that. I'd run through this scenario already, a million times, and my heart might never recover from the pain of having to think through it over and over, but I'd ruled it out. There was always that unusual crime that surprised you but it didn't fit the facts.

"She knew martial arts. Self-defense." I shook my head. "She's a capable woman. I just don't see this working so...efficiently without it being a pro job. There would be blood spilled, clothes shredded, maybe some teeth kicked in, and it wouldn't all be hers. There was almost no sign of a struggle, at all." I'd rapped my knuckles on the table for emphasis, and looked up at him, nodding.

"I see." He stared upward. "Okay. I agree with you. I know how good she is. I had the bruises, once, to show it."

"The police would limit my options severely. I'd be forced to go hide somewhere. Here's my one avenue. It is why I'm here in this town, except I hit a wall. I can track this Vetrov to a pinpoint source, if I can get into the database of the ISP provider but my one possible way in evaporated."

I wasn't telling him I'd never really had a viable way in. The ISP databases were meant to be sealed tight. Trying to get in was more likely to get the cops sniffing about, suspicious, than to gain me info. It's what I'd told Pieter and it was true. But Hugh might have better resources.

"Difficult. Once again, a warrant would get the police that." At last, he picked up the coffee and drank. After he put it down, he squeezed the cup with his fingers and his jaw muscles tensed then relaxed, then tensed. Little body signs.

Inside, I guessed, he was seething. Hugh was as protective of

Wren as a mother bear with her cub. Maybe we could be chums after all. I smiled, though I was sure it didn't reach my eyes.

We were both ready to rip the world apart to find her, even if from a distance our actions might seem as low key as a couple of men discussing the latest model car.

The sun was up fully now; the sky was so clear I could tell the day was going to fry.

"However," he continued, "I do have a contact. One day to try this. After that, the police have to be involved. This is going to be huge news and delaying will be impossible soon anyway."

He was right. The headlines would be everywhere. Big money attracted journalists. I'd either have to return to PNG or find a place to hunker down.

"I'm not leaving." I could feel a frown building. "If there's a chance I can help her, I need to be here. Understand?" I looked out from under my brows.

"Of course. Of course." I fell victim to that intense study of his again. The man dissected with his gaze so well he could do brain surgery with it. "That raises you in my estimation."

Huh. Good words, from him.

"Then let's get back to the place I'm staying. I can transfer the pictures of the beach, the IP address, and whatever else you need from me to get this rolling."

As I began to rise, he held up his hand, then seemed to take his time appraising me yet again.

"One last thing. There may be another reason for this."

I waited.

"Wren has a history of mental issues."

Now that was one surprise. "Wait...you mean the sleeping pills?"

"Partly." He tapped his cup and I listened to the rapid drum of his fingers. Hugh was not one to have nervous gestures. I went on high alert. "The man she was going to marry died one night while they were travelling in Europe. Stabbed to death. She still believes she may have killed him even though the police investigation proved otherwise. It's caused problems. She has a knife fixation."

"Okay." I blinked. *Wow.* "Meaning?"

"I'm worried she might have suicided or had some sort of breakdown."

Now that sent a chill through me to my stomach. My poor Wren.

123

The urge to make her safe intensified to the point of an ache in my temples.

I thought back. "If anything, she was happier these last few days. A little worried that night, about something, but not badly so." We'd laughed a lot. As well as having sex a lot. I couldn't see her as doing either of what Hugh said. Thank god. "No. I really doubt that."

He swallowed. "Good to hear. Thank you."

"No worries." The Aussie saying came easily to me after all these years. "Let's get this rolling." I stood and leaned over to shake hands again, holding his for an extra second. I figured he was hurting as much as I was.

We had a chance here. Once in the database, it wouldn't take more than an hour, surely. We had a damn chance.

I scrubbed my hand through my hair and gave Jurgen a thumbs up. That had taken us fifteen to twenty minutes to sort out. Every minute that passed was another minute she was with him, whoever he was. I could feel this deep in my bones. Somebody had her. Or maybe it was just my wishes coming to the fore, because I'd rather someone have her than her be in a grave.

Either though, *either*, threatened to demolish me.

I hadn't been sure how much she meant to me. Now I knew.

Whoever is up there organizing my life, the rush wasn't necessary. I could've waited.

*****

I was out of the car and staring as soon as we braked to a stop. This was a poor neighborhood and video surveillance cameras were unlikely. As dismayed as I was, I still thought of that.

The house was a corpse.

Stumps of black timber poked the sky. Corrugated roofing iron lay twisted and neglected. A surviving door, half dusky-gray peeling paint, half flame eaten, stood askew but attached by one hinge to a lonely remnant of brickwork that had once been the entrance.

Ashes crushed underfoot releasing a stinging scent of smoke that scoured my nostrils. I walked closer, stalking the remains via the vacant allotment next door. This had burned recently.

I squatted and stared some more. This was our answer. Destroyed.

Even as we'd driven up, from way down the street, I'd prayed we had the wrong address. Our plans for distant surveillance were a joke.

Number forty-five Gullway Street. The letterbox, a battered green metal box, stood intact to my right. Correct house and it was gone.

Hugh crunched across the blackened dirt and scabrous grass to stand beside me.

"I've done a check and this happened a week ago. A man died. No suspicious circumstances. The police have so far decided he set the house on fire with his cigarette while he slept. Seventy-two year old man. We'll check this out deeper but this was where the email was sent from and this to me..." He nodded slowly. "This says whoever kidnapped Wren was getting nervous and covering his tracks. It says he thinks this will create an impasse. He may be right."

"Yeah." I slid both hands to the top of my head and bowed my head, staring at the ground before my boots. "Fuck. I had hopes."

"It's not the end, Mister Glass but it is time to involve the police."

Optimist. Normally that was me too. He was probably faking it too. During this past day, I'd gotten to know Hugh well. Tight minded, he didn't let you in to see what he was feeling often, or even what he was thinking. But he loved Wren, in his own way.

Slowly, I stood, feeling as if I'd gained ten years and a mountain of weight. "I'm sorry."

Hugh stuck his hands in his trouser pockets. "Not all your fault. Our opponent is ahead of us. By the way, we found a tracking device on your previous vehicle. It's why I had you dispose of it. My men have also caught two men surveilling us. On extensive and somewhat brutal questioning, we obtained their client's details. All fake. He knew you were here, Glass. He's been watching you, Wren, and probably me when he could. Possibly since PNG. Whoever this is, he still has plenty of money and he has the brains to use it well. We need to get her back. Fast."

"Yes. Of course we do." Shit, my eyes were stinging again.

Hugh was assuming she was alive.

She is. She is.

"I want to kill this *fucker* same as you. I want her safe." Hugh looked at me, teeth bared in the first uncivilized gesture I'd seen him make. "I may not like what you are, but in this we're united. You go hide. Tell me where. We can see what we can do while the cops crank up their investigation. Expect a tidal wave of journalists to descend on this town."

I nodded, turned, and headed for the car, in a reverie of pain and regret. Where the hell were we going to aim ourselves with all that happening? Sitting on my backside, waiting, was not me. But here I was, with nothing to do.

What was *he* doing to her right now?

If she could get away from him, send a message somehow, we could find her. I bet she was trying. I needed to be here in case that happened. Getting bored was a minor inconvenience.

Until that time came, I'd wait, if waiting were all I could do. If.

The days wore on. The police knew there'd been a man with Wren at the beach and my need for anonymity became even more important. Though Pieter was raring to go and furious that Vetrov had perhaps taken Wren, my girl, as he now called her, I couldn't even let him join me. There was no point in endangering him too when the cops would undoubtedly have a sample of his DNA on file from the slave house in PNG.

There was nothing I could have him do.

The house used as a holding area for slaves, that Pieter had been to in Far North Queensland, I found it using his description. After a few days of watching the media and the police infesting the island and the media circling the town like vultures, I gave in and left to raid the house – myself and three of Hugh's men. Only to find it'd been pulled down and the property sold months ago. A new house was being constructed on the site. Something posh, from the looks of it. We turned our backs on beautiful Cow Bay with its now defunct undercurrent of human slave trafficking, and returned to the island.

Any skeletons buried at Cow Bay would have to stay buried.

Another dead end. Whoever had been on the property documents, they weren't going to be more than another placeholder for Vetrov, though Hugh was going to hand the info to the cops anyway. They'd been told she was searching for her father's murderer, just not who the mysterious stranger was accompanying her, except that I was someone helping her who was very unlikely to be the kidnapper.

The cops might connect me. It was a risk I had to take if we were to let their investigation be at all meaningful.

Despair fought with frustration as the days accumulated.

Too long.

Too fucking long.

She could be in China by now. Dead. Anything. I wasn't a man for the past and regrets but I damn well would've given my soul to turn back time and be holding her hand on that evening beach walk. My poor Wren.

CHAPTER 18
Wren

Last night, he'd yet again hurt me with various implements, this time while strapped onto one of his benches, before fucking my mouth. I knew the taste of his cum so well I could've started an ice cream stand and called it the ten flavors of the mystery man's cum. It had been, by my calculations, eight days that I'd been here.

The butt plugs had increased in size every few days until he seemed to have run out of sizes. I'd taken to screaming when he inserted the latest size. It was huge and I figured deafening him was a good payback. And I couldn't help myself. That too.

The pity of it was that he liked me screaming. Liked me crying too. I hated it. I hated him, even more, every time he made me give in and call him Sir, or scream, every time he made me orgasm.

Hating him was my opening mantra each morning. Call it planning ahead. Establishing a baseline. On most days, he would get under my skin and make me give up a piece of *me*. With my mantra of hatred, I reclaimed that part of myself. Or that was my aim.

It was all in the mind. Look on the bright side, glass half full and all that – while I was his, I couldn't sleepwalk. Even if knives were an even bigger fantasy than ever. I thought about sticking one in him often.

I jolted. *His?* Cut that shit.

Damn.

I'd never sworn, even in my head, so much as I had recently. Guess I had excuses though.

I lay there on my side, feeling the leather of my collar

absentmindedly and staring at the ancient Greek-style mural on the far wall, to the right of the entrance. It was the one thing of beauty in here, apart from the small pool that I'd never been allowed to use. This room was perfect for torture. He'd said so himself. A white canvas to echo back my screams, to show the spots of blood, to act as a backdrop to any activity so every detail was trapped in his eye.

Poetic bastard. The blood though, thank god, hadn't come true. One thing to be grateful for.

His blood would be okay though...come to think of it. I thought of how that would look on the floor, spreading.

The door opened. I sat up, tugging into place the white bra he'd returned to me with the matching lace panties. Wearing the bra while sleeping was uncomfortable but better than being naked.

He was in jeans, black shirt and boots. Did the man have no sense of villain decorum? It was the mask that added that necessary ingredient of monster. He'd done something new to it. Lenses reflected light off their surface. Cold slithered in, spiking when I sensed he truly focused on me. He'd added goggles to the mask? Why?

Anything new bothered me. It was the unknown. It was creepy.

As he approached, I went to my knees on the floor. Habitual now as well as sensible, even if I despised myself for submitting. His punishment for not kneeling had only been repeated twice before I decided my act needed adjusting. So now I kneeled. I was a poor actor. Every unexpected piece of humiliation he inflicted made me rear up and spit in his eye, figuratively speaking.

Today was the day I was kicking his teeth in. Resolution of Day Eight. Yeah, baby.

He was getting lax. I was almost sure of it.

"Good girl." He smiled and surveyed me a moment, a lanyard dangling from his hand, before walking to the wall point and detaching the leash using, yes, the key. Note to self: he has the key on him.

This happened at least twice daily when he took me to the showers and toilet. So far I'd had no opportunity to take him down. He never fully turned his back, and if I failed with a kick the consequences would be traumatic. I needed him unaware so I could do a full bodyweight kick to get him on the ground, then stomp on him and do some head kicks, throat kicks. Hits that would incapacitate the man. If I missed my mark, that leash would be my undoing. Long hair was a disadvantage in combat. A leash was far worse. One yank on it and I'd be down on the ground and at his mercy. The bodyweight disadvantage was a horrific problem up close...unless I had surprise and a weapon.

I practiced kicks and strikes most nights, sometimes hauling myself out of bed despite exhaustion. The tinkling of the leash as I moved, the smack of my hand or foot on the leather, I couldn't disguise that. I could only pray he wasn't watching me.

"Today, you're getting a treat." The switch from thinking about deathblows to treats was jarring, but I listened attentively.

"I'm taking you to the courtyard and letting you exercise and swim. I know you like swimming." He wound the leash into his fist and tugged. "But first, crawl over here." Then he sat on the bed and beckoned.

What was this? Wary, I crawled to him then between his spread legs.

"Hands at your back. Just let me touch you."

Words quietly said and so they shocked me. He'd done many crazy things to me and I was always off balance and suspicious.

"Nothing sinister, Wren. Now, please. And bow your head."

Please? A word he used rarely. I did as he asked and clasped my hands behind me.

His hands slid into my hair and began to comb it out, over and over. My anxiety lessened when he did nothing else.

"See. Nothing bad. Good, in fact. I like touching you, just touching. You're a beautiful woman and sometimes touch is what I need. Perhaps you too?"

Touching him? Hell no.

Still...after a few minutes, his fingers brushing over my scalp felt like magic. The incessant rhythm of his words and the slide of his fingers along the strands of my hair hypnotized me. I half-closed my eyes. Previously, I'd only had this sort of care after he'd done mean things.

"Up here now." I heard him pat his leg and looked up. "On my lap."

Fuck. This was too much like being a lap dog. My mouth twitched but he caught my thoughts, no doubt from my grimace, and tapped my cheek in a mini slap. I jerked, blinking up at him, disconcerted by his eyes being hidden behind glass.

"Just a reminder of who is in charge."

Self-evident but, as always, it brought me up short.

"Up."

Sighing, I crawled onto the bed and lay half across his lap. I curled up my legs into his side to get comfortable. He turned my head into him. I grimaced again but this time he couldn't see. My face was far too close to his cock for this to be relaxing.

The touching resumed, except now he massaged the muscles of my neck and back as well as sometimes playing with my hair, rocking my head and my body with the strength of his fingers, while talking about nothing much. I may have groaned in pleasure once, though I bit it off when I heard him go *mmm*, as if he liked me liking this. Oh the mindfuck in that.

I didn't like that he liked giving me pleasure anymore than I liked him enjoying giving me pain.

And yet...resisting was useless.

It went on and on. I relaxed and let the pleasure sift through my body. The murmur of his voice was never-ending and a background noise like the splash of a waterfall. This sort of gentle intimacy was more difficult to defy than his harsh discipline and kinky sexual mastery.

"That will do," he said at last. I roused from drowsiness. "We're having breakfast in the courtyard first. It's a sunny day and I've wound back the shutters."

Sunlight? Ohmigod, I needed sunlight. How I needed it.

My smile arrived despite him watching. He only nodded.

I followed him from the room like a happy puppy. A courtyard on the outside. Wow. Inside *me* was a bubbling mass of what ifs. Most of them revolved around one idea – escape.

All that intimacy we'd exchanged was nothing compared to the pain and humiliation he'd caused me.

First time outside. Courtyards had access to the sky. I could scream, I could climb walls. To swim he'd have to disconnect the leash. So many possibilities. I might not need the key after all. All I needed was to knock him out for long enough to get away and over the walls.

All this churned in my mind as we walked. I'd never even left the room before. My bare feet enjoyed the cool of the tiles of the corridor we walked down. The leash tinkled and there were no other sounds in this house. How quiet it was. Where was this place? We went up a flight of stairs then along another corridor. White doors led away, to either side. Closed though. Who did all the damn cleaning?

An open space to the left expanded into another enormous room with the far wall mostly thick glass. Beyond was a breathtaking vista of the sea and blue sky. I dragged my feet, slowing, to take it all in. In the center was an open square of inward-facing sofas where I glimpsed some sort of sunken area.

"I'll show you that another day. My Pit of Despair." He smirked in that evil way that said he found something amusing because it would not be amusing to me if I tried it. Oh man, I knew the way he thought.

"A pit of despair? You're joking? Is there a Mount Doom in your back yard too?" Joking with him, at him, was my one outlet of freedom, my one bit of equal expression. So far he'd allowed it, as long as I didn't insult him.

"Not yet. Give me time."

We continued on, him a little ahead but never enough to be sure he couldn't see what I did...like if I tried to launch a kick. One attempted on the fly wasn't good enough. The slight pause for set up would give me away, if he was watching. It was nerve wracking, forever looking for that opening. If I failed, a shitstorm of sadism awaited me.

And what if I missed it, the big chance, the one and only, because of nerves?

I never wanted to think back and regret not trying.

I bit my lip and eyed his broad back and the muscles of his arms. Nothing could change the fact that he was bigger than me. In the darkness of night, my resolve had been known to crumble. I'd curled up and wept a few times, because those bits of me he took, I wasn't sure they were the same after. I felt as if I was changing, atom by atom, brain cell by brain cell. Pavlov's bitch, that was me. After only eight days of this, I was worried he might eventually train me to like what he was doing.

We emerged onto a sheltered patio, the timber door huffing shut behind us, then went forward to the edge of the shade.

I looked up and around, daunted.

Oh boy. He was more than rich, this man was rich as hell. Maybe not as rich as me but enough to let him spend money on things the average person would find amazing.

The courtyard walls were two stories high. Only opposite us was there not house. Above the open area, two stories up, were enormous white louvres that ran across the width. Yes, he had opened them and I could see the blue of sky, some clouds, even a couple of seagulls. This was near the sea. Somewhere on the coast of Queensland. I couldn't have been unconscious for that long?

Any screams for help would go straight up to the sky, muffled by those louvre blades. I doubted his neighbors would be close enough to hear, unless their property almost abutted this building.

The pool was a twenty yards long, sparkling blue square, surrounded by a generous grassed and gardened area to one side. No way would I be able to climb the walls.

My plan was a little wonky.

He'd not have let me out here if anyone might hear me.

My courage crumpled, a little. I was here alone and how was I getting away? I needed superman. My mouth turned down. I needed Glass. I needed him holding me. Memories of how that had been, his scent, the murmur of his voice...laughter even... Stupid maybe, when on that last day I'd doubted him. Being here made Glass seemed more perfect with every passing day. I missed him so much. A wave of dismal sadness hit me, but I let it do its worse, shook it off then stood taller. I only had me. That would have to do.

The square columns holding up the roof of the patio section we stood beneath had circular metal handles both high and low. A casual observer might think them decorative. Their heights clinched what they were: anchor points for tying up people. He'd probably made people scream out here in the past.

Did he kidnap women regularly? Or take some of those who were destined for his sex slave trafficking? Or...was he into the BDSM lifestyle?

That could be a way to identify him.

"Done? Let's have breakfast." With another tug on the leash, he led me to a small sofa beside a rectangular table set with plates of fruit, bacon, sausages, and pancakes, and oddly, a pair of black gloves. Then he tossed a cushion to the terracotta-paved floor and pointed. "Kneel."

More kneeling? My knees were going to kill him all by themselves. I almost blurted that out but I bit back that unsafe reply and kneeled. My stomach was rumbling at me anyway.

The table was low enough that I could see the perfection in the presentation of the food. Beautiful plates and bowls, silver knives and forks, the fruit pieces were in cute ornamental shapes and the pile of sausages was topped off with garnishes.

I knew both student-level cooking and Michelin level. A chef had produced this.

Where had this come from? Delivered? If so, others came to this house.

He'd already speared a sausage on a fork and was offering it to me. After days of so-so food I might have kneeled for this without a command. "Did you cook this?" At the tilt of his eyebrow I hastily added, "Sir?"

"No. No more talking without permission, Wren."

I reached for the fork, he didn't normally feed me for god's sake, but he rapped my knuckles with a butter knife blade.

I snatched away my hand.

Fuck. Hurt. I sucked on my hand then took a bite from the sausage he was so insistent about offering.

Damn. So many questions. But I kept silent from then on as he fed both him and me. What was it with the feeding? By the time he was done I'd eaten far more than I should have and probably more than he had.

Ugh. Which meant begging to visit the toilet, an embarrassment I detested more than most requests.

That done, we returned to the table and I kneeled again on direction.

"Would you like to swim now? You can talk." He slid the table aside then leaned back on the sofa, eyeing me. "Ask nicely if you want to."

Where was that butter knife when I needed it? Ask nicely? Manners? Someone like him made manners repulsive. I wrinkled my nose, then rubbed it as if it were itchy.

"Yes. Please. Sir." *And fuck you again.*

I half expected him to read my mind and throw me over his lap to be spanked. Which would've had me both grinding my teeth and wet. I knew my stupid body's reactions well by now.

"Very good. No clothes, though. You'll swim naked. Stand and strip those off for me, girl."

I looked down at the cushion, just so I could squeeze my eyes shut with some privacy but then sprang to my feet and began to undress with as much speed as possible without ripping off clasps. Be damned if I'd do this like some striptease.

"Stop! Slowly. Turn as you do so. Show off that body of yours for your master."

Really? I took a deep, calming breath then I reached for the bra clasp and undid it, slow as seemed slow enough to please him.

"Stop again," he said softly, just as the cups were about to fall from my breasts. I held them on. "Wren, answer me. Am I your master?" He tucked the leash between his knees, picked up the leather gloves from the table, and drew them on. Then he waited.

No, you are not.

I shifted my weight from foot to foot.

Those eyes in the goggles, watching me – like being examined by some bug with lustful desires. It made me want to squirm in an uncomfortable way and smack him at the same time.

I swallowed. "Yes. Sir." That would do it, right?

"More, Wren."

He knew that I knew what he meant. I'd been over this sort of questioning before.

While staring at his boots, I added, "Yes, you are my master." My toes scrunched on the terracotta. My pussy cringed, as I uttered those words.

Could pussies cringe? I considered that, frowning, still looking floorward. Cringed, definitely. I was not turned on by him making me say that. My head was an unraveled mess today.

More sleep, less hitting things. Just for one night.

The leash tinkled and pulled at my neck. He'd tugged it. "I can almost see those thoughts of yours, little slut."

I fumed. I said *nothing* in return. I seethed without showing a single twitch of mouth or twitch *any* bloody where.

The man stood, unfolding in my vision so deliberately, so slowly, that it made him seem bigger. I shrank and he dwarfed me in his boots, his black gloves, and his clothes, and by his presence. It wasn't just height anymore. My lips parted and an invisible shiver ran up to my nipples.

"When you are silent like this, that talks to me too. You're being punished after you swim."

Oh. Mind reader? Or was he tuned into signals I didn't know I was giving? This confused me and...overwhelmed me. I needed to be able to hide how I felt about him. I needed that badly.

I closed my eyes. "I'm sorry, Sir."

"Not enough. Keep stripping, slut. Show off your tits, and when you're naked turn and bend over so I can see your cunt."

So dead. He was dead, but I was done resisting.

I did it all, including the last, bending for him to see everything, feeling as if I was two inches tall. Women did this in strip clubs all the time. It wasn't so bad.

They did it for pay. Because they chose to. Big difference.

Before, if he made me do humiliating things, he at least seemed to show appreciation. He'd touch me or say complimentary things. That had in some weird, mindfuckery way, made me feel less awful. How that added up, I had no clue. Stupid but true. This time, it was as if I was an object to be leered at, reduced to a fuckable body that meant little to him. I was shaking when I rose.

If he made me do one more horrible thing, I would hit him, no matter the consequences.

Being naked before him was nothing in comparison.

The worst of it was that when he undid the leash, he gave me no opportunities. He remained vigilant. To run, I needed to get to the door through which we'd come. He was squarely in the way and didn't take his eyes off me as I paced to the pool's edge. Poised there, I swung my arms back and leapt. That moment of awesome flight took me away, in that moment of no gravity, before my outstretched arms tore into the water.

Peace.

Water, slipping along my body. Bubbles rippling past. Beneath the water was another world.

I swam, aware of him pacing me as I did laps. After fifty, I went to the end to climb out and he squatted before me.

Water dribbled from my hair and dripped to the curved stone edging. Under my forearms the stone was a pleasant warmth, reminding me of all my past days of freedom, of swimming without having a man crouching over me and eyeing me like a possession.

"Keep going, Wren. I want you fit and healthy. Those lovely

curves of yours show the marks so well.

I panted, disconcerted, wondering if he had some strange reason for this, but I turned and slid under the water again. I wasn't that tired and swimming laps took me far, far away from here to my land of meditation.

When I did finally get out though, he'd best be on alert. I was hyped up by all this activity and by his latest humiliations. I counted the laps by going *fuckhim one, fuckhim two*. It was fun and satisfying, and not at all meditative. My cursing was a small victory that only I understood. Better than none.

When he let me leave the pool, he threw me a towel, watched me dry myself then walked onto the grassed area where he'd left the leash. He'd turned his back.

The towel slipped from my fingers. A small breeze curled over my wet skin and my nipples crinkled in.

This. Was it. I hesitated for all of a second, feeling a surprise tinge of sadness and regret that I had to do this, hurt him. I obliterated the thought and took that chance.

One stride, then a flying kick. An uncompromising, totally unsafe kick that I couldn't pull back from once committed to. I took that stride, felt the grass give, soft under my feet, and I launched, feet first. Full body weight. All of me, aimed at the base of his neck.

I could *feel* the strike before I even contacted.

And he sidestepped. *No* was all I had time to think before a side blow slammed me off course to hit the grass rolling. He'd reacted fast. He'd known.

My ribs hurting, I flipped to my feet, turning, and aware of him closing in...those shadows, the flicker of movement as I spun. My hands were up but too slow, as blows from those gloves thumped into my tensed stomach.

I staggered and folded to the grass, angry and still ready to fuck him up if I could, coughing out the last of my air. *Don't stop now. Not now!*

Kicks were best. Vision blurring, and wracked by painful gasps, I planted my palm and forearm to the ground and snapped a kick to his legs. If I could get him down...

Missed. He'd moved behind me. Rolling frantically to keep him in view, I was yanked short by his hand ripping into my hair and his other hand anchoring on the back of my collar. He hauled the front of the leather tight against my larynx.

I kicked at nothing, tried to turn.

My face was squashed into the grass, and again I struggled to get a kick back at him, any part of him, while my throat closed in from the steady pressure. I retched, and tried to claw at his hand.

"Stay." His knee thumped on my spine, grinding me down.

The strength fell away as I wheezed in tiny fragments of oxygen. Grass, dirt, and blood filled my mouth. Pain called to me from so many places. I wasn't sure where anything was anymore as the ground swayed. Out of instinct, I heaved back with my body and got nowhere. All his weight was on me.

I'd failed.

The words wandered in and I didn't care. Breathing was more urgent. The greenness before my eyes wavered, blood pumped like mud through my head, the greenness darkened. No part of my body worked as it should, and I gave up and slumped under him.

"Good." I heard that word grunted from close to my ear, then felt my hands wrenched behind me and fastened.

He shifted on me and the weight lifted. The tautness on my neck went away. I coughed and sucked in luxurious lungfuls of air. Oh god, breathing.

With that hair-roots-tight grip on my head and other hand wrapped about my wrists, he pulled me to my feet. I spat out grass as I was pushed and brought staggering to the edge of the pool, then left teetering there, flatfooted, and only just remembering how to stand without faceplanting.

"Go."

He shoved me. Aghast, I fell, unable to do more than plummet into the water. It closed over me, cold, blanketing sound, and I wrestled with the cuffs, wrenching at them while I scrabbled for purchase with my feet.

I heard him jump in after me. Without my arms for balance, I was lost. The tiles under me slipped sideways whenever my feet found them. Rolling, I saw the surface above. Was he drowning me? Was this it? I'd done something so wrong I was being killed.

Even underwater, I think I cried.

Life should be more than this.

The black, wavering thing hovering above the surface closed in and I was hauled out, dripping and gasping. I was held there, with the back of my head just above the line between life and death. I imagined him letting me fall again, watching me sink, then planting his foot on me and pressing me down, watching me as I wriggled on the bottom of the pool. I'd never been afraid of water. Now I was.

Spluttering, I stared upward. The goggles were gone, just the mask now. His eyes were an intense brown, his mouth a straight, cruel line, emphasizing how close I'd come to the limits of what he could tolerate. Only his arms kept me safe.

The abrupt rise and fall of his chest said I'd made him work for this.

"What do you want, Wren? Are you going to stop fighting me? Beg me to keep you. Now. Decide." How quiet his voice was, and here I was torn by dread and sorrow.

I moved my lips, fumbling for words. I was wet and battered, half woman, half drowned thing. "Please?"

"Please what?"

Even now, in this most vital of times, I hesitated. "Please, I won't fight. I'm begging you."

It wasn't in me to give in, but because my hesitation was so small, so infinitesimal, he missed it for once. Or perhaps he chose to not see. Perhaps, even he had his hopes sometimes blind him.

"You're begging for me to keep you, Wren? You need to accept that you're mine."

I blinked away water. *Keep you* sounded as if I would have to be killed, if I kept fighting, or sold off to others. I'd known resisting might have terrible consequences.

"I do. I want you to keep me." I swallowed past a throat burning from trying to breathe when there was nothing worthwhile breathing. "I won't fight you again."

I shut my eyes.

"Good. Don't close your eyes to me, Wren. Never, unless I say you can. You hide in there and I won't have that."

I made myself open my eyes.

The look that awaited me was fierce, with the promise of pain. I ceased to breathe, to think, for a few long seconds. He'd dislocated thought and numbed me to all that existed, except us...

When he only hauled me from the pool, and carried me across to the patio, to attach me to the columns, I was relieved. Each wrench and knot of the rope said I was alive. My arms were tied to a rafter above with a rope through the central link on the wrist cuffs. My ankles were tied to either side, to the base of the columns, spreading my shaking legs.

"I need to punish you."

Oh. I'd only heard him say the words. His boots moved past, squelching. I saw his hands as he pulled the shoes off his feet and set them aside.

He'd made the big square tiles slippery with pool water. More water dripped from the twists of my hair onto my breasts and my thighs, and ran down my legs to my feet. I hung my head and let myself simply inhale, exhale.

There was nothing I could do to stop him. For now, I accepted that.

Then he simply walked away and disappeared inside the house. Minutes later, returned, carrying a bag.

By then I'd roused, my muscles bruised but my mind reset from the battering I'd received. I'd lost to someone stronger and he hadn't killed me. Glass half full. Hadn't killed me, yet.

I whipsawed back to that time. Those few seconds had lodged in my memory. I'd lost badly, and fast. Even remembering devastated me. I'd be in rewind forever over this.

I needed to push this aside, but pieces of it had lodged in me, that blurred and panic-strewn moment where I looked up through the water at him — I was dying and he was leaving me there.

So evil. So him.

I'd never fought anyone for my life before. Never been hurt so deliberately and with such force. Sparring in a martial arts hall or with Hugh — those meant nothing in the face of this man's willingness to do whatever it took to make me...just plain give in.

From the overnight bag he'd deposited on the table, he pulled objects I recognized from previous days. He lined them up and, as I saw each one, it chilled me to my soul to think of what he might be planning to do after my little rebellion. Because, it wasn't so little. I snagged my lower lip between my teeth, wishing I were still strung out from the fight. I was too tough for my own good.

Cane, crop, paddle, belt, coils of thin rope, a leather flogger, the butt plug... *Fuck, what else?* I couldn't see. Then he moved, brought a chair over near me, front and center, and sat. My gaze was drawn to the table as slickly as a cobra might attract a mouse before it becomes dinner.

A lick of cold unfurled in me. Goose bumps prickled into being. *Metal.*

A whip where the nasty end was a shower of shiny strands of wire.

A row of curved metal crescents whose use I couldn't fathom.

The last staggered me.

Knives.

Edges sharp enough to cut the light.

The air jarred with viciousness. A knife harvested blood and pain like nothing else.

It caught my breath in its serrated fangs.

The ropes held me there, tight, in his gaze, while I struggled with my fascination. My toes kneaded the tiles and I wrapped my fingers in the twisted rope above, swaying a little and feeling the ache in my muscles.

Not fair. The man was a voyeur on his own perversions.

What was he thinking?

Whatever it was, I needed to be careful and not defy him. Not after what had happened. When my head was straight, I'd figure myself out.

My courage was all used up.

CARI SILVERWOOD

CHAPTER 19
Moghul

If only Chris knew who I had back here. The man was patiently waiting for me in the upstairs lounge. He thought I had some ordinary submissive in my ropes. Knowing he was close, gave me ideas. I'd love to show her off but there was no one I trusted. Not even him, with all the dirt I had recorded. All those vids of him fucking, flogging and tying up his two women with that friend of his helping. The police would be not be amused to discover a local accountant had a thing for kidnapping.

I leaned forward in the chair, rested my forearms on my thighs, and tapped my fingers together, thinking. Wren would be my undoing. What was the fun in a slave no one knew you had?

Lots.

The way she stared at my array of toys, all those little body signs. Interesting, considering her pristine past. Was there something I didn't know about her? The knives in particular had her mind churning. Her hands were doing stuff, her toes screwing into the floor while her face stayed in neutral – dead giveaway that something was happening in her head. Knives... I'd wondered.

Her reaction made me smile inside, though not where she could see. I preferred to appear unmoved. Unmoved was such a fucking understatement. Wren had no clue as to how meticulously I'd planned this. How much this victory meant. Inside, I was soaring.

Every night, I'd watched and heard her practice her Muay Thai. Every day, I'd seen her eye me as if wondering when to strike. It was going to happen, so I chose to make the outcome as guaranteed as

142

possible.

The goggles, I'd ripped off after her first kick. A tiny camera in the back of the strap fed a screen on the inside of the glass. Difficult to judge distances, but enough to warn me to dodge. They were a trick item bought off the net. I'd made sure to rile her by making her do things I knew bothered her the most. I'd pretended I was the cruelest master with little interest in her as a person. I'd hated doing that. My instinct, then and there, had been to reward the behavior, even if only with a *good girl,* and not to treat her with disdain. I was cruel by nature, just not that cruel.

Wren, watching her reaction...that'd had been like watching a fire catch hold, knowing any minute it might turn into a conflagration.

I'd fed her a large breakfast, stuffed her full, then made her swim, hoping to tire my athletic little captive. If her kick had hit her target, I'd no doubt have been the one on the wrong end of that fight.

But I hadn't been. Touch and go for a few seconds. If she'd hit me, I might not have gotten up again. What a fucking thrill it had been wrestling her down. There'd been a danger to us both, but I'd pulled my punches, used only as much force as I needed to. The padded gloves had helped.

Instead it was her who'd lost and was now strung up, naked, exhausted, and waiting for her punishment. I was going to enjoy this. My only regret was that throwing her in the pool had seemed to terrify her more than I had wanted or expected. She swam like a fish but had still panicked during those few seconds she'd been underwater. I'd only wanted to subdue her, to make her see she was never going to win. Mental domination as much as physical.

I let my gaze travel over her, savoring my victory, as well as letting my sadistic lust feed off the possibilities of her pretty body. Bruises were showing on her stomach where I'd punched her, but she had no signs of real injury. I'd felt her all over as I tied her up there, checked her color, her ribs. If there had been problems, getting a doctor involved would've been a nightmare....

I would've gone there. Surprise, surprise. I would have risked all rather than maim her.

A revelation, that.

I really wasn't cut out for this, not owning a slave of my own. I'd become more than obsessed with Wren, I'd grown fond of her.

I stood and selected both the crop and the cane from the table

143

then walked forward with the crop swinging by my side, as I warmed up my wrist and reacquainted myself with the weight and balance. "You will no longer practice fighting at night."

Her head swung up and she ran her tongue along her teeth, as if disdaining my instrument or my words.

Awake and feisty again. My cock that'd been at half-mast made its way upward.

"Answer me." I stepped over the ankle rope to get behind her then swung the crop across one ass cheek. I paused, appreciating the meaty *whack* of this first strike. The wobble of her ass was admirable.

She hissed, as if I'd startled her, her knees collapsing for a second as she rocked in the ropes.

One strike had done that. *Hmm.*

The swing of any implement meant to hurt had a certain quality that thrilled me. The ambience of sadism. I swished it again, only airward. Targeting girl's asses was fun, even when they were tied in place.

"I won't, Sir."

The automatic *Sir* heightened the scene, made me concentrate. Colors cranked up to full saturation. I squatted for a second and traced the red line that was appearing then placed a single kiss.

Then I stepped around to her front and asked again. "Are you sure?"

"Yes, Sir."

A fast response, and her eyes were wide and guileless. Had I really reached her, finally?

This time I did smile. I captured her face in the palm of my hand and tilted her up to me. Then I leaned in and brushed her lips with mine. "I'm glad I've not broken you."

"You didn't," she whispered. "Can't."

A small defiance?

I almost told her of my fear that I'd terrified her in the pool but held back. Some fear was good, and it wasn't right for me as her Master to say that. Besides, I saw no great fear. Just those pretty blue irises, searching my face. Tired though, she could barely focus.

What if I read her wrong?

Damn. Where had these doubts come from?

I needed to shut up. I wasn't her Dom. This wasn't a negotiated scene. Showing weakness, today especially, was wrong.

"Good." I kissed her again, unable to resist, pleased at how her eyelids sifted closed. My thumb found the corner of her mouth as I caressed her and I sneaked in my thumbtip. "Open for me, Wren."

She did, and even better, her eyes softened and I felt gentle suction and the stir of her tongue as she tentatively licked me.

That always got to me. Subs did it all the time, but for Wren to do it, better.

"Pretty girl." I swept some damp, tangled hair from her eyebrow.

Best visual, ever. Those lips and absorbing eyes. This captured girl, bound, legs spread, in my ropes. Her breasts with their enticing nipples, moving with each breath. I nudged my thigh between her legs and grabbed one ass cheek, clawing my fingers, pulling her into me. Her quiet moans warmed my thumb.

This didn't bode well for me not coming in my pants.

I released her and took a sharp step back.

Wren wasn't broken. Hallelujah.

Fucking her was on my to-do list with a vengeance but I'd promised to punish her and keeping my word was important.

I hit her ass, thighs and upper back, a neat twenty times, with crop and cane, switching hands when a line appealed more than a rectangle, or just to surprise her. When she jerked and tried to dodge, I grasped a handful of breast or gripped her neck to remind her to be still.

She quivered even more when I did so. "Good girl," I would whisper. The woman was showing her submissive side so well.

I'd chosen the right path.

Wheals blossomed into being on her paleness like carnal scripture.

There was a beauty in putting designs on her skin. Crisscross. Parallel. The cane was better for bruising. A flogger would let me work on more of her, so I fetched that and wove more prettiness on her.

Only so much skin could take...a woman could take. Now it was more a massage with force.

Wren became redder in places than pink, with a smattering of blue as punctuation. When I walked in and ran my hand between those spread thighs, I found her wet and swollen. I could give her pleasure, if I chose. No rules stopped me.

"Are you a naughty girl?" I murmured, sliding one finger into her, deep, fucking her nicely.

"Nooo," she breathed, though squirming on that finger.

I laughed. "Does any of this punishment turn you on?"

Her downcast eyes said she could still be embarrassed. Good to know.

"Some." The word slurred, trailed off. She was cruising in subspace.

"Uh-huh."

I stepped away, then smacked in some strikes so the falls of the flogger curled along her slit. Her squeal and jerk was as much a reward for me as her. From then on, I played with her pussy and breasts with the flogger and the crop. I tapped, I brushed lightly. I did some thuddier hits. I inserted the handle of the flogger and fucked her.

Mostly, she crumpled at the knees and moaned.

I made her come, at least once. I could tell it surprised her from the way she eyed me afterward, mouth open, drooling a little. Poor thing.

I smiled for a while after that.

It was all fun, even the pain. The screams had been the icing before her moans and wriggles.

I went up and down on my toes. Maybe I should get a few more screams from her?

The wire flogger waited for me, alongside the knives and the hooks. Using wire too harshly would be the work of a sadist without boundaries – a tantalizing idea.

Decisions, decisions.

So many instruments of pain, and only Wren to use them on. I had more than today though. She wasn't leaving me.

What was punishment if it didn't hurt and make her pee herself, just a tad? I grinned and fetched the wire flogger.

I circled her again, walking outside the columns she was fastened to, my bare feet padding on stone. A rainbow lorikeet swooped through the columns then outside and across the sunlit pool to a flowering tree. Birds already squabbled there.

I don't think Wren saw what I carried.

When I lashed out and struck the back of her thighs and butt, she screeched and tensed, grabbing at the ropes for dear life, dancing as much as she could.

No sub had ever volunteered for the wire. None had been game.

Was that blood? A line on her lower thigh wept red. This wasn't going to last. If I kept this up she'd be raw meat, not woman, and I wasn't a butcher. I struck her once more, a little higher, with a similar result – three bleeding lines. I guess I'd known, just the novelty tempted me.

"Wait!" Wren screeched.

I tossed the whip aside, sending it skidding across stone to the edge of the grass.

"No more. Please." She craned her head around. "Please."

"I've stopped." I circled and paused before her.

She wasn't done shuddering and was sucking in big lungfuls while hiccupping. Tears ran down her face. Guess I'd found her limit.

I'd conquered her; That much was certain. There'd been nothing but submission since I'd fought her down and proven she was mine.

She was so flawless without my marks. In a few days, a week, they'd be gone. The light bulb snapped on. *A tattoo.* I needed something permanent.

It was possible she might revive her fire and fight against me again. Not a real fight, she'd be too scared of what I might do to her if she tried that. Small rebellions were possible.

The important thing was that I had mastered her today. This would never go away.

I had her. I'd claimed a big part of her mindspace. She could kick all she liked at the psychological bonds. I had her. The echoes of this would last.

"I'm done punishing you." I went to one knee and undid the ankle bindings, unafraid that she'd kick me. She was past that.

I didn't rise to my feet, but I moved my hands up her body, holding her, here and there, as if claiming each part of her, then sliding further upward – from her ankles, to the outside of her thighs, to her gorgeous waist. Last of all I reached up and cupped her breasts, rolling each nipple between my finger and thumb.

The light touch on her nipples made her shrink away, so I crushed them instead. One or the other would work. My mouth was near her pussy. I blew warm air over her. The few whacks with the flogger and crop that I'd landed on her pussy had made her clit pop from its hiding place.

Clit torture? Hmmm. On my agenda.

I licked her, once, paused, breathed on her, then repeated.

The results...magic. She cried in helpless whimpers and her fingers wound and unwound on the rope above.

I leaned in and fastened my teeth over her clit in a firm yet not too cruel grasp, not letting go while I tongued her. Her groan was followed by a string of soft yet agonized curses, *oh fuck, oh fuck, oh fuck* before she degenerated into more whimpers.

I had a nipple clamp in my pocket. Impromptu. But was it torture or play?

Did it matter? I fished out the clamp with the small lead weight dangling from it and clipped it to her cunt just above her swollen clit, where I hoped she'd be sensitive. Even before the teeth closed on her, she was tilting her pelvis forward.

Today had hit the poor girl hard and I doubt she had it in her to resist any of the sensations I was feeding her. The flogging, the cane, my dominance, her surrender, these had made good and bad, pleasure and pain, mix together until extricating one from the other would require more brain cells than were currently functioning.

I had her mindfucked, infinitely. Nothing could've made me happier.

Whether it was from the effects of the clamp itself or the tapping of the weight, her sobs grew louder. My cock climbed up the hardness scale a few rungs.

I stood, leaving my finger squarely on that little button before slipping it back, ever so slowly, along her slit. I shoved my finger inside her. Her wetness...I drew in a breath...riveting.

"You're seriously moist down here. Your sweat and your cunt juices." I fucked her some more, listening to the sounds.

As I spoke her head fell back, exposing her neck to me. Rivulets of water trailed from her damp hair to shoulders and breasts. She groaned again, rocking into my fingers. Her weight made the attachments of the ropes creak.

"Do you want me, Wren? Inside you?"

I extracted my finger and moved my arm so I could get into her from behind.

She raised her head, staring, her lips parted. That might have been due to me pumping my slickened finger in and out of her pussy. My thumb found her little asshole and I wriggled it into her too.

"Say it. Say 'yes, Sir.'"

"I..." Her eyelids fluttered then closed.

I waited. Soon these responses would slip from her mouth automatically. Training, it was all training.

"Yes, Sir."

"I'm going in both these holes today, and you're going to beg."

That her eyelids squeezed down tighter and I could see the little movements of her eye muscles; That she panted like a bitch in heat, it spoke volumes: holding in her arousal, but unable to stop herself.

I leaned in, kissed her sweet mouth then dragged her head back by her hair, smiling at the sight of her exposed neck and the sheen from the sweat I'd made on her body.

"Mine. You're all mine, pretty girl." I bit her neck, in spite of her screams and wriggles – a bite that would make a wolf proud of me. The indentations from my teeth were bluing already.

Then I walked away from her and texted Chris, after washing my fingers clean. My phone was still going to smell exquisitely of Wren. Which was perfectly good.

I released her from her bonds and carried her to where three sofas faced each other across a square coffee table. Her weight and her scent had brought home to me how much I wanted to fuck her. Despite all the pain I'd given her, she curled into me after I let her drink some cold water. To rest her, and so I could admire how I'd marked her body, I petted her awhile.

It was time.

I threw a couple of the large cushions across the golden timber of the coffee table then kissed her forehead. "Enough. On the table on all fours. Then turn to me."

Her hesitation might've been due to the shaking of her arms. I waited until she obeyed. When I had her before me, I wrapped black bondage tape around her eyes and a little above. It bunched up her hair but it was her body that'd get to my guest, and her adorable mouth.

"This man who's coming is a friend but nervous about being seen. Don't say a word to him or I will punish you. Be good and I will reward you."

Punishment would be a word of great weight to her now.

I had her head down, ass in the air, with her body half on the coffee table and half on my lap, when he arrived. The door closed silently, slowly. Chris paused after taking one step onto the patio. He thought this was deep roleplaying and knew I wanted no names said.

If some slipped out, I would deal with the consequences.

I wasn't sure if he'd recognize her with her face half covered. I didn't care.

What I most wanted, what made my dick happy, was to show off Wren while I fucked her properly for the first time.

I waved. "Come on over!" He paced toward us, steady, checking her out and perhaps surprised he didn't instantly recognize her from the local kink community.

When Wren went to push herself off my lap, I fastened her in place with a hand in her hair. She shifted on her knees. I guess she wondered what was about to happen. Naked, bleeding, newly whipped and flogged, with her thighs wet from her own moisture and her pussy on display to this stranger she could hear advancing.

Wondering, for sure.

I could've told her. More fun. Much more fun.

I was high as a kite in topspace. Flogging her, making her submit, had made this day rise above all others.

My one hesitation came when I looked down at this woman and wondered about my motivations. Showing her off was one thing, sharing was another.

I ran my fingertip around the whorl of her ear, pushing aside strands of her hair. She was such a small fragile creature, compared to me...and a new emotion tiptoed in alongside my need to dominate her. I wasn't sure I liked it.

CHAPTER 20
Wren

Here was something new. Something that filled me with dread. Another man had arrived. I'd thought I couldn't imagine anything more embarrassing or terrible than what had happened, but this was it. If I'd known this was about to happen, before he blindfolded me, would I have objected?

How?

I had nothing left. I was used up and devastated, hanging on by a thread. Only the thought that eventually I would be by myself and be able to go through this in my head kept me going. My muscles hurt – my legs, arms, and back, everywhere he'd flogged and hit me. At least whatever he'd attached to my clit had fallen off and he'd not noticed.

The man wasn't infallible. *Yay.*

The sad part – I no longer believed that, not where it counted.

Footsteps came from the direction of the door. They drew closer, a little louder, deliberate. A heavy man. A friend of my abductor. He wouldn't be allowed near me if he were a good man, surely? My new effort to straighten on my arms and turn was frustrated yet again by *His* hand in my hair. Not that I could see, unless I ripped off the blindfold?

No.

"Stay."

I stayed.

What he'd done to me... I shivered. I wanted no more of his punishment. The sting from his last marks said I was probably bleeding.

"You've got a new captive?" the man said, in a soft yet deep voice

— an assured voice. I smelled cologne on him.

My abductor only smelled of sweat, same as I must, and faintly of the chlorine from the pool. What struck me most was that this stranger had no qualms about seeing me here. None. I couldn't appeal to him for help. That conclusion trampled me even lower than dirt.

Their words seemed distant while I curled in on myself. Funny. Feeling lost shouldn't be anything new.

"As you can see, she's well prepared. I had to punish her." His fingers traced down my back, brushing over hurts. I winced. "But now she's ready, for us." All his gentler touches made me see future pain. Did he know how he affected me?

Probably. A chill trickled in, one that flipped from fear to arousal, and back to fear. I was a fucked-up mess.

He understood me, intimately. More than Glass did, probably, certainly more than any other man. If he wasn't a mind reader, he was so good at what he did that I'd begun to doubt my ability to second-guess him.

Like I often did, I felt such a traitor. I'd never talked to Glass, never said goodbye. I'd just walked away that night. If I had a choice, I would be back in Glass's bed and in his arms, in an instant. That *had* to be what counted.

"I can see she's well flogged, yes." The new man chuckled. "But, *us?* You didn't mention sharing her."

No. Oh no. I'd suspected this was his aim but hearing it in words drove home what was about to happen. I tensed my thighs and my back, ready to twist and leap away, caught up in my first thought — *run.*

Running wasn't an option. Nothing was.

"Up to you. You can sit there and watch only, if you want. Turn around, girl. I want your head bowed before my guest. In case he wants to join in." He addressed his friend, "I'm going to fuck her but you can use her mouth if you want to."

All I could see while I stayed frozen was the black cloth of his pants under the lower edge of the tape. Where had my life gone? Where had *me* gone?

But I didn't think I could take more punishment and stay sane.

"Go." He tapped my head.

I drew in one shaky breath then turned, feeling my way over the table with my palms. *What am I doing, what am I...* Then a man's hand on my shoulder stopped me. I flinched.

"You've found me. So...she likes the attention of an extra man?" The stranger was ahead of me. With the blindfold on, my senses of smell seemed heightened. I smelled man beneath the cologne. To my dismay, *He* began to stroke the seam between my lower lips. A man behind me. A man to my front. Every time his finger slipped over my pussy entrance, a petite moment of desire ripped me away from the *now*.

I found myself arching. I wriggled to get just a little closer, craving what he did. The effect of his training? This wasn't my own body anymore.

As he kept working his fingers on me, over me, into me, I gasped and catalogued my reactions, yet couldn't stop myself. My eyes rolled up. The throb of the myriad hurts and bruises brought me back to him with every thump of my heart. It held me in thrall despite the subtlety of his touch.

Then, not subtle. Two of his fingers speared in and I groaned. *Instinct, it's only instinct.* Animal response. Sensations climbed, curled inside me, blotting out thought.

"Beautiful," the stranger murmured, his hand tightening in my hair and dragging me forward an inch. With the jolt of electricity, he stroked my breast where it hung down

He chuckled and his fingers stilled partway into my pussy. "Tempted?"

"A little."

"She won't say no."

So true. Because I couldn't.

He thrust into me once more and again I quivered. Thick fingers. Deep. *Fuck.*

I was *His*, whether I wanted to be or not.

"If she doesn't want this then I guess it's too bad. Don't speak, pretty slave, you know what you've been told."

Bastard.

My thoughts were so scrambled I may have whispered that. The stranger guffawed, but he didn't tell. He only pulled up my head and kissed me, his hard lips crushing onto mine while his harder hand used a grip on my breast to haul me even higher, then keep me in place.

He ended the kiss but kept the hold on my hair, his fingers twisting in my roots. I heard the sound of a zipper. "You've convinced me. She can suck my cock a while."

"Use a condom."

I heard the packet caught and ripped open by the stranger, but felt *his* tongue on my pussy then inside me as he held open my ass cheeks, then the probe of something artificial and solid at my asshole. Everything entangled. All of this seemed to happen at once, in layers and bites of sensation that tugged my attention this way and that, until I might've been a mile underwater, and not known it.

Too much. My thoughts scattered. Under my eyelids was blackness and a spattering of colors as my eyes tried to see where there was nothing.

The rip of the packet, segued into a plug being screwed into my asshole. I gasped at the feel of that and at the fingers deep, then deeper, in my pussy, at that tongue licking my clit, at the hand in my hair forcing me down. The blunt plastic feel of a condom-sheathed cock touched my lips and squashed them aside. More fingers at the corner of my mouth, making me open wider. The cock sliding in over my tongue, opening my mouth up to the limits, choking me. I needed *air*.

Pleasure flooded me. *He* had his mouth on me, playing with me, fucking me with something that wasn't fingers, moving my clit from side to side with tiny nudges, sucking it into his hot mouth, licking some more. *Oh god, fuck, oh god.*

I crept, soared, and was bludgeoned by fingers, cock, tongue, and the throbbing marks on my skin, into rising to the glorious heights of a building climax.

Nearly. There. I tensed, unable to do more than feel and make primitive noises, so absorbed in what was being done...

I heard the ring of a phone, inches away. Then the stranger spoke, quietly, with his head low and near me, as if he wanted my moans and choked sobs to transmit to whoever he'd found to tell about facefucking some anonymous woman while another man licked and licked at her and made her come.

Under the blindfold, I had my eyes jammed shut. I whimpered in a muffled way, my mouth full of dick. I *was* going to come, couldn't help it. Inexorable desire had me in its grasp.

While his cock thrust in and out of my mouth, I listened to the noises of that carnal slop and slip of his cock, as he used my tongue and my drool to get himself off, even my throat when he fucked me deeper and shoved my mouth down onto him. I sucked in his words while I was being sucked on and he took my mouth.

"Kat. Yes, it's Chris. Were you asleep? Got Zoe there? Put her on a leash. Get her ready for me. Get her to get *you* ready. I want you both leaning over the hall table, when I get back, head down, ass out. I've got a girl with my cock halfway down her throat but I'm not coming in her amazing fucking hot mouth 'cause I've got you two. If you're not wet as hell, I'll spank you both first." I could hear the grate of lust and amusement in his voice. "Fuck!" He hissed when my teeth grazed him. My tongue curled over the head of his cock and he slowed.

He answered some phone comment, grunted then said, "Yes. Yes, she does. Yours is hotter? I'll get you to prove it. I'm going to choke her with it and count the seconds. If you can beat the time, I'll be nice. Yes. I can be. Guaranteed. Means I won't cane your pussy more than ten times."

His chuckle sounded positively evil.

"Stick the phone where I can hear you lick Zoe. I want to hear some sexy noises." While he talked he thrust into my mouth. I felt like a hole in a wall made only for blow-jobs.

The licking of my clit was making me schizoid – concentrate on one end of me, or the other? I shut my eyes and knew precisely where that tongue lapped, explored, what those fingers were doing to me. The phone drew me back.

He slowed and didn't force my head down as deep or as fast. My mouth ended up with just the fat, mushroom-like part of the head poking inside.

"What are you doing to her? No, no fist fucking her, Kat. Bad girl. Not until I'm there." He stared down at me and I dared to bite him, using enough force to squash in just below the head of his cock by half an inch.

"Fuck. Those teeth..."

He liked it? Damn. I let go and he shoved my head down and my mouth onto him, deep, and stayed there, his cock pulsing.

At that same moment, *He* sucked my clit into his mouth, rammed the plug in as far as it would go, then stretched my pussy wide with a third finger to join the others shoving into me.

It hurt, it hurt, then...all the good and the bad muddled together and paused. The big bang theory made real. I burst into crazy-headspace orgasmtime, my back trying to bow despite my head being shoved balls-deep onto the stranger. I gurgled and cough-grunted until the spasms died away.

"Hell." He held me there still. "Hell." Dirty talking his women on the phone, while I suffocated.

Need to breathe!

My nose tried but I wasn't getting much air. I moved to grab this man's hands only to find my wrist cuffs had been linked at my back. I tried to kick but my ankles were caught. He laughed then licked at my too-sensitive clit. I squealed in protest.

"Got that? I want two pussies waiting for me when I walk in the door. Damn, girl!"

The grip on my hair tightened to excruciating level and I felt his cock twitch and swell. After one, long, almost agonized gasp, he dragged me off him and his thick cock from my mouth. My drool spilled from my lips and I coughed then inhaled, struggling.

"Fuck, fuck. You almost did me in, girl."

"It's good that you decided that."

The stranger paused before replying though I heard him zip himself up, while cursing under his breath. "Why?"

"Because I've decided I'm too damn jealous. I don't want another man coming in her mouth or anywhere. Could you excuse me for a while? I'll talk to you after I take care of her."

"Sure." The sofa creaked as he stood. "I understand. Thank you though. She was...inspiring. How about I come back in an hour? Being Sunday, that'll give me time to duck home then come back."

They were ignoring me so I collapsed onto the table and curled up on my side.

"Great. And thank you."

"No worries. An hour."

I listened as he walked away, only half awake. Whatever happened next, would happen. I was only a pawn in this man's game. The plug was still inside me. I didn't give one fuck.

"Hey there."

He was talking. I was getting good at ignoring things from behind my blindfold. I was comfy, if naked. Warm outdoors and my mind was full of sleepiness even if my body burned here and there. If he wanted to fuck me, I didn't care.

"I've done a lot to you, I guess. I can see you're tired."

Yeah? I mumbled something nonsensical.

"But that doesn't mean I'm going to excuse you."

I drifted off, distantly feeling him rearranging me so my butt was presented to him, maybe.

Don't care.

His cock entered me. I knew it, felt the surge as he carved his way inside me, pushing in.

Too tired to care. It became background, bland, nothing, I was being handled and manipulated and I may as well have been a crate of apples.

"Oh fuck. This is no good."

Hah. I smiled lazily and grunted my reply as I felt him withdraw.

The blindfold was undone, unwound. There was light out there beyond my eyelids and I didn't care about that either.

A bite on my ass had me erupting off the table, screaming. Only to find him shoving me back down. On my stomach, with my upper torso twisted aside, I rediscovered the linking of the wrist cuffs. I squirmed and glared back at him.

Only to find, him, looking at me. That mask. Those deep brown, menacing eyes.

Shit. Hello again, fear. I looked at the floor, at anywhere but him. Fear, the monster I'd forgotten while drifting off.

"Do not ever think you can ignore me, girl." He smiled and went to one elbow on the table, until his face was a foot from mine. His fingers sneaked to my one breast that was in sight and clamped onto the nipple. Though I cringed, he pinched it with his finger and thumb. "Fall asleep while I'm fucking you? No. Damn. Way."

I held in the squeak though the pain increased, only to find not only had the multiple pains bounced me back into consciousness, I was also hyperaware of him controlling me.

And, *save me from myself*, I liked this. Wide-eyed, I shuddered.

My lips parted as I strived to keep my breathing normal. His sadistic playing with my nipple while he held me down had sent a line of hot arousal screaming straight through me.

This was not something I wanted him to know.

While he pulled me to my feet, I thought some more. This was different. It wasn't like the other times when he made me become aroused. This had been like turning on a tap. From la-la land to where I was now, aching for him to put his cock in me. I squeezed my thighs, sending a pulse to my clit.

The fatigue was overriding my normal responses. This wasn't me.

"I want you on your knees, over the table."

Getting ideas from the stranger? No, he wouldn't have heard the phone orders that man gave.

I did as he asked, I walked my knees into position on the hard floor and he slipped me a cushion. I poised, my upper body above the table. Leaning over was tantamount to saying I want you to fuck me, and even if I did, the wrongness was disgustingly...*wrong*.

I bowed my head, appalled I was such a slut as to want him. Tears prickled my eyes.

"Down." With his hand in a *V* on my nape, he forced me to bend until my breasts touched the timber, then he pressed on the small of my back until I was flattened to the table.

I lay there, exposed, wanting to wriggle my ass, but resisting. He was seconds away from fucking me. I could feel the slight well of my moisture down there, my body lubricating my pussy, an advertisement of my sluttiness.

"To teach you not to go to sleep when I'm fucking you..." Funny, but I could hear amusement. "This."

His teeth met on my butt. I screeched, couldn't help it. His teeth worried at me, and I was terrified he might take out a piece. Then he moved up my back to the side of my spine, to my shoulder, tens of bites, while I keened in my throat. Some bites worse, some small.

I heard him whisper, *mine*, once or twice. This was a sadistic ownership ritual.

He was marking me, owning me.

Nothing was more personal than bites, except his cock inside me.

No matter how I screamed and tried to thrash, he pinned me to the table with those large hands.

By the time he was done, I was covered in bites. Each of them throbbed in time with the others, and with my pussy. My back, ass, and thighs were on fire again, and I was having trouble breathing, yet I was sure he toyed with me. He could do far worse.

"You're not bleeding. Just bruised. Shhh."

After I'd gulped in some air, he slapped my ass once.

"Let me see that pussy coming up."

Confused as to what he wanted, I arched my lower back.

He slapped me again then took my thighs in his hands to pull my butt even higher. The head of his cock probed for my entrance, and he thrust inside in one heart-bursting slide. Then out and in again. Each time he jammed himself all the way in, he hit the butt plug and I awakened to the weirdness of that with him inside me too. It hurt. His cock seemed ten sizes too big to fit in me.

Then he'd withdraw and plunge it in anyway. I tried to claw at something but my restrained hands only found air.

"No! Can't! Please. You're too big."

"Too much?" He chuckled, though already a little out of breath. "I've been waiting all week to fuck you. It's the butt plug, taking up space. I can fix that."

Then he slowed in his thrusts, pulled out, and I heard a condom packet rustle, then the liquid squeeze of a bottle.

No. Not at all a good sign. A whine started in my throat.

"Come to me, baby," he muttered, wriggling the plug as he slowly pulled it out, stalling a few seconds, when I tensed and whimpered. He called the butt plug *baby?* The last, widest part, as it exited, made me want to bite the table. "It's out. Now, my turn."

Oh fuck. I squeezed my eyes shut.

"Don't worry." He leaned in and kissed beneath my ear. "I'll go slow."

His hands opened me wider, pulling apart my cheeks. I could tell he was looking at my asshole, his latest target. I wanted to squirm away, wishing I'd done this before just so it wasn't *him* taking my ass for the first time. Then his cock touched me and began to push inside. I could tell how it dilated me, fraction by fraction. In some more, and more. And, *fuck it*, more. Something that size wasn't meant to be there.

"Don't forget, push out," he croaked.

I was affecting him that much? I have to admit, that thought was gleeful even while my asshole burned as if he had chili on his cock.

His cock's journey all the way in was like some medieval torture. How could anyone like this? My body squeezed down on him as if trying to reject it.

"In," he gasped, his bodyweight pressing me down. "Done." He humped me a few times in tiny increments of pulling out and going in. Butting me into the table. A half inch of toying with me, sliding into my ass. All I could do was bite my lip and squeak.

He stilled and I felt his fingers brush at my nape. "Not liking it yet? Hmm? I can fix that too, pretty Wren. If only you could see yourself with my whip and bite marks all over you. I'm going to get some pictures of you like this."

He did another slow thrust with his hand under me, massaging over my clit, and *damn*...my eyes snapped opened. That was. *Nice*. The warm glow of awakening lust had me listening to my body. His cock in my ass was the most possessive thing ever. He thought his bites had owned me; I'd had no clue how this would make me feel. I felt an extension of *him*.

I huffed out air and let out the first muffled groan, despite drawing my bottom lip between my teeth to try to keep my noises to myself.

"There you go," he whispered, laughing.

Why was he laughing so much, when I was hurting? But warmth was swelling from everywhere down there. New nerves had popped into being. My ass curved higher and his fingers sped up in that damn merciless rhythm that had me rocking back into him just to get nearer both cock and fingers. My nipples, constricted into tiny buds that dragged on the table as he shoved into me. His movements became bolder, harder, more violent. Flesh slapped against flesh.

I was going to come. I was...

I shut down thought, tensing, on the very, very edge...and he sank his teeth into my shoulder again, only now I could hear the strain in his own panting. Those fingers hit the right speed on my clit and I bucked, spasming down onto his cock, coming crazily.

"Good girl," he gasped.

I was done. My muscles were jelly. Mouth open, I tried to catch up on breathing, but was seized by the fury of him thumping into me. I lay there shocked as I was swept up by pleasure. He took my ass and shoved his cock in so far his balls squashed in against me.

He took me and he stayed in there, pushing into me as if there was further to go.

The grunt as he hit his climax made me smile. I shouldn't like that but I did.

After towing me to a shower out in the garden and rinsing off all the sweat and grime in a horrendous torrent of cold water, he dried my body with a big fluffy towel and carried me back to the sofa. At last he allowed me to close my eyes. Snuggled on there, lying on a dry towel, I listened while half-awake to the sounds of him tidying up whatever the hell the equipment was that he'd dirtied. Everything, it had seemed.

Except the knives, a small voice whispered to me.

Mmm. Next time.

I wasn't cuffed anymore, but he'd clicked a leash onto my collar and attached me to the sofa somewhere. In my muddled state, it almost seemed an act of caring, of compassion. I yawned. Besides, now wasn't the time for escaping.

Maybe never, that same voice whispered.

I told it to fuck off.

He came to me after he was done cleaning up and cuddled me into his chest, spooning and facing outward to the swimming pool. I allowed myself to peek at the garden and the sunlight and to wonder if I'd ever call myself free again.

"You were good for me." He caressed my neck, over one of the bites, I imagined. When it tickled, I shivered and hid my shoulder. "We're going to talk when you're recovered. Tomorrow will do."

"About?" I murmured sleepily.

"Our future. What you will be to me."

Alarm bells rang but they were far away ones. I snuggled back into him and sighed. He was evil, I knew that, but I was getting used to his brand of evil.

"Always know, Wren, I have no qualms about hurting you if you defy me, or if I just feel like doing it."

I guess that should've scared me, but it didn't. I was done being scared, today.

Finally, I closed my eyes and, while he petted me, everything washed away.

CHAPTER 21
Moghul

When Chris returned, I met him at the front door, after turning off the security alarm that'd reset when he left, to the tune of bing, bing, bing, as I hit buttons. Wouldn't do to just let anyone wander in. Which reminded me, time to get the cleaner in tomorrow. I'd have to lock Wren away in the basement.

One day, I hoped to be able to let her loose. One day, I wanted to be able to trust her.

I led the way to the open living area looking out over the sea and opened the section of glass that led to a small balcony. It was windy but I leaned on the brushed steel and glass railing and waited for Chris to settle into his own space.

For a while, we just watched the sea and the sky.

Seagulls and terns wheeled above us. The slope below was naturally terraced and covered with trees as well as raw red-brown rock. Though they'd no doubt split away from the cliff slope millennia ago, the chunky boulders seemed fresh and not eroded. Nature took a long time to do its work.

Made me wonder how long it'd take Wren to decide kneeling at my feet was satisfying, to be happy to hug my leg for reassurance when she needed it.

"Get done what you wanted to with her?" Chris had a mild smirk and, from his damp hair, looked as if he'd showered in a hurry before returning. I'd bet a million he'd used Kat and Zoe every which way. Andreas was away on business, so he had them all to himself.

"I did."

I planned to fuck her again tonight. Best to remind her of her submission. My dick wanted to do that too. I had a hard-on just thinking about her naked, and I'd only seen her five minutes ago.

Small epiphany. I wasn't a teenage boy with too much testosterone and no brain. Did I really expect this woman to be only my slave and toy?

"You said you wanted my help planning a munch? Something special, this time?"

I wrenched myself back to the present. I did, didn't I? I had to think to remember. Sidetracked by Wren, again.

"There's an Australian zombie movie coming out and I thought we could do some zombie effects. Dress up. That sort of stuff. Want to be in charge of sourcing some kink-friendly make-up artists? I know your friend, the lady who's Klaus's partner had her finger on the pulse of the local film industry."

"Jodie? Yes, she did, she does, just they don't live here anymore. I can see what I can find out." Then he eyed me. "Is that all?

I could've phoned him to ask all that, and we both knew it. He'd waited for nearly an hour for me earlier. I never hesitated once I made a decision but today was going to be a first.

I turned to put my back to the railing, assessing this man I might one day hand my business to. For a price. I had enough evidence on him to send him to jail for a thousand years, even if Kat, my distant second cousin, or whatever, would now deny it all. He'd abducted Kat. Zoe had once been a girl in training, ready to go to a House, before he bought her. That he was saving her from a worse situation wouldn't help him if the police were informed.

After all this time, Zoe was still kept secluded, so I figured she still wasn't quite ready to lay her neck under his shoe and call him her Master.

That scenario was what I could see happening with Wren. I saw submission in her and then she'd yo-yo back to her previous defiant self. I was patient. I was like Chris, prepared to wait a long, long time for her to come around.

Once I told Chris who I was, he would have evidence on me. No coming back from that unless I had him killed. Once I told him, he might want to kill me.

I didn't have a weapon on me. I figured I knew him. If I was wrong, I was about to find out.

"No. That's not all, Chris. I have a proposal for you that will shock you."

I'd dropped my laidback king of kink persona. He'd notice it, but I'd rather be me. I could barbecue a prawn or a snag with the best of them, talk cricket and footie, eat takeaway food that was one hundred percent fat and batter while swigging a stubbie of beer, but underneath I was a far more calculating and educated man than most realized. I liked it that way. Secrets were my meat and bone.

"But before I tell you my proposal, I have to give you some facts. I know they will also shock you. You're going to be angry. You're going to want to hit me possibly. Don't. Think first. I may not be who you thought I was, but I'm also no worse a man than you are."

"Fuck. You're freaking me out with this talk." He frowned but nodded. "Go on."

I wondered if his mind had gone to those crimes he'd committed. Abduction, rape, murder, assault. Most guilty people went there when anything seemed off. I'd never proven he murdered Scrim, my guard, but I was pretty certain it was him and Pieter.

I'd sneak my way into his head by telling him things only Vetrov, my other persona, would know. Make him follow the tracks, the clues. That way he might be less inclined to erupt because he'd unraveled half the facts by himself.

"When you come to that munch," I slowed, "maybe you could bring both Kat and Zoe?"

Gotcha. His eyes had widened and his face hadn't moved a jot since I said Zoe. There was anger there already though, I was sure of it.

What I'd said threatened him and his reaction was more extreme than I'd hoped.

Not good. Plan B.

"Yes. I know about Zoe. I'm not reporting you to the police. I'm not telling anyone. One of the reasons why I'm not is that woman in there." I thumbed sideways, pointing across the living room to the center of the house.

He glanced across. "You'd better explain. Who is she?"

I bet he was hoping like hell this was going to turn out for the better. He had no idea.

"She's Wren Gavoche."

There. I'd handed him my own head on a platter. If I was wrong, I might have to kill him. Somehow. I'd manage or I'd fail. This was the crucial point I'd had to accept. Chris wasn't a wholesale murderer, though. Not like I could be, given the right circumstances.

He took a breath, and only blinked once – keeping me in view in case I turned into an alien maybe. "You're messing with me. Wren Gavoche? The missing millionaire?"

"Yes. You must have seen pictures of her?" I pulled out my phone and scrolled to the latest pics I'd done of her back, and of her sleeping on the sofa, curled up like a kitten. Serenity, that was the best word to describe her expression. I took a moment to admire her, smiling inside, before I tossed the phone to him.

"You're telling me I just had a blow job from a woman the police have top of their missing persons list? Every cop in the country wants to find her...and her kidnapper. *You.*" As he looked, thumbing from photo to photo, I watched him, and he looked up to check me too. His jaw worked. "What are you planning to do with her?"

"Keep her." Nice to know he was concerned. Society might think I was fucked up. I could order someone killed, but if they were in my house, under my law, I cared for them. "I'm not a monster. I'm still Moghul. Your friend."

"My friend...and kidnapper."

"Same as you."

"You could've told me before I let her go down on me."

I shrugged. "I figured it wasn't one of your hard limits, considering..."

His mouth twitched. "Fuck you."

He was right, of course, I had thrown him in deeper and it'd been intentional. I'd reinforced my hold on him with that act.

"And how the fuck do you know about Zoe? How? Wait, did you get her through him?"

Ahh. Getting there. "Who? Vetrov?"

Oh the pregnant pause at that.

"Yes. Him."

"Not exactly. You know that I run Kinkaverse. That I'm a businessman with a foot in many worlds, so to speak." I waited for him to nod. "I have many illegal businesses too."

Chris straightened and turned the phone over and over before throwing it back to me. "Why are you telling me this?"

Would the clues piece together? Had he a hunch as to who I was?

"I'm telling you because I hope to sell you most of my businesses. I want to retire. I'm a distant puppeteer to many. No one knows me. I can show you how to do the same."

The corrugation on his brow deepened and he studied me for the longest time. "You're not...him?"

"Vetrov? Yes."

"No. No." He shook his head, despite having asked me directly. "Impossible. He's Russian or something."

"Easy to fake online." I pretended nonchalance and crossed my feet at the ankles as I shifted my back into a more comfortable position on the railing. "If you're wondering about the past, I didn't know you when you were at the House. I had to have assurances. That's why all the videos."

"I've done your accounting for years," he said in a quiet voice. "Years. You bastard. You fucking bastard. You run those slave houses? Have men and women killed because they do the wrong thing by you? For petty bloody reasons, from what I could tell. Your guards torture the women. What. The. Fuck. And you expect me to..." He swept his hand out. "Take over? I'm not that man. I don't understand why you'd think I am. I feel...betrayed right now. I thought you were a friend and now I find out you're the man who had me doing all sorts of shit to Zoe just to get you assurances? Where's the porn library of vids you took to keep us in line? You going to hand those over?"

I waited, to let him run out of steam.

"No. That would be stupid. You don't have to take over from me, but consider this – if you did, you could run things your way. Yes, you've done my accounts and for that reason alone, I know you're not squeaky clean, Chris. You knew all those things were happening and swept it under the carpet like it wasn't there. Figure out your head. You've got months to decide. I'm not going anywhere soon. *Then* give me your answer.

"Just keep this in mind. You're the only man I've ever told about my other businesses. The only man I've ever considered as my successor."

His expression was stone, for ages then he nodded once and stalked away. I let him go. He knew the way out. I'd hear from him again. I was sure of that.

If only I was as sure of Wren. My previous thought was spot on.

Deluding myself that she could be or would be happy simply trotting at my heels was wrong. I had done exactly the same as a teenage boy might — I'd sniffed after the object of my desire like some damn animal. In this, the main difference between me and a boy was that I could get my hands on her, keep her, and hide her away.

I could do it even if she hated me. I didn't want her to hate me.

Would I be content in her situation? No and not simply because I hadn't a submissive bone in my body. Therefore, I should assume she wouldn't be either.

And what were the consequences of that? My house would be in lock-down forever.

Fuck.

I lauded myself on my skills at staying on top of any situation, but I'd never done this before. There was a chasm of difference between the consensual negotiated power exchange between Dom and sub, and this.

Underestimating the opposition was the biggest flaw anyone could commit in business yet here I was in the kidnapping business and I'd ignored that rule. I had to find a way to bind her to me that didn't involve rope or sadomasochism.

I rubbed my chin. Where was the damn fun in that?

"Woman..." I chuckled. "You're making my head hurt and you're not even here."

Eight days was nothing. I'd barely begun.

I had to get her to like me... I turned to look out to sea again and watched those long waves roll in. I imagined her by my side, enjoying this, could even smell her hair, feel my arm about her waist. Damn, it would be better if there was love.

That, now, that was a tough problem that I'd never solved.

Flying to the moon, fighting a land war in Asia, governing a small country, all those were easier than love.

CHAPTER 22
Wren

That night, he gave me painkillers before leaving me, but my bruises and hurts seemed twice as bad when I woke after midnight. I lay there processing what had happened. I lay alone in my dimly lighted room, my fingers playing with my collar and the link where the leash connected. My brain was working again. I recalled what he'd done and his words.

For me to keep you, Wren...

My heart had squeezed in at that moment, and coldness had swept me. If I disobeyed him badly, if I dared attack him, he was prepared to dispose of me.

The stranger had only proven that by what he'd said. *You've got a new captive...*

New. He'd had other women here and they'd gone elsewhere or died.

I'd been sympathizing with him. He did care for me in some twisted way, but if he couldn't have me, he would kill me or sell me. I was a mere owned thing to him. I had to remember that.

If I ever tried again to escape, I needed to be more than sure of succeeding and I needed to kill. To kill him, I'd need him facing away from me, because I must not see his eyes. Stupid not to acknowledge my weakness.

He could hold me with them. One look from him, alive with condemnation, with that strength he held over and above mine, and I'd falter and my knees grow weak. If that happened, I might die, not him.

I had to remember the man I'd been so close to being in love with: Glass. So close the difference between being in love with him and not being in love had become impossible to see...or to feel. I kept him fresh in my mind by recalling how he'd felt as he cuddled me, how safe I'd felt on that beach after the plane landed, even after he 'flip-flopped my butt', as he termed it...remembered even that last time in the restaurant when he'd shoveled food in his mouth and I'd had an *ohmigod I love this man even when he's fricking eating* moment.

My doubts from then were paltry, stupid. The yearning to be in his arms got to me at the dumbest of times, made me blubber like a baby in the darkness some nights, but it helped too.

If I ever got back to him, I'd say those words – that I loved him. That I might one day say those words, it was my talisman that kept me hoping and strong.

I had to stay strong.

The days wore by and I learned how easily *he* could break that resolve.

I kneeled to him every day. Every night I made my resolve again: *stay strong.*

One day, after hours restrained in his basement area, he visited me. Night had fallen, yet I was led away from the room I'd lived in for weeks. He showed me to a luxurious bedroom. His, I assumed. I noted the main features as I padded across the tiles and thick rugs. My little silk dress swished against my thighs.

The color scheme was a mix of cream, bronze, and gold, with hints of azure and emerald. Ocean view, a huge solid-glass window I'd need a crowbar to break. Sofas, wall-to-wall TV opposite the bed, and the bed...was different. The height off the floor meant there were steps at the end. Beneath the bed was a space walled in by bars.

Hell. This was a cage. A cage under a bed. I could see pillows and bedding.

"You're sleeping here from now on."

"Oh." I glanced at him and back to my new home. The big open room with the hard leather bed seemed wonderful compared to being in there. Such perversions as this shouldn't shock me anymore.

"Don't like it?" One eyebrow tilted and his lips almost managed a smile.

Did he expect a yes? Some days I still felt ornery, or bratty as he called it.

"Nooo," I drawled out. "It looks claustrophobic. I'd rather..."

He shook his head, slowly. "Good. I like that you don't like it. There is no *rather*. If you're good, one day you'll sleep up top."

Fuck. I stayed silent and merely looked dubious.

Seriously, being good should now be my priority. Sleeping next to him was a step closer to freedom.

"Here." He crooked a finger and climbed up to sit on the bed.

I followed, trying to look happy. He was going to spank me, something I found exceptionally humiliating. I'd rather be strung from the ceiling naked and whipped than be spanked but I guess he'd figured that out.

"Lap." He pointed.

My sigh was close to silent and I obeyed, wriggling across his lap and wishing I wore something other than this pale blue dress. My matching panties were as good as a gift from the gods, since it was rare he gave me underwear. They weren't likely to stay on.

"Your ass would inspire a poet."

Huh. A compliment. The man was slipping.

I felt him hook his fingers under the elastic and slide the lacy fabric down to my upper thighs, so that he no doubt had a clear view of my pussy. Knowing he was looking made me feel wanton. I nestled my forehead against my arms and waited for the first strike as he circled his palm over my butt cheeks.

Then, nothing happened, except more playing with my butt. After a few minutes, I simply *had* to wriggle against his legs. Lying like this was a hot trigger for me. Positive reinforcement? I detested spanking but had found I liked the position once I was there. He'd given me a hundred incredible orgasms after being hurt and I couldn't help myself. No blame, no shame. Except it was easier to think that than to really forgive myself for getting turned on.

I understood why but hated myself too.

"You couldn't tempt me more than you do now, woman."

Uh. Okay. Stick your finger in me already. I buried my eyes and nose in the quilt and huffed. I might, hopefully, suffocate.

The darkness made all the sensations he evoked the only ones in my head – nothing else but him, stroking me, teasing me.

He ran his finger down the cleft of my ass, pushing aside each cheek, going feather light across my asshole then almost to my slit. I wriggled again, impatient for a more intimate touch. He'd called me woman? Not slave or some diminutive? I rubbed one thigh against the other, trying, in an obvious way, to encourage that finger to go inside me.

"Want something, Wren?" His big hand snuggled down onto my neck, squashing me harder to the bed.

I grunted, hazing out but then remembered to say, "No Sir."

"Are you lying?" He shook my neck.

Crap. "Yes, Sir."

His laugh was energizing and my eyes snapped open.

"While I have you here, I thought I'd ask you some questions. We can have a chat."

What the? A chat while he threatens to either spank me or do, something, nicer... His finger dipped lower.

"My finger is now very wet. Tsk, tsk. Your fault."

No kidding.

That same finger was circling my entrance, in smaller and smaller orbits.

I grunted again, nearly inhaling quilt in an attempt to calm down as he snuggled his finger onto me, the whole length of it resting over my slit while the fingertip swirled at that perfect place for making me want to hump something. I felt the expanding warmth of arousal as he nudged at my hole ever so damn sneakily.

"Are you listening?"

I made a noise, at best, and he snorted.

"You've never asked me my name, Miss."

Now I was awake. He would tell me this? I swallowed down my lust, stilled that primitive urge to fuck something, even if it was only a finger. What I'd been reduced to was... I didn't know how to express it. Sad?

I wanted to be with Glass again. His question reminded me of my old life. Of when I had choices.

Finding out his name could be important for when I was free. When. And how likely was that? If he told me this, it would be a milestone. To not have told me yet, it seemed to follow that he thought I might reveal it to someone else.

When he told me his name, would that be the day he thought I was truly no longer free?

Dread made my heart beat faster but I was compelled to ask. Curiosity killed the kitten, perhaps.

"I never heard you say I could ask you. Sir."

"Hmm. You didn't. I can't tell you it anyway. Not my commonly known name. You may already have guessed I am Vetrov?"

Thank god. He wasn't telling.

He *was* Vetrov.

Relieved that wasn't his real life name, I lowered my head, having arched up my neck to hear his announcement. Though...even knowing he was Vetrov was scary. I'd guessed but it wasn't the same as knowing. So this man on whose lap I lay ran slave houses, perverted ones.

Hope dwindled ever more with each passing day.

"I knew," I said hoarsely.

"Yes. You're smart. I don't like it as a name. You can use Master for my name, for now, if not Sir."

Master? Ugh. No.

He stroked my nape and began to talk. "I'm sure you still hope to escape me, Wren. I understand that. I understand, but I will not condone it. Trying to escape is futile. You'll learn that I want you for more than sex or someone to play with. I want you for a companion. Someone to share thoughts with."

He must be joking. But...but, wasn't this good? I shouldn't disdain such an idea. I needed sustenance that was more than food or I'd end up a giggling fool staring at walls. I had to embrace this opportunity even if I never gave up on freedom.

"I'd like that, Sir."

"Master."

I squirmed inside, hating this next level of dominance he enforced.

"Master."

"Good girl."

His touch, his hands on me, played with my head. The man could massage like an angel. He'd kept his hand between my legs as if to hold me in place but kept those fingers still.

"I've taught you to like the whip, haven't I?"

True. He'd made my appreciation for pain soar, but saying it to him seemed like another betrayal of myself.

"Answer me. I will know if you lie."

He couldn't know. Could he? He might. The doubts got to me lately.

His fingers between my legs reminded me of what he might do.

Was that the faintest stir of his finger? Eyes shut, I listened to everything in my head, feeling the pulse of blood in my female parts and the weight of his arm on my thigh, and terribly aware of the spread of my legs before his gaze.

"Answer me, sweetheart. I know it's hard for you to say."

Oh fuck. Sweetheart? Impromptu tears welled and seeped onto the quilt. Mind-fucking-reader.

He was a master of mindreading, if nothing else. I blinked into the quilt, torn.

"Yes, it's true."

"Thank you. I love you when you're honest. It pleases me. I want you to suck on my finger while I make you come."

Love. The word fell past me. He dared say that?

His finger arrived at my lips and I opened.

He tasted glorious. The only way to describe this. His finger in my mouth said possession and man and a whole bunch of things that stemmed from everything he'd ever said or done to me.

Training.

I didn't fucking care.

Liking this *didn't* make me bad. I was just a victim. I was...

I sucked as he thrust his thumb slowly into my entrance and started toggling my clit in time with my sucking on his finger. I ceased sucking, he stopped too. I began again and, *damn*, I groaned and managed belatedly to suck on his finger while he played maestro with my clitoris. He tasted of chocolate biscuits as well as him and I vaguely wondered if he'd eaten Tim Tams while my body gathered up all the sensations unfurling in my now not-so-private parts and sent them thrumming into me, awakening my nipples. They poked up and rubbed on the dress. Awakening his cock too until his erection dug into my stomach.

My one power over him.

"Good girl," he murmured as I writhed on his lap. "That's it. I reward you if you suck. You worked that out so fast."

Put in the coin, Wren does what he asks. I was prostituting myself for a finger fuck.

No. Not so. And thinking took too much from me. I shut down and *felt*.

"Yes. Be mine. Let me fuck you while you show me your little wet cunt. Keep going. Let me see you come. That's my favorite after seeing you cry when I whip you red." I felt him bend and bite the hair at the back of my head, then he moved downward and bit my ass.

I squealed.

Whipping.

Mentioning that while he stuck that thumb deep inside me and I sucked on his finger, it made me fuzz out more than a little. Time blurred. The two ends of me, mouth and pussy, connected in some glorious fucking circuit and sensations built and spilled lust, a monstrous, expanding storm of lust.

The hold he had on the corner of my mouth, his cock sticking up at me, that had been *in* me so many times...I needed...needed....

I groaned and squeezed down on his finger in my pussy, bit the one in my mouth, feeling that relentless force take me up and *throw* me at the universe. Gasping, squeaking, spasming on him, and unable to stop until I wound down into a feeble limp heap of spent woman, and then, then...I knew he had me.

"There. Beautiful, as always. You're mine, Miss Wren, Just proved it there."

I didn't have the energy to weep. I was too busy gasping.

He left his finger in me until he knew I was done and I sighed at its removal, feeling that suction as my pussy clamped down a last time, regretting the emptiness in me and the loss.

"My turn." He moved me off him then shifted me further onto the bed. "Turn over and look at me."

Vulnerable after the orgasm, yet I rolled over and faced him. I'd be flushed, red of cheek, but I made myself return his gaze. Be damned if I'd be ashamed.

The amused triumph I saw there was worse than a leer. It always fucked with my head – that he could bring me to climax in spite of my distaste.

"I'm not going to tie you down today. You're going to do what I ask you to while I fuck you. Bend your legs up and show me your cunt."

I hesitated, squeezing shut my eyes for a second, and made to wriggle down my panties, only to have him growl at me.

"No. Leave those. I like them where they are."

Halfway down my thighs?

Slowly, I bent my legs until my knees were up to breast level and I was peeking at him through the gap between them and my underwear.

"I like you, like this." His voice purred harshly, like he was a big, hungry jungle cat. "As if I caught you walking down a hallway at a party and pushed you into a bedroom. And now I've got you all messed up because I made you come while I pinned you down. You've tumbled onto the bed and opened your legs to me. You want me to stick my cock in you, don't you girl? Me, a stranger. Because..." He swept his gaze over my body, studying my exposed pussy then wandering up to my breasts, then to my mouth, my open mouth. I licked my lips as he shook his head at me, seemingly dismayed at my display of my cunt. "Such a slut."

He'd done it again. Turned me the fuck on. I *was* a slut.

"Open your legs some more. Tell me you want to get fucked by this stranger. A man who's going to split you open with his dick, to come on you, in you, to make you scream, even though all the other men at the party will hear you being screwed and know you're ready for them, if they choose to walk in on us. They'll all hold you down and make you suck them off. Make you turn over and let them ream your ass. While another fucks your mouth."

Oh god. My head would explode soon. I shouldn't *like* this.

He stood over me and unzipped his pants, pulled out his cock, then stroked his hand up and down the shaft.

Rapt by his words and actions, I watched him and thirsted for his next words.

"Beg me, slut, so I can get this done then invite the others in to rape you as well."

How *dare* he? This was sick, demeaning, and I was possibly going to come from his dirty talk alone. My heart did overtime, hammering away at me.

I couldn't. Shouldn't.

I wriggled my butt, conflicted, and then...I let my thighs fall open.

He still didn't touch me, only watched as my legs parted, stretching my panties. He waited until I'd stopped moving, then observed me leisurely, as if I were a done deal, something assured. His piece of pussy for the night.

"Beg me. Put your hands down here and hold open that naughty little cunt so I can see a hole to aim at. Beg me or you get nothing." He leaned over me. "Beg or I'll call in all those men who will fuck you so hard you'll bleed and have cum all over you, be spilling it from your nose, your cunt, your little asshole – any hole they can find.

He'd made that up...and it spoke directly to my perverted soul.

I gulped. I shook from the tension. I loved this. My clit throbbed, ached, and I needed him in me so badly. My pussy entrance felt as if it had cracked open, gaping, inviting him in.

The man had a thing for rape and corruption.

And I?

I was an innocent and such a whore. I was everything he said to me. Everything.

For the first time in my life, I embraced my sexuality, my every dirty corner and hole, every part of my femaleness, my fecundity. This was what people did. They fucked, they procreated, they exchanged cum and fluids, and all to the glorious accompaniment of screams and weeping and roars of male dominance, of flailing limbs and pumping cocks and wet, engorged pussies.

But, I still I couldn't say this.

My brow furrowed and I squirmed under his looming presence. This wasn't my fault. The last dam inside me broke.

"Please?"

"What? I can't hear you. Louder."

"Please." The words didn't want to leave my throat. Saying more would kill me.

"What. Do you. Want?"

I sighed out a mountain of angst. *You bastard.* Where had this dirty pervert inside me come from?

"I want..." I paused, terribly humiliated, fidgeting. "I want your cock in me."

"Then show me where you want it."

No. I couldn't. But I would. I had to. He made me. I angled up my pelvis and put my fingers around my butt to reach in and hold myself open for him to see me in the most intimate way.

"Of course you want it there. Sluts always want cock."

Not me. I closed my eyes.

"Open your fucking eyes."

Scared, I snapped them open.

Without touching the rest of me, he placed his cock at my slippery entrance and stuck it into me, just as he'd said, sliding in all the way, with ease. Like a man doing a whore.

I groaned at the penetration.

"Take your hands away," he snarled. "Put them above your head and don't move a fucking inch."

Then he simply used me. He fucked me hard, made me immerse myself in all the awesome feelings of just being fucked. I was shoved across the bed as he banged me and I ended up moaning, my head upside down, as he came, my arms and hair dangling down.

Upside down, half hanging off the edge, struggling to breathe, annihilated.

I hurt. He'd bruised me with the pounding of his hard male body against my softest parts. I had finger marks on my hips from where he'd gripped me for the last flurry of thrusts, and all I wanted to do was lie there, eyes shut, my eyelids twitching, remembering exactly what had happened and how I'd been his thing to fuck. I replayed it in my mind, as if it was the best thing ever.

Which it had been.

He slid up the bed, turning my worn-out body over so he could spoon into me, then muttered, "You pleased me. Now you have to lie there and be fucked by the ten men lined up outside the door."

When I only whimpered, he laughed and bit the side of my neck.

"Such a good, good girl."

I slept in the cage under the bed from then on. It was comfortable and let him pull me from it easily if in the middle of the night he wanted to fuck me. Sometimes, I even wanted him to.

Weeks went by, and more weeks.

What was Glass doing? Hugh? They hadn't found me. It seemed they never would. Maybe I was forgotten, declared missing, presumed dead. It happened. I wasn't sure of the official time but perhaps it was after a year that it would become a legal fact and people could pretend I was gone forever.

I was history, almost. A lost person. I was his. I was becoming accustomed to that. Unless, I found some answer, some completely unknown, impossible answer. I could've managed to kill myself, I guess, if determined enough, but that wasn't me.

To be honest, he had me thoroughly entangled in his web. Most days, he fucked me or made me come, or punished me...

I squeezed my eyes shut, remembering those times, feeling again what he'd made me feel, and I grew aroused and wet. My reaction wasn't something I could say wasn't there, it was me, and that was the crux of my problem. I was trapped here and I feared I'd lost sight of the way out.

CHAPTER 23
Glass

Months had passed since the night she went missing. Too much time for me to stay near where she'd vanished. Though it'd been a terrible decision to make, I'd left and gone back to Port Moresby, but now I was back.

I'd wracked my brains and looked for loose ends. Vetrov must make mistakes. I'd tried to track down the men we'd killed at the House where Wren's father had died. What a shithole den of sex and torture that place had been. They'd all been local men, or foreigners based in Papua New Guinea. I'd asked every man I knew who might know anything at all about a man like Vetrov. I'd ended up exchanging info in alleyways with assholes I'd not trust to not feed me to a wood chipper if I annoyed them, along with my dog and my children, if I had any. Nothing. All kinds of nothing.

Hugh wasn't even on the job anymore. The trust had pulled him off security.

I braced my arms on the window and looked out at the night, at a street full of run-down apartments in the old south end of the town, somewhere where no one cared if a stranger arrived with a mean attitude and a habit of hiding his face. The cops had mostly given up looking anyway.

I wouldn't. I crunched my fingers into the ancient paintwork, felt flakes of the paint turn to powder or cut away under my nails.

"Wren."

Just saying her name brought heart-ache. I couldn't even go out on the rocks to fish anymore, and that was something that used to bring me peace. The last time I tried, I'd thought she was with me and turned to say something, only to remember she was gone.

I could feel her absence, see those glossy red lips of hers that day we met and the flick of her dark-as-sin hair.

Girl...where are you?

I wasn't sure why she'd affected me so. I mean...I'd had girlfriends who'd lasted longer. Maybe it was just the way she'd disappeared, or the man I thought had her? No, it wasn't that, I knew it. I loved her and if she was still alive, I held onto hope. If she was still alive, maybe one day I could hold her again.

I looked up above the streetlight at the dark sky and prayed to the stars.

CHAPTER 24
Wren

It became my routine, to be used as his toy, until the day he introduced something new.

I'd been past the big room so many times, and looked longingly out to the sea and blueness, or even to the dark gray clouds of storms, and this day, he led me in.

"Come." He unclipped the leash and gestured. "We can lie on the sofa next to the viewing window. I've decided you've progressed enough to be allowed this."

Watching him from the corner of my eyes, I crept forward, taking small steps. I'd been restricted to such a small part of the house for so many weeks that this was...I drew in a breath and looked around...like a dream.

When he sat on the sofa, I was still unsure, so I kneeled at his feet. Though I'd done this a hundred times, I knew how wrong this was, kneeling to him, but I accepted it was my lot, for the moment. It was my life, for the moment. When that moment would end, I didn't know. I was waiting, in limbo, and in limbo, it was fine to be his obedient creature.

I survived.

"Up here."

He patted the sofa cushion and I crawled up there and nestled beside him, with my head on his chest. I'd been there before, with my head on him in that convenient place on men's chests that seemed made for snuggling. It was somewhere safe, I'd found, as long as I behaved.

"Now." He kissed my hair. "Thank you. You're pretty in that dress."

I looked down my body, seeing the length of ivory material and my legs stretched beside his legs further down. It was a beautiful garment. Simple, perhaps Indonesian style, with fine embroidery on the bodice. I wore no underwear, but this was still far more than he gave me to wear most days.

"I thought I'd let you begin to read again."

Really? I made myself not look up at him. Reading was something I loved. It had always been my relaxation, my fantasy world, and my way of escape if the real world became too stressful.

On the coffee table beside the sofa, there were stacks of books. Greedily I perused the spines, reading the titles.

"Pick one."

My heart thumped harder. How silly, to get excited over a book or two, something that should be my right. How pitiful that I was reduced to this.

I sat up and pretended to have to think but I knew which one. It was a book I'd often thought of reading but had never felt as if I could devote enough of myself to. It was a book that needed to be consumed over many wonderful days of reading. I had time for it now.

I slid the book from beneath the pile and drew it to me, cracked it open, praying he wouldn't interrupt. He pulled me a little higher up his body and peeked over my shoulder.

"*War and Peace*? That's the last book I would've thought you'd choose."

"Why?"

Oops. I waited for a reprimand.

"Good question. I know you were studying at university. It's just a monstrosity of a book. I grabbed a whole lot of different ones from my library. Never read it myself."

Were. A small pain started in my chest. *Were studying.* The past tense. I hated him for all of five seconds.

War and Peace. Forget him, even if he made a good pillow. I smiled and began to read, only to recall that nearby was that view of the sky and ocean I'd yearned to see for so long. I glanced across and at the first sight of blueness through the glass, I found myself inhaling – peace. My mind floated. Waves, wind, the sea on the horizon, it was like the fresh smell of storm-wet air.

But it couldn't feed my mind. How I needed words, stories, something to make me think.

Dreams, I needed those.

I turned back to the book.

Again I read the first words. I closed my eyes. He could punish me, but I needed to know.

"Why?" I asked him. "Why now?"

"Why now what?" The only sign of displeasure was a tug at my nape hair.

Do it. "I thought you meant to dispose of me. Why let me read?"

"Why would you think that?"

"The others. That stranger who was here. He mentioned other girls. They're not here now so..." My throat seized up.

"You think I killed them?"

"Or sold them off." His shirt shifted under my ear and I listened to the *lub-dub* beat of his heart. Not speeding up – that had to be good?

"No. You're the only girl I've had brought here. There's been no one else, Wren. No one..."

What was he thinking? I peeked at him and found he was looking at me, almost sadly. For the first time in weeks, I didn't feel the need to duck away.

"I'm not sorry I have you here. Don't think that. From now on, if you're good, I'll reward you with things like this."

Things that should be mine anyway. Tears threatened. The book was safer. I looked down at it. "Okay. Thank you, Sir."

I'd remembered to say it, this time. Now... *Chapter 1*

"Well, Prince, Genoa, and Lucca are now nothing –"

"Can I read it too, love?"

I jolted.

He'd asked me permission. Said, *love*? Had he changed into someone else overnight? But no, he'd spanked me this morning for some minor infraction, presumably because he just wanted to. When the sadistic urge overcame him, his face looked *hungry*.

A thrill had unraveled then, waking me. What we had wasn't simply a predator and prey interaction, it was more, much more. Prey was not supposed to like what happened when the wolf consumed them.

"Sure." I let him help me hold up the heavy volume so we could both see the page. This was odd, yet promising, in some way. I was a human being to him, not just a fuck toy, as he sometimes called me. This felt like that day he first allowed me out to swim in the sunlight, and look how that had turned out.

How did I even know he told the truth about there being no other girls?

I don't.

I never will.

I couldn't trust him. I needed to remember that.

From then on, each day brought some new present, because I wasn't stupid. I responded to his reward and punishment scheme well. Defying him brought the bad things. Being good brought me presents.

He let me sleep on the top of the bed, some nights, only cuffed and tethered. I considered, fleetingly, kicking him or trying to strangle him in his sleep but both were stupid ideas.

I was allowed in the kitchen, to help him prepare food. I'd never been much of a cook and neither was he. My one restriction was not being allowed near anything dangerous like a knife. I could only eye them from across the kitchen. I could mix and stir and sit with him while we found something new to cook.

Alas, there was no concentrate of arsenic among the herb bottles.

The first day we cooked, I thought of throwing smoking hot cooking oil over him but decided it wouldn't help me, unless I hit his face and eyes. Too much room for error. I feared failure.

Besides, I couldn't face hurting him in that way. What he'd told me had come true. He hurt me but not terribly. He even made me like it. Burning off his face wouldn't likely free me, in any case. If he knew my thoughts, he'd rethink my future qualifications as his slave.

University exams would hold no terror for me after this. *Haha.*

Even in the face of my morbid internal jokes, I found I enjoyed learning. That was me, a learning slut, as much as my need to one day escape was a part of me.

Sometimes, I found myself smiling at the messes we managed to create. Stir fry goop earned a place in my memory. Both of us were notorious for burning things that weren't supposed to burn.

Then there was the day he let me sit with him to watch movies. I could pick which we would watch. I used to love horror movies, but my taste for those had changed.

The first movie was one I'd seen before. *The Lord of the Rings*. In the middle, I jolted alert, realizing how ironic it was I was settled at *his* feet with him combing his fingers through my hair and that I was loving it and happy. My last boyfriend, before Glass, had refused to watch fantasy movies with me, declaring them stupid.

Fate had a way of playing jokes too.

All these rewards were his way of training me. He knew I knew that. One day, I bitterly told him so. That outburst earned me time on the spanking bench. Afterward he unstrapped me and put arnica on my throbbing, bright red ass. I knew precisely how red it was because I checked out the marks in a mirror in the bathroom.

As I smoothed my hand over my whealed and warmed skin, I caught sight of my face and the collar on my neck. I looked freaky, spaced out, spellbound.

The marks he put on my skin fascinated me. I wanted them to last for days, so I could feel them and see them, again and again.

Yet another *Twilight Zone* moment, brought to you by the letters S and M.

The next day, after I swam, he offered to get me a puppy.

Holy shit.

I was drying myself. To give myself time to think. I went to my knees and clutched his leg, wrapping my arms about it and getting water on him. Luckily he wore drip-dry surf shorts and was barefoot. The hairs on his legs were coarse and exciting under my fingers.

I looked toward the sofa, unfocused.

A puppy.

A puppy would be like allowing another prisoner into my world. Disconcerting, even if it brought me comfort.

"No, please Sir." I craned my head back and searched his expression to see if this would be a dangerous time to say no to him. His eyes were clear of the hunter. "It would remind me of university and..." I wriggled, thinking. So true.

"And? Would it make you unhappy?"

"Yes."

To my surprise, after only one long, calculating stare, he accepted my lame excuse. Perhaps it was all down to how well I clutched his leg. He liked that, same as I liked doing it.

I was going to Hell in a handbasket, express postage.

A few days later, he said he would mark my back, permanently, with a sign of his ownership.

By then I was good at hiding my emotions.

I couldn't let him do this.

Not. At all. It brought me tears again, that night, in my cage beneath his bed.

A mark seemed irrevocable.

Where was *me*, if I was his?

CHAPTER 25
Wren

On this day, he had me go into the large dungeon room where I'd slept for so many weeks. Nervous, I followed.

Was this to be a tattoo?

He stopped beside the spanking bench I'd been strapped to many times.

"You must not move during this. Understand?"

A machine of some sort was plugged in via an extension cord to a distant power socket. It didn't look at all like a tattooing machine.

"Wren?"

I glanced up, shifting from foot to foot. Today he'd allowed me to wear underwear – red bra and panties. I'd been wondering if he had some color coding for my underwear and had mused that red could be for the days when he was super sadistic. I prayed I was wrong.

"Wren. Pay attention."

Though accustomed to his attention, his gaze was greedier than ever, as if he found this especially exciting.

"I'm sorry, Sir. I understand." I barely blinked in case I missed something. Running would be good. First, I needed to snap my steel leash.

"Up." He patted the leather.

He meant to mark my skin.

Me. My skin. Did this seem worse because it was different? I'd had him inside me. Why did some letters or a design on my skin mean so much? I tried to sort out my head while I crawled onto the bench and he strapped me down. Arms and hands to the front, then legs and ankles and waist were fastened down. On all fours but lying across a padded bench.

As the last strap was cinched in, he said, "This mark will mean you're mine."

Yes. That was why I feared this. Another step, another slide down the stairs. This was ownership.

Be strong.

"I thought, for a while, of using a knife to cut a scar on you. It would be satisfying but I'm not sure if it would scar enough."

To cut a scar? My toes curled and I gripped the padding that my arms rested on, jittery, wishing I'd had the guts to do something other than lie down and let him immobilize me.

What knife?

From the corner of my eye, I watched him bring over a stool and a wheeled tray. I was struck by the absurdity of this as I hadn't been for weeks. *My masked master, in a dungeon, about to torture me.*

I almost giggled, though desperately unhappy. What else could I do? Fastened down, barely able to wiggle, it was like waiting to be sliced and diced. I was meat. A victim, yet again. A thing.

The familiar ache in the middle of my forehead bored in.

No way was I going to fucking cry for him, not today.

Now he'd gone behind me, where I couldn't see what he was doing.

"I'll try a small scratch with the knife. Just to test you," he added dryly.

And that made so much sense. Not. We both knew he did it because hurting me made him happy.

A glint attracted me. There was a small, all-steel knife, waiting to be used, in the middle of the tray to my right. The clatter and scrape of metal when he retrieved that knife was replaced by silence.

I listened deeper.

His breathing, my breathing, then the padding dipped, as if he rested his elbow. Something made contact just above my ass and I tensed. Only a pen, from the coolness and soft scratching.

"Here is...perfect," he murmured.

Then the scraping began. I'd rather cutting than this annoying, continuous scrape as the knife's tip wore away my skin. Nausea coiled in my belly and I tried to squirm away. It awoke nasty feelings that made every part of my body feel wrong.

At last the scraping stopped and I let go of the fold of leather and padding I'd held onto to stop myself whining.

"No. I don't like that. The other tool is an electrocautery handpiece. If you're wondering, I've practiced."

I gave a small grunt. I didn't care to talk in case his concentration slipped. Electrocautery? I'd wondered at the familiarity of the device. He was going to burn me? Though I'd not used one, those were made for surgery, for cutting straight through skin. If he used the wrong setting, or the wrong pressure, I'd be sliced open and need stitches to fix it.

Worried, I tried to turn and look.

"Be still." He slapped my butt.

Moving would only make the chance of a disaster higher. I bumped my chin into the leather and inhaled, long and slow. Sometimes, by doing that, I could make my pulse slow and my blood pressure stay low.

Not today. *Thump, thump. Thump, thump.* I'd probably blow up a sphygmomanometer.

"Good. It'll start soon. The word I'm writing on you is *mine*, if you're curious."

And that was reassurance?

His voice went up and down in volume as he pottered about picking up the handpiece and fiddling with stuff back there, chatting as though this was the equivalent of a visit to the hairdresser or tattoo shop.

The first blistering tap of the point of the device shocked me. It burned then was gone. I could feel a traveling, continued burn, hear a faint sizzle, smell my own damn skin burning, but it was bearable, swiftly moving over the skin above my ass.

Mine had only four letters. Thank god he hadn't gone with something like *Master's slave girl.* He'd need a bigger ass in that case. I shut my eyes and breathed through the pain. The heat spread, more like a bad sunburn than anything. As torture went, this was five on a scale of one to ten. My dentist did worse.

"Good. This is going really good." Then a minute later. "Almost done." Then, "Done."

So quick. A minute of that and now I had this man's word burned into me. This wasn't like the mark of a belt or a whip. It was permanent and it would unsettle me to see it in a mirror.

189

Something cool, that stung for a moment, was wiped over the word on the small of my back.

He undid straps, methodically, moving around me. On the little three-foot-high table on wheels was the handpiece, a tube of ointment, some swabs stained with spots of blood, and the small knife.

A weapon. That was a weapon.

The thought flickered on and off in my brain like a faulty neon sign.

The last strap came off and he squatted before me, smiling. He was fucking *smiling*.

His mistake was a huge one. I ran through the ramifications, the pluses, the minuses.

Dare I?

Dare I not?

Really, did I? Last time still haunted me. What would he do this time if I failed? I'd told myself not to look in his eyes and here he was, a foot away.

I did not want to be his forever.

"Wren, I'm going to tell you my name and show you my face now." His fingertips pressed up beneath my chin.

Ohhh crap.

This was that day. Now I knew, I had no choice.

"Why?" I grimaced and levered up onto my elbows, pretending I needed to stretch.

"Because, I guess, I trust you."

Well, that was interesting. I'd never heard him vacillate like he just had in that sentence. He wasn't sure if he should, but he was. I wasn't the only one who made bad decisions.

I couldn't do this with his brown eyes looking into mine. Staring at me. Just couldn't. My hand found the knife, sneaking like some ninja disembodied hand, then found the handle.

Be silent. Don't rattle it. Metal sounds will alert him.

I shut my eyes and I whispered, "Don't tell me your name."

"Why?"

"Because you're wrong."

"What? Elaborate on that."

I'd not said *Sir*. Oh well. Last time ever I'd have to.

Now or never.

I stopped my breathing and swung my hand in a vicious arc, across where his throat was.

The catch of skin and his gasp had me ripping open my eyes to see him clutching his throat. Blood on his fingers. Yes! The arc of the sweep with the knife ended with a *slap* as my wrist met his palm.

My reaction was half horror, half pleasure, half *what the fuck did I just do*, with a paltry, *ohmigod, I'm sorry* tacked on at the end.

I jerked to free my hand but his fingers closed on my wrist.

He glared and his hand left his throat. A nick, only. A leak of redness, barely that. A true wound there would spurt. Rickety trickles of blood branched into the creases of his neck.

"Fuck," I whispered, horrified by my failure and the stark potential for death. I'd done that.

The features of his face deformed; his anger turned molten.

I'd done bad.

I'd never seen him angry before. My second attempt to free my hand and scramble backward brought me to the floor, flung there, spinning, my arm almost pulled from its socket. My wrist was caught in his hand, burning where my skin had twisted in his grip. The knife, he pried from my fingers, and sent it skipping and skidding across the floor. I watched it go, appalled, as if the loss of the weapon signified the end of my life, the universe, everything.

Maybe it did.

Wrestling with him was useless, but I tried. I'd lost all my reasons for being good.

Reasons meant zilch.

His strength obliterated my efforts to pull loose or kick or bite. Blood smeared my left hand when I tried to punch his face. I'd deflected into his throat instead and made him cough. Though both my arms were no longer mine and being dragged back as he swung behind me, I grinned that I'd gotten in one strike and I'd made him bleed.

"Little bitch," he muttered evilly, his chin gouging my shoulder as he cursed me through his clenched teeth. "Bitch."

"Fuck you too!" I spat, jackknifing onto my knees to rise, only to be kicked down. His technique of sitting on me was happening again. Terrifying and pitiful, but he outweighed me by two.

What was he going to do? Whip me? I could take it. He'd said he wouldn't harm me. I'd curse him out as he did it, even though he lashed me a hundred times. I vowed I would, while I nearly tore muscles in a ferocious attempt to worm myself out from under him.

Our irregular pants and curses and the screw of my muscles and skin under his proved the final punctuation of the fight.

He straddled me, my arms bent back painfully. My face met the tiles and was smooshed there. The pain got to me. "Stop, stop, stop. My arms! Hurting!" Dislocating my shoulders scared me far more than any whip.

He didn't say a word. I only heard his harsh breathing then he climbed to his feet and walked away.

My first jerk to free my limbs told me he'd hogtied me, linked my wrists and ankles together.

Damn.

He strode back, hands full of ropes and a bag of something I had no doubt was diabolical.

"Fuck you." With my face to the side, I spat at him.

Without speaking, he turned me over, slapped me across the face until I stuttered to a halt and stopped swearing, then he wriggled a metal gag into my bleeding mouth. I glared as if my eyes were fire and tasted the sweetness of blood. The straps clicked together at the back. At one spot, my lips had been caught and jammed between the metal and my teeth, but he didn't seem to care. After my ankles were unclipped, I was hauled to my feet and marched from the room and along the hallways to the big viewing room.

What I'd done had thrown him into incandescent anger.

I didn't know he was capable of being this angry. He'd always met my efforts to rile him with calmness then measured punishments. Regrets arrived, late and useless. My mistake had been catastrophic and worse than before. I had no possible defense. I hadn't meant to wound. I'd aimed to kill.

"You stupid, stupid girl."

I wavered on my feet then swallowed, strangely relieved to hear speech. If he took off the gag, maybe I could talk my way out of this...somehow.

I *was* stupid if I believed that.

I could see the monster in his eyes.

We'd reached his so-called pit of despair. The drop over the railings was a full story onto tiles. He wouldn't, would he?

I shook my head, making weird guttural noises, and drool spun away then dripped from my chin to the floor.

Slowly, while staring, his breathing slowed. I could still see his teeth past his taut lips but some of the wildness had gone. Locks of his ragged black hair had flopped over the mask. The scruffy look was always carefully maintained – a persona of rawness. Now, it was pure fucking scary menace.

"When I first planned to take you, I meant to use these on you."

From the bag, he pulled a handful of five-inch-long hooks.

The blood drained from my face and hands, leaving me shivering. He wouldn't.

I imagined them, the points popping into my skin, then sliding into me, and my nausea from earlier kicked back in, snakelike, coiling in my stomach, making bile rise to my mouth.

"These are suspension hooks. People do this for kicks. The hooks are sunk into them, in their backs or chests, then they're pulled into the air by cords attached to the hooks. You've earned a session."

"Uh-uh!" Legs trembling, I took a step away, only to be halted as he grabbed my neck and pulled me back in, despite the dragging of my heels.

"No, girl. You're not going anywhere. Not for some time. I was a kind master until now. I hope you're very sorry, because this is the punishment I'd decided was too much for you. I haven't decided yet how long I will leave you strung up. It could be a long time." He touched his throat. "A very long time."

The room fuzzed in and out as I struggled with the concept of staying upright and not fainting. I wouldn't give him the damn satisfaction.

CHAPTER 26
Moghul

The points of the hooks called to me from where they dug into my palm, but I only clenched my hand tighter.

The worst part of me was snarling that I should hurt her badly. I'd made a rule, years ago, to never let that *me* out of its cage. Nevertheless, she needed punishing.

I turned her, face first, over the railing so she bent at the stomach and had to stare down into the pit. Her little squeaked *no* was clear despite the gag.

As I knelt and clipped each ankle to the railing so she had her legs spread a few feet apart, I asked her leading questions. "What's wrong? Worried I'll tip you over?" I ran the point of a hook up the back of her thigh as I rose, stopping it at a fleshy part of her lower back, to the left of the *M* of the brand. "Here? For starters?"

"Mmm! Uh-uh!" She shook her head, violently, looking at me from her upside down position, the gag making her mouth a neat *O*, rendering her even more accessible, more objectlike.

I swabbed her back with alcohol in the places that seemed best, reaching over the rail to get her upper back.

With my finger and thumb pinching the skin into a fold, so I could insert the point of the hook, I paused to think, I could suspend her by the hooks then fuck her mouth, a good way to underline her mistake.

I could...

But should I? I knew her tolerances by now.

She'd tried to cut my throat. An inch deeper and I'd be struggling to breathe through a hole in my windpipe, with blood filling my lungs. She'd have finished me off soon after.

Volatile little bitch.

I looked down at where my fingers waited for instructions. The hook gleamed with light all along its length. This spoke to the sadist in me like nothing else.

I knew her tolerances, if not her deepest wishes and thoughts. There was terror in her eyes. Far more than from anything I'd ever done to her, even the half-drowning in the pool.

I glanced through the rails. She hung with her hair swishing lightly from her movements. Drool spooled in a thin string from her mouth. Red-faced, she retched once then stared at me, then away, blinking crazily.

Violent, volatile, unconquered bitch. I *had* her at times. I could make her into the sweetest submissive, then she flipped and became what she'd been a few minutes ago in the room. Would I ever get her past this? I might. With the hooks.

This little biting metal thing in my palm had the potential for change.

Stringing her up might kill who she is.

It might change her for the better.

Or would it make me into a monster so that I could never reach her? What I'd done so far hadn't worked.

I closed my eyes, closed my fist on the hook until the point bit me.

I needed distance. I should think about this some more and let my anger lessen.

Being her monster had never been my aim. Well, not lately, not really since that first time I saw her in the boot of the car.

Her wanting to kill me was a result of how I'd acquired her and kept her.

I released the ankle ties and pulled her upright, then I clipped on her leash and led her to the bedroom and put her into the cage beneath the bed. There was no point in speaking at this stage so I said nothing, only removing the gag and shutting the door before I went back to the viewing room.

On the balcony, the wind rocked me. Maybe, if I stared out to sea for long enough, the answer would come to me.

The sting at my throat reminded me of what might have been.

The endless roll of the waves reminded me of the world outside of my microcosm of perversion.

I crouched and put my palms to the glass, looking through the faint smear of salt that drifted in on the air when the wind was high. Then I leaned my forehead on the hard surface.

Like all my decisions, there was only me to confer with and this one had me in a vice.

Pretty Wren. I thought I had the key to your soul when all I had was a hammer. You're too sweet for me to ever think of destroying and I'm too selfish to want to destroy myself.

There wasn't much of a choice after all.

CHAPTER 27
Wren

Looking out through the cage door was an exercise in terror and meditation. I tried hard to stop my mind from running around screaming but being at his mercy, trapped in here with my hands at my back and nothing to do except wait for his decision, was making my imagination go berserk.

I knew what he'd intended to do. Why had he stopped?

To arrange something worse?

To control himself? I figured that could be it; though he hadn't said anything, he'd looked calmer when I dared to examine his face.

I shifted to lie on my back and study the underside of the bed, pretending this was somewhere I wanted to be, somewhere nice, like a cubby house where I'd hidden as a child, until my arms and shoulders went numb. I told myself to breathe slower and think of daisies growing on a green hill on top of a deserted island. The visual helped. I could smell the sea after a while, and the flowers. I could feel the breeze.

Then some distant noise would trip me back into the present.

What would he do? He was planning some punishment. He always did.

If he used the hooks on me, I'd withstand it. I wasn't some wilting daisy.

Except...the thought of them going inside me, then out again, and him hanging me up in the air. I shuddered.

I'd tried to cut his throat. Another man would've killed me for that.

I kept recalling my reaction after I'd cut him. As well as triumph, I'd been sad and had an absurd need to say *I'm sorry*.

I guess...I liked him a little, pitied him even, because I wondered if loneliness had made him kidnap me. And I feared him. Hardest of all to admit, I was in awe of how he could make me *feel*.

But most of all, I think I hated him.

Even now, I was unsure of that.

Foolish me.

When I heard the bedroom door open and his footsteps approach, I tried to keep my breathing steady. This was why I'd lost my taste for horror movies. Something was coming and none of the possibilities were good ones. When he squatted in front of the bars and looked in, he shadowed me. I was low. He was high. I was tied up and he was free. All that time he was away, he'd been thinking up how to punish me. Couldn't be much more ominous than this.

I looked out at him, seeing the parallel lines of his fingers, the size of his legs, the hairs on his arms, and the stretch of his shirt over his chest. Mercy wasn't in his makeup.

I trembled and felt my nipples peak.

My own private nemesis was out there.

This was no time for defiance. I swallowed down my reawakened pride and croaked out, "Sir?"

He opened the door, and reached in. With the utmost gentleness, he placed his finger in the center of my forehead, then traced a line down my nose to the tip, bumped over my lips, slowly, then trailed back to where they met. When he ran his finger along the seam, I opened my mouth, but all he did was shift his aim to draw a slow line over my eyebrow, from the middle to the outside, before doing the same on the other side.

Then he grabbed my collar and dragged me from the cage.

That he didn't speak scared me. I was taken to the shower and made to clean up, my hair thoroughly washed and combed out with conditioner in it, then rinsed again. Using gestures and handling my body, he showed me what he wanted. New underwear waited for me on a table. He let me dry myself then had me dress. The underwear was straight from a package but with the shop labels removed.

Things seemed to be turning out better than I'd expected. Had he forgiven me? So unlikely, and still he didn't talk.

At his hand signal, I reluctantly kneeled.

Alarms went off in my head a half second before he grabbed my hair and pulled me forward onto my stomach. While he pinned me there, he cuffed my hands again and settled a ball gag in my mouth. Then he put a canvas bag over my head and cinched it closed at the neck with a drawstring.

Where before, I might have protested, now, I stayed quiet and submissive.

I was in the dark, and gagged, though the ball of the gag seemed to have a large hole through the middle. Holes in the canvas let in pinpoints of light and some air.

I could breathe, sure, but he'd never done this to me before. New things scared me, on this day more than ever.

He walked me somewhere, through places in the house that sounded and smelled different, into a huge echoing space. A car door was opened then what sounded like a trunk. When my legs hit the bumper of a car, I panicked and tried to run, even though I was blind, and made all of one step before he had a hand on my arm.

I was forced to my knees, the concrete abrading my skin as I tried to wriggle away. He was taking me away from the house. Not good. The pounding of my heart and the rasp of my breathing, the scuffle of my feet and his shoes, my curses, the click of the ankle link – all these happened and none of them altered his course of action. Nothing I did made him speak, or swear, or acknowledge that anything I did mattered to him.

A moment later, he scooped me off the concrete and rolled me into the trunk, then slammed it shut.

Quiet, no noises past my desperate gasps. I counted seconds.

He walked around, entered the car, and started it.

I was fucked. So fucked. I coughed out my anger as tears and sweat ran down my face. The trunk was lined with something soft that took my head butts without noise. After a while I stopped trying to yell through the gag because it made it difficult for me to suck in enough air.

I cried silently off and on as the car drove along roads, waited for ages, somewhere, with the engine off, then drove some more. Scared was an underestimation of the power of this situation. I despaired endlessly.

The car stopped again and I heard the door open then he came for me.

First, he unlocked the collar and took it off. My neck seemed too bare, wrong, without the encircling weight. That was enough to send me reeling. If he didn't want me anymore...

I blinked in the darkness, striving to not go there. I didn't want to follow that thought through, to the end. I took a big, extra-shaky breath and the bag sucked onto my face.

Stay calm. It's the only way to survive this.

There was hope, always...wasn't there?

Though he didn't remove the bag, he searched for my mouth with his hand, feeling over the hollows and bumps of my face. Through the canvas, I felt the press of his mouth over mine, and then he whispered, "Goodbye."

No. Oh no. My heartbeat stuttered. Gargled words left my mouth. If he heard them or understood them, I received no reply.

I could've translated, if he'd asked, if he'd wanted to know.

What are you doing? You're not leaving me? Please. Please don't leave me here.

Begging? I would've gone down on hands and knees and licked his feet, kissed them, prostituted myself out for his ten imaginary friends, if he would've kept me.

Nothing. He picked me up and held me tight to suppress all my struggling.

I was carried to another car and left in the trunk, the lid closed on me.

When it opened again, perhaps a half an hour later, torchlight swept over the bag on my head. They held my arm still and injected me with something.

After that, nothing mattered.

A succession of blurred, faraway images paraded past, people, lights, engine sounds, the rocking of the surface I lay on. Men carrying me. Drinking water. For hours, minutes, days, the world was a series of distant fragments that had nothing to do with me.

Then I was left somewhere, still bound, vaguely knowing I was abandoned.

Slowly, I awakened and stared into the inside of the bag. At some point in time, the bag had been removed but now it was back.

Booted feet thumped on timber, echoing. Waves splashed and surged below.

A man grunted then put his hand on my shoulder then my neck.

The drawstring was undone but when he dragged off the bag I couldn't bear to look and see who had me.

Where was I this time? Somewhere worse than *his* house, I was certain. Perhaps I should pretend to be dazed?

With my eyelids mostly lowered, I began to lick my lips then stopped, not wanting to draw attention to any part of me that might give a man sexual ideas. Which was stupid. All I had on were a bra and panties.

CHAPTER 28
Glass

Wren?

Then I said it out loud, I whispered it, "Wren?"

I hauled her to me, my tears threatening to spill.

Her eyes seemed to struggle to focus even when I gently directed her to look at me. "Who?"

"It's me, Glass."

At last, I saw a smile waver on her lips.

"Really? It's you? Your hair's darker. He gave me back to you? I don't understand..." She whispered that then sobbed once and swallowed it down. "It is you? Untie me? Please?"

The doubts, hesitations, the apprehension in her tone, they cut me like a jagged knife sawing at my guts. Whatever had happened to her had changed her, and I'd not been *there* for her. My fault for letting her go out alone.

My regrets of that night were ingrained, like a dirty DVD track.

Rain check. Now is now.

"Give me a sec." I'd nearly lost it despite years of training. I drew my knife, searching the cuffs for a spot to cut. All metal links and a key lock.

Pieter was behind me, to the left, keeping tabs on the situation.

I had to get her out of here. Was it a trap? I'd wondered, when I got the text.

I considered cutting the leather but there was a key connected to the cuffs by a ziptie and I cut that instead. As I unlocked the cuffs at her back and the ankle ones too, I surveyed the inside of this small warehouse. The access was either from the sea past two big sliding doors, or where I'd come in, from landward. There was a lot of miscellaneous cargo in here – crates, boxes, sacks. Nothing that said a big company, this was someone's small freight shed. The door padlock hadn't been properly closed.

While I worked on the cuffs and helped her to her feet, Wren watched me but said nothing. Maybe she was afraid this would go wrong too? Why had he let her go? The poor girl could barely stand and I caught her under the shoulders, steadied her.

"It's okay, I've got you."

She turned her face into my chest. Her body trembled.

A single electric bulb had been on when I came in, and I'd ducked in the door then sideways to the right to avoid being silhouetted. Pieter had gone left. Going out, it would be a dead certainty that I'd be framed in the door. We could shoot the light but that'd leave a bullet in the roof.

"See a light switch, Pieter?"

"*Ja*. By the door."

"Hit it before we leave."

"Will do."

"I'm getting you out of here, fast, Wren, baby girl." I almost choked up again, at being able to say her name, to touch her again. "I'm carrying you out. You have to be quiet, okay?"

She nodded, her eyes red-rimmed from fear or crying, both probably.

When I'd first surveyed the warehouse, I'd felt a disconnection from reality.

I'd seen a woman, curled up and tied, with a bag on her head, lying on a central layer of boxes, like some perverted sexual display. My chest had hurt. I hadn't *known*, couldn't let myself be sure. I'd walked over, trying to be professional and scope the environment for bad guys, but I'd hoped *so* fucking hard. Every step had been a step toward both doom and euphoria. What if it wasn't her? What if it was?

What if.

I'd been on the last scrapings of hope.

It was Wren.

I wanted to kill him, whoever he was, but first, safety. If I failed her now, I'd kill my fucking self.

I had to keep looking at her, leaning against her side to reassure myself with contact as I talked to the others with the commlink. "It's her. Be alert. We're coming out. Have the car ready."

I'd brought Jurgen, Pieter, and four other men to cover me, but still I felt awfully vulnerable. What if there were explosives, a sniper? I'd only risked it because the text had mentioned her, or I'd thought it had. They'd said a live cargo called W was here, waiting for me. It'd been enough.

W meant only one possibility, to me.

"It's you." I smiled down at her as I carried her to the warehouse door. I kissed her forehead as she smiled back. Pieter turned off the light and went out, I followed. I had a Ruger at my waist and the guys had their favorite tricked-out weapons, from assault rifles to HKs but nothing would guarantee me getting out with her if half a battalion of someone's men was going to ambush us.

The journey down the jetty to the next cover took forever, and went through puddles of light and darkness, past at least five good ambush points. I jogged most of the way.

Wren didn't feel any lighter. There was good and bad in that. With her snuggled into my chest I felt like Thor and ready for anything, but carrying sixty plus kilos at a run took its toll. I was breathing hard by the time I hit the agreed evac spot. Pieter and Jurgen flanked me the last ten yards.

Around a corner and there they were – the two Land Rovers with drivers at the wheels and the engines running.

"In." Pieter gestured and held open the passenger door to the first Land Rover, his eyes on the surroundings, his rifle in his hand.

Once I exited that warehouse door, my men had covered us but I could've had a hundred enemy eyes on me. Every stride, exposed to bullets, and if they were coming I couldn't even duck, not with my girl in my arms. Worst feeling ever.

The second vehicle followed us as we pulled out, engine roaring, tires spinning fast over gravel but not enough to squeal. Discreet as possible, professional.

"Police?" Pieter queried. In the flicker of streetlights, I could see the raise of his brow. The man had every reason to want cops to stay a thousand miles away, but he was still suggesting it.

"No," Wren said, from where she snuggled into my side, her arms around me, mine around her, inseparable. Pieter had thrown the spare bulletproof jacket over her, then taken off his own and placed it over her as well.

Good man.

No man could ever ask for a better group of friends and for that I am eternally grateful.

My heart ached as she raised her head. She seemed much more fragile than before.

"No?" I asked. "But soon?"

"Soon. I guess. Now, I need just to be with you and safe. Please?" Her grip tightened.

"Sure. Rest. I'll get my doc to check you over though. Okay?" When she frowned, I frowned back. "Say yes, or..."

Fuck. Stop with the threats.

"Yes, Sir. I mean, fine." Then she snuggled back into me. I felt the warm huffs of her breath sneak through the layers of cloth and vest.

Puzzled, I watched her for a few seconds.

At her statement, a shock had vibrated in, and echoed.

That *Sir* had been automatic, like one of my men responding to a command. She'd never said that before she was taken. Never to me. And she'd caught herself, I'd seen that before she hid. She knew it would seem odd.

What had he done to her?

I should get the doctor to see her soon, though I wasn't sure I could even get hold of him this late. She'd been raped, almost certainly, maybe hurt in other ways.

I looked at her, curled up and holding onto me for grim death, like I was the only thing keeping her from floating away. The jacket had shifted and barely covered the bottom of her panties, so I inched it downward.

One night, a few hours of peace, then I'd make sure she was seen.

This had been Vetrov and I doubted he would leave any clues a doctor could find. I'd seen enough forensic crime programs to have some idea as to what was possible. The man would never have set her free if he'd only recently left semen inside her. It was a stark, horrible fact. Best to face it than ignore it.

We'd get past this. Maybe she'd need a psychologist? I'd have to contact Hugh. He might know more about how to treat kidnap victims. I had to find out if she knew why he'd released her. Had to be sure this wasn't some ruse. Though nobody sensible would dare attack my compound without a few armored cars. Vetrov, I knew he was smart.

We just needed to get through those gates.

I'd never feel safe until we found him. Never. But he was in Australia and I was in Papua New Guinea. My resources weren't the best outside my territory. I'd still need Hugh, no matter how much of a reticent bastard he'd become. Wren must have some new facts we could use to find Vetrov.

I patted her as we rocked through the streets, but my pistol was loose in its holster and Pieter's eyes stayed on the street. No chances.

I'd make sure she was safe, well, and that the man responsible for doing this to her was dead. Fucked over first if possible, but dead would be enough for me.

ASAP.

We swung around a corner and our street appeared, at the end of which were the gates to the compound.

My back itched and my stomach tightened into a painful ball as we drove those last few hundred yards.

I slumped a little as the gates shut behind us. *In. Home. Thank god. Thank whoever was watching over us. Thank my men.*

When we were all out and standing on the internal street outside my house, I gave them all a nod. "Thank you." Then I looked them over, slowly, meeting their eyes. "I owe you one."

Apart from a few murmured words, they were silent as I carried Wren up the steps and into my house.

Fuck it. Home.

Now to get her right again. Poor girl.

Whether it was the leftover effects from drugs she'd been given, or pure adrenalin letdown and fatigue, she was asleep. I gently shut the door behind me with my heel.

"Never letting you go again, girl," I whispered, looking down at her, feeling her precious weight in my arms, watching her lips as she breathed and feeling her small hand stir against my chest. This time I let the tears come. "Never."

CHAPTER 29
Wren

That night, I think I woke fleetingly, twenty times, and every time Glass was there beside me, ready to hug me and talk me back into sleep. Wasn't *him*. I was safe, in Glass's house.

When a hint of morning came, sifting through the shutters and striping the walls, the floor before me, the bed quilt, my first thought was how bare my neck felt, as were my wrists and ankles. Reminders that reached into my consciousness.

My back burned, where he'd branded me. Had Glass seen the word yet? That brought me to tears.

Reminders. They'd fade with time; they had to. I nestled into Glass and fell back into a restless slumber. So strange, to have someone beside me like this – someone I could trust.

Strange to know that once again I had choices.

*****

I sat on the edge of the bed in my newly adopted white shirt – one of Glass's so it engulfed me like a snowstorm. The doctor was nice, gentle, a man who clearly sympathized easily with his patients. He possessed a soft, smooth voice and would wait for my answers a long time before he'd prompt me. I needed this. It was difficult to talk about how my life had been for the last two months.

Two months. A bit more, really. I'd lost track of the days. His advice had slotted into my head, neatly, like something pretty pasted onto paper. Sentences that meant important things I should remember.

You seem in good health, Wren, apart from the bruises and small scars, though the brand will need daily treatment to ensure it won't become infected.

He'd told me it could be removed by a plastic surgeon when I felt ready for such a procedure.

I'd nodded. I would do that, one day.

The blood tests are to check for various problems including diseases such as hepatitis and HIV and to ensure you're not pregnant.

I doubted he had any such diseases. The man controlled his life so precisely. Still, I agreed to the tests.

I'm taking this swab to check for evidence of semen.

Even though *he* had always used condoms. The doctor explained he should be thorough, and I agreed.

I need to comb through your hair, in case any of his hairs have been caught in yours.

Again this was for DNA. Though he wasn't the police, it seemed he could access such tests. I agreed again. I clearly recalled *him* washing my hair but it was worth trying.

We both, the doctor and I, regretted that my pubic hair had been shaved often, as it meant there was no opportunity for his pubic hairs to be trapped there.

All so professional. He'd summed up the results of my abduction with some poking and prodding and blood tests.

As he packed away his stethoscope, he gave me more advice. Even the methodical way he handled equipment reassured me. I'd had to insist twice to shoo Glass from the room. I didn't need him in here.

"One last thing, Wren." He studied me, and I studied him too, thinking how elegant his peppered dark hair seemed. All part of his air of competence.

"Yes?"

"You're going to need to see a psychologist."

Oh.

I'd thought of that, though as yet it hadn't seemed urgent.

A tiny frown line appeared between his eyes. "Sometime soon would be best. I'll give Glass some names. If you don't return to Australia soon, you should ask him to contact one of them."

"Okay. I will." I watched the door shut then I let the gown fall to the floor and returned to the bed. I pulled the cool sheets up over me and ignored the shaking of my arms.

So odd. Of all things, I most noticed my wish to go back to not having to choose. I wanted to hide under the sheets and not come out until I was who I used to be.

Shock, I guessed. Psychological. Not physical. I was fine in my body. The doctor was right as far as that went.

The idea of seeing someone and having to talk about this horrified me. I would weather it with Glass's help, at least until I knew I wasn't going to shatter if I went outside his house.

I'd been through this before, the dislocation, the weird surrealism the world assumed after a catastrophic event. I'd been under his spell for months, based all the push and the pull of my existence around him, as if he were the center of everything. I'd succumbed to his every command, every day, and I'd schemed to escape from him most days too.

Now he was gone, I felt loss. Bereaved even. The loss was as if a tumorous blackness had been removed, but it was still a loss.

When Nathan had been murdered, I'd ended up hospitalized, partly due to my father's influence. I'd lost our baby even, one of my biggest regrets, and I'd been too drugged out, too deep in sorrow to even pay attention when it happened. Sad times. A time I never dwelt on, but now, I had that same feeling. I was no longer a part of what was real.

I'd get over it. Logically, I knew this. I had before.

Funny though. I had Glass now instead of him and suddenly I craved my sleep medication again. I was afraid I'd get up in the night, and end up somewhere I didn't want to be.

Glass didn't understand or know all of this but he stayed by my side, all of that first day. Most of it I spent in bed. Not surprising, I suppose.

The pile of books Glass brought, to help me relax, only resulted in me staring at them for ages as I tried to make myself pick one to read.

"None?" he asked, from where he sprawled behind me.

I shuddered and pushed the book piles away and off the bed. The piles fell, like toppling skyscrapers, to the floor.

"Not yet. Maybe tomorrow."

"Okay." Then he put his arm over me and pulled me into his body. He kissed my hair and I imagined him biting me there, on my neck, before he held me down on the bed and entered me from behind. When he didn't, I shivered and stared at the quilt.

Things were wrong in my head.
It was only a day. Only. I needed time to heal.

CHAPTER 30
Glass

Nightfall and Wren was no better, though she'd had her ups and downs throughout the day. I didn't mind being her babysitter. I had a business that nearly ran itself by now due to having rearranged who did what during the time she had gone missing. I could rely on Pieter to kick butt if it needed doing and Jurgen filled in for pilot duty when I might have stepped up. We had spares. Shifting people and illicit cargo into and out of the top end of Australia was lucrative as hell.

All I needed to do right now was to get Wren well. To do that, I was beginning to think I would need someone who knew how to treat post-traumatic stress syndrome. But like she'd told me, it was one day only.

"You can't hide in here forever." I hadn't even convinced her to sit out on the balcony with me to get some sun.

I shifted the tray with her meal onto the small table near the shuttered French doors. Then I perched on the bed beside her. At least I had her lying on top of the made bed, instead of under the sheets, and in a little yellow dress I'd found in the closet. It was a casual dress an old girlfriend had thrown on after swims. Beachwear, loose and see-through, but no one was here to see except me.

"I know. Tomorrow, I promise I will talk to Hugh." She drew in a deep breath. "Not sure what else."

"The Australian police will be wanting to speak to you." I looked at her from under my brows. "You know that has to be done."

She shuddered and rubbed her arms. "I don't want to go back to Australia. *He* is there."

Whenever she mentioned him, in that emphatic tone, I had to take a moment to get myself composed. Feeling useless wasn't my normal thing. Finding him was a priority, after I was sure she was safe. If I could do these in unison, even better.

"Maybe they will come to you."

"Strangers? How would we know they were really police? What if they were his?"

So paranoid. "I'll know. We'd arrange it somewhere safe. It would have to be away from here. Besides, you told me he said goodbye to you."

"Yes, he did. I'm sure he doesn't want me back. I'm scared, though it doesn't make sense." She shrugged.

"Understandable, but I'm here. You've got me to guard you. Okay? Tomorrow, we have to record what you can remember about everything..." Where she was, how she was taken, so many things I wasn't going to say, yet. "I'm sorry, but the cops would be doing this anyway and, if there's a chance you'll forget something important, we need to get on top of this."

"I know. I'm still me, Glass. I want him caught." She frowned and looked at the lap of her dress. "Just promise me you'll not get hurt. I couldn't stand it if hunting him ended with you hurt."

"I won't do anything reckless. I'm ex-SAS, Wren. All my men are ex-military and could take down Hugh's security with their little fingers. You know that."

"Huh." Her mouth distorted, tweaked up, as if unconvinced.

"Well...those and a few assault rifles."

She smiled weakly. "Sure. Thing is, he is..." She scratched at a clean spot on her dress as if something was there. Just to get time to think, I figured. "Thing is, he's very particular. A perfectionist. You're not going to find any clues. He scrubbed me down before he let me go. Washed me, my hair. Changed my clothes. He's that sort of man."

Her stare was too direct, for her. As if she was seeing something in the past when she saw me.

"Wren." I took her hand. "I need to say this. I'm sorry I wasn't there for you that night. I failed you."

My forehead ached but any pain I felt was deserved. I'd ask for her forgiveness but that was self-serving. What hurt me was that I had caused her to be hurt. I doubted I would ever forgive myself. If

I'd been there, they would never have taken her.

"You? Sorry?" She shook her head and sniffed. Her hand in mine shook, visibly shook. "No. Don't be. It was my stupid fault for being there and his fault, not yours. Don't say sorry, please?" Her hand shifted in mine and slid down to grip my fingers. "You're my damn hero and I need that. No more sorries. Okay?"

I nodded. "Okay." Any doubts I had could stay buried. "We can only try. And he does make mistakes. You said you almost got him with the knife. That's why he released you. Right?"

"Yes. I did. Maybe, there could be something he's missed."

"So long as you try. Now roll over and let me put this ointment on your back."

I didn't say why or what I was talking about. We both knew it was for the brand. I had to apply this twice daily or risk an infection. I could do this, even though seeing that word made my stomach gnarly.

After she was in position on her stomach, I pushed the dress a little further, up past her butt.

There it was. *Mine.*

How fucking warped was a man to want to put that on a woman just because he felt like it?

I unscrewed the tube and squeezed some of the white ointment onto my fingers, then applied it to the angry red letters. She hissed once then was quiet.

I could see the point of this, yes. I could see myself doing it, to be truthful, but only if she wanted me to. And a tattoo would be safer and prettier.

"The doc said you might get this removed with surgery?"

"Mmm-hmm." Her reply was soft and said into her forearms. Guess having stuff rubbed on this was somehow relaxing and I'd thought it'd hurt like hell.

I wanted to ask her to exchange tattoos one day, but it was too soon. I'd be happy just to see this *Mine* gone from her skin. Struck by an impulse, I leaned in and kissed her ass on one side. She shuddered at that.

"Hey. Sorry. Didn't mean to bother you."

After a few seconds' silence, she said, "It was okay. I liked you doing it. Please, Glass..." She wriggled, rocking a little on the bed as if what she was about to say was uncomfortable.

"What?" I put my hand on her ass, covering much of the pretty lace of her panties on one ass cheek.

Sex was out of the question, I knew that, but it didn't hurt to look. I'd been happy that she hadn't decided all men were bastards and I should be kept at a ten-mile distance, like some leprous creature. We could ease back into sex. I could be gentle. Every moment she let me touch her I was grateful. Our relationship had barely been off the ground before she vanished and if anyone was at fault for that, it was I.

Wren made an exasperated noise. "It's just. You didn't bother me. Apologizing for kissing me bothered me more. Don't *ask*. I want us to be like we were before." She peeked back at me. "Understand?"

I was stunned. "I'd thought you'd want me to be gentler. I thought sex was off the agenda. Surely it is? Did I read this wrong?"

I tried not to look accusatory but the suddenness of this astounded me.

"No." She sighed into the bed. "No. See. I was turned on after you kissed me. And now, after talking, I'm not. Sorry. Don't ask me why. I don't get myself. I'm all fucked up."

Damn. Anger came from nowhere. "No, you are not fucked up. He was. I don't want to hear that again." I screwed up my mouth. "Don't you apologize either. Got that?"

I'd gone too far.

"Yes, Si– Yes. I got that. Thanks."

And now she thanked me? I shook my head then hauled myself up the bed to lie beside her. Still thinking, I rearranged the spaghetti-thin strap of her dress so it fell over her shoulder where it was supposed to.

She turned her face to me but stayed on her stomach. Her next words were soft. "You used to be assertive, Glass. I still like that."

"I can do that. No problem. I'm going to be here for you. We will figure all this out. Next time you want sex, I'll be sure to be assertive. I'll pounce. But you remember your safeword. Sand?"

"What? Oh. Yes. Safeword. I guess I can do that. But pouncing...is good."

"Hmm." I stirred her hair about her ear.

Pouncing on her, today, would've so screwed with my head that I'd need that shrink.

I didn't tell her that though. Was it normal to want sex so soon after something like this? I had no idea. If she didn't want to talk to a shrink, maybe I'd make that appointment for myself. One of us needed to sort out what was going on in her head.

"Can you cuddle me properly?" she whispered? "Like put your arm over me."

"Like this?" I rested my arm over her, though trying not to squash her to the bed too much.

"Yes. I guess." She wriggled closer, under my arm. "You can press down if you want."

Why did this send a chill through me?

CHAPTER 31
Wren

I woke, for the second morning aware that he wasn't here. There was sunlight out there, past my eyelids, traffic noises, birds. No Glass though, I could tell his warmth was gone and the dip in the bed was less than if he'd been here. What if he was here? What if he hadn't meant to let me go and came back? Could Glass truly defend me or would he get in?

I half expected to open my eyes and see him above me, smiling that malevolent smile, with two pairs of black leather cuffs in his hands, ready for me. When I opened my eyes, a tremor swept my body. The room was empty.

The thing was, I'd always seen the bad news, the massacres, the murders, the rapes, the children abused, and I was aware the world wasn't perfect, but now I'd had it up close and personal...twice, if you counted Nathan. I wasn't in a bubble.

Now I knew for sure the bad things could get in.

The man down the street might be a serial murderer, the kid in the car coming toward me might be on crack and googling maps instead of driving straight, the gang on the corner might decide I was a good easy victim in my lonely lit-up house one night. Someone could walk up behind Glass as he took me through a crowded street, put a gun to his head, and shoot him dead with a bullet to his brain.

Nobody was safe. *What if.* One mistake, one piece of bad luck was all it took.

Back there, in *his* house I knew the dangers and it was all him. Knowable danger. Controllable, to a degree, by my behavior. If I was good, he was kind, mostly. Even when he was bad, he kept it within his rules, his limits. He'd let me go after I tried to kill him. I remembered...being content at times, happy, and that sort of thought confused me so much.

I'd been safer back there, than out here in the world. I felt as if I was surrounded by darkness and evil here, in Glass's house. Not because of Glass, no, he was my hero. But heroes died sometimes, didn't they?

I was scared. Scared to get out of bed. Scared of bleeding, of people I loved dying, of things happening I had no control over.

Fuck this. I was no flower.

The door banged open and I jerked, the white sheet sliding off my shoulder by a few inches.

Glass entered, carrying a tray of food.

Smiling wanly, I slipped off the bed until my feet hit the floor and ran to him.

"I can take that."

He held the tray above my head. "Nooo. This is my job. Besides, after this you're going to be eating with us all, downstairs. You're coming to the market with me after this too."

I screwed up my mouth and reached for the tray. He raised it.

"Okay?"

I jumped higher, pretending I would grab it.

"Wren..." His glower was real and I grinned but subsided.

"Okay! Meanie."

"Good. I figured blackmail would work." The warm, friendly glow I'd gained from the bit of fun slowly faded. I'd almost forgotten what it was like to joke.

He slid aside shutters and opened the French doors, letting in the sun and the breeze, before sitting opposite me at the glass-topped round table. The delicate timber chair creaked. I cocked a skeptical eyebrow. It often amazed me when a big man like him didn't collapse the chairs he sat on.

"However." He waggled his own eyebrows. "If you don't wear something less pretty and see-through, I'll be fighting off the passersby."

I looked down at my panties and a lightweight white T-shirt – the best he could do at a moment's notice last night. The night before I wasn't sure what I'd had on.

The words he'd said resonated badly and I shrugged without raising my head. If I wore this outside, I'd get raped, if Glass wasn't there. That imagery had flung me back to *his* house. No point telling Glass that. His words had been innocent and a bit of fun.

Everything had hidden meanings.

"We will have to find me more clothes." I smiled quickly. "But I'm rich, so it's fine."

"Mmm." He picked a croissant off the center plate and munched down, spraying flakes of pastry. Messy and so like a man. "We have to fix that. You're not going to be able to send any of your money until we get onto Hugh. All your credit has been cancelled."

"Oh."

"Don't worry." He squeezed my hand and I prayed he didn't notice how cold my fingers were. "It's easily fixed and I'll lend you some of mine until you can pay me back a few million."

As always, Glass, just by speaking, by his assured tone, made me feel good. The man didn't deserve all this craziness I'd brought him.

"So, we'll phone Hugh, because you have to tell that bastard what's happening. He knows you're here. I had to inform him. But you need to talk to him. If you don't, he will bring down Armageddon on us to make sure you're happy."

That would be Hugh. I nodded and picked up a piece of toast and put it on my plate, then unscrewed the lid from the blueberry jam. "Sure. I can talk to him."

Hugh. I ran a wave of calm through myself by imagining. Desert island, palm trees, waves, and shit. Talking to Hugh would be something. I wasn't the *me* he used to admire. I wasn't sure who I was anymore.

After we'd eaten, Glass put the call through then spoke to him first, leaning back in his chair, but keeping his hand over mine. While I listened, I watched his hand.

"Yes, she knows the police are necessary just don't push her, please. You haven't seen how things are. You're not here."

Meaning I was a ball of nerves.

"Yeah, we have some medical tests that should be back today, I'll send you those and I'll send you a transcript once Wren tells us more. Of course. Yes."

He slid the phone across the table and I stared at the glowing screen a moment before I picked it up.

"Hi, Hugh."

"Hello, Wren."

Semi-formal as always.

"Tell me if there's anything you need me to do. Before you say anything though, I'm getting you access to your bank accounts again. We'll do it through the trust, so to start with, the police won't know, but we can't keep this a secret for long or we will be prosecuted for obstructing justice. Two days tops. Okay, sweetheart? Tomorrow you need to come back to Australia with me."

Sweetheart? A new word for Hugh, at least when talking to me. *He* had used that word. The association with then and now made me feel ill.

"Hugh, I..." I leaned on the table, hand up high hiding my face because tears were dribbling down it, fingers propped on my forehead. Glass must have noticed but he only gave me another squeeze. "Tomorrow?"

"Yes."

I stared at the phone. "I can't. No." Then I pressed *end* before I could hear his reply. "He...he wants me to go back to Australia."

"If you don't want to go, you don't have to. Stay with me as long as you like."

I was standing at the edge of a whirlpool, and all it would take was one push...

*****

Moghul

A storm was coming. Dark gray on the western horizon. Rumbling. I took another big sip of chardonnay, eased back into the chair, and propped my crossed ankles on the railing. The house was empty since she'd left. Me, I was behaving like a fucking love-sick puppy. I couldn't be bothered eating and those two nights when I knew she was traveling back to PNG I'd sat up watching movies. *Lord of the bloody Rings.*

Memories, and all that crap.

I chugged down the last of the wine in the glass and reached for the bottle, dragged it from the ice bucket.

My vow to completely forget her had come unstuck within half a day. Sure I wasn't having her watched, but I was damn curious about her fascination with knives. Why? It bugged me not to know. I put

219

my hand up and felt the scratch on my throat. *Bitch.*

Had to know. So far the investigation was costing enough to buy a small town in Sweden due to a strange trail in Europe that apparently needed bribes galore. I'd waved my detective onward, via text.

"Mush. Go Prancer, go red-nose reindeer. Go detective! And fuck." I was drunk. Shit. First time in years and all over a woman.

Her eyes though...the way she wiggled that ass. How well she snuggled into me when I was being her Mr. Nice Dom. I could do that. Be nice. I'd perfected so many roleplays over the decades. I sucked in a breath, coughed, and slugged down some wine. *Fuck. Yeah.*

I pointed at the storm with the one finger left over from holding the glass. "Fuck her. Wasn't roleplay, even *ifff* she didn't know it." I'd loved being her big bad carer. "Fuck."

It'd showed first when Chris came over. Big bad fucking Chris.

My head threw something at me, a niggle, something was wrong with the picture and I squinted as if I could see her giving him that BJ.

What was it?

I frowned and my mind delivered up him talking on his phone. Which I hadn't been able to hear.

But she could've.

I hung my head backward and chuckled. All my careful shit and preparations, cleaning her up, and what if Chris had said something that could lead her back to me? I fumbled for my phone, wriggled from my pocket, and nearly dropped it to the tiles where it would've, given my luck, bounced through the gap at the bottom of the glass and then plummeted twenty yards to the rocks below.

I speed dialed Chris and gathered my wits. Needed doing. I ran my fingers through my deranged hair and remembered that at least now I could stop dyeing it and let the brown grow out.

Found a plus to her going. No hair-dyeing crap.

He picked up. "Yeah? Moghul?"

"Yes. It's me. I need to know something." The horizon tilted and I swallowed. Two bottles was my limit nowadays, clearly. "When you were with her, you talked on your phone. Did you say anything at all that might identify you?"

"Why?" Big huge fucking pause. "Isn't she with you?"

I could tell, even drunk, that he was trying to be nonspecific.

"No. She went home."

"Then why haven't I heard... Okay. Look. Let me think. I didn't know who...it was. I don't think so, except I said my name – Chris. That was it. So long as you're okay, I'm okay. She never even saw me."

I figured, he meant if they couldn't find me, they couldn't find him.

"I'm fine. Thanks. Bye."

End.

I slumped back into the chair. His first name? He was right. There were a trillion Chrises out there. We were good.

Except I had some more drinking to do. I picked up the quarter empty bottle, studied the label, then I stood, and threw it outward to the storm.

Wherever it smashed, I couldn't hear it.

I was done with her.

One last time though, just in case the Chris thing triggered something. Yeah.

I sat down and tapped my phone on my knuckles, giving myself a good, long time to change my mind.

Then I dialed my man in PNG.

Wren was like bloody Dom-nip. I guess I needed time and maybe somebody else to whip.

As if I would...

CHAPTER 32
Wren

As we drove past the hotels with their razor wire and through the government road block checking for ID and vehicle roadworthiness, I knew I would never be comfortable or happy here in Port Moresby, but Australia was worse. Or it seemed worse.

We went past a car with a *Baby on board* sticker in the rear view mirror only this one showed a pistol rather than a baby. Said it all, really.

Glass's friends might be okay with guarding me short term but it wasn't going to last. I had to brace myself and see Hugh, see what was possible without a return to my country of birth. Had to organize my own security.

"Ela Market." Glass pointed out the casual beachside market and Jurgen slowed and slotted the vehicle into the nearest vacant spot.

When I slid from the seat, the late-morning humidity was already making my T-shirt stick to me.

"Come on." Glass tugged at my hand. "Something to take your mind off that interrogation. Buy yourself a bunch of taro or a tribal mask."

I scoffed. Tourist stuff. I'd done the rounds of a market like this months ago. The sun was good, though, beating down on my body and making me feel alive. We stepped along the dirt and bitumen aisles, checked out the huge bunches of bananas, the shells, the handwoven baskets, and exchanged greetings with the sellers. Glass had an easy rapport with most people, but I couldn't dispel my unease.

The interrogation, as he'd called it, had brought it all back. Jurgen had been kind and Glass had been in the room to keep me centered, but question after question about my abduction had blasted away all happiness. Despite the brightness of the tropical sun, the day had become ominous from then on.

The questions had lodged in my head.

How long did it take to get there? What was the house like? Did you hear addresses, names, details about anything that might identify anyone? He recorded audio, wrote things down too. Then, after the general questions, he'd gotten into precise times, days. The time I'd met that man and been forced to give him a blowjob. Though aware of Glass listening, I'd answered. I recalled his name, Chris, and had thought a girl of his had been called Zoe.

The names had made them pause. At the end of it all, that had been the only clue that seemed worthwhile. Jurgen had sat back and made a rueful face.

"We'll go over it again," he'd said. Then we were done. Like the doctor, my ordeal was summed up on paper, to be filed away like a parking ticket.

Life was full of ironies. Someone could destroy you then afterward it was only scribbled words, if that, if anyone bothered.

I watched my sandals as I walked, heard the grit crunch under my soles and the chatter of others about me.

Behind us stalked Jurgen and Pieter. Armed, somewhere, somehow, though I hadn't spotted a gun on either of them. I guess they could always stomp on any attacker. They were a constant reminder of bad things.

"What about a walk on the beach?" Again Glass prompted me and I smiled and followed.

Ela beach was a rock and sand-strewn curve where ocean washed onto land in a desultory way. Like much of PNG life, the ocean was laidback. The hot weather made everything slow down.

We waded into the water that was a few degrees cooler than the air. Barefoot, we had to dodge the sea urchins, while we talked about how pretty the sea was and avoided serious topics.

"Thank you." I twined my fingers in his and tried to swing his arm.

"For what?" Glass stopped walking and turned to face me. "You don't need to say that. I'm here for you, no matter what."

I shook my head, staring at the ripples around his legs, feeling the freshness of the water on my skin, and the smooth surface of a cowrie shell under my toes, yet still the world crushed me. Realness versus what was in my mind.

"I need to thank you, I think. Because..." I shook my head again. "I don't think I can stay here much longer. I don't know where to go, and I'm scared of losing you if I do that, if I leave."

"Hey." He levered up my chin, in spite of my resistance. I scowled, trying to look aggressive, trying to say *we're not one anymore*, despite my heart saying the opposite. "Wren, you're looking too far ahead. Day by day. Remember? There are things you do *have* to do, and other things, like what you said, that you can discuss some more. I'll help you as much as I can and, damn, you're not going anywhere without me, unless you make me leave your side. Come here. I'm going to do some pouncing."

With a hold on both my hands, he drew me closer. I could tell he was watching and waiting for any protest. The hesitance took some of the *zing* from this but I desperately wanted exactly this – to be made to be close. I needed to know how important I might be, to him. I wanted force.

"There. Got you in my trap."

Yes, you do.

With great deliberation, he twisted my hair around and around his hand then he bent to kiss me.

My eyes stayed open long enough to see the *need* in his. *Yes.*

His lips on mine, his grasp on my hair, and his other hand at my hip, freed me and let me wander far away from my bleak past and future. And when he kissed me, I was his, because he'd dared to take me.

He wanted me for who I was, fucked-up head, or not.

At first he was considerate, soft, pressing his lips to mine then breaking away. I smiled from the intimate distance of a fraction of an inch, my lips moving on his as I murmured. "Forgotten how to do it?"

He smiled back, amused menace resonating in the twist of his mouth and eyebrow. "Fuck you, Miss Wren."

By several degrees of delicacy and violence, his kissing escalated.

We traded dominance, exchanged tongue-deep kisses, until it was my turn to swear and wriggle against him. The hard length of his cock against my stomach made me wish it was in me.

"Have a problem?"

"Something down there is sticking into me."

At that he snorted. "Patience is a virtue."

"Bastard." I wriggled again, deliberately toying, and kissed him with my tongue dipping between his lips, then I bit him.

From the flare in his eyes, I'd roused his nastier half. *At last.*

"Bad girl."

"Mm-hmm."

His fingers clawed into my hair, awakening familiar, delicious pain, and he dragged me onto him. Every muscle of his body was wrapped around me to keep me still or pressed against him. As he bent me backward, I had to part my thighs or risk my back snapping from the pressure. I whimpered. How I'd missed this.

He ground his mouth onto mine with enough force to make me gasp.

Then his phone rang.

Coitus interruptus? Well kissus interruptus.

I nearly giggled.

While he fumbled in his pocket, I opened my eyes. People were watching us, even if Jurgen and Pieter were being polite and not looking.

I didn't care and tucked myself into Glass's side.

"Hi, doc. Yeah. Yep. Yes, she's here." A long pause and with his next words I could hear the terseness in his voice. What had the doctor said?

I waited while he said goodbye then looked at him.

"What? It was about me, wasn't it?"

"Yes." He'd slipped his arm across my shoulders and now he stroked my arm. "I can tell you when we get back. Might be best?"

"And wonder what it is that can be so bad that you're worried? I can see you are. Tell me now, please." I put my hand up and touched his. "Please, Glass."

"Okay." He nodded slowly. "Okay. One of the tests was a pregnancy test." Frowning, he eyed me.

"No," I whispered. "It's not possible."

"He's certain. He even knows how long it's been. You're five weeks pregnant, Wren." His brow was wrinkling and unwrinkling. It was fucking with his head too. "But, it's just a baby. Remember that.

Just because it's his..."

I registered his fingers still stroking mine. His explanation sank in. How easy that was to say. No. Wait. A man, for a man to say that to his girlfriend, or whatever I was, about another man's baby, it *must* be painful.

"I'm...I need time to think. God. This is crazy." Crazy on top of yet more crazy. "Let's go back to your house."

I might not have morning sickness but throwing up was on the agenda.

"Of course."

What was I going to do with *his* child? His baby?

Once back at the house, I ended up on the bed again, staring at the ceiling, then I moved to the small secluded balcony, and looked out over the razor wire on the wall. In a haze of *what the fuck is happening with my life*, Hugh contacted us.

I have to keep this baby: my one thought as I pressed Glass's phone to my ear.

Whatever I said to him, when I hung up I could recall details but not exact words.

Gently, Glass took the phone from me, then pulled me around the table to sit on his lap.

"Baby girl, I wish I could take all this away from you, but I can't."

The sadness in his voice made me tear up. I refused to wipe them away, feeling them trail down my face as I lay there with my head resting on Glass's shoulder.

"He said I can sign papers at a lawyer's. Barratt and Bailey? Tomorrow at ten AM. I don't have to go back to Australia yet, he agreed to that."

"You didn't tell him about the baby?" He played with my hair and my eyelids drifted down. I wished I could stay there, with him petting me, forever.

"No. I didn't. Couldn't. Tomorrow. Okay?"

"Sure. He needs to know. You realize, Wren, that's partly *his* DNA the baby will have."

"Oh shit." I opened my mouth and let out a breath. I'd missed that. DNA was evidence. "That's true."

"Don't worry about it. We can ask the doctor if there's a safe way to get a sample. It may help..."

Track him down. I finished the sentence.

I had *him* inside me still.

That wrecked me. It was as if he could reach out and touch me, even here.

The steady heartbeat under my ear and the solidness of my man's body, his hands on me — that was all that was keeping me from floating away.

"I just wish..." And here was a crucial statement if ever there was one, but I said it anyway. "I wish it was our child, not his."

I had always wanted children, just not like this.

Glass stiffened. "Wow. I'm honored. You have no idea how much that means to me, Wren. I wish it too. I thought, since we were barely together, before, that I'd lost way with you. Maybe. You know?" He breathed close, into my hair and I shivered.

I'd said too much, dived in, but I didn't care.

"You've lost nothing. I heard from Jurgen how you waited for me, how much you tried to find me, how you went back there, after months, to see if you could do something." I took a big breath then plunged in. "Maybe this is too early to say the love word but I still want to try and see if we work out. I do."

"Me too."

We breathed together, for a while, and my cares lifted away. I needed to be near this man.

"Wren, this child, it's half yours. To me, that's what counts. I'll stand by whatever you want. Okay?"

"Okay. Thank you."

"It's nothing. It's what anyone with sense would say."

I snorted and smiled. Glass's *nothing* was better than most people's everything. Then I drew his hand up to my face and kissed his fingertips. I pulled his hand over my eyes and hid under there. Peaceful, that was how I felt with Glass holding me, at peace.

CHAPTER 33
Moghul

At two-twenty PM the first text from the surveillance summed up her situation nicely.

The subject is five weeks pregnant. Staying at the house of previously mentioned Male One. She will be with Male Two at ten AM tomorrow for legal matters. Paper signing, etc.

I stared at the screen for ages before tossing it to the bed and heading out to the pool.

Pregnant.

The baby had to be mine.

Two things stood out as important.

First. I'd left evidence inside her, and therefore would have to change the brand of condoms I used, or stop fucking my women so hard. Haha.

Second. Damn. That was mine. Wren was having my, *our*, baby.

A hundred and fifty laps was enough and I stood in the water, leaned on my forearms on the edge of the pool, with my chin resting on my arms, and I stared at the patio where I'd once whipped and fucked her.

The sandstone was warm and as relaxing as a massage after that long swim.

How...how could I possibly leave her with Glass with my child growing in her?

Fate was toying with me and having another laugh. I never changed my mind after deciding something this important. Yet I'd already reversed a little and had her watched. And if I hadn't done that, who knows what would've happened? Could they get my DNA just from her blood?

Wet, I padded to the laptop, dried my hands, and googled if you could extract the baby's cells from the mother's blood. Seemed like it would be possible, later in pregnancy due to the baby shedding cell-free DNA, but not yet. What better reason could I possibly have to retrieve her?

I could have her killed and her body disappeared, but that was as likely as me buying the moon. The thought that she might have an abortion made my gut twist. Such a decision was possible and, as things stood, I had no say in what happened to my child. Fuck that.

This was as good as a sign from above, if I believed in anyone above, that I should have her. I'd thought her an impossible puzzle and thought not to hurt her so much that she would no longer be Wren, but this was a sign saying, *try*.

A big, neon, fireworks-display, orchestral accompanied, sign.

And it was what I'd wanted all along.

I walked back to the room naked, still dripping, and picked up the phone, sent the text.

I want her back.

Say again?

I want her back. Do it.

Impossible. Before it was her and one man. Now it's two separate security operations. Man One's and Man Two's. Impossible.

I thought for ten minutes, lying flat on my back on the bed. I never changed my mind. Now I'd done it within a few days over something ridiculous. He probably thought I'd gone mad.

Name a price.

I'd need far more than five men. Twelve or more. Someone will get hurt doing this.

Name a price.

Two hours later his answer arrived.

Men will die. But it might be possible due to inside info. One million now. One more when it's done, successful or not.

I read it, did some maths, and sent my reply.

Money will be transferred by ten AM tomorrow. Do it. Do it successfully or no second payment.

Received. I'll text you when we have her.

Well, well, well. Done. I whistled as I walked to the kitchen, did a quick spin on my heels when I entered, and smiled.

I opened the fridge.

Bottles of wine, milk, and not much else except ancient salad and three-day-old chicken. Time to order something appropriate for a celebration.

I speed dialed the restaurant.

"Hi. I'd like to order your Greek pizza with aioli, garlic bread, and some of those barbecue buffalo chicken wings."

CHAPTER 34
Glass

Watching Wren, in her businesslike black dress and those sinful high heels, disappear up the steps to the lawyer's, played with my heart. Badly. I didn't quite trust Hugh.

The man had been great for a while but the long waiting time after her abduction had turned him against me for some reason I hadn't fathomed. If anything, I suspected it was my criminal activities. If ever there was a man with a broomstick up his ass, it was Hugh. Funny, because I'd seen him skirt the law to keep Wren safe.

I leaned against the Land Rover and Jurgen stuck his head and elbow out the window,

"We're good? Just waiting for her to come out?"

"Yup. She's got her phone. I told her to contact me if she needs backup. I can run up those stairs and beat Hugh to a pulp if I have to." *If he makes her cry.*

I'd never seen her cry as much as she had during the past few days. Though that was an expected side effect.

"If she's in there more than an hour, we go in."

Jurgen pulled a face and screwed up his ugly nose. The bar through his eyebrow glinted silver. He pointed up the street and his multicolored arm tattoos flexed along with his biceps muscle. If he weren't big and male, I'd call him out for prettying himself up. "We've got the back covered. The underground garage entrance is that next gate up that you see."

"I know." I crossed my ankles and let myself wonder if Hugh would give in over Australia. Wren wanted to stay away entirely.

That was impossible, even I knew that.

He'd insisted on seeing her alone except for the lawyers. I owed him some time with her and she wanted to talk to him too. They had years of history and I was the recent man that really should never ever have had the slightest chance of getting near Wren. She was pretty, rich, clean, and she was...innocent. No longer though. No longer innocent. I still felt a tearing at my inner self whenever I thought of how much blame I carried. She'd said not to worry myself, but my thoughts never went away.

I sighed.

Why did life have to be so hard for a woman like her? Unfair. Me, Hugh, sure. We deserved everything thrown at us. Her, no. She was my angel.

The metal gates to the underground car park began to roll up at the same time as my phone buzzed with a text message. I scrambled into the car and two black limos roared out. No three.

Sam, a blond, clean-shaven, clean-skinned man who looked like a boy band member next to Jurgen, had our engine going. "Is that her?"

Why would it be? But, I frowned at the message.

Going to another address where the lawyer is caught up in work. See you there.

The address was a couple of miles away and the limos were going the right direction.

I slapped the back of the driver's side seat rest. "It's her. Go. Wait. Jurgen you drive, switch with Sam. Sam, go in and check the office. Make sure this is all okay. We'll pick you up on the way back." I watched as he hopped out and ran for the stairs. "Now we can go."

I got on the comm to the others to make sure they followed then sat back. If Hugh was trying to pull some stunt with this, Wren would give him an earful. She might be teary but she still had backbone.

CHAPTER 35
Wren

This was not one of Hugh's usual vehicles. A black sedan, sure, and it was clean, but the insides looked rough, like the car had seen use for years.

When Hugh and the lawyer's receptionist both informed me that Mr. Bailey was tied up at other offices and we were going to have to drive there to do the documents, I was fine with it. I had no reason to think Hugh would do anything wrong. He never had.

But when I reached for my phone, I found someone had swapped my phone for another. The password was always the same for my phone. Hugh had badgered me to change it, but knew I kept using the same one. Slick and rapid theft was one of his specialties. When?

I stared at the phone, the car jogging me sideways. "Hugh, what are you doing? You've got my phone, haven't you?" I cocked an eyebrow at him, smoothed the skirt of my dress, all the while wondering if I should pull the Beretta from the handbag.

To use on Hugh? No. Silly.

In the front seats, past the glass partition, were his driver and a guard I recognized from years of having Hugh and his men shepherd me around. He was as old as Hugh and had babied me from when I was nine or so. Lollipops had been his specialty back then.

"We're going to the airport." Hugh's steady gaze brooked no argument.

Fuck that. I'd had enough of being meek.

"No. We are not. Glass will be following us. He won't allow this if I don't wish to go. I won't allow it. You can't even have a passport for me."

"Glass is following a different set of cars. I can get around the lack of passport. You know that in a place like this." He jerked his chin at the passing streets of Port Moresby. "I can do what I like with the right connections."

I nodded. "Okay. Yes. You probably can. But this is kidnapping, Hugh. Are you prepared to do that? Just to get me to go to Australia and talk to the police?"

"By the time we get there, you'll have agreed with me."

With my knuckle to my forehead, I bowed my head a moment. "No. You have to see that I cannot go there."

"Why?"

I choked up. "I *can't*. He is there. No matter how much you say you will guard me, I can't. I just can't. Not yet."

I watched him take that in. He shifted on the seat, sighed, looking a perfect gentleman in his suit, with a silver tie and silver cufflinks.

"No, I don't want to kidnap you, my dear. You know that." For the only time ever, I think I saw tears in his eyes. "I want you away from him, from here. If you need to go to a different country I will arrange that. Just don't stay with him. He isn't a safe individual."

Glass? I was growing to love that man but somehow I doubted Hugh was going to see the light. The strain of this on top of everything else was telling on me. I drew a shaky breath.

"He, Glass, was there for me. Yes, he made a mistake in letting me get kidnapped, but he was there. I know he came back, stayed in Australia, even though it was dangerous for him. He was there again even two weeks ago."

"Rubbish."

I shrugged. "Jurgen let it slip. His hair color is still dark. That disguise was for me. It's only washing out now." I quipped, needing to make light of this, "Any man who will dye his hair for me has my heart."

The car was pulling to a halt. Past a row of cars and trucks, I could see the tail of a big commercial plane taxiing off the runway.

"I didn't know that. I missed it. The trust took me off you, your security, a month ago, since you seemed gone." He tilted his head, looking morose, with his mouth downturned. "I'm sorry, Wren. I should've been there too."

"Then you can sympathize with Glass. Hugh..." I took a breath to pace myself, my voice trembling. "I think, I may, be coming to love Glass. I know that's outside your realm of –"

"Stop." He held out a hand. "No need. I understand now, in a way. Now that I see you, and have heard you speak. Your emotions are in your voice and how you react. You always were a little wild. The man appeals to that side of you." He put his hand to the side of the door and opened it. "So. You're not going to leave?"

I shook my head, firmly. "No."

"Okay. I will sort this out for you, as best I can." He ran a hand over his close-shorn hair. "I will."

"Thank you, Hugh."

"No need. It is my job. We'll return to the lawyer's, meet Glass there. However, before I forget to say this, Wren. I've always been proud to be your man. Proud to guard you, no matter what ups and downs we faced and I hope to do so in the future. Thank you."

Wow. I smiled.

"No. Thank you." I reached over and gave him a brief half hug.

As he went to climb out, I recalled that Glass had told me to tell him about the child. "Wait."

"Yes?" He leaned in.

"I'm not sure this is the best time but Glass said it might be important to you, and I know it will be, just maybe not in the way he thinks." Shit, how did I tell him news I was still struggling with?

"Go ahead."

"Hugh. I'm pregnant. With that man's child. Five weeks." As he blinked at me, clearly shocked, I went on. "I'm going to keep the baby. I've decided."

"That's. Damn. That's... There are ramifications to this."

Hugh swearing? I had hoped for more sympathy than *ramifications.* While he said something more, two men in suits approaching the car caught my attention. His? I opened my mouth to ask but what Hugh had said made me stop.

"What? Say again?"

"This changes everything. If he's still watching you, and discovers this, you're in a hundred times the danger."

He meant the DNA? Really? Why? I hadn't connected that with increased danger. I had no logic to my terrors about *him* coming to get me. He was like the bogey man or Freddy from *Nightmare on Elm Street.*

"We need to go. You're not as safe as I thought." He twisted to slip back into the car.

One of the men beyond raised a weapon and shot Hugh, twice.

From the sound, one bullet hit Hugh's back, the second hit the side of his neck and sprayed blood at me, splattering on the seat and across my dress, my face. He crumpled and slid from the car but somehow managed to slam the door.

Despite my vision blurring, my training kicked in.

Where were Hugh's other men, other cars? I ripped the Beretta from my bag. I had a universal lock control in the back and I slapped the button, heard the locks click down. The attackers had been joined by others on all sides, but if we gunned the engine we could leave them behind.

I had to go. *Fuck the world.* I had to leave him behind. Dread thumped through my head in big nasty boots. The guard in the front of the car had his gun out. The driver had pressed the accelerator and we jerked forward then stopped as another vehicle crossed in front and blocked us.

"Reverse!" I screamed.

The guard in front raised his weapon and put a bullet in the driver's head. More blood, this time spattered across the driver's window.

Ohmigod.

I wrenched open the partition an inch and shot the guard twice while he was turning. Blood sprayed the windscreen, one shot went straight through his head and pocked the glass. It held. Bulletproof, of course.

The world cracked. My heart seemed to pause. Hugh was out there but he'd have a vest on so maybe he'd be okay...and I...I...

No, he wouldn't be okay. *Don't panic. Do.*

Plan: get to the driver seat and accelerate out of here. But as I pushed the partition all the way open, someone held Hugh up to the back window, slammed him there, really. His face bloody, there were new wounds on his head from being assaulted, I guessed. Seconds before, they hadn't existed. He was dazed, out of it, his eyes mostly shut, blood pulsing from the main hole in his neck. He needed aid, fast, or he'd die. I could hear the scream of words from the man holding him.

"Open the fucking door or I kill him. Open it now!"

I counted five men on that side of the car and the man in the front was somehow still functioning, though I couldn't see him, only hear his moans and the scrabble of his hands on the upholstery.

I shrank into the seat, my hands shaking, though they gripped my pistol. My jaw and my head ached. Everything, all the death, all the blood, the violence, seemed to pour into my head and make it pulse. From the way darkness encroached, people crowded the car behind me. Could I hear sirens? I wasn't sure. If I could hold out, they couldn't get me.

These men were his. They had to be. They would take me back to *him* if I let them get hold of me.

I looked to Hugh for some answer, but there was nothing. I wasn't sure he was alive anymore. The blood smearing the window, the red trails bubbling down the glass, made it difficult to see him.

"Decide!" the man screamed. He ground a gun into Hugh's head. "Come out or he dies!"

There are two endings to this story. From here, the reader may choose to read the darker Thorn Path, which begins at Chapter 50, or continue on and read the next chapter of the Blade Path.

Though some of the words are the same, the decisions are not.

"...The flutter of a butterfly's wing can cause a typhoon halfway around the world" - Chaos Theory.

CHAPTER 36 BLADE PATH

BLADE PATH

Wren

The man was bluffing but would Hugh forgive me, if he wasn't ? If he could, Hugh would tell me to do this. He mightn't even be alive. I might give myself up for nothing. He'd tell me to do this. I just needed time. The airport security or the police would be here soon.

Unable to speak at first, I shook my head while staring into the angry face of the man holding the gun to Hugh.

"Last chance!"

I couldn't do this, could I? I wavered, first one side, then the other. These men were determined and I could hear no sounds of rescue, no sirens. The gun was so close to the back windscreen that I could see his finger on the trigger and it was blanched white. A vignette of death and I was the pivot. I was the decider.

If I said no, and he fired, *god*, I put my hand to my stomach. It wasn't just me anymore. I had my baby to keep safe. Yet, what sort of person would I be if I put Hugh in more danger? He was much more than a guy who helped guard me. Giving myself up didn't mean death for me or my child. There was hope for me, but for Hugh, if I said the wrong words?

I didn't know anything for certain. If I could flip a coin to do this...

It was me though, only my decision.

I couldn't condemn him. "Don't shoot! Don't. Shoot. Please. I'll do it."

I was giving myself to these men. A terrible decision, but morally it was surely the right one? Funny, but I prayed they were *his*. At least then, I knew where I was going, and that he valued me as a person. If they were merely terrorists or random criminals, I was only a pawn or a money source to them. I bowed my head and moved along the seat until I was near enough to reach for the door. My hand seemed unconnected to me, and a million miles away.

"Stop! The gun! Put it on the floor."

The Beretta shook while I stared at it. By putting it down, I was sealing my fate. I listened again for sirens, for any sign of help coming.

"You have three seconds! Three..."

I didn't look at him, but I placed the gun on the floor then unlocked the door. A man hauled me out.

At the bang of the gun, I jerked and turned.

No. He wouldn't have. No. I refused to believe, clinging to hope.

But he had. Hugh slid down the smeared window, boneless, then off the trunk, and flopped onto the road.

My hand was at my mouth and I choked on sobs, my nose running with tears. He didn't move at all, or breathe, but his blood meandered down the glass and dripped from the car's bumper.

*****

Glass

"She's gone, man." Jurgen's words made me angry enough to punch him, but I didn't.

I leaned forward, staring through the windscreen and down the street to the car park entry.

The police swarmed over the ambush site, lights flashing, uniformed officers checking for evidence. An ambulance had taken away one man but the rest of the bodies had been left, clearly dead. Most of the casualties seemed to be Hugh's men. I had no idea how the attackers had managed it.

Outnumbered? Out planned? Maybe betrayed?

Who had diverted us? Hugh, or whoever our enemy was? Wren was gone and, from snatches of overheard conversations from onlookers, she'd been their goal. For some reason, Vetrov had let her go, then come back for her.

CARI SILVERWOOD

"She's not gone, Jurgen, just missing. This time I'll find her."

"Sure. We will. I want to get these guys too." His quiet assurance helped. He looked up from where he'd been reading something on his phone. "Remember how you told me to give Pieter the notes with all the answers Wren gave us?"

I waited, frowning.

"Well, Pieter texted me before we started this, as we were rolling out the gate. The name Chris, he remembers it from when he was working for Vetrov in North Queensland."

"And? We need more than just that."

"I think we have that more. Jazmine has seen the notes too. He asked her about the name and it triggered a memory. Chris helped her and Pieter escape. She thought he was a good guy, in a way. The other guards at the time said he was supposed to be an accountant on Magnetic Island. Pieter's found an accountant who works there with that first name. It has to be him. He dug, found out when he graduated from university, found an old picture on the net. Jazmine says it's him. And Zoe, the other name Wren heard Chris say, that was one of the other girls held with Jazmine."

I sat back. "Shit. We can do this. I can be in Australia tomorrow. At the island the day after. I can pay this Chris a visit. He knows Vetrov. He has to."

"Yes. And we're coming with you. Me, Pieter, Sam, anyone else I can convince, along with all the weapons we need to take out this bastard."

I stared. "You'll be fucked if the cops find you."

"You think that's going to stop us? We have to get Wren back. Shut the fuck up and plan shit like you always do."

"Huh." I sucked in a breath then grinned. "Doing it. Get us back to the compound. We're going hunting for bear and Goldilocks."

"Now you're talking." He started the engine. "I always wanted a bearskin rug."

Think positive. Planning was the key. I was getting her back, no matter what I had to do.

240

CHAPTER 37

Wren

I was in the back of a van when they told me they weren't allowed to drug me – within a few minutes of being dragged from the car and thrown there. My wrists had been ziptied, my mouth gagged, and I was jammed up against the back of the front seats. Three men were in here with me, all well dressed and normal. If big, well-armed, and menacing when they deigned to look at me, could be thought of as normal.

The worst of them had leaned down and smiled. I knew evil smiles well. He had them down pat.

"No drugs for you, but no one told us not to nail your hands to your pretty thighs if you annoy me."

I shuddered and leaned away.

"Are you going to be good for me, Wren?"

I nodded. Did he think I'd say no?

No drugs. They were probably his then. *Good.* I shuddered. Or maybe bad.

I guessed that *he* knew I was pregnant. The man wanted his child alive and healthy. Did he have a heart, after all?

Nails in my legs? These men were putrid thugs. I didn't know if the threat was real. If they did that I'd end up with an infection where the nails went in, and how cheerful and clinical was I to be following that idea to the logical end?

Damn idiot-fucking assholes. I'd behave, because these men were vicious. They'd find a way to make me be good, no matter what Vetrov had told them.

And my poor, poor Glass, he'd be blaming himself again.

Hugh is dead.

I tried to calm myself. No use exhausting myself worrying over the past – he'd have insisted I mourn him when I had a better opportunity.

Woman up. Grow some lady balls. I could hear him say that. He'd say it just like that in his stiff accent just to shock me. I smiled sadly.

Everyone around me was dying, and all because of *him*.

The men took me places and I tried to stay alert and to think because that was the smart, Hugh-logical thing to do. Not that it helped much, but it did make me feel proactive.

Positive thinking.

I lay blindfolded and gagged in a plane, in the trunk of a car, and the back of a van, and said nothing. But my mind, my mind was on fire. This time, he'd really pissed me off.

They delivered me on time, apparently. Or so *he* said when he opened the trunk and found me.

It was nighttime.

"Hello, Wren. I hope they treated you well?" The familiar roughness of his voice had my full attention in an instant. I felt his hand on my hair, saw torchlight through the blindfold. He lifted my head as if examining me then the light seemed to travel down my body.

I growled when he pulled my legs apart.

"Quiet. I'm not doing anything to you." Then he gathered the skirt of my dress upward, exposing me all the way to my lower back.

He was silent and I guessed he was looking at his brand.

"That looks good. You seem unharmed. Treating you badly is my prerogative. As is treating you well, from now on. Welcome back, my girl."

Arrogance. I seethed.

I was fed up with being his pretty girl to play with.

Then he pushed up the blindfold. I could see him. The real him. No mask.

Remember this.

He laid down the torch and the light bounced off the roof of the trunk — and he kissed me, with his hands cradling my face. Mine were still tied at my back. He kissed me as if I were something delicate that might break. I considered biting him but no, I had to play it cool, act as if I was cowed.

He'd killed Hugh. That was enough to keep my fires burning, tamped down, but burning.

"Welcome back. My name, Wren, is Moghul."

Then he slammed shut the trunk and drove me to his house. All the way there, being bounced around against the carpeted trunk, I ran his face through my memory. He didn't look a monster without the mask. Brown, artfully scruffy hair that on another man would make me itch to set right, and his eyes, such warm eyes. I'd seen hardness in them before and I'd felt fear. Not now. Not this time.

I'd nearly cut his throat and he'd only let me go. What would he do if I castrated him? He had limits, this man. That didn't make this right, but it gave him a weakness, which had to be good.

I smiled grimly.

Moghul. An odd name.

He'd looked...contemplative, as well as quietly triumphant.

I wanted to wipe that smile off his face. Just because he knew how to play my body like an instrument, didn't mean he could make me his. Shit was going to happen. I was going to make sure of that. The man had killed Hugh by proxy. He deserved to have a truck fall on him, and then some. Every time I'd tried, I had gotten closer to killing him. This time it would happen.

Think fucking positive.

Bambi time, for a while. I had to pretend, but this time I wouldn't miss.

CHAPTER 38

Moghul

When I let her out of the trunk, the garage doors were wound down, trapping us in the huge space with the expanse of concrete and the BMW, the corvette, and my vintage motorbikes.

I studied her, stepping away to take in all of her. She swayed a little but seemed able to stand. All that time in the dark and tied up would've played havoc with her muscles and balance, plus her hands were trapped behind her back.

I tsked, smiling sadly, thinking of all the perverted things I could do to her...if I could get her in the right mindset. I knew more about who she was now.

She was barefoot on the cold hardness of the concrete. The black dress was pretty and swerved in at all the right places, curved out at all the right ones – her breasts and hips. I'd burn it. She needed no reminders of her past and it must be filthy. Her hair had been squashed by the blindfold and I wanted see it hang free and clean and beautiful.

I stepped in and untied the blindfold, then dropped the cloth to the floor. I removed the gag then locked a steel chain-link collar on her neck and clicked the leash to it.

"I'm putting my cuffs back on you also, but you're going to walk with me up to the viewing room without me binding you apart from the collar. Is that understood?"

"Yes, Sir." Her reply was soft, meek even.

"Thank you for calling me Sir."

One eyebrow rose, as if she were surprised, but holding in her reaction. Holding back was not good. I wanted to see her emotions raw. She'd regressed since I'd let her go.

The last text had underlined how little time I had. Glass had tracked down Chris. If Chris was at risk, I was at risk, and Glass had arrived a half a day ago. The man had turbo charged his way here, taking risks of detection to fly farther down the Queensland coast than he normally would. According to my intel, the rest of his men would arrive later today.

My man had done the trip the safe way, and so, this came down to mere hours.

I had the equivalent of a special forces team ready to raid my house, once they had my address, but right now, Glass was vulnerable.

I'd told Chris and offered him alternatives, offered help. I could've told him to eliminate Glass but I'd lost my taste for ordering or performing homicide. Guess I'd never had one. With business...I'd just disconnected from what I'd told someone to do. It had been like firing an employee, necessary, nasty, but someone had to make the decision. My first and only personal kill a couple of months ago had convinced me of the wrongness. I was done with this dirty business.

Whatever Chris decided, it was his affair; I was done.

If he dealt with Glass, he could have my business, do what he liked with it. I'd extracted what money I could and I had other reserves in banks and real estate in half a dozen countries.

Yet the ground was cracking beneath my feet. With only Wren to take care of, for the first time in my life, I was unsure. She carried our child and I'd come to realize I loved her as much as I could love anyone. Would that be enough for her?

I led her away and into the hallway, only to see the devastation in her bearing – red-rimmed eyes, the sway in her gait, the lowness of her head.

"Come here." I scooped her up and carried her to the bathroom.

Her lack of aggression encouraged me.

After making her drink some water, I stripped her naked and urged her under the warm jets. I helped her wash, smoothing the soap and shampoo over her body, becoming reacquainted with her curves, her secret places. I stood naked under the water with her and held her to me but it was impossible not to do more than feel. I sneaked kisses and curled her hair around my hand, made her stand still while I used my mouth on her neck, her shoulders, and her plump nipples.

Was it half an hour? More? I took my time.

Though at first expressionless, she began to shiver at my touch and at my bites on her nape and breasts...she succumbed, even opening her legs when I slid my hand there and cupped my palm over her mons, slipped my finger partway inside her.

The collar on her neck drew my eye. With my chin on her shoulder and my hand between her legs, I studied how the gleaming metal links rested on her skin. I'd bought that and placed it on her.

"Mine," I murmured, kissing her below her ear.

She shook, but kept her head down.

Hiding? Later, I would make her look me in the eye.

After drying her, and being sure she was stronger, I led her to the viewing room. Both of us were naked and a little damp, but that was fine. The aircon would dry us.

Knowing what was in there, I picked her up before the entrance and carried her in, then I sat down on one of the sofas with her cuddled into me and half on my lap. The equipment was behind her and I'd made sure she couldn't see it. The block and tackle, the ropes and hooks. I surveyed my preparations, feeling the distilled excitement that S and m gave me, and wondered if I was about to do the right thing.

I breathed in, out, closed my eyes and simply absorbed the need I had to cradle Wren.

I had to care for her. I'd always done that as a Dom to my submissives but this was new to me. When I had her like this, with her head tucked into me, my arms around her, I had to suppress my strength, torn between cuddling her gently and an insane yearning to hold her so tight we'd merge, and I'd become a part of her – flesh, bone, blood, mind.

"Talk to me, please. Tell me everything. I need to know. I want to take some of your pain, if I can."

She stiffened and I braced myself for the storm.

CHAPTER 39

Wren

How dare he? Take some of my pain? Hah. So ridiculous.

There was pain, and there was what he'd made me endure, which needed a whole new word.

I was supposed to be pretending to be soft and overcome, like a baby fawn. Fuck that.

"Your men..." How could he be so *fucking* patronizing? "Killed my friend, Hugh. How could you do that to us and then dare to say what you have?"

I bristled, feeling ill, wanting to tear myself away from him but sure he wouldn't allow it. There was *nothing* he could say that would delete the past.

"I'm sorry."

Even that, even though by saying it, he admitted guilt. He must know how vicious those men could be? I could imagine him telling them to *get the girl, do whatever you have to*. Palming off blame wasn't going to work when Hugh had been murdered.

My anger petered out and sadness arrived, an unwelcome guest, but I had no real say this time. It overcame me.

I sobbed. I sobbed into his chest, the man who was to blame for kidnapping me and killing my friends because I had nowhere else to go. He was an evil fucker. I hated him, but I had, once, liked, pitied, and respected other parts of him in the most appalling mish mash of fucked-up emotions ever. Now, hate had become the marauding monster.

Revenge was for the weak or something? Best served cold? I needed revenge and I'd take it hot, cold, or flambéed with cognac and blood.

"It's not your fault, Wren. I don't know what they did but I didn't tell them to do it specifically. I'm very sorry. I'm not a good man but I'm sorry that happened. I don't want to hurt you. Not like that."

The truth? No. Excuses. I shot into incandescent anger.

"They shot him! Then they demanded I give myself up or they'd kill him! And when I did, they shot him anyway!" I couldn't help seeing it again in my head. The gun. The blood. The abrupt *bang*. The way Hugh's head shook at the impact yet nothing else of him changed. The blood still meandered down the glass, as he slid off the car. "They shot him." I gasped a few times, my throat having trouble figuring out whether to breathe or choke on my tears, before I found my voice again. "Your men...Moghul. *They* did it."

"Whatever method they used, it was not mine. I've given you enough leeway. Calm down."

There was a rawness in his voice that I'd never heard before – not just anger. Sadness and anger? Didn't *matter*. He was a sanctimonious bastard, trying to dodge responsibility.

"Yes, I wanted you. I made mistakes." He laughed, bitterly. "Most of them lately were because of you. I need you in my life and I'm not letting you go, Wren. I'm also going to care for you. I'm the only man who truly understands who you are."

Sheer goddamned arrogance.

"You? You! Hah!"

I held my breath. After his last instruction I would surely be punished for that, but nothing happened. Something was holding him back.

"I noted that on my list, for later."

"Oh." Survival mode kicked back in. "Sorry, Sir."

"You will be."

"Oh." Damn. He was only inches away and looking happy at the prospect of torturing me.

I wrenched my thoughts into line. What did he know? Was I right to fear myself, after all?

Fuck him.

"How," I ventured. "You've barely talked to me. Glass knows me, understands me, not you."

"Glass?" He chuckled and his eyes narrowed. "You think he's wonderful? Glass was there when your father died. He led the team that assaulted my House. He may have fired the shot that killed him."

"What?" I blinked, dumbstruck.

"What I said. Glass is not who you think he is."

Glass? My man, my hero? I stared at Moghul's chest, at his nipple of all things. I couldn't get my head around this. Yet it made total sense. It explained why Glass had first come to me, the unease I'd felt when he led me around town. That feeling he was concealing something.

"True?"

"Doubting my word?"

"No. I don't." I stared down at my breasts, avoiding his eyes.

Glass might've lied to me, I'd even suspected that something was wrong, but what he'd done since, it meant more. If he was in front of me, sure, I would question him, and I was sure he'd confess. Probably on one knee, before upending me and flip-flopping my butt. He was still my man.

"You think telling me bad news about Glass will somehow make me like you instead?"

He wrenched my chin upward. "Apologize. Now."

I gulped, paralyzed, as always, by him staring me down. His rules, his house. I was dancing on the edge, talking back to him.

"I'm sorry, Sir."

"How many apologies is that now? You've forgotten how I expect you to behave. I can be fair. That doesn't mean I'm weak." His fingers tightened and he held me there a while longer. My angry self drained away, second by forceful second, until all I could fixate on was Moghul looking at me.

"I'm sorry." Repeating that had slipped out.

His smile was mean. "I think it best I go on to the next step."

I shivered. *Next step? What is this?*

Nothing I would like.

Confused and frightened of what was coming, I said the one thing that might stall him. "I'm pregnant with your child."

"I know. It's why I decided I had to have you, little Wren."

"Then you can't punish me. It might make me lose the baby."

"This next isn't punishment. Think of it more as a test. I'm going to be careful. You can stand this because without this we will be *nothing*. I don't want to be your nothing, Wren. I want all of you. And I will do anything. Fucking anything to make it come true."

And then, I glimpsed that part of him I'd often seen, the Machiavellian sadist.

This was the man I'd tried to knife only days ago. I could still see the scratch on his neck when I looked. Why wasn't he afraid I'd do it again? He wanted to be everything to me.

A weird notion arrived, front and center. Did he think he was in love with me?

That would be almost too sad. My brow wrinkled as I tried to think through that.

Bad was good. Good was bad. Hugh was *dead*. My mind up and dumped me into a swamp where none of my ideas would come to an end.

Forget. Think. Dwelling on my misery wasn't going to help.

"Look at me, Wren."

On cue, I raised my head, the sofa upholstery rasping against my ear as I did so, and locked my gaze on him. It was easy to do, far easier than disobeying. As I looked into his eyes, at the darkness of his gaze, I sank thankfully into that waiting space. I knew I was doing it, recognized the feeling. The carousel of gibbering that had filled my head only seconds before died away. Maybe I was best not thinking.

I needed this.

"Put your wrists at your back."

I hesitated.

A familiar transformation had come over his face. That omen of sadism: *I want to do things to you that I'll like, though you may not.*

I realized I wanted to pain. Needed it. *He'll do it to me anyway.*

I could struggle crazily, maybe get hurt in the process, or I could let myself go. I wasn't going to win and I could feel that submissive mindset, just a breath away, like I could cocoon myself there and lose the anger, the sorrow, just for a while.

"My baby?" I whispered.

"You'll be fine. Trust me. Be good."

Trust? That was the problem.

While I was debating with myself, he grunted then manhandled me onto my stomach and locked my wrists together. I'd barely resisted. This close, I knew I couldn't win.

"Forgetting how to obey? It'll come back to you soon. Very soon."

I was already breathing easier, slipping into calmness. This would happen. I guess I trusted him with my body, even if he had the morals of a rat.

Moghul stood and pulled me to my feet.

I could see what he intended, now. The ropes hanging from some sort of block and tackle affair beside his pit, the steel table, the row of hooks, the bottles and swabs. I swallowed.

Oh. Oh fuck. Maybe I had energy left for fear, after all.

CHAPTER 40

Moghul

I led Wren over to where my equipment waited and made her climb onto the table. As her stomach met the cold stainless steel, she winced. I smiled. That was the least of her worries.

"Keep your eyes on me. This is *not* punishment. I think you'll like this. However, if you take your eyes off me, I will be displeased."

"Yes, Sir."

I wanted her focused, absolutely, on what I did, not on what might happen in the future. The now was important. Despite her recent rebellion, that softness came over her that submissives often showed when they were in their happy place.

I ducked to her eye level. "That helps?"

It took her a moment, but she answered. "Yes."

"Good. You know I like hurting you, but this, though it may hurt, I think you'll like it. If I'm wrong, your screams will tell me."

"Screams?"

"Yes." I straightened. "Good screams."

Though I'd researched this, done needle piercings, and even tried using one of these big seven gauge hooks on a sub, I was no expert. Which was partly why I'd opted to fill my pit with water, and why I planned to take some of her weight with ropes. I didn't expect this to fail but adding in fallback safety mechanisms was always worthwhile.

The pit had other uses too.

Slow and steady.

The four hooks shone where I'd lined them up on the tray.

"Be very still while I place these." I swabbed her back with alcohol and drew an X on the places I intended to pierce her. High on her back. A common place for suspensions. As I worked I filled her in on what I was doing.

"Hook suspension has quite a history. The Mandan tribe used it as part of their Oh-Kee-Pah ceremony." I went on, steadily doling out the info, in a bass voice, making it a rhythmic thing so she could sink into the moment.

I was pleased at how well she was responding. Her slow breathing and the lack of focus in her eyes, all said she'd hit subspace already.

"Here." I found the poster of the young woman at a suspension convention being suspended from four back hooks, unrolled it and hung it from the railing surrounding the pit. "Look how happy she is."

"Incredible," she whispered.

"Keep looking at me. Nothing exists but you and me. Remember that."

Wren was going to love this. My final act before the test begun. This was something that compelled me. Wren was never going to commit herself to me unless I forced the choice. Once she decided, she'd mentally be prepared. I'd push it, make it a habit. I'd make her see she should be mine.

If I was wrong, so be it. All or nothing. Life was meant to be lived, not sleepwalked through.

The water in the pit was so still it looked like glass. Once I suspended her over it, there might be blood, when I played with her. Blood was such an odd liquid, a symbol of life as well as death.

I'd not told her all I meant to. That would have to wait. She'd seemed too unsettled and angry for me to tell her about her fiancé and his death. It was a devastating piece of information and what I was about to do would be devastating enough by itself. From the reports sent to me of her psychiatric evaluation, I needed her calm before I told her.

Later, when I knew she was one hundred percent mine.

"I'm pushing in the first."

"Mmm." She grunted, once, as I pierced the skin with a needle in preparation for the hook.

When I popped that hook through her shoulder blade skin, and out again, she reacted so beautifully it took my breath away. The way her breathing altered, the flush on her face, the little wriggle she did against the table. This had aroused her. The woman was such a masochist.

CHAPTER 41

Wren

When he said, "I'm pushing in the first," the room paused. I tensed, feeling connected to the table by the pressure of the most sexual points of my body, as if they bore all my weight.

My blood seemed to pulse stronger, and I became aware of the erotic...undertones of this act.

Moghul, shoving metal into me, while I was bound.

I needed to stop fantasizing. My arousal shocked me.

The thick hook sinking into my skin beneath my shoulder blade sent a wave of pleasure cascading through me so quickly I gasped, and I was almost coming before I grasped what was happening. I bowed my head and shut my eyes, feeling him push it out the other side, determined not to show any signs of how this affected me.

"Hmmm." He stopped before me, stared a moment, then retrieved the next hook.

On the second hook, I gritted my teeth, but not from the pain, from the effort of concealing my reaction.

The third made me arch a miniscule amount before I caught myself, and I squirmed to relieve the building tension. My clit seemed ready to electrify the table. If it swelled more, if there was more pressure. I gasped and put my forehead to the cool table.

Three in me. *God. Why was I getting off on this?*

"Last one." He pinched up a fold.

Fuck. The metal was inside me already. I keened as it penetrated further, arching my back despite him leaning on me. Then the hook popped out the other side, and I was coming before I could stop myself. Full-on shuddering and gasping.

Controlling the aftershocks was harder to do; not panting, even more so.

I found him before me, once more at eye level. "Did you just climax?"

I blushed hot, wanting to hide.

"Wren, answer me."

"Maybe. I guess...yes?"

"Ahh. Good. I was right."

"Arrogance was always your best feature," I mumbled from where I lay, recovering, trembling, reminded of the presence in my back of something foreign.

He chuckled. "Now I just have to tie your legs and hoist you into the air over my pit."

I managed to think that through. "Above the pit?" That thing was deep.

"Don't worry. I filled it with water."

So now I only had to worry about drowning if I fell in as well as my body hanging from hooks.

I squeezed shut my eyes.

"Wren. Look at me."

I snapped them open.

He tied my legs with rope, as he'd promised, doubling them over, and attached the rope above, then linked more red rope to the eyelets on the hooks. He hoisted me up from the table. I was still in that stomach-down position, with my body taking the strain where the hooks entered my back and the rope bound my legs.

Did he know what he was doing? Would the hooks tear out? I might fall...

I shut my eyes, unwilling to look at what seemed miles below when I had no way of saving myself if I fell.

Nothing happened, except the pull translated into a stretching in my shoulder blades that changed as the seconds passed and pumped me full of a soft, buzzing energy.

Safe, for now, I was safe. Then he swung me over, so that I was just able to see into the pit. Yes, there was water up to a few feet from the top. A full story deep.

Why? What macabre deviousness came next? I hoped he didn't have a thing for drowning and breath play.

My hands were still tied and he'd said he'd free them.

Pain? There was none. I was floating. Surfing on air. Happy. My dark thoughts had been banished, but they waited, circling at the back of my mind.

"My hands?" I croaked, tugging at where they were held by the leather.

I swung slightly, focusing on that feeling of being fastened to something and pulled upward, while the rest of me was elsewhere, scattered beyond where my body ended.

He showed me a big, shiny knife with a blade that curved forever.

The cuffs had a metal link he couldn't cut.

He placed the knife at my neck, near where I'd sliced him. "Look at me."

What was this?

I looked, fearful, my bottom lip in my teeth and my neck curved away from that sharpness, though my muscles there were weakening. I couldn't hold my head up forever.

"I won't cut you, unless you move. Don't fucking move."

He trailed the knife about my neck, before he drew it lower and made sinuous sweeps. I felt the blade encircle my nipples then he ducked under me and sucked on each, one nipple then the other, while the knife wandered elsewhere. I wondered how he knew how hard it pressed and when to stop so it didn't cut.

With him licking at me, and mouthing me, holding my nipple in his teeth, my arousal climbed.

I whimpered as the tip of the knife tapped my clit and pricked me. When I squirmed, he tsked.

"Be still or I'll slice you, make you bleed."

But he'd already sunk his metal claws into me.

I guess I thought I could hold back, and keep part of myself contemptuous, even if he manipulated my body, but I failed. I drowned in his dominance as he teased me and threatened in his softest, most wicked voice. He fucked me with the knife hilt and made me squeal. I caught myself, eyes shut, grunting while he used that knife hilt inside me, as well as his mouth, teeth, and tongue on my flesh.

By the end, I was a limp, quivering mess of a woman, swinging at the end of his hooks and ropes.

Sweat ran down to the tip of my nose and dripped into the water along with a little blood.

He stood beside me, looking down at the water, with his hand resting on my back. "Blood dripping in water makes me think of seeds of pain."

His words fluttered past and died.

A poet. A vile poet.

I had nothing left to give and simply rocked there, head down, recovering.

When he released my wrists, I did nothing more than lick my lips and twine my fingers together. He swung me out, further over the water.

Below was coolness. My parched throat could taste it from here.

The knife spun past, beneath my gaze, to plop into the water and spiral down into the pool, finally coming to rest at the very bottom. Lying there, smiling at me in its silvery dominance.

"Fetch it if you want to. The ropes will come loose if you pull the dangling strand. The hooks will hold you until I return. You won't bleed, much, if at all. Hooks, if they tear out, do little permanent damage. A scar or two, at most. The skin heals. It happens sometimes. Four will hold your weight. One will not.

"You decide. Stay here, and I'll claim you in an hour. I'll be outside, at the pool."

He was leaving?

Then he came into view, crouching to look me in the eye. "Let's see how much of a rebel you have in you now."

Was this a challenge? I heard his words but had trouble deciphering them. The orgasm had addled my already fried brain. I licked my lips again, thirsty.

What did he mean? That I could get loose?

The knife, down there, beckoned me, like a demon with promises of Hell.

If I had it in my hand...

CHAPTER 42

Wren

How long did I hang there? I wasn't sure. The effortless existence had consumed me.

The knife waited for me.

My arms hung down before me. I'd grown tired of clasping my hands together. The knife lay at the bottom of fathoms of water. Could I swim that far?

Why had he left it?

I could use it to escape, of course, if I made a superhuman effort but I was so tired. Even here, I could shut my eyes and sleep, cradled by ropes and hooks.

Knowing how he thought, he expected me to fail, and that somehow to him that would mean he was right.

Why now?

He was desperate...yes. The baby must have made him rethink his approach.

If I could get loose, why not just walk out of this house?

Because I'd still have him to contend with. He'd catch me again and haul me back. He might not think I could do this, but I could, even though the thought of killing him came with a whole other burden of guilt.

He was between me and Glass. Me and my life. My *child's* life.

Perhaps this was more of a trap? His punishment, if I tried, might be extreme. What did it matter? It had always been this; I could see that now. Me or him. He was too obsessed to ever give me up.

What did it matter when I was yards above, spun out and tired, with hooks in my back?

All this was pointless...

I was never one for giving up.

When I pulled on the dangling rope end, the ropes fell away, leaving the indentations from the coils on my skin. As my weight fell only on the hooks, I jerked to a stop, and screamed.

Fuuuck. Lightheaded, I waited for the pain to settle.

Blood dripped into the water; warmth running on my skin.

I should've let myself down gently. My legs seemed filled with cement.

How could I remove the hooks? Though I could contort my body and touch them, the weight pulling on them made removing them impossible. Unless...

I was hanging lower than the railings surrounding the pit and there was a ladder at the side, going down into the water. I'd need that, if I fell in. After five or ten attempts, I managed to swing far enough to hook my legs over the railing and sit there. For ages, I waited, breathing through the reawakened burn from the hooks. My legs shook. I was fairly sure I'd torn my skin more.

The baby. If I harmed it. Mouth downturned, I cupped my stomach. Was this right?

Yes, it was. The alternative was staying with him forever, as his slave. My child needed a proper father.

I looked past my shoulder at the water. How long could I hold my breath? I was tired, possibly losing blood, my limbs shaking. Who knew?

By extreme twisting, by gritting my teeth and whining and trying over and over, I extracted the hooks. The slippery thickness in my fingers combined with the slide of the metal as I pulled, almost had me fainting. Odd, really, after all he'd done. Three of them were out and I stopped to catch my breath.

At the final hook, blackness closed in from the edges of my vision, and I felt myself fall.

I woke, swinging backward, headfirst. The hook must have ripped out, because the rope was above me, dangling. My legs slid from where they curled over the rail and I plunged into the water, upside down, my arm knocking against the side of the pit.

Coolness. Confusion. Bubbles and blood drifted away.

Flailing, I found the surface, righted myself, and sucked in a lungful of air. When I next had a thought, my fists were wrapped around the ladder.

I looked down, careful not to slip my feet off the rung. My legs were blurry, a yard deep in the water. Far below lay the knife. Blood spread around me in a pale pink tide. I'd blacked out. Swimming down was stupid.

Stupid or brave or reckless. Pick one.

Brave, I liked brave. Moghul wasn't winning.

I dived and arrowed down through the water. My eyes on the knife, I zeroed in on that dark thing wavering at the bottom of yards of water. Fainting was *not* happening. My fingers closed on it and I swooped into a turn, pushing off from the bottom and kicking.

The trail back up was marked with swirls and spots of red.

CHAPTER 43

Chris

I took a moment to rid my mind of worry before I knocked. Behind this door was Glass, Wren Gavoche's lover, a man on a mission to rescue her from Moghul. From what Moghul had said, Glass was prepared to call down the Apocalypse and the Four Horsemen if he thought it would help. I understood that need to protect someone you loved. It was why I was teetering. Help Moghul get rid of this man, or turn the tables?

Yeah, I could read between the lines. Just because he hadn't suggested I murder Glass, didn't mean that wasn't what Moghul wanted done. Clean hands? I called bullshit.

I was about to be Moghul's little yes man, his dirty right hand ass-wiping man, in exchange for a crap load of money. Millions and millions of money.

Was I even capable of thinking of running a sex trade business? Most of his illegitimate ones were based on that. It was depraved, a whole level of nastiness past what I'd done with Kat and Zoe.

There would be no going back, past a certain point. This man was likely to take my head off, if I set a foot wrong. Which was why I'd deployed men in the apartments to either side, ready to blast their way in via explosives planted on the walls. It was amazing what money, big money, could accomplish, once someone gave you the right contacts. My own little instant mercenary army — five men who knew how to kill people, dispose of them, and clean up afterward. Like caterers with benefits.

I could kick a man's balls up through his teeth but compared to them I was a fluffy teddy bear. I wondered if Glass knew Wren had given me a blowjob. He must.

"Fuck," I muttered. "Let's do this."

I knocked.

Glass answered. The man from the surveillance videos, though he'd dyed his hair again to get into Australia. A macho guy with tattoos and a plain no-nonsense attitude. Straight as a stick of bloody explosives, I'd bet. Sandhurst qualified and SAS special forces. I hesitated. The button in my pocket would signal to my men.

Did I really want to go this route? Murder, to protect my ass, protect the business Moghul had given me...and Moghul's ass too. All because this man was fucking heroic enough to want to get his woman back from her kidnapper?

I let my hand relax at my side.

"Yeah?"

"Hi, I'm Chris Garrick. Can I come in? I've got things to discuss with you."

"Things?" His eyebrows rose.

"You know who I am. I know you. I can give you Moghul's aka Vetrov's address."

At that, his eyes widened, then he looked suspicious as hell, and he drew a pistol from behind his back and trained it on me. "You turn around and step in here backward. Raise your hands. Sam will pat you down."

I glimpsed the one man who'd come down with him rising from the sofa. On the coffee table in front of him were a couple of unwrapped sandwiches. The rest of Glass's men would arrive in a few hours.

"Sure." I turned and did as he asked, raising my hands and praying I wasn't about to get a knife or a bullet in my back.

I hated the decision I'd been forced to make. Be a murderer or be a traitor. Then I thought again. These guys weren't likely to leave Moghul alive. Unless he employed his own army, he was duck food. Guess I was both, either way – a murderer and a traitor. Only for some reason, this way seemed a smidgeon nicer. This way Wren would end up free.

I stepped backward through the door and waited while Sam patted me down. He found the signaler, my phone, my gun.

"What's this?" Glass held up my signaler while still covering me with the pistol.

I considered my answer.

"Be careful with that. That was my second choice. Press it and five men blow their way in here and shoot you dead. I went with the better choice." My mouth twisted. "I like a man with morals who knows how to love."

"Oh?" He smiled suspiciously. "And that's you too, I suppose?"

"No." I shook my head while checking out the rug at his feet. Then I looked directly at Glass. "No. My morals aren't so good, but I'm an accountant. I like things tidy. I'm evening out the balance of good and evil in the world...for once."

"Uh-huh. If you'd said you were an angel I'd have beaten you before I let you out of here. I know what you did to Wren."

"I'm sorry, man. I didn't know who she was, or why she was there."

The silence stretched like a rusty strangling wire.

"Okay." He sniffed and made a face like something smelled bad to him. "Help me find her and I'd even forgive you if you were a fan of that Bieber kid. Take a seat. Wait, before you do, is there another button on this that turns off your fuck-'em-all-dead squad?"

I chuckled. "Give me my phone and I'll get them to stand down."

He tossed it to me. "Type good and fast. My trigger finger has mayonnaise on it and might slip."

"I'll show you the message before I hit send."

Chalk up one slightly wonky Good Samaritan point.

CHAPTER 44

Wren

Climbing up the ladder happened, step by wet step. My feet, I had to tell them what to do, on every single rung, or they forgot. How much blood had I lost?

I found myself face first on the cold tiles and my knees slipped as I scrambled to all fours. Somehow, I'd scaled the railing. Under me was a puddle of red and pink water. *Jesus.* It always looked worse when you added water.

The knife was beside my hand. I stared, gathering energy, then fumbled to pick it up. I rose to my feet, by stages, like an old woman, breathing hard.

Where was he? The pool? This was what I had to do.

I padded onward. The one time I looked behind me, I saw a trail of pink footprints.

Water makes blood look worse. I'm fine. Maybe a little dehydrated.

I'd had a whole pool of water and I'd not drunk any. Typical me.

I found him on the patio, kneeling, staring out at the pool. His strong shoulders and the bulk of his arms daunted me but I reminded myself of my purpose and banished my fear. He wore black drawstring pants only, and seemed to be meditating – not something I'd ever seen him do before.

Fatigue made my eyes feel scratchy. My brain swam. All my pains came and pounded at me at once. My whole body throbbed, even my feet. Yup. I was fine.

Not the time to make a mistake. Be careful.

I swallowed and walked onward, my feet squeaking on the tiles despite my caution, until I stood over him, poised, the knife held in the right way for slipping between his ribs. If I miscalculated, he'd beat me, or kill me.

Shit happens. I was done with being his victim.

My breathing rasped so loud.

"You know I'm here."

"Yes." His tone shocked me; it was bitterly hard.

"Why?"

"Because...this way, I know. All or nothing. I want you, all or nothing." He laughed, and again it was harsh. "I brought you to this. You've got the knife. Decide. I predicted you'd get this far but you're bleeding more than I expected. I need to fix that."

"It's not as bad as it looks," I said, bemused, wanting to disconnect. I didn't want his pity or his care. Why had I spoken? The more he said the harder this was to do.

Over his shoulder, I saw a tablet lying before him, and on the screen were four squares of camera footage. One showed the viewing room, others the trail of my footprints.

Moghul waiting passively, for me to strike? What was the trick?

Kill, or be his.

Glass was waiting for me.

I had to do this.

If he let me. My grip on the knife crunched in.

He wants me all or nothing.

Then it was fucking nothing. My stomach rebelled as I swung. I knew my anatomy facts and the lie of the ribs, I thrust the knife into him side-on and prayed.

It slipped in with a *thunk* at the end, like carving a roast that breathed...and was human. He jerked forward, scrabbling at the knife and plucking it out, releasing a gout of blood.

"Wren!"

He folded forward, the knife dropping from his fingers, blood pouring down his back. Before I released it, the hilt had shuddered in time with his heartbeat, like the needle in a cardiac injection. I knew the feel. *Christ.*

This is wrong.

I'd buried the blade in exactly the right place.

I staggered away, mortified by the result. I tripped over my feet to fall in a heap, dizzy, gulping down bile. For a killer, I was bad at following through.

"God! Damn!" He half-coughed and groaned out the words.

With my palms on the tiles to steady myself, I raised my head.

Was it a triumph, the pinnacle of my achievements, to see him die, sprawled out on the tiles gasping? No. I was horrified. This man had been such a force in my life for so long, and I'd brought him low. It sickened me. A single blade in the heart had done it.

It didn't seem possible, or right.

He'd almost told me to kill him. No. Still not right.

I'd retreated backward in fear but now I sneaked forward on my knees, watching the last of his breaths. A building storm of grief behind my eyes made me feel as if my head was about to explode.

His mouth opened and he stared, unfocused, but I think he knew I was there.

I inched forward, still on my knees with tears slipping down my face. "I'm sorry. I'm so sorry it came to this. I didn't..."

I couldn't say I didn't mean to kill him, because I had.

"I didn't want to do this." I closed my eyes. "I just wanted you gone."

I leaned on my hands again but found my arms wobbling. Even my legs felt like they weren't part of me. A thin sound echoed in my head.

Moghul coughed and I looked at him, through a gathering smear of light.

"Don't blame yourself. It was me. Now I know. You always were good with a knife."

Then he smiled, and took a half breath, and stopped. Just stopped, and breathed no more. I was free, finally.

I lay my cheek on the tiles because my head had become too heavy to hold up and the world slowly toppled off its axis and teetered away into the blackness of space.

CHAPTER 45

Glass

According to Chris, this man Moghul kept to himself. Whatever empire of evil he commanded, he separated it from what happened at home. The chances of us meeting anyone except him or Wren should be tiny. Didn't matter a lot. We took no chances.

The small charge blew in the locks and we entered via the front door and a high window after tossing in flash bangs. The neighbors were a quarter of a mile away and his driveway long and concealed. We should be fine unless he'd connected his alarm system to the police station. Which wasn't at all likely.

We swept through the house as fast as we could, but the place was a fucking maze. The one house plan had come from Chris, if reluctantly. But he'd googled it. This mansion had been a local celebrity while it was erected. If only we'd thought that through, with details from Wren, we could've tracked down where this house was located. No need for Chris. Parts of it were unique, especially the huge louvre system above his two-story garden.

The cops would've figured that out eventually. We just hadn't had the time. For a perfectionist, like Chris thought this man was, he still made mistakes. Maybe Wren had knocked the poor man off kilter.

I nudged open a timber-and-glass door that led out to that very pool area. Two bodies lay at the very edge of the roofed area. Even from the doorway, I could tell one was Wren, one a man.

"Wren!" I took off at a run, accelerating, wishing I had wings despite my legs going like pistons.

She lay on her side on the sandstone, naked. Still and white, and a yard away from a man who was clearly dead. A large pool of blood colored the tiles beneath him. From the glance I spared him, and Chris's description, the corpse was Moghul. Someone had killed him. Could Wren have done it? The fucker was big and fit.

I prayed my men were clearing the area, because I didn't have time. I went to one knee beside her, unsure at first how much of the blood was hers and how much was his.

Her foot rested in the bigger pool, which came from a wound in his back. The rest of the blood seemed hers and under her shoulder.

"Wren? Baby?"

I knew basic medic training and checked her carotid pulse, her breathing. She was alive and stirred as I talked to her. Pale, and that could be from shock or blood loss. The few wounds on her back weren't enough to kill her, surely. One of them, a deep L-shaped tear, was still leaking blood – a little arteriole squirted tiny but strong geysers of blood. I put pressure on it and checked under her again. Not a lot of volume. Freaky, but I could stop this easily.

Her pulse was fast but had good strength, as far as I could tell.

Pieter arrived and squatted next to me. "We're good. No one else is here. How is she?"

"Lost some blood. Give her a drink if she's conscious enough to swallow. Wren?"

We managed to get her to sit up enough to swallow some water from a canteen safely, then I let her rest her head on me and pulled out my throwaway phone.

I shut my eyes for a second, only. Safe. I had her back. The unease at seeing her semiconscious prodded me.

"I have to get an ambulance here, Pieter. Double check the house on the way out. I'll stay until the last moment. Leave me the Veedub Golf."

We had two vehicles.

He nodded, gave Wren and the dead guy a once over, surveyed the pool area. "Okay. I guess you'll be right without us. You meeting us back in PNG or up north?"

I held up a finger to silence him as I contacted the emergency services and told them there was a woman screaming about a bad accident at a house. Gave the address, hung up.

I crouched over her and she blinked up at me then gave a small smile. "Hey there. I have to go soon, Wren, but I'll stay until the ambulance arrives. I'll find you and visit you as soon as I can. Okay?" Her eyes closed again. Had she heard? An ache started up in my chest. "Fuck. I hope that's enough. I can't stay, Pieter. Not to go with her to the hospital. They'd jail me. I'm going to do my disappearing act here, then figure out how to see her after. You –" I nodded, looked at him. "I think you're all fine to go home. We're done here. That bastard is dead."

"Yeah, he is. Wren knifed him from the looks of it." He stood, gestured at a knife lying a few feet away. "He must've let his guard down. Take care, man. Keep us advised. Ja?"

"Sure. Ja. Go. Now. I don't want you all in trouble with the law. Here." I handed him my Steyr assault rifle. Take it back with you. I'll just keep my pistol. In case." He walked away. "Oh! Rig the door so I hear it if anyone comes in!"

"Okay, boss."

I watched him file out with Sam, Jurgen, and two other of my men then I cradled Wren until I heard distant sirens. Thank heaven for ambulances and their warnings, though I would've scaled the wall if I had to.

They took her to the mainland hospital, flew her over by chopper. I watched it go overhead. By then I was on my way back to the mainland anyway. Wouldn't have been wise to be stuck on the island with the cops going crazy.

Within a few days, they declared her kidnapper had been found. Two days after that, her police guard at the hospital was replaced by security sent by the board of trustees set up for Wren's finances. They switched her to a posher hospital even. Her father had thought of everything, almost, except how not to die, and how not to behave like a prick. The new head of her security, Jon, was a protégée of Hugh's and I'd met him before. We got on well and it was a simple matter to sneak into her private hospital room.

Anyone else would've been sent home by now and she was due out tomorrow. I needed to see her before she flew south, to Sydney, or went back to university.

She was asleep. The blue curtains let in a muted morning light and made her look like the angel I knew she was. Her wounds were clean, healing, and stitched, but something had happened last night that Jon said they'd not told her about and that she was sedated but coming out of it. The doctor was due to inform her today.

Someone who loved her should say it. It was my job.

The nurses were due in soon. Jon figured I had forty minutes, tops, but I wasn't waking her, not when she looked so sweet. I swallowed down my sad tiredness and pulled up one of the armchairs. How much pain did my girl have to face before the world decided she needed a break?

Head bowed, I was staring at my fingers, wondering how to do this, when she spoke.

"Glass?"

All the vows to be quiet and gentle vanished. I stood and leaned over her, blinking madly to clear my eyes. "Damn, girl. You are the toughest chick I've ever met."

"Me?" She moved further up the pillow, wincing. "Kiss me, you big idiot."

So I did, a soft but heartfelt kiss. I wished I could give her all my strength through that kiss and lingered a while.

I stopped myself from telling her I'd heard what the media had figured out she'd done — how she'd released herself from those fucking cruel hooks, then dragged herself down to where he was while losing blood. It was awesome and horrible, and when I'd heard it on the news, alone in that apartment, I'd sworn enough to have the neighbor yell at me to shut up. The hardest thing ever, was to find out something like that, to not be there when your girl was hurting so badly.

But I couldn't say it, because that'd put her mind back there, and make her remember. Instead, all I said was. "Yes, you're brave, and I'm proud of you."

I reached up to cup the side of her face and stroke her cheek with my thumb.

"You know you're safe now. He's gone forever."

"I know. Yes. I do know that."

She was quiet for a while, staring down along the bed, her odd little expressions making me wonder. But I let her be, figuring there'd be times like this when she needed to get her thoughts together.

"I'll be out of here tomorrow, the doctors said."

"Uh-huh." I leaned in and kissed her again, once. "Wherever you go, girl, just know I intend to be there. Legally, if possible."

Wren frowned and played with my fingers.

For a second I wondered if she intended to tell me she was leaving me. Breathing got difficult.

"Legally. That can't be here, right?"

"No. I've got a track record here, due to my activities in PNG."

Oh damn. She had a university to attend.

"Hmm. Well, I figured...I've got enough money to support us both, anywhere."

Shit. "I'm no toyboy."

Her eyes narrowed. "If you were, I'd kick you to the curb. Pick where. You can figure out an alternative career." She said "career" as if it was dirty. "You don't need to be a criminal, Glass. That's my one stipulation for us staying together. Say yes, or I hit you with a fucking pillow."

I paused, stunned, then I grinned. So be it. She was right. Why risk arrest, jail? I could start clean in Europe. Somewhere. Passports were possible.

"Wait, wait, wait. You have a course to study."

Wren sighed. "Yeah, I know. I think I'd feel weird going back there. I think...I should be able to find a place in the UK. I know I can. So, pick a country. I'm on holidays for months yet, and until I get that sorted."

She still wanted to finish that. It would be kind of interesting to watch her finish that degree. I'd be damn proud of her.

"Norway?"

"Uhhh. Cold, but it'll do for a start." She grabbed my hand again, sneaked hers inside mine. Are you going to be a good father?"

Man. Oh, man. It was time. I drew in a long breath.

"Wren." I nodded at the bed sheets like my audience was there. Eye contact, man. Then I raised my head and looked at her. "I've got some bad news. Really early this morning, they did an emergency ultrasound on you. I know they haven't told you. Jon said I could, before the doctor."

The change in her face tore me up.

"The baby?" She sucked in her lip.

"Yes. I'm sorry, my girl." I squeezed her hand. "The baby...isn't alive." Saying died just seemed too much. Too many people she knew had died.

"Oh god." She turned her face into the pillow. "I know...I mean...I know it was his, but I wanted this child. It's hard not to..."

"It's fine to be sad. I know you wanted it. I know." Then I rose from the chair and covered her with my body and gathered her to me, giving her the best comfort I could. When I heard her cry, I only patted her lower back, and kissed her cheek. "Maybe, maybe one day, we could try too. You know?"

"Oh Glass!" She peeked at me with those pretty blue eyes, with tears spilling and wetting her eyelashes. "That would make me happy, *so* happy, but right now, I need to cry. Just keep on hugging me, you big beautiful man. I need you so much. I love you so much."

"You cry all you want. I'll be here for you for as long as you want me to be. Longer, if I have any say in it."

Her answer, *good*, was muffled and soggy sounding but it made me smile.

Wren was still in there. She just needed to heal.

Listening to her sob, and not being able to fix her troubles, was the most difficult thing I'd ever done in my lifetime. I let a few tears out myself, though I'd not admit to it. We'd get past this. We would.

CHAPTER 46

Glass

While I toweled off the sweat from my bike ride through the village, Wren barely looked up from her latest book. Since we'd come here to Cyprus, she'd not gone outside except to a few restaurants.

"Coming for a walk on the beach?" I lifted an eyebrow at her but she had her nose in the book again.

It was great that her fascination with reading had returned but last night she'd still had a crying jag that I figured had left me shaken inside as much as her.

All the quiet talks we'd had might have helped her but it was time to branch out. The moping around had to stop sometime and be buggered if I was going to let her get entrenched in the psychiatrist path as some sort of crutch for her sanity when there were simpler methods I could try first.

"Okay. Enough's enough." I grabbed her ankle and hauled her to me along the bed until I had her under me, with her butt perched on the edge.

"Glass!" She struggled and sat up on her elbows, but I rested my palm on her, making sure she couldn't rise any higher.

"I get that you like books and that you need time to get your head straight." I nudged her under her chin. "But this is Greece. I think you need sunshine."

"Sunshine? Is that like a prescription now?"

"Yes." Her pout was laugh worthy but I managed to adopt a stern expression. "I haven't been fishing here yet and I'm going now, this afternoon, and you're coming too."

"What if I say no?" Her mouth twisted, as if she was wrestling with a smile.

At last, a hint of that mischievousness I'd been missing since she'd killed Moghul. He was a hard man, as close to evil as I'd come across perhaps, though I guess I might be biased. Coming back from that had involved a truckload of crying. I was cool with her needing that but now, nope. Time had come for more to happen.

"Saying *no* means, one, I get to tan your butt until it's red. Two, I get to come back and dump the worms I'm going to buy for bait all over you and this bed."

I grabbed her hips and pushed her down into the mattress, bouncing her softly off it a few times.

"Worms?" She made her face run through every look from nose-wrinkling, to rolling her eyes, to grimacing.

"Worms, yes. You'd like some?"

"Ugh." She tossed her paperback aside. "Insufferable man. Fine!"

"Good. Wear that new yellow bikini and keep those cute little ass-revealing shorts on too." I let her go and straightened.

"Yes, Sir!" Wren said sarcastically then she sat up and saluted.

"Oh hell. You girl... You just..." I shook my head slowly, trying my best to look unhappy.

I hadn't spanked her for so long. We hadn't even had sex but maybe, just maybe, she needed this. I sat myself heavily on the bed and hauled her over my lap, bottom up. Her protests and wriggles to get free were minimal, revealing even.

"Something tells me you want this."

She only turned her head to peek at me, her bottom lip already sneaking between her teeth, her eyes unblinking.

"I haven't seen your ass like this for ages." I circled my palm on one cheek, then shoved up both sides of the back of her shorts and panties so I could see more of her most gorgeous, smackable, and naked ass. "I might need to break you into this slowly, hmmm, Miss Wren? Have you forgotten what it's like for me to spank you?"

I leaned down closer to her face, my elbow propped on the bed, while I kept on playing with her butt. "What's this? I found a hole. A wet, wet hole." Then I wiggled a finger under the denim and into her pussy. When I shoved my finger deeper, she shut her eyes, curled her tongue tip onto her lip, and made a small noise.

"Did I hear a squeak? Do you like my finger up inside you, Miss? Hmm?"

As I pumped my finger into her a few more times, curving it in slow, taking my time in the best possible way, she sighed.

"Oh yes, I do, it's...nice."

Simply having my finger in her was such a possessive act that I could've crowed like a fucking rooster. I pinched one lip of her labia between my inserted finger and my thumb. "Answer me. Have you forgotten?"

"*Mmm.*" Wren squirmed and whimpered, then she whispered, "I haven't forgotten, Sir, what's it's like when you spank me, though it was flip-flopping, I recall."

It was too. *Wow.* So long ago. It seemed years.

"Sir again?" I could take that label, keep it even if she wanted to do it this way. "I like Sir coming from you."

I kissed her, sweetly, playing a little with her tongue and amused at the moans I was getting from her. Then I pushed myself up off the bed again and removed my finger from her cunt.

I raised my hand. "For that first smart ass remark and because I can't resist."

I smacked my hand down on her six times. Every slap awakened me. Skin to skin...seeing the wobble of her pretty female flesh and the pinkness coming out...her yelps too.

Damn, those yelps and whines were so sexy. Why hadn't I done this already? I could comfort her to hell and back, hold her, late at night, when I felt the shake of the pillow from her crying softly. We could talk and talk, and talk some more, but *this* was us. This was how we started, and I wondered if we didn't both need this to get us healing.

Even I had my scars. Who wouldn't, after that?

War was war, but when someone you loved had to kill to stay alive, the hurt and fears ran deep.

I pulled her upright and set her before me with my hands curved into her waist, amused and also fucking happy at how fast she was breathing and how low her eyelids dipped. I kept her there a while longer, watching and feeling all those little movements of her body, even the shift of her small feet with the red toenail polish, appreciating this woman, appreciating how she gave herself to me.

We could fuck now, but no, I wanted to get her outside, not get me into her. My cock swelled at the thought. I grinned. Okay I wanted both. This first.

"You, love, are almost edible. I could use you as bait. Think of all the mermen I'd catch."

Her small smile said more to my heart than any words. Yes, this was the key. For both of us, connecting was more than sex, it was kink.

"You liked me doing that? Getting all dominant on you?"

Her eyes opened fully and she blinked at me for a few seconds. Her toes curled in the rug, then she said one wonderful word, and it was "Yes."

"I thought so. Me too." I squeezed her waist. "I feel more alive after spanking you than I have for weeks."

"I could help you with that?" She glanced down at my rising cock, where it was putting a dent in my shorts.

I laughed. "Later. If you earn it."

For a second I imagined myself making her kneel, then making her take out my cock and suck on it. Holding her head and getting a blow job from her. She'd make all those little groaning and humming noises I loved. But I wanted to do this right and a BJ wasn't how I wanted to restart our sexual relationship.

I stood. "Later. Let's go see if this hotel has fishing gear we can hire."

After talking to the receptionist, we ended up with all the gear we needed and it was only a fifteen minute walk along the sand to an inlet where, supposedly, fish could be caught on the late afternoon tide. I didn't really care if I caught nothing, just having Wren hold my hand as we strolled along, talking about shells and the color of the sea, us, a happy couple again – that was my reward.

Sunshine and spanking, that was what Wren needed. I could deliver those in spades.

When we reached the inlet, I threw out the line while she pottered about on the shoreline or climbed some of the rocks to sit and watch me. I didn't catch anything, story of my fishing life, but I didn't mind. I had a dark-haired siren up on the rocks calling to me with the late sun painting her thighs with gold and haloing her head. I waded ashore, tossed the rod to the sand, and beckoned to her.

"Take off those shorts and let's have a swim!"

I had plans, of course. Even with the cool water lapping at me it'd been agony watching every lithe flow of her muscles as she walked and the sway of her breasts as she bent to pick up something from the beach.

I took her by the hand and drew her out into water that came to just below her breasts. Though the last other people had left the small cove a few minutes before, I turned her so her back was to the shore before I murmured, "Don't move."

Her eyes lit up.

Then I tugged down both cups of her bikini top, until her pink-brown areolas peeked out.

"What are you doing?"

"Turning you on, of course."

I bent and kissed her while thumbing around and around her nipples, slowly, agonizingly slowly, from the way her breath hitched. Her nipples tightened into hard buttons and I pinched both between finger and thumb.

"How far can I go without you coming?" I kissed her neck, then her ear, biting her softly.

"Without? I don't know. I don't want to come here!" Her answer was breathy and she was already wriggling forward, rubbing on my poor long-suffering cock. "Someone might arrive and –"

I chuckled. "No, no one can see anything. There's no one here. Pull down my shorts and take out my cock. Unless you're safewording?"

"Safeword? Ohhh. I'd forgotten I had one."

When she looked indecisive, I decided to up the stakes. "Would you rather I strip you naked first?"

"Shhh!" I felt her hands fumbling at me. "This is crazy."

When she had her hand wrapped around my shaft, I put my hands under her butt and lifted her higher, made her spread her legs and put them around me.

"Now put my cock between your legs."

"You can't do that!" she whispered urgently. "We'll get arrested for screwing in public."

"Do it."

Her brows tweaked inward but after one long sigh, she did as she was told.

I inched aside the crotch of her bikini bottoms, so there was nothing between us, then thrust along the natural groove formed by the lips of her pussy. The slide of her on my cock had me stiffening even more. "That feels awesome."

Wren giggled. "I can feel you getting harder."

"Mmm. Before I was chocolate bar stiffness, now I'm iron bar. All your doing."

I hoisted her a little higher and stuffed myself along between her legs, almost, *almost* dipping into that well of slipperiness I could feel giving way under the head of my cock.

"Oh god." She groaned. "Would Sir like me to eat his iron bar? Lick it? Tongue it?" She hugged my neck, put her mouth to my ear, and whispered, "I'm good at that."

"Sir," I grunted. "Would like to stick his iron bar *in* you. Don't tease or it'll go in your other hole, right here, right now."

"Eeek! No! Bad man."

I grinned. "Yes." I did some more little slips and slides right on that entrance spot. "Fuck."

"Yes, Sir. Fucking is good." She gasped. "Oh god. I need you in me. Just not here. Not here. You've no condom anyway."

"I know," I growled that word between my teeth as my cock pulsed against her willing little cunt. A hand job just wouldn't be enough. "I was going to make you come but I've changed my mind."

I reached around and found her entrance, stuck my finger up there. I bit her neck, and the upper curves of her breasts. Though she protested and squealed at each bite, Wren leaned back in my arms, as if to give me easier access. Her pussy entrance was clenching in down there, greedy for cock, and I had to pull back or risk ending up inside her, all accidental like. So tempting.

It was getting desperate for both of us. Mostly for her soon, I decided. I was going to make use of that massager I'd bought days ago. Finally.

"I'm going to put you down then we're walking back to the hotel room." I stared at her. "I'm going to tease the fucking hell out of you with that vibe massager thing until you're begging me to come. But I'm not going to let you to come until after I fuck you from behind, while you stand bent over at the window with your little black dress on."

"Oh." Her eyes were wide. "All that and I can't come?"

"Nope. And if you do anything while I fuck you except be a good girl and stand still for me, you won't get to come until tomorrow morning, when I will find a deserted beach, tow you into the water and do your ass. So be very careful and tell when you're close."

"I don't know if I like this game." She wriggled side to side. "Did I ever say you were bad, Sir?"

"Uh-huh. And you know what else I'm doing?" I nudged her nose with mine. "I'm prescribing fucking every day from now on. As well as a walk in the sun. Kink, fucking, and sun."

"Wow."

"You know why? Because I can see the happiness in you, Miss Wren. More than you've been for so long. The sunlight is in you, your face, every wriggle, every smile I've seen. I want more of that. Looks like I made up a good prescription."

"Yes," she looked down as she answered. "I know, Glass. I never thought this would make me feel so good. It's a little crazy really." She curled her tongue out onto her top lip, as if thinking, then licked along her mouth. "What if I disobey? Some days I might not want to walk...or to get fucked...or even kinkiness. Do I get spanked?"

The little minx liked spanking. "Hmmm. I might need to think of something you don't like. Minced worms for breakfast?" I started lumbering to the beach with her still up in my arms, like some leviathan creature rising from the depths...though at least I'd caught something tasty.

In my head, I laughed at my idea. I needed to go fishing more often.

"Ewww! Yuck, yuck, yuck. That would be disgusting! And unhealthy."

"Then, I might just make you stand in the corner naked while I watch you, then paddle you with that spiky kitchen utensil I saw in a drawer."

She was quiet. Too quiet.

I sighed. "You like that idea too. Damn. I'll just have to tie you up and ignore you."

"Awww."

I checked and Wren looked sad, as in lost puppy sad.

"Good. I found your weakness."

"Meanie." But she put her arms around me even tighter and whispered, "Love you," in my ear.

"Love you too, my pretty luscious lipped wench. You'd better put my cock back in my pants and get down or we'll scare the wildlife."

Wren snorted.

The sun might have been setting, but around us seemed brighter than it had been for many months.

CHAPTER 47

Wren

I laid the book by my side and smiled up at the pinpricks of the stars. The crescent moon was distant and small and still drifting above the horizon. At this time of night, this rooftop pool was breezy and a few cicadas and mosquitoes had somehow found their way up here, but it was surprisingly quiet too. There was only an elderly couple across the water, sipping red wine and being served a cheese and fruit platter, as well as two teenager girls having fun chasing each other in the water.

Glass had done exactly as he'd threatened to, made me wait forever before I could come, teasing me endlessly after he fucked me. I'd loved it. Seemed as if it didn't always matter to me so much what was done but rather that it pleased him. Remembering his absorbed stare and the way his hard-on had come back while I pleaded with him...it gave me goose bumps. I surreptitiously put my hand between my legs and squeezed in on it.

Luckily Glass had fallen asleep on the sun lounge beside me. If he knew remembering had turned me on, he'd be amused in that infuriating way of his. Which would be hot, come to think of it. I sighed but decided not to prod him. The massager had given me a sore clit already. High speed was more like way-too-high speed.

I picked up the book and smoothed my hand over the wrinkled cover.

War and Peace.

One more page to read and I was done. I wanted to savor this, all by myself. I flicked to the last page and turned it into the overhead light.

I read the words, slowing at the final line, almost breathing them in, then I slowly closed *War and Peace*. For a while, I held the heavy book to my chest, looking up at those stars.

Glass didn't understand what this book meant to me. I didn't quite understand either, except that I couldn't dismiss Moghul or his effect on me with the wave of some magic wand.

I'd needed to say goodbye and this book had helped me to see that if I looked beyond the avalanche of his arrogance and sadism and immorality, there had existed a man who had something worthwhile to him.

I couldn't sum up those qualities, or him, easily, couldn't put them in a neat box and declare *there it is*, but there was something good beneath the monster.

"Time for bed?" Glass sat up, yawning, then scrubbed his hands through his hair.

"Sure." I gathered up the magazine I'd also brought and padded after him, toward the glass door.

He paused to point past my shoulder. "You've left your book."

"It's okay. Sometimes when I'm finished with a good book I like to leave them. It's like I'm passing on the fantasy." I smiled and ran up to him to take his hand. "Maybe you can buy me a new one?"

"Okay." He nodded, smile lines crinkling around his eyes. "We'll go browse some bookstores tomorrow."

"Thank you." I went up on tiptoes and kissed him. "Thank you for everything."

Then I walked away, leaving the book under the stars again – those tolerant, serene, and distant stars.

Goodbye Moghul.

CHAPTER 48

Glass

Europe. Amazing that I'd never done a lot of touring here until Wren decided we should. I'd been to the usual tourist places that all Brits go to but never skied down the Swiss Alps or paddled a kayak in the Greek isles, visited the Coliseum, or this... Damn the view was enough to give me a hard-on.

Mountains and more mountains. Crystal-clear air that you could see forever on and snow on those mountain tops across the valley.

I set down my glass of apple cider on the crooked terracotta step. The stuff was okay but beer was better. Wren could keep her cider all to herself. Some monk, or someone medieval-ish, had built this place and it'd been refurbished so often the floor had more ancient floor beneath it and the old goat pen down the slope had a chunk of ancient Roman tessellated mosaic next to the feeding trough.

Fucking amazing history, though I wasn't keen on falling off the mountainside if I staggered out the back gate, drunk, and didn't watch my feet.

We would move on in a month anyway, if I knew Wren. Wanderlust? Or some weird need she had to explore? It didn't matter to me. Happy times, either way. My prescription for kink, sex, and sun had worked well.

"You can come in now!"

The delivery must be installed. What the hell had she found? A six-foot Grecian love goddess statue? Last time it'd been a gothic table with dragons for the legs. I'd show her what I'd bought at a street vendor yesterday, after I saw whatever monstrosity she had in our bedroom. Mine was perhaps not as authentic, but it was the sort of item I liked to collect.

I'd get her hiking tomorrow. We both needed the exercise.

I sauntered through the house, amused by her impatient yells.

"Where are you?"

"Coming!"

"No you're not. If you were, I'd know." Then a giggle.

Cheeky thing. I shook my head and stepped through the bedroom door, bracing myself for a gothic nightmare object.

"Wow." Our bed was gone and had been replaced by a higher bed, stunning really with the Japanese-style quilt and the fine leaves curling up the black metal bed posts. "Very...Oriental."

But most stunning of all was the black-barred cage beneath the bed, on which the mattress and bed base rested. Even that followed the Japanese theme, with the bars slightly curved yet elegant, and a stork in different positions forming the main posts of the cage and the legs of the bed.

"A cage?" I raised my eyebrows at my girl, where she kneeled beside the bed, wearing a delicate white dress. "So innocent. So virginal." I smirked my best evil smirk as I stalked closer. "Is this a hint?"

Wren cleared her throat and looked up at me. "Only if Sir wishes to make use of the cage."

Fuck yeah, I did. I'd been so careful around her, not pushed the kink too much, letting her show me the way, to a degree. I'd let out some of my perverted side and so far she'd loved it when I took the initiative. Calling me Sir had happened naturally when we were in the bedroom, and sometimes elsewhere.

Our relationship had begun with kink and the hell I'd let that other man inhibit what we got up to. But I was still careful with her. Maybe too much so.

I rubbed my chin. "Did you okay this purchase with me?"

"No." Her eyes widened and she shifted on her knees in an obviously guilty way. "Should I have? I don't think Sir has asked me permission to let him decide what I spend."

Well, well. "Permission?"

Permission mightn't have been set up but...I could see her brat side coming out here. "You used Sir in that sentence, which makes me think you like the idea."

She had a safeword, *Rincewind*, if I recalled right. As I pulled her to her feet, a pair of tits showing erect nipples through her dress enhanced that doe-eyed look.

"Damn, that's see-through."

Wren looked down and smiled. "Of course."

"Does a cage get you going? If I say I want to see you in it? Maybe fuck you in it? Are you my little slave today? Hmmm?" I nudged up her chin with one finger.

"I guess...Sir. Yes. If you wish. You like the cage?"

I laughed and cruised my gaze down her body. "I think I like the idea of you in it, some mornings, yes. You realize I'm going to have to order you in there, if I think you've been bad?"

"Mmm." She took a big breath, making those tits rise.

"Pull your dress up so I can see your pussy, little slave."

"Oh, fuck." Her hushed swearing had the hallmarks of lust.

"Did I say you could swear?" I bunched my hand in the back of her hair, then wound it about my fist, and made her stand on her tiptoes. Wren whimpered.

I cursed under my breath. "Those little noises. My hard-on just got harder."

She snorted. "Good to know."

"Dress!"

"Oh. Sorry."

I extended the arm holding her so I could watch her properly. As she gathered her dress in both hands, slowly, the hem crept upward. Minx, she was teasing me.

I gave her a shake. "Faster, little slave."

She gasped, then snickered, and sped up the climb of the hem. It ended with just a hint of her pussy peeking out at me. The split of her sex had to be one of the most enticing things a man could see, except if she was bent over the other way and showing it off.

"Damn. No underwear?" I blew out a breath. "A little higher. I need to test your wetness." I eyed her tits too.

She arched a brow but shifted her dress a few inches higher.

"Are you wet enough for me? Well?"

"I don't know, Sir." The way she nibbled her lip and squirmed made me sure she was. My Wren was feeling the heat. I'd bet her fortune she was dying for me to touch her.

"Put two fingers between your legs, and run them between your pussy lips, along that cunt of yours, then show them to me. If they're wet, I'll only spank your cute little ass. If they're not wet, I'm going to spank that pussy until it is wet *then* fuck your ass."

"Ohmigod. That's so ho –" she whispered. "Yes, Sir."

"Don't forget, it's my ass to fuck if I want to fuck it." I murmured that then moved in, towering over her, bending her neck back so I could look down on her. I pressed my dick closer too, rubbing it against her stomach, as I spoke. "Slowww or fast, with a twelve-inch dildo, or with my fingers. Remember that."

She nodded fast and went, "Mmm. Yes. Please."

I grinned. Ass fucking was one thing I knew she loved. This punishment was going off-course quickly.

"Feel your pussy. Now."

She did as I asked, lifted her dress an inch higher and slid her fingers between her legs and along her pussy while I watched, then she showed me them. Her juices glistened on those fingers, a strand stringing across from one finger to the other.

"Now that's what I call wet," I murmured. "I'd like to bend you over that bed and stick my cock in you, but I have other things to do first. Duty calls."

Her mouth downturned. My cock twitched but it could wait. I had an itch to do things to her. This cage made me want to tie her up to something and fuck her until she couldn't lift a little finger. Using her hair, I turned her around and pushed her toward the bed.

"You're not coming until I'm happy with you. First I need to punish you for spending money I never said you could spend. And for buying that dragon thing." I almost laughed out loud.

"Heyyy." She tried to turn back to me, so I smacked her butt.

"Go! Bend over that bed and stick that butt out."

When she'd wriggled up there then wriggled the dress up above her thighs, then wriggled her pussy against the quilt so I could see her slit shining with moisture...damn lot of fucking *hot* wriggling, after all that, I was finding it hard to breathe.

I chuckled to myself and found the belt in the new bedside drawer. At least she'd put it back there. I doubled it over.

"Count out the strikes while I make your butt glow red, little slave." With the folds of her dress in my hand, I squashed her lower back to the bed.

I began with it hard and surprised her, made her yelp. "Punishment is *supposed* to feel bad."

"Owie!" She did that wriggle. Lord, I could watch her cunt move when she did that, forever.

"Don't try to distract me. Damn you're such a slut."

When she sucked in a breath as if to protest, I grinned and went to town on her ass, whopping her with the belt low on her thighs where she'd love it as well as higher up on her ass. I made her a pretty canvas of white, red and pink, and she made the room echo with squeals and yelps, then at the last with panting and moans.

"You like this." I traced a stripe mark with a fingertip then whacked the flat of the leather along her pussy.

"Fuck!" Wren sank into the bed, her eyes slammed shut, and she damn well quivered.

"You better not come." I ripped off all my clothes and tossed them aside, let my cock out to point at the girl it wanted, like some bloodhound on the trail. I turned her over, and let her see it.

"My cock wants inside you. Get off your clothes."

Then I stroked my shaft while she pulled the dress over her head. "Good."

With one hand, I pushed her onto her back on the bed, then straddled her and whipped the belt around her wrists and tied it, towed her off the bed, her tits swaying, her nipples enticing me so I had to pause and suck on them both while two of my fingers ended up halfway up her cunt.

She groaned and leaned into me, shuddering.

"No coming. Get in that fucking cage."

I forced her to her knees, my cock slapping across her mouth at one point. She opened and sucked in the tip of my cock. I pulled out fast.

"Fuck, girl. No sucking me off until I say!"

"Please?"

"Uh-uh."

I urged her into the cage and slammed the door then went in search of the red leather collar, and leash I'd bought, but not showed her, desperately looking in shopping bags and under discarded clothes.

Where the hell did it get put?

It was in that same drawer I'd found the belt in. Figured. I went back to her and opened the cage. Too crazed to introduce her to the collar properly, I just hauled her over by her hair and stuck my cock in her mouth for a few sucks, pumping it in there, while I strapped the collar on her neck and buckled it.

"You go girl," I said, in awe of the hot pulse of lust drawn from my cock by her mouth greedily licking and tonguing me. "Enough!" I finally managed, groaning as my dick left her mouth.

The cage was high enough to fuck her on all fours, if I went inside, but hell no. Something more depraved called me.

I clicked the leash on the collar and took a turn through the leather of the belt between her wrists as well, then attached her to a spot on the cage wall a few feet inside and to the right. That left her on all fours with her three quarters of her body outside the cage, and her head hidden inside.

She liked hiding her head when she came. This time she had no choice.

"That's what I like. A slave who knows I only need to fuck her cunt. Are you my little slave, the one with the wettest cunt, the one that sucks all the cum from me when I tell her to?" I slapped her ass.

"Yes, Sir. I am."

"Let me hear you beg."

"Pleeease fuck me." Then she whispered. "I'm going to die in a minute if you don't. Please Glass. Please, Sir." She'd gone down onto her elbows and had stuck that butt out even higher.

I laughed and shoved my cock in, deep, gliding all the way in, feeling her wetness smooth the way, and more liquid squeeze out to wet my balls.

I suppressed a groan, knowing I wasn't going to last and wondering what else I could do with this cage. I fucked her hard and fast, even hearing her curse once when she slid forward into the bars, but she only moaned some more after that. Her body tightened, her squeals and panting stopped as she built toward orgasm, putting out little grunts. As she came, I felt her walls clench in on my cock. I rammed my cock into her even further — so far I figured my balls were nearly in her too.

The climax hit me like a fucking tsunami.

I caught my breath, and leaned in to nip Wren on the shoulder, laughing at myself. Tsunami. Oriental bed and cage. Yeah, I was on a roll.

When I'd pulled out and cleaned up and came back to her, she was still sprawled half collapsed onto the floor, half inside the cage. I went to one knee and looked in at her. Her eye opened, as she peeked at me, then shut. From her breathing she was only just coming down. Sometimes she took a while.

"Guess my slave needs to be left her here with my cum dripping from her as punishment too."

"Uhhh. Can I call Sir a bastard?"

"Nooo." I bent over her butt, eyeing those red lines. "Because this happens." I bit her squarely in the middle of one ass cheek.

"Eek!"

"Look at that. Such a great tooth mark."

"Tooth mark? One only? Top or bottom? Is Sir some mutated Cyclops with only one tooth?" She smirked at me.

I tsked. She was still tied, still with that gorgeous red embossed collar on her neck.

"I think my slave needs more of something."

I pulled her legs over and apart a little, so I had access to her cunt, then I inserted three fingers into her, working them in slowly while I watched her face and massaged her clit around and around, up and down, with my thumb.

She squeaked and writhed her butt, as if to get away. When I held her down, she watched me, frowning, her mouth open." I don't think... I can't do. Another."

"We'll see."

I grinned malevolently. I'd not tried to get a G spot orgasm from her yet. I wondered if I could.

I wriggled those fingers higher, searching, waiting to see what happened. One particular area made her head fall back as she sighed. Her walls moved in on my fingers. I kept rubbing there.

"Good?"

"Mmm."

It took some time to work her into the right state, took a lot of bites on her inner thighs, as well as lots of hard labor with my fingers, my tongue, but it was so worth it. Seeing her arch and scream three times in a row then beg me to stop.

"No more. Please."

I smiled. "Fun times ahead," I said, kissing her belly. "Now I know I can do that."

She groaned at me blearily, still lying twisted where I'd dragged her from the cage, on her back, her hair wrapped across her face and neck. "I was right," she said hoarsely. "You are a ba..."

"Hmm?"

"I mean. I mean, Sir is an angel."

"Of course I am."

"A bad angel, if that's possible."

"I'm sure it is." I lay down beside her and kissed her neck. "What do you want for dinner? I'm cooking...which means ordering from the shop."

"Really?" She licked her lips. "I'm so thirsty. How about just fruit and a cheese platter? You can have that ham and roast meat too, if you want?"

"Sure. I can make that myself. I'll get you some water then it's in the shower with you. ASAP. You stinky, sweaty thing."

"Pffft. Your fault. Glass?"

"Yeah?" I paused in the middle of rising.

"Thank you. That was amazing. I wasn't sure you'd like it...the cage."

"Hmmm. You need to worry about me liking it too much."

"Ohhh. Oh my." Her mouth stayed open.

I chuckled and left her to think.

Later, we settled down to the cheese, fruit, and meat platter, along with some mulled red wine, outside at a timber table. Sitting on one long bench together, we could watch the stars come out over the mountains. It was cold, but we'd rugged up.

I didn't think I'd ever been as content as I was at that moment.

I put my arm over her and squeezed her shoulder. "Come here. Sit on my lap, woman."

"Woman?" She waggled her eyebrows. "Not sure I agree with that diminutive insult.

"It's not an insult. It's what you are, just as I'm a man. Now come here or I'll make that ass even redder, and do it out here in the fucking cold."

"Well. When you ask nicely like that."

Once I had her comfy on my lap, I rested my chin beside her ear, feeling her breathe, smelling her hair. "You're not allowed to change your shampoo without asking," I whispered. "You smell too good."

"You're such a dork sometimes." I could hear the smile in her voice. "You said you bought something today too?"

"Yes." I reached over and pulled the package closer. "Found it at an antique shop type place."

"I know you. Bet it was that guy with a street stall."

"It was an upmarket stall." I unrolled the white cloth, revealing a magnificent curved blade. "I think it's Arabian. Niello engraving, see?" I traced the dark markings. "Solid silver blade. It may not be antique but it is beautiful."

"Ohhh. A knife. I do agree. It's very pretty. Can I touch it?"

"Sure. Best to keep it in the cloth when you handle it."

I placed the cloth and the knife across her hands then had one of those moments that make you want to facepalm. A knife like this, after what had happened to her?

Though I watched her carefully, it seemed not to faze her. As if to see the blade in the moonlight, she raised the knife.

"I might start a knife collection."

"Antique knives would be great to collect, Glass. I've seen some before but it never seemed...the right time. There's a lovely shop in Paris. I'll take you there."

I wrapped up the knife again and set it aside.

"Glass?"

"Yes?" I kissed her cheek.

"Do you think we could try, as in...try to have a baby? Before I start university next year?"

She had London lined up for university. "Won't it interfere?"

"It would, but I don't care. I can defer again if I have to. I'm in no hurry to get my degree, but I would..." She wriggled in my lap. "I'd really like to start a family."

What a big idea for this night. The best idea.

"Yes. Wren..." I breathed in, with my nose on her neck and my arms close about her. "Sweetheart, I'd like that too. I really, really would." I chuckled, thinking back. "It's lucky then wasn't it?"

"Huh?"

"That we forgot to use a condom earlier."

"What?"

"I told you that you had cum dribbling from your pussy." I started laughing again and couldn't stop, even when she tried to elbow me. "I did!"

"Bad man. I'm definitely with a bad man." Then she laughed too. "And I love you for it. Guess the cage was a hit. Made you get all impatient."

"Oh yeah. It sure did that."

I held her tight, squeezed her to me. The two of us keeping each other warm on a cold night, with the stars above. Romantic. Like something out of a movie.

Sometimes it takes a long time to find the person you're meant to be with. I'd finally hit the jackpot.

A memory nudged me. Here I was like this, with Wren, and I'd still not told her how I'd deceived her. Bad. If I didn't say this now, it'd bother me for the rest of my days. "Got something to tell you. I hope you won't hold it against me, though I guess I'll understand if you do."

"Oh? What is it?"

It would kill me if this broke us. *Here goes.* I relaxed my arms and made myself not hold her to me like she was my personal life buoy.

"It's about your father. I lied to you, by omission. I didn't tell you I was leading the men who shot him." When she only tensed and stayed silent, I went on. "We were rescuing Pieter and Jasmine. I know she's on your bad list too. Now..." I held up my hands, letting her loose to jump up if she wanted to go. "Now say what you need to."

She sat up and looked at me. I searched her face but didn't see anger. *Thank god.*

"I knew most of that." She shook her head. "I knew. I should've told you that Moghul revealed this. He thought it would make me like him more, I guess. I don't blame you. I don't. My father was a douchebag of the worst kind. We both know that. I've heard what he was doing to Jazmine when he was killed. Horrible." Her face screwed up into an expression of distaste. "It just took me a while to see that looking for his killer was ridiculous. I had to connect the dots in a way that made sense to me. He was my father. No matter what sort of person your father is, you're connected to each other. All my emotions were so messed up after he died."

"That's understandable, Wren."

"And that you *might* have killed him? It's like knowing you put down a rabid dog that used to guard me. Sort of. Kind of." She frowned. "One that bit me too. I hated him some of the time.

Jazmine?" She shrugged. "What she did to my brother was terrible and from what I heard from Pieter, she paid her dues many times over. I know Pieter loves her. Still, if I ever meet her, I may do something awful to her. Providing Pieter lets me. But you, Glass, I forgive you. How could I not forgive my man? Does that help you?" Her voice cracked as she spoke. She stroked her hand down the side of my face then smiled. "Say yes?"

"It helps. Pieter told you about her?" Damn that man.

"Mm-hm. I promised him I'd wait for you to bring it up. He seemed to think that best."

"Okay." Pieter had overstepped. He should've told me. He'd read Wren correctly though. In some ways, she'd forgiven Jazmine. "I don't think I've quite earned you. But I don't care. Come here." I wrapped her in my arms again and squeezed. "My heart's galloping off into the sunset right now. I needed to say that."

Wren giggled. "Love you," she whispered.

"Me too, baby, me too. Which reminds me. You know we've skipped a step?"

"Oh?"

"We should get married first *then* have babies."

Wren giggled. "I guess I got carried away too." She elbowed me in the ribs. "Well?"

"What?" I angled a brow at her.

"You're supposed to get down on your knee and ask me."

"It's too damn cold, besides, I like this method." Then I pushed her off my lap and pointed. "Kneel."

Her eyes went wide but she shuffled to her knees and waited expectantly. At least she wore jeans.

I leaned down and cradled her face in both my hands, smiling when she turned her head and nuzzled into my palm. "I don't have a ring yet, but imagine one. Do you, Wren, my little submissive girl slave, wish to marry me...one day soon, before I change my mind?"

She twisted her mouth and harrumphed. "Please. No joking."

Ah. I cleared my throat. "You know I adore you, girl. Will you marry me?"

"I –"

"Wait." I shook her head with my hand, thinking back to the cage and us, to everything. Impromptu too, but I figured this would mean as much to her, if not more. "Will you also accept my collar?"

"A collar? Really?"

"Uh-huh. I want to make sure I can chain you up, so you don't run off with a furniture salesman."

"Shhh!" Wren frowned adorably. "Seriously. Ahem. Yes, Glass, Sir, my man who I adore with all my heart. Yes to both. I want to marry you and, yes, I want to accept your collar."

"That smile is so beautiful, better than any Mona Lisa." I traced her lips. "It lights up my world, you know. Come back up here before you freeze." I patted my lap.

She climbed up and snuggled in again. After a while she stirred, lifted her head from my chest, and shivered. I rubbed my palm up and down her arm.

"Best we go in. Too cold out here for a little thing like you."

She shifted on my lap. "Could I see your knife again? Before we go in?"

"Sure. Anything for you, my love. Anything, at all. If it's not a real antique, I thought I'd get your name engraved on it."

"I'd love that. Thank you."

She tugged the blade from the sheath again and moonlight flowed along the metal.

"Beautiful," she said softly.

If this wasn't the civilized twentieth century, I could see Wren as some warrior princess leading a charge against her enemy – her teeth bared and her screaming.

What man didn't want a wild warrior princess kneeling at his feet?

CHAPTER 49

Chris

I sat back in the broad leather chair, put my elbows on the arm rests, and surveyed the computer screen with all the opened docs as well as the 'real' paperwork on the desk.

What did you do with something like this? There were places as far afield as Europe, Russia, and South America. Christ, I was just an accountant.

I tapped my fingertips together, feeling like that big glowing eye from *Lord of the Rings*.

Sauron?

Yeah. Him.

To be or not to be. To keep this empire of evil, or not? I needed time to decide.

I had plenty of time.

I sighed and rolled the chair back, walked to the door, and exited. From the sounds, dinner was being prepared in the kitchen.

I locked the door. Some things were best kept private.

The End

Following this is the alternative Thorn Path ending.

CHAPTER 50

Wren

The man was bluffing, but would Hugh forgive me, if he wasn't? If he could, Hugh would tell me to do this. He mightn't even be alive. I might give myself up for nothing. He'd tell me to do this. I just needed time. The airport security or the police would be here soon.

Unable to speak at first, I shook my head while staring into the angry face of the man holding the gun to Hugh.

"Last chance!"

I found my courage and screamed, "No!"

At the bang of the gun, I jerked.

No. He wouldn't have. No. I refused to believe, clinging to hope. No one was that barbaric.

But he had. He released him and Hugh slid down the smeared window, boneless, and vanished from sight.

I'd killed Hugh. How could I have done that? What sick, spineless person was I to do that?

My hand was at my mouth and I choked in sobs, my nose bubbling with snot, as I watched his blood move down the glass.

"Next!" The man outside had a little girl, his fist curled in her floral dress, and she screeched as he sat her on the trunk, with a thump, and as he shook her to get her to be quiet. "Next!" He yelled to me. "Out now or she is next. Then I get another, another, another."

At the last words, despite the girl's cries, a hush fell inside my head, dislocating me from the outside.

I couldn't do this, condemn her too. Couldn't let him kill a bunch of kids, while I sat in here safe. Why should I be worth more?

I shifted along the seat toward the door, watching him follow me, the gun swiveling so he could turn.

I put my hand on the door lock. Whose hand was that? It couldn't be mine. It seemed a million miles away.

"The gun! Put it on the floor."

The Beretta shook while I stared at it. By putting it down, I was sealing my fate. I listened for sirens, for any sign of help coming.

"Want me to start shooting kids!"

I didn't look at him, but I placed the gun on the floor, then I unlocked the door.

*****

Glass

"She's gone, man." Jurgen's words made me angry enough to punch him, but I didn't.

I leaned forward, staring through the windscreen and down the street to the car park entry.

The police swarmed over the ambush site, lights flashing, uniformed officers checking for evidence. An ambulance had taken away one man but the rest of the bodies had been left, clearly dead. Most of the casualties seemed to be Hugh's men. I had no idea how the attackers had managed it.

Outnumbered? Out planned? Maybe betrayed?

Who had diverted us? Hugh, or whoever our enemy was? Wren was gone and from snatches of overheard conversations from onlookers, she'd been their goal. For some reason Vetrov, had let her go, then come back for her.

"She's not gone, Jurgen, just missing. This time I'll find her."

"Sure. We will. I want to get these guys too." His quiet assurance helped. He looked up from where he'd been reading something on his phone. "Remember how you told me to give Pieter the notes with all the answers Wren gave us?"

I waited, frowning.

"Well, Pieter texted me before we started this, as we were rolling out the gate. The name Chris, he remembers it from when he was working for Vetrov in North Queensland."

"And? We need more than just that."

"I think we have that more. Jazmine has seen the notes too. He asked her about the name and it triggered a memory. Chris helped her and Pieter escape. She thought he was a good guy, in a way. The other guards at the time said he was supposed to be an accountant on Magnetic Island. Pieter's found an accountant who works there with that first name. It has to be him. He dug, found out when he graduated from university, found an old picture on the net. It's him. And Zoe, the other name Wren heard Chris say, that was one of the other girls held with Jazmine."

I sat back. "Shit. We can do this. I can be in Australia tomorrow. At the island the day after. I can pay this Chris a visit. He knows Vetrov. He has to."

"Yes. And we're coming with you. Me, Pieter, Sam, anyone else I can convince, along with all the weapons we need to take out this bastard."

I stared. "You'll be fucked if the cops find you."

"You think that's going to stop us? We have to get Wren back. Shut the fuck up and plan shit like you always do."

"Huh." I sucked in a breath then grinned. "Doing it. Get us back to the compound. We're going hunting for bear and Goldilocks."

"Now you're talking." He started the engine. "I always wanted a bearskin rug."

Think positive. Planning was the key. I was getting her back, no matter what I had to do.

CHAPTER 51

Wren

I was in the back of a van when they told me they weren't allowed to drug me – within a few minutes of being dragged from the car and thrown there. My wrists had been ziptied, my mouth gagged, and I was jammed up against the back of the front seats. Three men were in here with me, all well-dressed and normal. If big, well-armed, and menacing when they deigned to look at me could be thought of as normal.

The worst of them had leaned down and smiled. I knew evil smiles well. He had them down pat.

"No drugs for you, but no one told us not to nail your hands to your pretty thighs if you annoy me."

I shuddered and leaned away.

"Are you going to be good for me, Wren?"

I'd nodded. Did he think I'd say no?

No drugs. I guessed that *he* knew I was pregnant. The man wanted his child alive and healthy. Did he have a heart, after all?

I would've deserved that anyway. The nails in me. Punishment for my impossibly bad sins. Unforgiveable sins. What I'd done to Hugh swamped my head, in waves. *Why'd I do that? Why? Fuck. Why.*

Round and round and round went my thoughts.

I'd killed Hugh, a man who would do anything for me. I'd casually let him die.

And Glass, he'd be blaming himself again. I couldn't seem to set the world right. All those I cared for died, half the time because of something I did, or neglected to do.

They took me places and I cared as little as I had when drugged.

I lay blindfolded and gagged in a plane, in the trunk of a car, and the back of a van, and said nothing. Why bother?

They delivered me on time, apparently. Or so he said when he opened the trunk and found me.

Nighttime. No extra light had come in the trunk.

"Hello, Wren. I hope they treated you well?" The familiar roughness of his voice had my full attention in an instant. I felt his hand on my hair, saw torchlight through the blindfold. He lifted my head as if examining me then the torchlight seemed to travel down my body. This was his routine, I guessed. He felt safer accepting illegal cargos at night.

I grunted when he pulled my legs apart.

"Don't worry. I'm not doing anything to you here." Then he gathered the skirt of my dress upward, exposing me all the way to my lower back.

He was silent and I guessed he was looking at his brand.

"That looks pretty. Healthy. You seem unharmed. Good. Treating you badly is my prerogative. As is treating you well, from now on. Welcome back, my girl."

Then he pushed up the blindfold. I could see him. The real him. No mask. He laid down the torch and the light bounced off the roof of the trunk – and he kissed me, with his hands cradling my face. Mine were still tied at my back. He kissed me as if I were something delicate that might break. My breath caught. No mask. Again, he whispered, "Welcome back. My name, Wren, is Moghul."

Then he slammed shut the trunk and drove me to his house. All the way there, being bounced around against the carpeted trunk, I ran his face through my memory. He didn't look like a monster without the mask. Brown, artfully scruffy hair that on another man would make me itch to set right, and his eyes, such warm eyes. I'd seen hardness in them before and I'd felt fear. Not now. Not this time.

Moghul. An odd name, but appropriate for a man who tossed aside society's rules as if they were trash.

He'd looked...contemplative, as well as quietly triumphant.

Hope had awakened at that.

Hope... Why? I was a stranger to myself.

CHAPTER 52

Moghul

When I let her out of the trunk, the garage doors were wound down, trapping us in the huge space with the expanse of concrete and the BMW, the corvette, and my vintage motorbikes.

I studied her, stepping away to take in all of her. She swayed a little but seemed able to stand. All that time in the dark and tied up would've played havoc with her muscles and balance, plus her hands were trapped behind her back.

I tsked, smiling sadly, thinking of all the perverted things I could do to her...if I could get her in the right mindset. I knew more about who she was now. The facts from Europe had helped me see.

She was barefoot and would be feeling the cold hardness of the concrete. The black dress would be the one in which they'd taken her. It was pretty and swerved in at all the right places, curved out at all the right ones – her breasts and hips. I'd burn it. She needed no reminders of her past and it must be filthy. Her hair had been squashed by the blindfold and I wanted see it hang free and clean and beautiful.

I stepped in and untied the blindfold, then dropped the cloth to the floor.

I removed the gag then locked my chain-link steel collar on her neck and clicked the leash to it.

"I'm putting my cuffs back on you also, but you're going to walk with me up to the viewing room without me binding you apart from the collar. Is that understood?"

"Yes, sir." Her reply was soft.

"Thank you for calling me Sir."

The shock on her face also pleased me.

There'd been time to think since I'd made the decision. Nothing was certain. I'd come to terms with that.

The last text had underlined the fragility of our time. Glass had tracked down Chris. If Chris was at risk, I was at risk, and Glass had arrived a half a day ago. The man had turbo charged his way here, taking risks of detection to fly farther down the Queensland coast than he normally would. According to my intel, the rest of his men would arrive later today.

My man had done the trip the safe way, and so, this came down to mere hours.

I had the equivalent of a special forces team ready to attack my house, once they had my address, if they could get it, but right now, Glass was vulnerable.

I'd told Chris and offered him alternatives, offered help. I guess a simple solution would've been to eliminate Chris but I'd lost my taste for ordering or performing homicide. I'd never had one. With business...I'd just disconnected from what I'd told someone to do. It had been like firing an employee – necessary, nasty, but someone had to make the decision. My first and only personal kill a couple of months ago had convinced me of the wrongness. If I couldn't stomach it in front of me, it was dishonest to make others do it. I was done with this dirty business.

Whatever Chris decided, it was his affair; I was done.

He knew if he dealt with Glass, he could have my business, do what he liked with it. I'd extracted what money I could. Besides, I had nest eggs all over the place, in half a dozen countries.

Fate could play her hand without my further interference.

The ground was cracking beneath my feet. There was only Wren to take care of now and for the first time in my life, I was unsure. She carried our child and I'd come to realize I loved her as much as I could love anyone. Would that be enough for her?

My revelation of the day was one I'd always been too selfish to understand. Some people demand of you the ultimate sacrifice, before you can deserve their love. When your heart beats with pain at the thought of losing someone, you've found that person. I'd found mine.

I led her away and into the hallway, only to see the devastation in her bearing – red-rimmed eyes, the sway in her gait, the lowness of her head. I needed more than this. More than my distant persona. More.

"Come here." I scooped her up and carried her to the bathroom.

After making her drink some water, I stripped her naked and urged her under the warm jets. I helped her wash, smoothing the soap and shampoo over her body, becoming reacquainted with her curves, her secret places. It was impossible not to do more than feel. I sneaked kisses and curled her hair around my hand, made her stand still while I paid homage with my mouth, to her neck, her shoulders, and her plump nipples. I stood naked under the water with her and only held her to me.

Was it half an hour? More? I took my time.

Whatever thoughts filled her head, I was pleased I could cast my spell over her still. Slowly, the confusion and worry faded from her face and she melted into my caresses and my dominance. I'd had her obedient and willing before, and I could do so again. When near me, she was mine. She parted her mouth and shivered at my touch and at my bites on her nape and breasts...she succumbed, even opening her legs when I slid my hand there and cupped my palm over her mons.

The silver gleam of the collar on her neck drew my eye. With my chin on her shoulder and my hand between her legs, I studied how the metal rested on her skin, basking in the fact that I had bought it and placed it on her.

"Mine," I murmured, half to myself, kissing her below her ear. It wasn't quite true, but close, so close. "Thank you, again."

She bent back her neck and stared at me. Puzzled, I was sure.

I could, perhaps, have taken her further and made her come but it wasn't the right moment, not at all.

After drying her, and being sure she was stronger, I led her to the viewing room. Both of us were naked and a little damp, but that was fine. The aircon would dry us quickly.

Knowing what was in there, I picked her up before the entrance and carried her in, then I sat down on one of the sofas with her cuddled into me and half on my lap. The equipment was behind her and she couldn't have seen it. The block and tackle, the ropes and hooks. I surveyed my preparations and wondered if I was about to do the right thing. I needed to settle things before I began, in any case.

It'll wait.

I breathed in, out, closed my eyes and simply absorbed the need I had to cradle my girl.

I had to care for her. I'd always done that as a Dom to my submissives but this was new, revelatory. Before I'd only skimmed the surface of what I could be to someone. With Wren, when I had her like this, with her head tucked into me, my arms around her, I had to suppress my strength, torn between cuddling her gently and a futile and insane yearning to hold her so tightly we'd merge, and I'd become a part of her, flesh, bone, blood, mind.

"Talk to me, please. Tell me everything. I need to know. I want to take some of your pain, if I can."

At that, I felt her shudder and I braced myself for the storm.

CHAPTER 53

Wren

How dare he? Take some of my pain? Hah. So ridiculous it almost made me burst into tears.

There was pain, and there was what he'd made me endure, which needed a whole new word.

"Your men...they killed...made me kill, my friend, Hugh. You bastard," I whispered that last part, then I drew strength. "How could you have that done to us and then dare to say what you have?"

I bristled, feeling ill, wanting to tear myself away from him but sure he wouldn't allow it. There was nothing he could say that would help me.

"I'm sorry."

Except that. It assuaged a little of the guilt somehow. Maybe because by saying it, he admitted guilt and took on some of mine.

I sobbed. I sobbed into his chest, the man who was to blame for kidnapping me and killing my friends. I couldn't reconcile it at all. It was just me, my response to him, evil fucker that he was. I hated some of him, liked, pitied, and respected other parts of him in the most appalling mish mash of fucked-up emotions ever.

A notion bubbled up that made me want to giggle crazily. Was this how married couples felt after a million years together?

"It's not your fault, Wren. I don't know what they did but I didn't tell them to do it specifically. I'm very sorry. I'm not a good man, but

I'm sorry that happened. I don't want to hurt you. Not like that."

Could I read truth in his words? No clue, no fucking clue. Either way, I shot straight into anger, a whole world of incandescent anger.

"They shot him! Then they demanded I give myself up or they'd kill him! I chose the wrong thing, the stupidest, most selfish thing, and they shot him." I couldn't help seeing it again in my head. The gun. The blood. The devastation when the man carried through on his threat. The abrupt *bang*. The way Hugh's head shook at the impact yet nothing else of him changed. The blood still meandered down the outside of the glass, until he slid from view. "They took him and they shot him." I gasped a few times, my throat having trouble figuring out whether to breathe or choke on my tears, before I found my voice again. "Your men...Moghul. *They* did it."

"Not by my specific orders, but yes, it happened as a result of what I wanted. I can't change the past."

There was a rawness in his voice that I'd never heard before – not just anger. Sadness and anger?

"You. I wanted you. I take responsibility for that. You should know by now that I'm honest. I've made mistakes." He laughed, bitterly. "Most of them lately are because of you. I need you in my life and I'm not letting you go, Wren. I'm also going to care for you. You see, I'm the only man who truly understands who you are. I know the real you."

What the fuck? That scared me.

What did he know?

A dark thing stirred at the back of my mind. A place, a circumstance, a history, I'd avoided since forever. There was a time when I knew I might have done bad things, no matter what I'd been told.

Was I right to fear myself, after all?

"No," I whispered. "You're lying."

"I'm not. I'm going to tell you the truth about yourself."

What truth? My heart stuttered like someone had turned off the switch. "You're lying..." I swallowed. "You're fucking lying!"

"You don't swear at me. Never. I'll reserve punishment for this until after. Caring for you means showing you what you are. Who you are." He pulled up my chin so I had to meet his gaze. "You're more than you think, as well as less."

I scrambled, pinned there by ideas, by thoughts, as well as his hand. He had plans and I didn't want to see them happen. I said quietly, "I'm pregnant with your child."

"I know. It's part of why I decided I had to have you." His grip on my face began to hurt. "I love you Wren, whether you want me to or not."

Love? Him?

"Then you can't do anything bad to me. I might lose the baby."

"You're dictating to me?" He laughed. "I can do as many bad things to you as I want to. What comes next isn't punishment anyway. I'm going to be careful. You'll be fine. You're young, healthy. You can stand this because without this we will be *nothing*. I don't want to be your nothing, Wren. I want all of you and I will do anything to make that come true. Fucking anything."

And then, I glimpsed that part of him I'd often seen – the devoted sadist.

I looked away and tried to calm myself. What was coming, if not punishment? I didn't like the sounds of any of this. To stall him, I'd ask what I absolutely did not want to know. Ever. But what choice did I have?

"What is it then? What do you think you know about me?"

"These are facts. I'll tell you *then* you're allowed to think about them but you're not to blame yourself.

"First. Glass was there when your father died. He led the team that assaulted my House. He may have fired the shot that killed him. I don't know. To be fair, I'd have done the same thing, concealed my involvement by distracting you."

Glass? My man, my hero? I blinked, staring at Moghul's chest, at his nipple of all things. I couldn't get my head around this. Yet it made total sense. It explained why he'd first come to me, the unease I'd felt when he led me around town. That feeling he was concealing something.

"It's true?" I could hear my own puzzled tone as if the question was said by someone else.

"Yes. Your father was a man more perverted than I am. That's also true. What you make of that's up to you."

Yeah. I shrugged. *Old news.* That meant nothing to me...

He patted me lightly, doing more of his *caring*, I guessed. The feeling sank in though and it helped me, no matter the who and the whys.

Damn.

Tears started and I blinked them away. Glass had lied to me, but what he'd done since must mean more? His dishonesty paled in comparison with what I'd seen him do since then. He was still my man...and I was still here.

"Okay." I gulped. "Go on." What else did he have?

That last fact, yes, it was truth. I'd deal with it later. Poor Glass, he'd probably hated doing that to me, once he and I had become lovers.

"Second. This is in your past. You've always been afraid that you killed your fiancé, Nathan. He was stabbed to death. The police blamed a home invader or a burglar. They never caught him. You were hospitalized for months afterward, partly because your father insisted. Powerful man, your father, he hated your fiancé, from what I can tell. My detective dug all this up and more. You had a child and she was stillborn. You were on drugs for sleeping problems for years afterward, off and on, though you had problems before the murder. The pathologist speculated to my man, not on paper, just verbally, that your sleep disorder contributed."

Contributed? What?

I was listening and checking off facts as he went. Which of these was the one? "Tell me."

"The murder, it wasn't murder. It was manslaughter. You killed him. You used the knife on your fiancé. The forensic report was subtly altered to say a tall man did it. Old footprints were attributed to a thief. Blood was found on a doorknob that wasn't actually there."

My mind went blank.

"Digging that up took a lot of money. Your father protected you, I suppose."

Or the family name. That. It wouldn't have been me.

"We all have crosses to bear, Wren. Me, you, Glass. No one is innocent. No one. Now you know your hands aren't clean."

Crosses to bear. Yes, and I was crumbling under the weight. Had he done me a favor by telling me? How? But I'd always wanted to know what truly happened to Nathan.

My dark place was real.

This would be why I'd had flashbacks, for a year after his death, of knives rising and falling. Of blood.

It had been me all along. Why had my father lied to me?

I'd killed Nathan, my sweet, innocent Nathan. He'd barely graduated from being a boyfriend. An architecture student, a beautiful person. I'd planned a family with him, against my father's wishes.

How quaint. My mouth twitched. I'd been pregnant then too.

The coincidence was so ironic and so awful. I put my hand to my stomach. And now I carried another man's child. I was sure I was going to pay for this later but right now I was numb. I'd suspected this for so long, been told I was wrong. And now, Moghul, my worst enemy, had somehow become a sort of perverted friend. Why did he have to be the one who found this out?

I was wrecked. Crying, what was that? It was impossible. I had no tears for this.

I wanted to curl up in a corner and wrap my arms over my head and do nothing. Inside my head was a wasteland.

The blood on my hands was real.

"No," I whispered. "No. I can't..." I shook my head.

Here I was, snuggled up to the man who'd kidnapped me. The man I'd tried to knife only days ago. Why wasn't he afraid I'd do it again? Maybe he was? Nothing was the right way up. He said he cared for me and that he was truthful, and I guess he was, he did. He'd only hurt me physically in ways that I, in my own perversion, loved. Even his punishments only jarred me, made me think, made me look up to him afterward, and that was *so* wrong too.

Bad was good. Good was bad. My head up and dumped me into a swamp where none of my ideas would come to an end. They circled me, endlessly, like sharks and flotsam and zombie babies and yeah, stuff. Mess.

I clawed my hands into my hair and groaned out my frustration. "Let me go! Please."

"Shhh. I'm going to help you. I want you to keep your eyes on me. Don't be afraid of me or of what will happen. Do you hear me, Wren? All you need to do is listen to me. Answer," he grated out the last and I flinched.

Fuck.

I nodded, my hands still in my hair. He nudged them away.

"Words, please, Wren. Look at me."

My whirling thoughts slowed. "Yes. I heard you."

311

I raised my head, the sofa upholstery rasping against my ear as I did so, and I locked my gaze on him as he'd asked. It was easy to do, far easier than disobeying. As I looked into his eyes, at the darkness of his gaze, I sank thankfully into that waiting space. The carousel of gibbering that had filled my head only seconds before died away. I needed something I could do without having to think.

I needed this.

His smile warmed me. "Put your wrists at your back, Wren."

Even as I watched and listened, that transformation sneaked over his face and his voice became a deadly purr. I remembered what that meant from so many previous times: *I want to do things to you that I'll like, though you may not.*

I welcomed that. I wanted to be hurt. Needed it. It was a relief to know this was coming.

I put my hands behind me and he locked my wrists together. His arm muscles pressed on me from above and below, and my bewilderment sank me. I liked how that felt.

For a fleeting second I entertained a doubt. How traitorous this was to Glass, accepting this man's dominance over me, but...I could do nothing about that. There was only me here. And Moghul.

"This is only until I have you ready. Then, I'll release your hands. I don't want you panicking."

Panic? He said he knew me but I had nothing left inside. I'd used up my emotions, my strength, whatever it was that drove me. If he wanted me to stand up and be flogged, I'd crumple in a heap.

Moghul wormed his arm out from under me, disentangled our bodies, and stood. Then he helped me to my feet but kept a hand on my arm.

I could see what he intended now. The ropes hanging from some sort of block and tackle affair beside his pit, the steel table, the row of hooks, the bottles and swabs. I swallowed. Maybe I had energy left for fear, after all.

"Wren, look at me."

I swung my head. "Why? Why this. You said –"

"Keep your eyes on me, remember."

"Yes."

"This is *not* punishment. I think you'll...like this. However, if you take your eyes off me again, I will be unhappy."

Unhappy snapped into place in my head and made all sorts of weird connections that came together and summed up like a jigsaw puzzle. I didn't want to make him unhappy. Oh yes, I'd fallen back into fucked-up land where what he wanted mattered to me.

I took my lip between my teeth and I didn't take my eyes off him. Watching him watching me was keeping me functioning. I needed this, I reminded myself. I could feel my eyes widen, the room soften. A familiar, ingrained response.

He ducked low, to my eye level. "That helps?"

We both knew what he meant. I drew in a breath and admitted it. "Yes."

"Good. You know I like hurting you, but this, though it may hurt, you will like it, a lot. If I'm wrong, your screams will tell me."

I blinked. *Screams. Oh.* Well then. That was okay.

"Lie on the table on your stomach." There was a small portable step. He held my arms to steady me as I obeyed. With my wrists cuffed, at the last, it was more allowing him to lower me, and then adjusting where I lay.

My skin stuck to the table and the steel was cold.

Like this, I couldn't always see him as he moved about.

On a tray was a row of hooks. They were thick – far bigger than any needle that ever went into a dog. I knew my needle sizes and sixteen gauge was the biggest I'd seen. Whatever gauge these were, they were far bigger, and thus, far more fascinating.

Those were going in me?

This wasn't punishment? I was beginning to understand. Last time he'd threatened me with these he'd been angry. Moghul, when he simply was being sadistic, I trusted him not to hurt me too much. If he said I could take this, I believed him.

I'd learned to trust him. That, by itself, seemed more perverted than anything else in this room.

The anticipation had me on edge. I'd taken pain before, but this was new. Having a ton of metal hooked into me, how would I react?

"Here." Moghul unrolled a poster and attached it to the railing around the pit, so I could see it. "See how happy she is?"

The smile on her face as the young woman dangled from hooks in midair was...ecstatic.

"Wow," I whispered.

"Keep looking at me. Nothing exists but you and me. Remember that."

But when I couldn't see him, I sneaked looks at the equipment and the woman too. As he swabbed my back with some sort of alcohol and drew on surgical gloves, I saw how total Moghul's concentration was on his task. I was the center of his universe.

He told me what he meant to do while he worked, forewarned me.

The weariness of my days of travel, and the battering I'd taken from all the other things, too many to recall, were thrown to the background. The chaos faded, vanished, gone. I rocked when he pushed me. My eyes varied from full-on alert to a humming sort of calm when I half-closed them.

I listened and his words embroidered the peace, like stitches weaving on a tapestry.

Words...

He would push metal through my skin, so the hook went deep into my subcutaneous area...human skin was strong...people did this for fun. Lots of people. I wouldn't bleed, much, if at all.

The patter reassured me.

Four hooks in total.

His explanations didn't remove all fear, but they added layers of excitement, reassurance, trust.

I need this.

When he said, "I'm pushing in the first." The room paused. He cut me with something and I gasped. I tensed, my mons and my breasts were naturally three of the main places of pressure between my body and the table. As if they bore all my weight.

My blood seemed to pulse stronger, and I became aware of the sexual...undertones of this act.

Moghul, shoving metal into me, while I was bound.

I needed to stop fantasizing. My arousal embarrassed me.

"Ready?"

He'd actually asked me?

I eyed him, blinking slowly, and nodded, alert for the prick of sharpness at my back.

The sink of the thick hook into my back beneath my shoulder blade sent a sizzling wave of pleasure cascading through me so quickly I gasped, and I was almost coming before I grasped what was happening. I bowed my head, eyes shut, feeling him push it out the other side, determined not to embarrass myself.

"Hmmm." He stopped before me, stared a moment, then retrieved the next hook.

On the second hook, I was gritting my teeth, but not from the pain.

The third made me arch a miniscule amount before I caught myself, squirming to relieve the building tension. My clit seemed ready to electrify the table. If it swelled more, if there was more pressure. I gasped and put my forehead to the cool table.

Three in me. *God. Why was I getting off on this?*

"Last one."

Fuck. The metal was inside me already. I keened as it penetrated further, arching up my back despite him leaning on me. Then the hook popped out the other side, and I was coming before I could stop myself. Full-on shuddering and gasping.

Controlling the aftershocks was harder to do, not panting, even more so.

I found him before me, once more at eye level. "Did you just climax?"

I blushed hot, wanting to hide.

"Wren, answer me."

"Maybe. I guess...yes?"

"Ahh. Good. I was right."

"Arrogance was always your best feature," I mumbled from where I lay, recovering, trembling, as I felt again that multiple presence in my back of something foreign.

He chuckled. "Now I just have to tie your legs and hoist you into the air over my pit."

I managed to think that through. "Above the pit?" That thing was deep.

"Don't worry. I filled it with water."

So now I only had to worry about drowning if I fell in as well as my body hanging from hooks.

I squeezed shut my eyes.

"Wren. Look at me."

I snapped them open. *Looking. I was looking. Yes, Sir.*

He tied my legs with rope, as he'd promised, doubling them over, and attached the rope above, then linked more red rope to the eyelets on the hooks. He hoisted me up from the table. I was still in that stomach-down position, with my body taking the strain where the

315

hooks entered my back and the rope bound my legs.

Doubts rushed in. Had he done it properly? Would the hooks bend or tear out? If I fell...

My fears died away.

The pull translated into a stretching in my shoulder blades that changed as the seconds passed, pumping me full of a soft, buzzing energy.

Then he swung me over, so that I was just able to see into the pit. Yes, there was water up to a few feet from the top. A full story deep.

Why?

My hands were still tied. He'd said he'd free them.

Pain? There was none. I was floating. Surfing on air. Happy. Though I knew that the darkness waited for me, it could wait...

"My hands?" I croaked out, while tugging at where they were held by the leather.

I swung slightly, focusing on that feeling of being fastened to something and pulled on, stretched out until I was full and scattered, expanding beyond where my body ended.

My thoughts obliterated.

"Yes. I'm doing it. I'm freeing you."

He showed me a big, shiny knife with a blade that curved forever.

The cuffs had a metal link.

"You're wondering? There is this." He placed it at my neck, near where I'd cut him. "Look at me."

I did, but I curved back my neck, though my muscles there were waning in strength. Holding my head up forever wasn't happening.

"You like knives, Wren. I'm just showing you their dangers."

Then he snaked the knife about my neck three times. I counted, still in my haze and I wasn't afraid. He trailed the blade over me, drawing complex curves and lines, encircling my nipples before ducking under me and sucking on them while the knife wandered elsewhere. I wondered how he knew how hard it pressed, when to stop so it didn't cut.

With him licking at me and mouthing me, and holding my nipple in his teeth, arousal was impossible to deny.

I whimpered as the tip of the knife tapped my clit and pricked me. When I squirmed, he tsked.

"If you move too much, I might cut you."

But he'd already sunk his metal claws into me.

The hooks declared their presence. They curved into my back, claiming me, taking up more room in my skin than they should.

If moving wasn't good, staying still was exquisite. The knife was going around my clit, tapping, prodding lightly, pressing. The flat of the blade or the tip? I couldn't *tell*, only knew that my pussy was slicker than moments ago and now, he inserted the knife between those lower lips.

I wriggled, such a small wriggle, because the haze was dissipating and being replaced by lust and a need to be fucked. *If that went in me. Oh god.* I sucked my lip in, focused on all the places of me that were under his control.

The knife slid in a fraction more, parting my lips.

I hung my head and groaned, straining at the cuffs.

"Very pretty, Wren, with this in you. If only you could see the blade in your cunt. Are you going to come for me again? All strung up and hooked. All mine. I'm going to fuck you with this knife and you're going to come beautifully because I know you're my slave. You're mine like it says here." He wiped wet fingers across my back then my inner thighs. "That's you. Wet. Wanting this. I could fuck you with a baseball bat and you'd suck it in. Open this pussy wide and let me fuck you."

Then it sank deeper into me. The blade, the hilt? I barely stifled another groan. Didn't matter. As the knife forged deeper, he put his mouth over my clit and tongued me well. Sloppy wet, slippery kisses on my clit. Deep fucking with the knife, so deep it hurt, then out, then in again.

"Your cunt can take this all the way in."

It was so hard though. Not like a dick or a dildo. The hilt, for sure. Wide, hard plastic, made for a man's fist to hold, not for inside me.

"Open up. You can take it. Open that cunt." He pushed it in some more.

I was moaning loudly, swaying on the hooks, my pussy clenching onto this strange object, my body striving to push my pussy at his mouth and the knife all at once.

He kept fucking me with it, going ever deeper, messier, wetter, sliding it in like he was some machine made only to fuck me. Then he jammed it inside me even higher and left it in there while he licked me in one long slippery line that ended with him putting his whole mouth over my clit, then biting it, toggling that swollen button.

There. Oh fuck yes, there. I writhed on the knife, on his mouth, on his tongue, and on the hooks.

The ropes creaked as I came and arched higher. I floated on evanescent lust, my thighs parting as if I were about to split in two from the knife inside me, coming and crying out and shaking. Slowly I came down, the orgasm waning, and I collapsed, my every muscle limp, my mind shattered.

I heard the shuffle of his feet. Then he came to my head and shoved his cock in until I gagged. For the first few seconds, I could barely comprehend what was happening. The slop, slop, slop of his dick entering, thrusting, and withdrawing over and over, his hands on either side of my head, and the bump on the hooks from my body jarring – it added up to a surreal mind-blowing experience.

Facefucked while hanging from hooks. It turned me on and made me feel like a disgraceful whore, which turned me on even more.

When he was done, drool and cum dripped from my mouth.

The hooks, the ropes, they cradled me, sweetly.

He crouched before me, smiling and watching for a while, as if the sight of me red-faced and messed up pleased him... Of course he liked seeing me like this. The man always had. I tried to stare back but my neck muscles were done and I slowly slumped until all I could see was the floor through the tangled locks of my hair.

He took a firm hold of my hair and levered back my head.

Though words rose up that I might speak, none went to my tongue and I stared back wearily.

"Nothing to say? You look so adorable like this, my girl. You look fucking destroyed. Don't forget this." He slapped my face lightly. "Don't forget you're mine."

Then he straightened and walked back around me, leaving me stunned.

He released my wrists and I did nothing more than lick my lips and twine my fingers together. He swung me out, further over the water.

Below was coolness. My parched throat could taste it from here.

The knife spun past, beneath my gaze, to plop into the water and spiral down into the pool, finally coming to rest at the very bottom. Lying there, smiling at me in its silvery dominance.

"For you, Wren. Fetch it if you want to. The ropes will come loose if you pull the dangling strand. The hooks will hold you until I return in an hour or so. There is bleeding but barely a trickle. Hooks, if they tear out, do little permanent damage. Four will hold your weight. One will not.

"Decide. I'll be at the pool."

I heard all his words but had trouble deciphering them. Thinking wasn't my best thing, right then. Nothing, I was best at nothing. My brain was fried. I licked my lips again. Thirsty.

What did he mean? I could get loose?

The knife, down there, beckoned me, like a dodgy car salesman with oily words, or a demon with promises of Hell.

CHAPTER 54

Wren

How long did I hang there? I wasn't sure. The effortless existence had consumed me.

When I had my feet on solid ground again I might bounce into space with each step.

The knife, which was it? Demon, I guessed.

My arms hung down before me, where they'd ended up after I grew tired of clasping my hands together. I squinted, as if by doing so I could see the knife more clearly there, at the bottom of fathoms of water. Could I swim that far?

What did he expect me to do?

Escape?

He didn't want me to, but I had the choice. Why though? Why now?

He'd never wanted me to escape before.

A knife said killing. It said blood. I didn't need a knife to escape him did I? The answer came instantly. *Yes.* Because if I could somehow get loose and walk out of this house, if that were possible, I'd still have him to contend with. He'd haul me back here. I knew that, even if the thought of killing him came with a whole other burden of guilt. His death didn't call to me as it had. My hate had dwindled, somehow. He wasn't an enemy anymore. He was a force of nature.

He was also between me and Glass. Me and my life. My child's life. I knew that, saddened as I was.

I doubted he really thought I would kill him. Perhaps it was a test then? Or a trap.

What did it matter when I was yards above, spun out and tired, with hooks in my back?

All this was pointless...

I was never one for giving up. I suppose he knew that too.

The ropes on my legs were well tied and based around the cuffs, the pressure distributed so evenly that all that remained, when I undid the knot and they fell away, was the indent from the twirl of the coils on my skin. The jerk, when my weight fell only on the hooks, made me scream.

Owie. Lightheaded, I waited for the new pains to settle.

A moment later, blood dripped onto the water from my back. *Drip, drop, drip.*

I should've let myself down gently. My legs seemed heavier than a tombstone, filled with cement.

Halfway there. How could I possibly remove a hook in my back? Though I could stretch my arm and touch them, the extreme weight of my body made pulling them out impossible. Unless...

He had me hanging lower than the metal railings that surrounded the water-filled pit. There was a sectional ladder I'd need, if I fell in the water. I could swing, now that my legs weren't attached above. After five or ten attempts, I managed to hook my legs over the railing and sit. For ages, I remained there, breathing through the reawakened burn in my back. I tried to quell the shaking in my legs. I might've torn my skin more.

The baby. God. I cupped my stomach. Was this right?

Logic said yes. Besides, I *had* to.

I carried on. I released the ladder and it slid down into the water, rattling only a little, its lower end seeming to quiver with the rippling of the water. If I was at the bottom, I could use it to climb out. How long could I hold my breath, in this condition? I was tired, losing blood, my limbs shaking.

By twisting, by gritting my teeth and whining and trying over and over, I extracted the hooks. The slippery thickness in my fingers combined with the slide of the hook as I pulled, almost had me fainting. Funny, really, considering what I'd endured. I plucked them out, I shook, and more blood ran down my back, but I wasn't stopping, not now.

At the final hook, of course, I fainted.

Blank.

When I woke, I was swinging backward, headfirst. The hook was gone, I thought, ripped out, because the rope was up there, dangling. I'd not felt it tear. My legs, my far, faraway legs, slid off the railing and I fell into the water, upside down.

Coolness. Confusion. Bubbles and blood spiraled away.

By throwing my arms about, I found the surface and sucked in a lungful of air. When I next had a thought, my fists were wrapped around the ladder. My knuckles were white. Letting go meant drowning. *Remember that.*

Upwards? I craned back my head, dizzy. There was light and air and maybe freedom up there.

Down? I looked down, careful not to slip my feet off the rung. My legs, all blurry, a yard deep in the water and there: *the knife.* Blood spread around me, tinting the water with little swirls of red. I was blacking out already, here and there, swimming down was stupid.

Fucking stupid.

I had a baby inside me but what choice did I have? Let us both remain here as his for the rest of our lives? What if this harmed the child? Which was worse? Living in his prison or dying? Then there was the best possible result – living free, with my baby in my arms. It couldn't happen if I didn't do anything at all.

This was as awful as my decision about Hugh – it was impossible to be sure which was right.

I dived and arrowed down through the water, determined. One target. I kept my eyes on the knife, zeroed in on that dark thing at the bottom of yards of water, like some robot on a mission. I always could swim well. Fainting was *not* happening. My fingers closed, and I swooped into a turn, pushing off from the bottom and kicking.

The trail back up was marked with curls and blots of red.

CHAPTER 55

Chris

You're fucking tough for a prissy accountant. The words of my helper, a giant of a man in jeans and green camo shirt. I wasn't small either, and he'd seen me kick a man halfway across a room. I guess he'd met all sorts and I was small potatoes. He had three friends to back him up too.

My helpers, courtesy of Moghul.

I stood there, watching them deal with the mess like they figured this was no worse than a day at the supermarket. I was cool on the outside too, but on the inside, I was rerunning the last ten minutes, thinking through what Moghul had said.

Your decision. Do as you see fit. The business is yours if you want it, want to fight for it. I want my hands clean from now on. However, I'd advise seeing him before his friends arrive later today. You really don't want them around. Not if you want to be in one piece after.

His advice had been terribly suggestive. Glass's friends were SAS and sundry assorted ex-military types. Armed to the teeth, I gathered. And so...this had happened.

I'd knocked on the door, all polite, recognized Glass, even minus that blond mohawk the original pictures showed. I'd told him who I was. His buddy, Sam, sat on the sofa at the far end of the room, near the window, same as the surveillance pics had shown.

"Hi, you're Glass, right?"

"Yes. You are?"

I think he knew from square one. Suspicion had been there, in his voice, his face. Expected, but the guy was still confident. He had years of war and killing in his history. I was a paltry accountant who dabbled in martial arts and liked BDSM and, lately, women who came to me via nefarious means. Only two specific women, but I guess he'd know that too.

I'd killed only one man, close up. I knew I could kill, but I was sweating this.

This man wasn't bad, just a guy looking for his woman, and Moghul had her.

Me, I had four men outside this unit, waiting for my go ahead. Press a button on the device in my pocket and they'd come charging in. This was my choice, not theirs. They'd only scoped the unit and made the assault plan.

Let Glass live and he'd demand what I knew, threaten to expose me if I didn't say. Moghul would go down. Maybe I'd be okay, maybe not. Moghul wasn't my best friend but...there were fucking millions at stake here. The properties he was handing me, alone, made it an incredible gift. Even if I wound up all the dirty businesses he ran. I'd seen a summary, had the rest on a computer file. So much to go through, it would take days.

The good thing to do would be to give up Moghul. But I didn't know this Glass from a bar of soap. Moghul was like me, hard, but fair. He'd take care of Wren, no matter why she was with him.

My past wasn't precisely clean. My future could be cleaner. A few words, tell him Moghul's address, and I was done. My chances of coming out of the alternative unscathed were crazily impossible to predict. Microseconds, only microseconds, all it took to sway this, one way, or the other.

"I'm Chris Garrick." I stared into his eyes. Should I, could I, do this? I wasn't a killer. "I have some information for you."

"How'd you find me?" His hand was behind his back and I guessed he had a pistol tucked back there. Guessed he could draw it and shoot it faster than I could hit him...maybe.

"Vetrov." Ahhh, that piqued his interest. "He thinks I'm running away. I'm not a man who runs. He told me you wanted me. I can tell you where he is, for a price. Mostly for just leaving me alone."

"Come in. Then turn around, lift your arms."

The hallway of this apartment block was deserted. We owned most of this floor. I fingered the button through the cloth of my pants pocket.

The things you can arrange with a shitload of money at your disposal. I guess he never figured on anyone being organized, so quickly. It had surprised me too. Moghul must have put these guys on standby.

I pressed the button.

The boom rocked the room, as the planted charges blew access holes in the wall to either side and behind him.

While I looked shocked and stepped away, he was already pulling his gun. Maybe he would've shot me before I did anything. Maybe not. The bullets in his back distracted him. My kick got him a second later. Lucky they didn't accidentally shoot me too, but then, these guys knew their business.

Now this. A blood-splattered room. A body being stuck in a bag.

I guess I was a killer.

Time to make myself scarce and make use of all the ways to hide that Moghul had clued me up on. I took out my phone to tell Andreas it was plan A, after all.

CHAPTER 56

Wren

Climbing up the ladder happened, step by wet step. My feet, I had to tell them what to do, every single step, or they forgot. How much blood had I lost? It was just the day, my mind insisted. Just all the...stuff.

Whatever.

I found myself face first on the cold tiles, wet, and my knees slipped as I scrambled to all fours. I'd left a puddle of blood and water. *Jesus.* It always looked worse when you added water.

Blood...spreads.

The knife! If I'd dropped it? But it was beside my hand. I stared, gathering energy. Steel handle, with ribs all down it for grip. No wonder that had hurt going inside.

I rose to my feet, by stages, like an old woman, breathing hard.

Where was he? How could I do this? How could I not try to kill this man? I studied my trembling fingers. I wasn't stopping. Fuck this. Only one thought impaled my mind. This was the only way out. Unless I wanted to stay forever.

Forever. Forever. I counted my way with the word, padding onward. The one time I looked behind me, I saw a trail of pink footprints.

Water spreads blood. I'm fine.

So thirsty.

I found him on the patio, staring out at the pool. His strong shoulders, the bulk of his arms, and his stillness reminded me of a perfect sculpture. He kneeled, wearing black drawstring pants only, as if meditating. I trudged onward, my feet slapping the tiles, until I stood over him, poised, the knife held in the right way for slipping between his ribs. Odds were I'd catch it on one. Then he'd beat me, or kill me.

My breathing rasped so loud, I knew he must hear me.

"You know I'm here."

"Yes." His tone shocked me, hard, like he'd said it through nails.

"Why?"

"Because...this way, I know. All or nothing." He laughed, and again it was harsh. "I brought you to this. You've got the knife. Decide. I know you so damn well. I predicted you'd get this far but you're bleeding more than I expected, girl. I need to fix that."

"It's the water," I whispered.

Over his shoulder, I saw a tablet lying before him, and on the screen were four squares of camera footage. One showed the viewing room, others the trail of my footprints.

Moghul waited, passively, for me to strike? I wavered. Yes, I got this far, but killing him was no longer easy.

Kill, or be his.

Stupid me.

You can't live with a force of nature.

Glass was waiting for me.

I had to do this.

If he let me. My grip on the knife crunched in.

His head dipped a little. "I have to tell you this. Chris sent me a text. Glass found him and arranged a meeting. I'm sorry, but he's dead."

What? Who?

"Chris?" I frowned, completely lost. Why would that matter?

"No, not Chris. Wren, Glass is dead."

Oh yes. Today was a good day. I swayed, resisting collapse, because I'd never rise. "What?" I said, huskily.

"He's dead. It's only fair that you know."

Fair? Fair? How was this fair? I sobbed and caught myself, put my hand to my mouth. "No!"

"It's true. I'm sorry."

More stupid sorries. I raised the knife, knuckles clamped on metal, trembling with rage and weakness, dying to hit him.

"Did you tell him to kill Glass? Did you?" I thought I'd screeched that but it came out muted. Tears poured down my face and I didn't even feel sad, just lost, just fucking demolished. If this was grief, I wanted my money back. I dropped my knife hand, letting my arm flounder at my side, and nicked my thigh.

"No. I did not. Wren. I need to stop the bleeding."

But he didn't turn.

He gave no excuses. If nothing else, he was honest. Telling me that had made me want to kill him. He must have known that. He must. Killing him too...why? Everyone I cared for was dead and I wanted to add another? My heart hurt so much. Glass was dead. I'd never see him again, be in his arms. There was so much more I needed to do with Glass. So much more life.

I wiped at tears with my arm, struck by a storm of misery. Some of this was his fault. It *must* be.

Stung into motion, I lashed out and the knife stuck an inch into his upper arm. When I tried to pull my hand away, I found he'd turned and grabbed my wrist.

His glare was steady, but I glimpsed anger.

"Do you really want to kill me?"

"No!" I staggered back, sobbing, only to be brought up short by his hold. "No." I put one hand to my face, wanting to hide. I didn't want to kill him. I wanted to die.

"I thought not."

"You were never going to let me go." I whispered that to my hand, not expecting him to hear.

"You think I'd just give up?" he snarled, his grip crushing my wrist, and I gasped, feeling the *throb, throb* of blood through my arteries, beneath his fingers. "Leave you to exist with another man? You weren't meant for that. What a waste that would've been. No, I was never going to let you go." He began to methodically twist the knife from me. "Never, fucking, ever will I let you go."

Then he released my hand. I heard the knife clatter to the floor.

There was no one left. For a woman who had everything, I had nothing. My legs wobbled and gave out and I went to my knees with a thump. Pitiful, but my face seemed to dissolve in tears and snot. I wept, folding up. My forehead bumped the floor.

I was so cold.

He could do what he liked to me. I didn't care, at all.

Despair was a place with no address, no pretty flowers on the table, no hugs, no one worthwhile. Only me.

His fingers touched my back, prodding softly then pressed a while. No words were spoken and my crying degenerated into a sad dribble of tears.

"You're coming with me. Just that little bit of pressure has stopped the bleeding. I don't think you can have lost that much blood. It's a small tear. I don't know why it bled as much as it did."

I heard him say that and more, as he carried me somewhere. My stomach and my eyes hurt from the crying.

"It was the water. It makes blood spread, stops it clotting," I said quietly, shivering and making my teeth chatter.

"Maybe. Once I get you to drink, and I stitch this, and you rest, we'll see. I'll get a doctor if I have to. I think you're mostly exhausted. Which isn't exactly a surprise. Say okay."

As he walked, my body shifted against him, reminding me of being in a boat at sea.

Say okay. An instruction. Maybe I needed those, just for a while. That he was going to stitch me made me feel better, if anything. I didn't care if it hurt. I did care that he wanted to do it.

"Okay." Then I added more, because it was niggling at me. It was like I held the last piece of a jigsaw puzzle or something. An indefinable itch. "I'm sorry I cut you."

I was. Because, I guess, he'd become the only rock in the burning swamp of debris that was my life. I didn't love him. I wasn't sure *like* was more than a small percentage of my thoughts. He was just big and monstrous enough to fend off everything else that might happen in the near future.

"It'll heal. You chose. That was worth getting cut over."

He thought I'd chosen him. I hadn't, though. I just needed someone now. Someone like him...

I shut my eyes.

Glass had died. How was that even possible? He was a mountain. Indestructible. I'd not even been there. He was supposed to be my hero and rescue me and now I wished he hadn't tried. Maybe, if he hadn't tried, he'd be alive.

After he stapled the wound in my back, Moghul left me in the middle of his bed then climbed in with me. I cried, as quietly as I could, for what seemed like hours. My pillow grew progressively wetter. Where did I fit in the world without Glass? What was I doing *here*, in this man's bed?

I should've killed him, but those words had already lost their power. Maybe I could've done it...if I'd struck him before he'd told me Glass was dead.

And then...then I would've been so alone.

Moghul shifted and his arm fell heavily over me, his hand ending a few inches from my nose, pushing my pillow against my face.

"Shhh, enough. Go to sleep."

"How?" I blinked at the darkness.

"It'll get better. There's more to me than there seems." His thumb stroked my forehead.

"Seems?" I laughed softly, my tongue loosened by weariness. "You seem big and scary."

"Oh, I am, but that's how you like me, Wren. That's what you need. Go to sleep."

For a few bleary moments, I considered protesting but his warmth and the weight of his body and words, helped me fall into oblivion.

More of his words filtered in and barely registered.

Tomorrow, we fly out early. In a few days, I may have something amazing to tell you.

CHAPTER 57

Wren

By whatever ways and means it was made to happen, I never found out, but the next morning, after being awakened and after my shoulder had been cleaned and my hair dyed blond, we took off from the local airport in a small private jet.

I, Wren Gavoche, missing rich girl, with my hair in a scarf and dyed, and with contact lenses in place that made my eyes water, was allowed through customs with barely a blink at my passport. Money talked, I suppose. It always did, since mankind's history began and the first coin was hammered out.

At that time, I was still, perhaps understandably, in a bleak world of my own. I could have exposed Moghul, as we were ushered through customs and given VIP treatment and accelerated processing of our passports to get to our plane. I didn't. I was consumed by the deaths of my friend and my lover, and also increasingly aware that the man into whose charge I had delivered myself, was the father of my child.

Had I delivered myself? Had I chosen Moghul in the middle of my grieving for Hugh and Glass? He thought I had, and with every passing day, leaving him became less and less urgent, less important, less something I wanted to do.

We ended up in South America, on the coastline, and the similarity to life on the coast of Australia helped me to keep myself together. I survived. Moghul, for once, treated me kindly if with the attitude of a man who brooked no disobedience from his woman. No spankings, no S and m...but I began to mourn the passing of that also.

I began most mornings by looking at his brand in the mirror. *Mine.*

A week after we arrived, I was lying on a towel-draped table, out on the rear patio, having my wound examined by Florencia, the one maid Moghul had so far hired. Our house was in a gated community with security guards and she was the only other human I'd been allowed near. Since I couldn't speak Spanish and that was all she spoke, we got along fine, according to Moghul.

Whatever she made of my steel link bracelets and neck collar, I had no clue. Only once did she examine the heart lock dangling from the new collar and then her only comment was a whispered, "Hermoso."

This morning, after giving me a stern look and instructions to be good, Moghul had gone on some mystery errand. After the garage door clunked down, I fidgeted. My desire to be my own person and leave him was reawakening. I could climb the wall maybe even circumvent the locks on the doors. The back gate, which only sported a padlock, led over to the beach. Every night I heard the waves roll in. Sometimes I'd dreamed of flying out over the walls, like a seagull.

I was being a thorough traitor to Glass by staying with Moghul, no matter how much I was... I searched for words to explain my need to stay and only ended up with tears dribbling onto the towel while Florencia dabbed my staples with iodine. I'd have to remember not to wear white. The yellow of the iodine would mark the cloth.

"Bueno!"

The buzz of an alarm said that Moghul had returned but the maid kept fussing over my back. All the secondary hook wounds had closed over to become only dots, but they seemed to bother her and make her want to attend to them as much as the stapled L-shaped tear. Another few days and those staples could come out.

When he stepped onto the broad patio, from the double doors toward the opposite end, Florencia curtsied and retreated into the house. A curtsey. It'd taken me awhile to get used to her doing that. Was it a local thing or just a reaction he elicited in young women?

I swear my nostrils dilated as he walked slowly closer. My reaction to his maleness was unmistakable, now that he'd left me alone for a week. When every day had meant sex, his mere presence now dictated that I moisten and become aroused when I was near him. It was disconcerting especially since he appeared to know how he affected me.

If this kept up, if he didn't make me do something like he always used to, I could see myself begging on my knees and offering a blow job just to get some action.

Wouldn't *that* amuse him.

"Cover yourself, Wren. We have a small visitor. Well she's more than that." He nodded.

"Oh?" I sat up and pulled up the top of my dress to conceal my breasts then pushed the straps over my shoulders. Moghul telling me to cover myself was a small miracle.

"You'll see." He smiled, speculatively. "I'll be back in a minute."

His deep voice had been welcome after Florencia's sharper, feminine one. And my insides had quivered. I suppose we, both men and women, have instinctual reactions to potential mates, only often we don't recognize them and we suppress our responses. I'd simply been awakened to my body's needs. I shouldn't be ashamed.

My main need now, was to decide, in this less traumatic environment, with a clearer head, what to do. I couldn't fight him anymore. I knew that. I was done with fighting, but there might be another way past his obsessive need to keep me as his.

And if not?

What were my real feelings for Moghul? So much had happened. He wasn't the same man I had first met. I wasn't the same woman.

A series of barks came from within the house, then a golden puppy shot from the same door Moghul had used, far down the patio. The small bundle, a cocker spaniel, ran around and around the garden, zipping between the shrubs, while I sat there stunned, with my mouth open.

What the hell?

I'd told him no once before to a puppy; did he think it would convince me?

Then a girl squealed and ran out after the puppy, her pigtails flying. Dark hair, and so small I guessed she was somewhere around two years old. When Moghul emerged after her and ran to scoop her up with her giggling at him, thoughts crammed in. Dread too.

No one else was here. No parents.

Where did you get a child in a South American country when you wanted one?

He stalked toward me and I stood, anger brimming, insults on my tongue.

"Moghul! What have you —"

"No. Stop there." He set the girl down but held her by one chubby hand then went to one knee to comfort her. She was staring at me, wide eyed, with one thumb wedged in her mouth. "I will not raise my voice to you here and now, Wren, but you will also speak respectfully. Apologize."

No please. No outs or alternatives.

I froze. My anger ground down. He'd not commanded me like this, not since we came here. It'd been more a guidance, for days.

My heart fluttered, and not with irritation, with a weird sort of joy. *Oh damn.* I cleared my throat. He was right. My anger was premature.

"I'm sorry, Sir."

"Good. This is Theresa. She is two and a half. You'll kneel and say hello." He smiled grimly at that, because we both knew it was for more than the child.

My gaze flicked to her and I couldn't help smiling. "She's beautiful." I went to my knees. "Hello, Theresa."

Though her fingers only received more chewing she nodded at me. Then I directed my question to him. "Where are her parents, Sir?"

This time it was he who seemed uncomfortable, his brow creasing and uncreasing. "Theresa, would you like to go play with the puppy?" Moghul pointed, smiling wider. "Look! Puppy!"

"Pup-pee?" After a last look at me, to which I nodded and

repeated, *puppy*, she raced away after the dog. It was sniffing grass and within moments they were chasing each other, giggling and barking.

"Her parents. Okay. One of her parents, the father, is dead, the mother isn't. What are your thoughts, Wren?"

I gulped. With a baby of my own on its way, seeing this child awoke a need to see her with her mother. "I think she should be with her mum. Why is she here?"

Was her mother a drug addict or something worse?

"Where is she from?"

"An orphanage in France. She is starting to speak French as well as some English. It's taken me a long time to find her and to arrange to bring her here. My man suspected she existed but she's had several foster families. None have kept her."

Suspected she existed. Those words stirred weirdness in my stomach. This girl was someone special?

My throat tightened. "That's sad. So... Why isn't she with her mother?"

Then he turned and went to sit on one of the big cane chairs that dotted the patio along with many hanging pots of flowers. "Come here, Wren. Sit at my feet."

There was something he held back. Knowing him and how mad he got with something that he wanted, my head was spinning. Why did he want this girl? But I went to him and kneeled on the pillow he gave me, then rearranged myself and sat with my legs to one side. He stroked my hair and after a moment or two of that and watching the boisterous puppy and child gallop and toddle about the garden, I laid my head on his lap. A while later, I succumbed and sneaked my arm around his leg, then I hugged it. This was strangely beautiful and peaceful – sitting here with Moghul watching these two young creatures.

I put my other hand to my stomach and smiled.

"Have you guessed, Wren?"

"Guessed?"

"Who the mother is." He stilled his hand on my hair. "Your father had her birth records falsified. But I don't want to ruin this moment

335

by saying more about that. I'm certain of the facts. I've had DNA tests run. I decided this child needed the love of her mother, but also, I have to confess, I thought it would bring me closer to you."

Ohmigod. I held his leg tighter. She couldn't be.

I could only whisper my next words, I was so afraid I'd guessed wrong. "Am I her mother?"

"Yes, you are."

I buried my face in his pants leg and squeaked out, "Are you sure. Absolutely?" I had to hear this again.

"Yes."

It wasn't possible. It just...wasn't, but I leaped up and ran to her, my steps slowing as I drew near.

How could this be? This little girl was the baby I'd thought stillborn? I wanted it to be so with all my heart. I'd grieved for her long ago and the tearing of my thoughts from one extreme to the other wrecked me.

In the curve of her nose and the color of her eye I could see myself. In the way she smiled so shyly and in the glee with which she played, I saw Nathan. I stopped doubting and I *believed.*

My child.

My baby.

Watery eyed, I drew in a shaky breath.

She stopped her playing, and shoved her hand in her mouth, as if afraid. I wondered at her past and what fears she might have, but when I went to one knee and held out my arms she ran into them.

I hugged her, carefully, and I whispered to her. "Theresa. I'm going to be your mummy from now on. Will that make you happy?"

What a silly question. She barely knew me. My heart was in my mouth as she raised herself on tiptoes and wrapped her arms about my neck. Then she gave my neck a baby kiss and whispered, *"Oui, maman."*

I cried then. Although I wept no more tears that day than I had at the death of Glass, they were far happier tears and I would gladly have bottled them and kept them forever to remind me of the day my first baby came back to me.

Maybe fate had decided I deserved something good after all that had happened. It was odd, to say the least, to have Moghul be the man to deliver her to me, this child I never knew had survived her birth, but perhaps that was his fate also, to be a perverted version of a fairy godmother. I think my love for him began from that day.

He never lost his taste for sadism and, if anything, once he had a basement room soundproofed and set up to his liking, he resumed our scenes with greater enthusiasm than before. I didn't mind, though; my initial reluctance had been replaced by a liking, a craving even, for his pain as well as for his dominance. My favorite time became those sessions out on the rear patio, bound and tied to the ceiling rafters, while he flogged me to the sound of the waves crashing on the sand.

I grew accustomed to the loss of Glass. He'd been a far gentler man than Moghul, a man who deserved to live, but I couldn't change what had happened. I took blame on myself because I'd led him to his death. If I'd not involved him in my ridiculous hunt for my father's killer, he'd be alive. My father hadn't needed justice, he'd needed a shovel for his grave then maybe some flowers, if I was generous.

After all the fearful things that had happened, I'd lived and had been given my two children. Fate played high stakes games. Once I might've thought Moghul my penance for my stupid search for the killer but now, he was far more than penance. He was my world.

When I considered the possibility that Moghul might die before I did, that I might survive him...I felt that potential loss as something annihilating and I wondered how I'd exist without him.

He was a part of me in a way that Glass could never have been.

A year after that terrible day when I'd made my decision, the day Glass had died, Moghul drew me to the walled-off section of the garden where we'd planted our crimson rose bushes, so that Theresa and Kegan, when he learned to walk, wouldn't end up with thorn scratches. Moghul had joked that he'd craft me a collar made of their branches with the thorns ever pricking me to remind me of my subservience. I still challenged him on my most unruly days and he never tired of punishing me for it.

The difference was that now I appreciated it as part of the give and take of our relationship. There were pluses and minuses to any marriage. I doubted any man, including my poor Glass, would have kept me away from knives.

Moghul did.

Knives were such a beautiful combination of light and dark, of good and evil.

Why they fascinated me escaped my comprehension. I think they always would, but they weren't essential. I had servants for chopping up things.

"Kneel, Wren."

I went to my knees, tucking the light fabric under me so the wild sea wind, blustering over the wall, didn't make it flail at my face.

I wore a flimsy red gown with an irregular hem, in honor of the journey I'd made, that day a year ago, from his pit of despair. Also it was in remembrance of Glass, though I hadn't told that to Moghul.

"This is my gift to you." As he spoke, he unlocked and removed the steel chain-link collar from my neck. Then he held out to me a new collar that lay across and dripped from his palms. This one seemed to be steel also, but it was in the form of interwoven thorns with a half-opened silver rosebud as the lock.

"You will always be my only partner in life, Wren, and this is a symbol of our struggles and our triumphs, as well as my mastery over you. Know that I will always be fair and reward you when you deserve reward, that I will punish you when needed and care for you for the rest of your life. I will never desert you. I will love you to the end of my days."

As I smiled up at him, tears welled in my eyes, blurring my vision. "It's beautiful, Sir. Thank you."

"Say your vow, Wren."

"I will be yours forever, Sir. I will obey you and accept your judgement in all things. I will care for you and trust you to love me and care for me." I swallowed as I thought over the last words. "I will love you to the end of my days, Sir."

"Bow your head so I can put the collar on you."

Then he locked it in place. The click of the key no longer declared my captivity to me, it quietly spoke of freedom with the man with whom I truly wanted to live my life. Though he'd begun as the man I'd loved to hate, he'd ended as my knight in blackened armor and the father of my children.

"Now put your head next to my foot with your cheek to the ground."

This was new, but I barely hesitated. I went lower and put my head at his feet, then his foot lifted, and I felt his boot press down on my head, with enough force that grains of dirt dug into my cheek.

"Just a reminder of where you belong. Under me."

I stared beyond the sole of his shoe at the grass stalks swaying and wondered at the change in myself. A year ago I would've snarled and rebelled, whereas now, I felt terribly comforted by where I was.

A little over a year ago, I didn't have *Mine* written on my back and I didn't understand the joy there could be in belonging to someone.

"Who owns you, Wren?"

"I'm yours, Sir. Always yours."

The End

To read the Blade Path ending go to Chapter 36

ABOUT CARI SILVERWOOD

Cari Silverwood is a New York Times and USA Today bestselling writer of kinky darkness or sometimes of dark kinkiness, depending on her moods and the amount of time she's spent staring into the night. She has an ornery nature as well as a lethal curiosity that makes her want to upend plots and see what falls out when you shake them.

When others are writing bad men doing bad things, you may find her writing good men who accidentally on purpose fall into the abyss and come out with their morals twisted in knots.

This might be because she comes from the land down under, Australia, or it could be her excessive consumption of wine.

Freaking out readers is her first love and her second love is freaking out the people living in her books. Her favorite hobby is convincing people she has a basement...though she really doesn't. Promise. If it existed it would be a terrifying place where you would find all the dangerous things that you never knew you craved.

If you'd like to learn more or join my mailing list go to
www.carisilverwood.net
Also Facebook & Goodreads:
http://www.facebook.com/cari.silverwood
http://www.goodreads.com/author/show/4912047.Cari_Silverwood

You're welcome to join this group on facebook to discuss Cari Silverwood's books:
https://www.facebook.com/groups/864034900283067/

Also by Cari Silverwood

Preyfinders Series
Precious Sacrifice
Intimidator

Squirm Files Series
Squirm – virgin captive of the billionaire biker tentacle monster
Strum – virgin captive of the billionaire demon rock star monster

The Well-hung Gun – virgin captive of the billionaire were-squid gunslinger monster
 The Squirm Files anthology

Pierced Hearts Series
(Dark erotic fiction)
Take me, Break me
Klaus
Bind and Keep me
Make me Yours Evermore
Seize me From Darkness
Yield

Pierced Hearts Volume 1 – contains books #1, #2 and #3
Pierced Hearts Volume 2 – contains books #2 and #3

The Badass Brats Series
The Dom with a Safeword
The Dom on the Naughty List
The Dom with the Perfect Brats
The Dom with the Clever Tongue

Cataclysm Blues
Cataclysm Blues
(a free erotic post apocalyptic novella)

The Steamwork Chronicles Series
Iron Dominance
Lust Plague
Steel Dominance
Others
31 Flavors of Kink
Three Days of Dominance
Rough Surrender
Blood Glyphs

Made in the USA
San Bernardino, CA
29 November 2015